# Legacy of Shadow

## by

## Craig Gallant

Zmok Books

Legacy of Shadow
By Craig Gallant
Cover by Michael Nigro
Zmok Books an imprint of
Winged Hussar Publishing, LLC, 1525 Hulse Road, Unit 1, Point Pleasant, NJ 08742

This edition published in 2016 Copyright ©Winged Hussar Publishing, LLC

ISBN 978-0-9903649-1-7
Library of Congress No. 2016935626
Bibliographical references and index
1. Science Fiction 2. Space Opera 3. Action & Adventure

Winged Hussar Publishing, LLC All rights reserved

For more information on Winged Hussar Publishing, LLC, visit us at:
https://www.WingedHussarPublishing.com
Twitter: WingHusPubLLC
Facebook: Winged Hussar Publishing LLC

# Prologue

The white dwarf was a distant glowing ember floating in the void, barely brighter than the scattered diamonds of the galactic disk beyond. The forgotten star bathed the system with the last emissions of its final, quiet eons of death. Orbiting the dying sun were the charred and lifeless remains of its children, their black and fractured orbs absorbing the feeble light, giving back almost nothing in return.

Aside from these last fragments, the system had died over a billion years ago. The millennia-long paroxysms that had claimed the planets' atmospheres were long extinguished. What life might once have thrived there was less than a memory for the vast celestial engine that continued to spin, oblivious to the tragedy that had claimed it. It was a catastrophe that had destroyed countless similar suns, and would destroy countless more as the inexorable forces of entropy marched down through time.

The largest remnant spinning though the silent parade, a dull and melted sphere, had once been the core of a massive gas giant before its voracious parent had devoured its heavy atmosphere. The relic wobbled along in an erratic orbit, still reeling from the grievous deathblow. Had any sentient being felt tempted to visit the dark corpse, it would have taken inordinate skill and stamina to keep station with the dead husk for long. The moon-sized craft that orbited the planet did not suffer the weaknesses or limitations of sentience, however.

Blacker than the most brutalized planetary remains in the system, the shape appeared more a hole in the star field beyond than something concrete and real. It's blocky, utilitarian shape was unmarred by the violence that had claimed its current home. The ship had kept its vigil for eons. Civilizations had risen and fallen out in the wider galaxy while it followed its silent, purposeful course through the ages.

Deep beneath the vessel's matte shell, whispers of thought flashed through ancient crystal matrices. There was no awareness behind these whispers. There was no conscious direction behind the thoughts. Patterns and duties set thousands of years ago continued in the silence of the giant hull. Translucent frameworks flashed in slow, steady rhythms as the cadences of the galaxy beyond were tasted, compared, and stored in memory stacks nestled in the heart of the sentinel.

Without warning, the hull vibrated with an imperceptible motion detectable only from the thin layer of celestial dust that shivered free, glittering in the faint light of the distant, dying star. A dim red light formed a rectangle beneath the dispersing motes. A hatch receded, dwarfed by the impenetrable darkness behind. The crimson glow brightened, and then was eclipsed by a spindly shape the matte black of the vessel itself. An armature pushed a bundle of tubes, dishes, and wires through the faint cloud of debris, bringing the instruments in line with the dull metal core of the planetoid below.

Time meant little within the echoing silence of the dead system. The insectile limb hung still and silent for what might have been an age.

Without warning, the instruments stabbed downward. Gravitic power relays and crystalline conduits flashed with a brilliant pulse of intense green light. For a moment, the flank of the giant machine leapt out of the darkness, its structure outlined in fierce jade glory. Massive doors and hatches were scattered across its huge surface, vanes and bulbs protruded here or there following no perceptible pattern. There was no sign of a window, sensor array, or lens of any kind along the entire, colossal length.

A beam of coherent light pierced the remnant atmosphere of the planetoid below. The column struck the slagged sphere in the middle of a wide field of melted craters. The dull surface, greedy for a taste of heat and light, absorbed everything the beam could provide. The lance of energy struck deep into the incredibly dense material, seeking out its core, interacting with ultra-rare elements that had been smelted down in the cosmic furnace of the system's death. Naturally-occurring matrices of heavy metals came alive within the crust of the planet, and the entire orb rang like the largest bell ever struck. Countless vibrations rippled through the material of the planet and were cast out into space.

Waves and particles of a million varieties spread forth, each following the esoteric rules of its type. Some wrapped themselves around the various dead bodies of the system and returned at once to their point of origin. These were ignored by the hulk floating overhead. Many stretched forth their ethereal fingers, and would not return for hundreds or thousands of years. The sentinel was infinitely patient. Some special few flew outward at staggering speeds, passing tachyons and luxons in their haste to reach the far corners of the galaxy.

The blazing column vanished without fanfare, plunging everything back into endless night. The planet below was silent and dark once more, save for a single glowing crater that quickly cooled and disappeared into the gathering black. Aside from the dim crimson glow from the open hatch, the entire system was dead once again.

The armature drew its bundle back through the hatch. Vague hints of movement within followed, shadows cast out into the void, and then a second shape emerged. A silvery orb slid out into the night and came to a smooth halt.

Again, an unknowable length of time crept past. When echoes of the swiftest waves began to return, the orb shivered. There was no other sign that some of the most powerful elements in the galaxy had been harnessed to a coherent, measured purpose.

The orb was withdrawn, the dull red light eclipsed once again as the hatch closed. Deep within the sentinel, whispers of thoughts returned. Ancient patterns were followed. The paths of the net cast from the dead system were studied rote, mindless precision. Data was separated, weighed, measured, and stored for some possible future purpose.
Nothing had been found.

There was no frustration at this lack of progress. There was no acknowledgment of empty eons sloughing by, except as yet another data point to be catalogued.

Colossal locks slid back into place, securing the huge hatch.

The leviathan had been created for a very specific purpose. It was a hunter, built to scent a particular prey, possibly the most dangerous prey the galaxy had ever known. Every system within the enormous hulk confirmed that this prey had not been detected. None of the ancient parameters so much as hinted at the prey's stirring.

But the sentinel was patient. It was singularly devoted to its purpose, neither restlessness nor anxiety designed into its temperament.

Deep within the massive hull the last stray components settled back into their cradles. Power slowed to a trickle as its fiery heart was banked once again, its full potentiality relaxing into a quiet, wary rest.

The dust began to settle once more over the dull black hull, and the dead system was plunged once again into the deathly stillness of a crypt.

# Chapter 1

The old Camry labored as they took a sharp turn, its speed hardly diminishing. The tires, which Marcus knew from past experience were probably as bald as the man driving, gave an alarming squeal before the car shuddered, swerving across the faded double yellow line a couple times, and settled back into its belabored roar for the approaching straightaway. A small sign, its faded legend, State Road 189, flashed past.

Marcus held onto the overhead handle with a death grip, but could feel the grin stretching across his face despite the fear. Glancing over to his friend he could see the brilliant white of Justin's answering smirk nestled within the black goatee and mahogany face, almost lost in the deep shadows. Only their headlights reflecting off the road lines, now coming in the staccato bursts of a passing zone, illuminated the interior.

"You're going to get us killed or arrested if you keep this up." Marcus strained around to look through the rear window. The running lights cast a ruddy glow into the wall of trees rushing away on either side. There was no one behind them.

Justin flashed a glance into the rearview mirror and giggled with a sound that Marcus had always found jarring coming from his tall, well-muscled friend. Despite the lack of pursuit, however, Justin kept his expensive shoe jammed on the gas, hunching over the steering wheel like a cartoon villain making his getaway.

"Right about now I'd welcome a little visit from Connecticut's finest." He shot another look into the mirror. "How's your leg?"

Marcus shook his leg in the foot well, twisting it back and forth. It still tingled as if asleep, but nothing like the fiery pins and needles that had downed him when the fat man had first shot him back in the casino parking lot.

"It'll be okay, I think. Still feels asleep." He turned again to watch their back trail. "What the hell do you think it was, anyway?"

Justin giggled again. "Don't ask me, I was too busy kicking the guy's ass and dragging your squealing self into the car to pay much attention. Mother of all tasers, maybe?"

Marcus shook his head. It had been chaos in the parking lot as Justin tried to push him out to the car. The fat man had appeared out of nowhere, blubbering on about being robbed and wanting his property back. Marcus had no idea what he was talking about and was in the middle of saying as much when the big man had pulled something out of his pocket, and then there had been a brilliant blue flash.

The next thing Marcus knew, he was in the musty old Camry rushing down the highway toward home, Justin giggling beside him.

"Well, whatever the hell it was, you owe me. I'm pretty sure that shot was meant for you, asshole." Marcus settled back into his seat, grinding his shoes into the matted carpeting, trying his best to ignore the foliage as it whipped past at high speed.

Justin gave him a hurt look, immediately dispelled by that lopsided grin.

He pulled something out of his breast pocket and tossed it into Marcus's lap. "I think he was probably after that."

Marcus picked the object up. It was delicate, but very heavy. There were chains attached to a solid central body, with several smaller items woven into the chains like a web; a strange, elaborate piece of jewelry or something similar. He reached out and turned on the dome light, bathing the interior in its cold, muddy glow. Holding the thing up, he almost dropped it when he got his first good look. At the center of the web of chains was a massive blue gem, star cut and glimmering even in the poor light. The smaller gems were clear, like diamonds, but picked up blue reflections from the central stone. The metal was silver, but polished to such a high shine it sparkled almost as much as the gems.

"What the hell is this?" Marcus breathed. It looked like something from a movie, around the neck of a queen, maybe. "How'd you get it?"

Justin shrugged. "The guy had a streak of bad luck. He was flat, and the hand was winding down. He asked if he could throw it into the pot to go all in, and I let him." The grin appeared again. "I might not have let him if I hadn't been sitting on three kings."

Of the two friends, Justin was the gambler, and Marcus left him to it. But even Marcus knew that it was highly irregular for folks in a high stakes back room game to accept anything like this piece of jewelry into the pot. "That's not like you." But he couldn't keep his eyes off the flashing sapphire jewel.

Justin shrugged again. "Well, to be honest, it was down to just him and me, and he asked, and … well …" Marcus looked over and was surprised to see his friend's grin turn a little sheepish. "I didn't know what it was worth, okay? I was embarrassed. The way the guy was acting, it was like he was throwing in his first born. I didn't want to seem like some rube in front of the other guys. You know how those New York jerks can get when they think they've got one up on you. So I played the big man, like I was doing him a favor, and we ran the rest of the game down." He snickered. "You should have seen his face, though, when I flipped my cards."

Marcus tried to force himself to lower the necklace, but a sudden flash of blue light blinded him and his whole body tensed. His hands burned as if they held live wires. His vision seemed to vibrate, patterns of light and shadow strobing behind his eyes. He had a feeling, even stunned with surprise and fear, that there had to be some sense or meaning behind the shivering visions.

It ended as quickly as it had begun, and Marcus dropped the necklace into his lap, his breath coming in harsh, desperate pants.

"He was muttering something over and over again about math, shaking that big dopey fat head like he was in a nightmare." Justin continued, looking over at Marcus's silence. His eyes widened and the car slowed. "You okay, buddy?"

Marcus shook his head. Whatever had happened, Justin hadn't noticed. He mumbled through numb, tingling lips, "I hate it when you call me that."

Justin's smile returned a little. "Man, you had me there for a second. You looked like you'd seen a ghost or something."

Marcus looked down again at the necklace, wanting to pick it up, but at the same time afraid. He generally didn't like surprises, and that one had been nasty. Maybe there was a battery or something behind the big blue stone?

"Oh, damn." Justin muttered, reaching up to adjust the rearview mirror.

"Things are about to get even more interesting."

Marcus turned, looking back down the highway, and for a moment stared at the oncoming headlights without understanding. As their own car started to surge away, however, he realized what Justin *thought* was happening. He collapsed back into his seat, checked his belt, and settled in.

"It might not be him." Marcus said the words because he felt like he was supposed to. There was no conviction behind them, however.

"No, sure. This time of night, on this road, it could be almost anybody." Justin hunched his shoulders again and the car rushed forward with a hoarse, angry howl.

"Might be Connecticut's finest, like you said." Marcus's eyes were fixed straight ahead, a growing sickness rising in his throat.

"If they catch me, they're welcome to everything I've got." Justin flicked his eyes into the mirror. "You didn't see that guy's eyes, Marc. Back there in the parking lot? There was something going on in there I don't think we want any part of."

Marcus was not one to run from a fight, and he knew Justin felt the same. But for some reason, as his guts wound up tighter and tighter, he felt like his friend had the right of it. "Well, what's he going to do, run us off the road?" He was trying to sound reassuring, but the question came out far too serious and sensible in his own ears, and his stomach twisted tighter.

For almost a minute the two men were silent as the trees streaked past. The old State Road wove gently from side to side here, following some old stream or colonial property line. There was nothing like the turn that had recently tortured so much protest from the tires. Unfortunately, the car creeping relentlessly up behind them was clearly in far better shape. There was no doubt how this chase was going to end.

"Maybe we just give him back the damned necklace?" Justin's voice was sharp as he spat the words out without warning. "I mean, what the hell do we need with something like that anyway?"

Marcus was nodding, ready to agree, but his mouth clenched shut, and he found himself unable to respond. The knot in his stomach and the burning in his throat moved nearer to each other, settling with a sharp pain over his heart.

He wasn't going to let the necklace go.

"Marc? How about it, man? We slow down, you toss it out the window, we move on?" There was a tightness in Justin's voice that Marcus had never heard before. His friend, usually the coolest head in any situation, was close to losing it. There was something foreign in the air that made no sense. When they were younger, the two of them had been in more than their fair share of brawls. Sure, they were a little old to be getting into fights on the side of the road at this point in their lives, especially against strange fat men. But the panic in his chest, and the fear in his friend's voice, belayed the confidence both of them should have felt.

Marcus turned, straining against the tight belt, and his lips pursed at the gleaming headlights bearing down on them. Swiveling back, he thought for a moment, and then looked at his friend, putting every ounce of conviction into his voice. "How much gas do you have?"

Justin jerked his head over to stare in disbelief at him, and then whipped it back to watch the road. "What the hell are you talking about?"

Marcus shrugged, momentum and sense-memory pushing him on. "Keep on driving, keep him behind us. The Mass border can't be too much farther. Granville's what, half an hour, max, on the other side? Hell, we drive him straight to the police station if he wants to follow us that far."

Justin glanced sideways again, brows drawn low over his glittering black eyes. "Are you insane? We just give him the damned necklace, and hope he doesn't tase one of us again, and I say we got off light." He turned back to the road. "The last thing I want to be doing when we hit that old bridge is drag racing with some crazy cracker with a jewelry fetish."

Marcus shook his head. Everything Justin was saying made sense, but something within him, tangled up with the hot, painful tightness over his chest, refused to consider giving up the gems.

Justin began to slow down, rolling down his window and gesturing for the car, now riding their bumper, to pass them. "Give it to me. I'll toss it at him and we'll be out of here."

Marcus shrank back against his own door, his head shaking of its own accord. Beyond Justin he could see the hood of the chasing car pulling up even with them; the sleek lines of a brand new Prius, gleaming from a fresh wash. The passenger compartment of the other car swelled in the side window, its own window a dark, gaping hole. It was him, of course. That feeling in the air thickened again, and Marcus knew it could not have been anyone else.

Even in the dim interior of the other car, there was no mistaking the crazed fat man, rolls of pale flesh piling up over his collar and pushing at his tie. The man was glistening with sweat, and his eyes seemed strange, as if they were all pupil. He was screaming something they couldn't hear over the howling of the engines and the roaring of the wind as Justin reined the Camry in even more. He was keeping one desperate eye on the road and the other on the Prius, and thrust his hand at Marcus, fingers clawing. "Give me the damned thing!"

Marcus shrank even further against his door, his hands falling to grasp the necklace. He was trying to marshal another argument when, past his friend, he saw the crazy fat man pull something off his own passenger seat and point it at Justin's head.

"Stop!" he screamed the word, punching Justin as hard as he could in the shoulder.

Between the warning and the sudden blow, Justin slammed on the breaks in confusion. Both of them were thrown against their seatbelts, faces precariously close to the windshield, when a gleaming ball of blue lightning flashed over their hood and slapped into the trees by the side of the road.

Marcus nearly wrenched his neck trying to stare at the impact point as they rushed past. By the sound and feel of the car, Justin had ground his fancy dress shoe back into the gas pedal with terrible force. They were leaping ahead again. Behind them, a flickering orange light in the woods sent a cold, crawling sensation over Marcus's scalp and down his spine.

Their erratic maneuvers had sent the other car swerving back into their wake, but now the man had his arm hanging out the driver's side window, and ball after ball of crackling lightning rushed past them. The energy disappeared into glowing tatters a couple car lengths ahead of them, and Marcus figured that the strange, exotic weapon must have a very short range.

One of the snapping, spitting orbs caught the rear quarter panel on Marcus's side and the entire car rang like a rusty old bell. The back window shattered, sending grains of safety glass shooting through the compartment. Tendrils of electricity crawled forward from the point of impact, one jumping from the lock to Marcus's elbow. He jumped away with a yelp at the sudden, burning pain. The lights of the car dimmed and then surged back, and an alarmingly diffident sound emerged from the engine before it struggled back up to its former roar.

"Holy shit!" Marcus screamed over the howling wind, slapping at his elbow. Justin struggled manfully to keep the Camry on the road, swerving back and forth to keep their attacker from pulling even with them again.

"He's playing for keeps now!" Justin gave the wheel a sharp yank to warn the Prius off, and then jerked his chin at the dashboard in front of Marcus. "Open up the glove box!"

Marcus looked at his friend in confusion. "What?"

Justin lurched across the compartment, one hand still on the wheel, and tore at the handle to the glove compartment. It fell open into Marcus's lap, napkins and paperwork spilling out, whirling around in the wild wind.

"Get it!" Justin screamed, wrapping his hands back around the wheel as the road ahead of them began to take a wider turn.

"Get what?" Marcus wanted to hit his friend again; he had no idea what he was supposed to do. He pawed desperately through the swirling papers, and then began to dig through the rest of the compartment's contents. A manual, a tire-gauge, and a few bulbs and fuses fell out onto the floor. There was a small box farther back that had to be what Justin was screaming about.

Marcus pulled the plastic box out and stared in confusion at the embossed plastic box top. There were two words there, but he didn't recognize either of them. It certainly wasn't English. Between the swirling wind and the pathetic dome lamp, Marcus doubted if he would be able to read it if it *had* been in English.

"For God's sake, will you just open the damned thing?" There were cords standing out on Justin's dark neck now, and his eyes were rapidly tightening with frustration.

Another ball of energy flashed past, this time rolling over the roof. Tiny branches of lightning lashed down to strike the windshield, dancing along the wiper blades and then the hood, sending the lights and the engine into fits again.

Marcus focused on the small box, trying to pry the lock open with fingers that had gone cold with wind and shock. When the latch finally popped open, something dark and heavy fell out into his lap, landing beside the necklace with enough weight to startle him. A pistol.

"What the hell?" Marcus looked back up at his friend. "What the hell are you carrying a gun around in your car for?"

Justin's sudden smile faltered and his eyes flicked between the road and Marcus's shocked face. Finally, as another shimmering ball snapped past, he spat angrily. "Just shoot him!"

There had been a few times when Marcus had fired a gun in his life. Twice at a shooting range while in pursuit of a particularly dark-minded young lady, a few times with friends out in the woods, and at one particularly wild bachelor party that had provided him with several memories he had planned to put to good use later in life. He just hadn't figured the advanced use of firearms would be one of those lessons.

"Just put the clip in and pull the slide!" Justin was screaming instructions while Marcus just stared at the gun and the clip, one in each hand. He had done this several times that weekend …

Another ball scorched past, glancing off the back window, shattering the safety glass and wrapping the driver's side in tendrils of electricity. What the hell was the guy shooting at them? This time the lights went dark and did not come back on, and the engine seemed to be struggling with itself as Justin shook the wheel with both hands as if he could force the car to continue. After a staggering pause, the engine came back, and they tore away from their pursuer again.

"Just do it!"

Marcus turned the pistol around, brought the clip up, a single round of ammunition gleaming in the uncertain light, and slid it home into the pistol grip. He looked at it for a moment, unable to remember what came next, and then quickly grabbed the barrel and tried to jam it down over the grip. It didn't move.

Panic once again rose in his chest. Marcus knew that they were going to die, and somehow it was going to be his fault. He struggled to bring the slide back, grunting with the effort. Two more balls of lightning flew past, both near misses that did nothing to calm his nerves. With all of his strength he tried to force the slide back, but it wouldn't move.

Justin glared over, looked down in disbelief, and then screamed at him. "The safety, you idiot!"

Annoyance at being called an idiot was immediately lost in the rush of shame and relief as Justin's other words registered. He flicked the safety down with his thumb and then easily brought the slide back with a satisfying click. He grinned, lifted it up to show his friend, and then realized what he was doing.

"He's back that way, Marc!" Justin jerked a thumb over his shoulder, and Marcus was embarrassed enough to just nod, swing around in his seat, and then try to draw a bead through the shattered rear window.

A part of him, suddenly breaking away from the noise and the chaos, reflected that it truly was odd that he should find himself in his friend's beat up old Camry, aiming a pistol through the remains of a window at an angry fat man he had never really met. The sliver of his mind stayed in that quiet place, contemplating the peculiarities of the universe, but a ball of energy struck the trunk a solid blow, lifting the back of the car up while lightning reached out to engulf him, and the rest of Marcus's mind decided that this asshole had a couple close calls coming his way.

Trying to get a two-handed grip on the gun despite the headrest that now pressed against his left shoulder, Marcus settled the aiming fin at the end of the stubby-seeming barrel back between the glaring headlights of their pursuer, then raised the gun up to where he could just make out the dark, shimmering windshield. Justin was slewing the car back and forth, probably trying to keep them alive, but it made it very hard to aim. He almost asked his friend to stop swerving, but then more lightning streaked past them, and he thought better of it.

Resting back against his seat as best he could, Marcus focused, brought the gun up, tried to steady it, and jerked the trigger. The sound within the confines of the passenger compartment was deafening. Justin screamed, flinching away, his shoulder rising as if to protect his ear. Marcus's own ears were ringing; all sound replaced by a constant, painful whine. The car behind them showed no ill effects from the shot.

"I'm sorry!" Marcus yelled, and then fired two more shots. This time the pain was nearly intolerable; his head pounded. Justin glared at him, but one of the Prius' headlights had flared out. The car swerved slightly. For the moment, there was no return fire.

"I think I scared him!" Marcus fell back into his seat, not even trying to hide the wide smile on his face. "He might—"

There was a deafening crack, like the loudest clap of thunder either of them had ever heard. Loud even over the dull whining in their ears. A bar of light flashed past the driver's side window, striking a tree far ahead. The tree detonated, throwing fire, splinters, and chunks of shattered wood in every direction. In a moment they were passing the toppling trunk, bits of burning tree hitting their car with a rush of fluttering impacts.

Justin screamed something Marcus couldn't hear over the ringing in his ears, but he could guess the meaning well enough from the context of the moment and the wild look in his friend's eyes. He struggled with his seatbelt clamp and wrestled his way clumsily into the back seat, careful not to point the gun anywhere he shouldn't. He fell into the cramped seat, scrambled up amidst the broken glass onto his knees, and braced the pistol against the seat back, his arms outstretched through the broken window. He half expected to get hit in the face with a nightmarish bolt of lightning at any moment.

With a battle cry that would have done his ancestors proud, Marcus aimed at his target's windshield and pulled the trigger with abandon. He felt as if his ears were bleeding from the painful battering, but he didn't care.

Sparks flew off the other car's hood, a hole appeared in its windshield, more sparks from the roof, another hole, closer to the driver, and then, far too soon, the gun made a dry, plaintive click, the slide locked back, and the weight of the gun seemed to mock him.

He took a breath, looked down at the empty gun, turned to look at the back of his friend's head, then down at the gun again. After a hesitant moment, he tapped Justin on the shoulder.

"What?" The road here was starting to meander more aggressively, forcing Justin to pay closer attention.

Marcus was pleasantly surprised that he could make out Justin's words despite the constant whining ring. His ears must have grown accustomed to the detonations. Or else he was getting used to interpreting through the incessant buzzing.

"Do you have any more bullets?"

Clearly Justin was having a hard time deciding whether he should keep driving or pivot around to try to strangle Marcus. The angry disbelief on his face was fierce in the tumbling flash of light and shadow. "I have three more clips, but they're all in the trunk! You're not supposed to need more than a single clip in real life!"

Marcus looked at Justin, wondering now if he was hearing him correctly. "What?"

"You're never supposed to need more than one clip in real life!"
"Says who?"

"Says *everybody,* you asshole! If you need more than one clip, you're screwed!"

Marcus nodded, sitting back against the cushions of the seat. "Well, they were right!"

Justin glared at him through the rearview mirror. "Who?"

"Everybody! We're screwed!"

Another beam shot past them, grazing the roof over Marcus's head. The interior of the car was lit brighter than midday for a moment before darkness returned, bright bars haunting their vision as they both blinked to clear them away. The metal was cut cleanly where the beam had touched it, the edges glowing an angry red.

A large rectangular sign loomed up out of the night and flew past them. Latching onto any mundane detail, Marcus came up short as his mind provided him with an image of the sign. He turned back to Justin, grabbing a fistful of his blazer and screaming directly into his ear. "The bridge!"

Fox Brook Bridge was an old iron truss bridge, its metal dark and corroded. Its rivet-studded flanks had always reminded Marcus of a stronger, more certain time, when things had been built to last, and looked it. The single-lane bridge spanned a wide, shallow river filled with tumbled granite boulders in a ravine that was deceptively deep.

As the bridge loomed up ahead of them, its yellow lights flashing their persistent warning, Marcus could only think of the ravine and the jagged rocks below.

"I'm going to shoot through the bridge, hope for the best!" Justin screamed back at him.

Marcus nodded. "Sounds good!" They weren't going to make it. There was no way they could make it. On their way southward a couple days ago they had taken that bridge at about twenty five miles an hour, and even then Marcus had felt a little crawling sensation in his gut as the rusty steel slid past. Now, at night, going by the feeble starlight and the erratic dancing illumination of the single headlight of the car chasing them? They weren't going to make it.

For the first time that night, despite the fear that had burned through him since the confrontation in the parking lot, Marcus felt a cold certainty grip him. They really *were* going to die.

The looming web of iron reared up in front of them, coming out of the shadows like a monster ready to swallow the car whole. The Camry's engine screeched beneath the hood as if it, too, could sense their impending doom. Marcus fell into the back seat and scrambled for the seatbelt. After several desperate pulls he had the belt across his chest, but his frantic search for the lock amid the broken glass proved hopeless, and he could only stare through the cracked windshield as the bridge grew larger. He thought he heard a screech beneath the constant ringing of the gunshots, but he couldn't be sure.

At the last minute, Justin brought the Camry around in a vicious arc, the tires screaming like the damned and the engine giving out a throaty roar. The bridge slid past the passenger-side windows, close enough that Marcus could see the pitted surface. He slammed against the door, the strap of the seat belt rough on his chin as he struggled uselessly to hold it tight. And then they were still, the car rocking back and forth, the engine panting like an exhausted animal. There was a plaintive creaking from various parts of the car. Pings sounded off as the engine of the tortured old Camry began to cool down. Justin was rigid in his seat, both hands clasping the wheel. Light from the approaching Prius gleamed off his scalp as he let his head fall forward.

They were facing back down old State Road 189, smoke and steam rising up all around them. The single headlight of their pursuer drifted closer and then came to a gentle stop, its hybrid engine inaudible. Dust and smoke danced within the beam of the headlight. The windshield was dark except for a series of small craters dashed across it, occasional branching cracks connecting them. Nothing moved within the shadows.

Marcus forced his hands to unclench and leaned forward slowly, as if he was afraid to draw the attention of the fat man surely regarding them through that shattered glass. In the front seat, Justin's breath came in heaving gasps barely audible over the remnant buzz of the gunshots. He looked up from beneath his lowered brow to stare into the darkness opposite them, his cheekbones twitching.

"I'm sorry." His voice was soft. "I couldn't do it."

Marcus gave a slight shake of his head, his own eyes locked on the other car. "Yeah, well, it doesn't look like I'll have too long to hate you for it."

A light winked on within the Prius' passenger compartment and both men flinched. A blue glow flashed rapidly on and off, its color reminding Marcus of the balls of energy the over-powered taser weapon had been throwing at them.

With a creak they could barely hear over the exhausted sounds of their own vehicle, the driver's door of the other car opened, rocking back and forth from a forceful push.

Again, an eerie stillness settled over the scene as they waited for the man to emerge. The area around the bridge was kept clear of trees. There was nowhere for them to run or hide. Behind them was the granite-lined lip of the little canyon of Fox Brook.

Justin looked back at Marcus from the corner of his eye. "Well, this is going to suck."

Marcus could only nod, staring at the swaying door, cold fingers of terror sliding up his neck and over his scalp. No doubt about it. This *was* going to suck.

# Chapter 2

Angara Ksaka hated Earth. She sneered at the thought, glancing up to adjust an overhead control that monitored local communications traffic. *Everyone* hated Earth. But the universal revulsion with which the rest of the galaxy regarded the nasty little dirt prison was vague and uninformed, whereas her loathing for the place was personal, particular, and very well-informed with bitter, all-too-personal experience. She snorted, shook her head, and went back to following the contact blips floating before her.

She couldn't count the number of times she had been forced to track her employer's ill-conceived attempts to flee his responsibilities to this out of the way pit. It was not as if he had a particularly demanding occupation, but he could be counted on, with the regularity of an atomic clock, to skitter off on one of his diversionary escapades whenever the perceived weight grew too much. And one of his favorite places to hide, no matter the opinion of the rest of the galaxy, was Earth.

Angara stretched her long body, luxuriating in the sensation of the malleable chagga hide covering of the intelligent command chair. The seat itself shifted beneath her, accommodating every move, supporting her body no matter how she twisted and turned. With a sigh, she settled back into a more comfortable position for flying, and checked the location of her employer, activating the tracking image with a flick of an eye. The image, appearing in the upper right edge of her vision field, showed two contact icons racing down the primitive road below. She shook her head. There had to be a better way for a young Tigan woman to make a living.

The old bitterness rose in her throat again and she tried to shake it off. It had been ages since her exile. She should be happy that they had let her take the *Yud'ahm Na'uka* with her when she fled. She had a ship, and that was more than most exiles were allowed. With that, she had been able to secure her current position, which was a stroke of luck, given her background. And at the moment, she should be spending more time thinking about *keeping* that position, and less on brooding over wrongs done to her in the distant past.

She focused again on the contact points. Who was it this time? More often than not, when Administrator Virri went off on one of his little jaunts, he would eventually run afoul of local criminals or other scum. He had a gift for seeking out the lowest form of life and then annoying it to the point of violence. If she was going to be honest with herself, his gift ran more to annoying anyone he met, the criminal aspect merely an added bonus.

Another thought forced itself into her cycling mind, and she called up several confidential reports with a twist of her right hand. They scrolled past in the air above her console and she glanced through, willing a series of key words and phrases to highlight themselves. When nothing did, she relaxed and dismissed the reports with a casual flip of her head. There had been no accounts of new Galactic Council interest in Virri or the city he nominally ruled. It would not be the first time they had dispatched Mnymian assassins to make a play against the cretin, finding him far from home.

Those few times she had faced the Council's hired killers in the line of duty it had been far more exciting than this mundane extraction was bound to be, but she found that she was not in the mood for a challenge today. Better to jump up, pull Virri's bloated tentacles out of the fire, and then return to Penumbra for a much-needed rest and refit.

Another look at the tracking icons showed that they were almost upon her. Reacting to her unspoken commands, the pilot's chair swiveled, bringing her down into her favored, prone flight position. Although she could fly her ship from nearly anywhere within, she preferred the intimate, hands-on experience of the command chair, looking out through the viewing fields at the world around her with her own eyes.

The walls of the shallow canyon swung into view as she banished the icons and other reports floating around her peripheral vision. Her hands balled into fists within the control fields, the energy there tingling against her skin like the grip of an old friend. A feral grin pulled at her mouth as she brought the weapons online. It was frowned upon to use galactic weaponry against earth Humans, no matter how lowly they were regarded, but when she was able to justify it in the line of duty, she allowed herself the latitude. How many beings across the galaxy would pay good money to be where she was at that very moment?

Behind her, the *Yud'ahm Na'uka's* power plant hummed low with anticipation of its own. It was not often that she could unleash the full power of the ship, and it contemplated the few moments of unbridled power and destruction it was about to experience with almost sentient relish.

Her tongue flicked out from between sharp teeth to moisten her lips. Her position did not offer many moments of satisfaction. She made it a point to enjoy every one that came her way.

*****

"Dude," Marcus muttered from the back seat of the Camry. "Your little getaway weekend sucks."

He could see the edge of Justin's responding smile in sharp profile. "Guarantee you forgot Clarissa for at least a little while."

The name caused a quick stab of pain despite the fear of the outlandish moment. His eyes were fixated on a car that would soon, no doubt, produce the man that was going to kill him. He shook his head; the unfathomable mysteries of the Human heart.

"Until you had to mention her, asshole."

The car in front of them shifted on its springs. The big fat man must be getting ready to emerge. The gun was empty, their car was dead. It all came down to this moment. Everything in both their lives had led to this little stretch of pathetic, backwoods road in the middle of Nowhere, Connecticut, and they were going to die here.

The rush of lights behind them was like a sudden, unexpected sunrise. The entire scene was cast in stark illumination. The ground around them, the trees off in the distance, and the car idling not twenty feet in front of them were all lit with brilliant, shifting light. It swooped and flashed, shadows sliding wildly all around, and a hurricane wind slapped against the Camry, churning billowing clouds of dust and smoke in all directions.

Marcus twisted in the back seat, looking out through the broken remains of the window, but all he saw were the swirling clouds and beams of sapphire and diamond-white light as whatever had caused the disturbance lifted up and over the car.

"What is it, a helicopter?" He shouted the words, although there was almost no sound. If it was a helicopter, it was some kind of bizarre, stealthy, government type.

Justin snapped out of his immobility, craning his head around the steering wheel and against the windshield, twisting his neck to look above them. His entire body froze as the lights speared down from overhead. He slid back into his seat as if his bones had turned to liquid.

"What? What is it?" Marcus reached into the front seat and grabbed his friend's shoulder, but Justin just flopped around, staring straight ahead.

Whatever was casting the lights seemed to move forward as the wild shadows shifted around them. Marcus could just make out the snout of something huge poking out from above the car's roof before it halted, hovering there above them, sending the tree branches whipping violently, dark clouds of dust and dirt swirling all around. Whatever it was, it was huge, and brightly lit, and still made almost no sound. A low throbbing tone seemed to make the entire car vibrate, but it was no louder than distant, gentle thunder.

The moment stretched on. The dark car across from them, its single headlight carving a solid column through the billowing clouds, seemed to shrink before this new threat. There was movement behind the shattered windshield, light from the hovering beast above them finally piercing the gloom. Marcus saw the face of the fat man pressed against the glass, his hands pushing outward as his mouth stretched impossibly wide in a scream of denial. There was more movement around and behind him, strange shapes writhing and curling in the shivering shadows.

A bolt of lightning stretched out from the hovering vehicle and Justin and Marcus both flinched down in their seats. A deafening roar engulfed their car, which shook with the fury of a primal storm. Both men screamed, reaching out to grasp anything that might offer some stability. The car continued to rock, sapphire and crimson lights flashing through their clenched eyelids.

The shaking of their car subsided, but the detonations continued as a series of thunderous blows landed, each accompanied by a hellish glare visible right through the steel of the car. Marcus could not control his curiosity any longer and pried one eyelid open just enough to peak through the windshield.

The car that had pursued them from the parking lot of the Happy Hunting Ground Casino was gone. Only a blasted and scorched crater remained, twisted limbs of steel reaching up into the chaotic swirl of lights above while tattered fragments of cloth flapped madly in the whipping wind.

Marcus reached out with a hesitant hand and tapped on Justin's rigid shoulder. One eye opened, wide and white in his friend's dark face, looking wildly around as if trying to piece together how they could still be breathing. Marcus raised one shaking hand to point out the windshield, and his friend gasped as the scene before them penetrated his panicked mind.

The lightning had ceased, and the object hovering above them began to move again, swinging wide around the clearing, away from the bridge and the burning crater, to settle beside the canyon edge. Both men could only stare.

The hull was a shining metallic blue, with silver details flashing along its flanks. With a body about the size of a school bus, something that looked like a head thrust out from massive shoulder-like assemblies that led out to a vast complex of wings, several on each side. It took a moment for Marcus's mind to register that many of the wings were not attached in any visible way to the hunched cowlings, but seemed to float independently of the vehicle and each other. A primary wing stretched out to either side, around which the others shifted and slid as it maintained its station above the ground. Each of these main structures housed a swirling ball of energy within a socket piercing them halfway down their length. The sockets were spinning furiously against the flow of the glowing spheres.

The head thrusting toward them was the same blue and silver as the rest of the vehicle, except the upper section, which was covered in a darker surface that glared and flared with reflected light and fire. It regarded them silently as if waiting for them to do something, but neither man moved, both pinned in place by the terror of the moment.

As if losing patience, the vehicle heaved upward, all of its disconnected parts spreading out for a moment, and then the wings condensed, the constituent control surfaces sliding into position around the main wings until these moved back against the fuselage, sliding into the large housings as the whole thing lowered to the churned and twisted ground. Clawed landing feet slid from within its body, and the enormous thing settled onto the ground. The balls of furious energy within the wings seemed to settle down, slowing and darkening as the wings folded back along the vehicle's hull.

Justin did not move, staring at the surfaces about fifteen feet above them. Marcus scrambled back into the front seat, staring up as well. His hand fell upon the string of jewels that he had left forgotten on the seat, and with a slight twinge he absently pushed them into a pocket as he settled back, keeping his eye on this mysterious thing that had saved them in such a spectacular fashion.

Beneath the raptor-like head, a light appeared as a section of the hull slid away to reveal a hatch whose size was lost in the vastness of the rest of the ship. A dim red light shone out from the interior, and a ramp slid down, digging a small trough into the roadside dirt. A shape rose up out of the dim lighting, standing at the top of the ramp, and the moment seemed heavy with significance he didn't understand.

The figure began to move down the ramp. Its movements were lithe and easy, and yet still managed to convey a clear sense of annoyance. As it stepped onto the dirt, illuminated by the softly pulsing lights on the vehicle behind, Marcus was surprised to see that it was a woman. He did not know quite what he was expecting, but a tall woman with long flowing white hair somehow missed the mark.

"Wow." Justin muttered under his breath, and Marcus knew that his friend had made the same realization. She stalked toward them at an easy pace. She wasn't running; nothing she did made it seem like she was in any sort of a hurry. She seemed irritated that she had needed to emerge, and impatient to be gone.

As she approached, they could make out more details. She was wearing dark, form fitting clothing. Not skin-tight, but more like a uniform, or exercise gear. She wore a belt that seemed to hold several pieces of equipment, none of which reminded them of a weapon of any kind. Only her face and hands were visible, both darker even than Justin's ebony skin. And her hair, flying loose in the wild, remnant wind, looked silver, picking up the glowing lights behind her.

She stopped about twenty feet from their wrecked car, her hip cocked to one side in an unmistakable sign of displeasure. She yelled something to them, but neither man could understand the words over the wind and the ringing in their ears. Placing her hands on her hips in irritation, she shouted even louder, but her meaning continued to elude them.

"Um … is that English?" Marcus was cold, shaking slightly; shock. He felt as if he were in a dream. "I'm not sure I understand what she's saying."

Justin shook his head. "I don't think it's English."

The woman did not stomp her foot, but somehow gave that impression nonetheless, and then shouted something yet again. This time she was loud enough they heard her clearly. Clearly enough that they could both say with confidence that it was not English.

"French?" Marcus's could not tear his eyes away from the figure, backlit by her strange, terrifying transport.

Justin snorted despite the fear and shock. "French?"

Marcus shrugged. "Canadians? I don't know, I'm guessing."

She just stood there, somehow conveying a dangerous, growing anger. "I think we need to get out."

"She saved our lives, yeah?" Justin's voice had the brittle edge of forced positivity. "I mean, she could just have easily have killed us too, right?"

Marcus nodded. "Yeah. I guess."

He forced his door open without taking his eyes off the strange woman. He grunted as he swung his legs out and levered himself upright. He was staring right at her face, and so there was no doubting her reaction when she saw him.

The black-skinned woman's eyes widened as he emerged from the car, staring at him in utter disbelief. Her mouth fell open, white teeth gleaming, incredulous. She was beautiful, some distant part of his brain noted. Her eyes were almond-shaped, her nose straight, her lips full above a sharp, defined chin. The hair billowing about her was pearly white, giving a further alien strangeness to her face. And she was not at all happy to see him.

The driver's door of the Camry creaked wearily as Justin pushed it open, and Marcus watched the woman's eyes slide to the side, widening even more as she watched him rise. Her hand snapped to one of the containers on her belt and she crouched down as if ready for a fight, but when Justin made no threatening moves, her eyes narrowed and she relaxed a little.

She looked both of them up and down, her mouth still open, her eyes widening again. A frightening realization dawned in them while Marcus watched, and she seemed to crumble, despair washing across her fine features. Her shoulders slumped and she turned slightly to look at the burning wreck nestled in the bottom of the newly-formed crater she had blasted into the old surface of State Road 189.

Marcus and Justin shared a confused glance. The large vehicle, whatever it was, rumbled softly behind her, strange and menacing. The blasted ruins of the car that had chased them from the casino burned fitfully in the last eddies of turbulent wind. The trees of the northern Connecticut forest whispered empty thoughts back and forth to each other. And this strange woman stood before them, exotically beautiful, clearly formidable, and obviously very upset.

"Um … thanks?" Marcus didn't know what else to say. That seemed entirely inappropriate and inadequate, but it was the best he had.

The woman glanced back at him; her eyes strangely empty, then to Justin, then back to the burning car. She moved to the wreck with a heavy, listless gait. She ignored the two men before her as she walked. She stopped at the edge of the crater, staring down, her dark face outlined in shiny highlights from the guttering flames.

Exchanging another look, Justin and Marcus moved around the Camry, walking together to the blasted crater. The twisted wreck at the bottom was barely recognizable as a car. A strange glowing void in the abstract mess had to be where the windshield had been, and Marcus tried to make sense of the twisted knot of blackened matter sitting, as best as he could tell, where the driver would have been. There was nothing Human there at all, and he felt his gut twist at this reminder of mortality.

The woman stood still, staring into the crater, showing no sign that she had noticed either man walking up behind her. The glowing lights from her vehicle and the dancing flames had a strange effect on her skin, making it seem more like a deep purple than black.

"Hey … um … like I said, really. Thanks." Marcus tried to sidle into the woman's field of vision without coming too close to the edge of the pit. "I really think he was going to kill us if you hadn't shown up. You did a good thing, here."

Justin nodded, although he stayed in the shadows beyond the crater. "We owe you our lives, miss. Thank you."

Something deep in the woman's violet eyes quivered behind the shimmering reflections of dying flames. She jerked her gaze back to Marcus, then to Justin, and back to Marcus. The flesh around them tightened, her pale eyebrows fell, and she pivoted without warning. Her hands caught Marcus in the chest and she pushed him violently backward.

With a startled cry, Marcus fell back onto his rear end. He tried to catch himself and only succeeded in taking some of his weight on the points of his elbows, cracking them against the old pavement. He looked up in a combination of fear and anger only to see the woman tilt slightly, one leg coming up to plant a foot on Justin's chest and push him down also. Both men were more startled than hurt, looking up at the strange woman looming above them, glaring down with undisguised hatred burning in her strange eyes.

She began to speak in loud, staccato bursts that would have been hard to decipher even if they had known the language. She shrieked, moving now in jerky steps, gesturing wildly down at them, then at the burning wreck, and then at them again. She pulled manically at her hair as she howled up at the sky, her voice never faltering as she screamed her nonsensical monologue into the darkness.

It seemed to go on for hours, and Justin and Marcus shared more than one sidelong look as she ranted and raved, now seemingly oblivious to them. Whenever it appeared like she was winding down, her staggering movements would bring her once again to the rim of the crater, where she would pause, staring down into the twisted mess at the bottom, and then she would be off again, roaring down at them as if this whole tragedy was all their fault.

Eventually, the woman ran out of energy. She stopped, seemingly in mid-rant, and her legs folded beneath her. She lowered herself gracefully to the pavement, her elbows coming to rest on her knees, her head in her hands, and she began to sob quietly.

Marcus looked over at Justin who could only shrug, raising his eyebrows in confusion. Pushing himself up from the highway, he dusted himself off and moved to the crumpled woman.

"Miss, do you speak English at all? Is there something that we can do to help?" He looked again at Justin, but there was no help there. She had to be military of some sort. Judging by the nature of her plane, she had to be high up on someone's chain of command. But she seemed to have completely lost her senses. Something about the way she was acting had set a dark and ominous thought stirring in the back of his mind, half-formed, giving only a vague sense of danger and unease. At the moment, however, they were all stranded on this all-but abandoned stretch of old highway, with a dead body not ten feet away, and the only escape available this odd helicopter-like thing, flown by a woman who had clearly checked out.

"Miss, if there's anything we can do, please tell us. I'm sure there are people who want to know where you are. Is there someone we should call?" He repeated the request, figuring that it might break through whatever depression had claimed her.

At last the woman raised her head. She looked up, her eyes red from crying, but cold as ice as she regarded him. She looked over to where Justin still sat on the tar, and he tried to give her a friendly smile. She did not return the expression.

The woman sat unmoving for several minutes, and although at first Marcus found this far more preferable to the anguished sobbing that had preceded it, but after a minute or two, the eerie stillness started to get to him. He was about to ask again if they could help when she unfolded gracefully to her feet. She looked down at Justin, and then reached out one hand. He hesitated a moment and then accepted the offered help.

She lifted Justin up, and then stepped back to look at both men. They stood side by side, waiting for what might come next. Her eyes had taken on a calculating look and she began to pace back and forth, looking at each of them in turn. She stopped, her expression vague, and tilted her head with a strange, sharp gesture. Her eyes seemed to fall out of focus, flicking rapidly back and forth as if chasing sparks that only she could see. Then with another tilt, she was back, looking at Marcus with eyes that had narrowed even further.

She spoke, her voice reasonable and calm, her words holding no more meaning than they had before.

Marcus shrugged, shaking his head. He didn't know what else to do. He didn't even recognize the language she was speaking, never mind understand any of what she was saying.

The woman cut off abruptly, shaking her head in undisguised exasperation. Her head fell again, her arms on her hips. When she looked up, her eyes were cold.

"Buteefu?" She said the word slowly, as if to a child, nodding her head as if urging him to follow along.

Marcus shrugged again. "I don't know what that means." Obviously, she was trying to communicate, but the sounds had been no closer to English than anything else the strange woman had said.

She sighed as her eyes closed, then opened again. Again, she repeated, "Buteefu?" This time she gestured around her neck, across her chest, with both hands as if gripping something.

Marcus looked over to Justin, but his friend looked just as lost. They both shrugged.

The woman spat something foul-sounding. Again her hands were on her hips. She looked up into the dark sky, her eyes closing, and her eyelids fluttered rapidly once again. When her head came down her eyes were open, staring straight at Marcus, and she said, clear as day, "Necklace."

Both men smiled, nodding, and Marcus said, "Yes! Necklace! ... Wait, what necklace?"

The dark face, still reflecting purple highlights from the burning wreck, did not move. The violet eyes did not flicker. She stared at him, then said, slowly as if to a particularly slow child, "Beautiful necklace."

Again the men shared a glance, and then looked blankly at the strange woman.

She closed her eyes again, then moved to the edge of the crater, pointed at the ruined car, then at their car, then flung her arms wide, looking from side to side as if searching for something, then again said, in her heavily accented speech, "beautiful necklace?"

The silence stretched on as both men stared at her, neither wanting to admit ignorance again. When Justin gave a slight gasp, Marcus jumped. "What?"

Marcus watched as his friend's eyes slid over to the Camry, then back to him. "Beautiful necklace?"

Marcus made a face. That had not been as helpful a comment as he had been hoping for. "Yeah, I got that part. What the hell does she mean?"

Justin gave a slight shrug, and then tilted his head toward the car. "Do we have a beautiful necklace?"

The jewels in his pocket suddenly doubled in weight as this little mystery, at least, became clear. "Oh, damn! The necklace!"

Marcus pulled the net of delicate chain and gemstones from his pocket and held it up with an innocent smile. "This?"

The woman's face transformed as the jewelry was held before her, but not in any way they might have anticipated. First, a deep look of despair came over her, and then anger boiled up to wipe that away, and finally, if they had to guess, a sneer of disgust. She spat again, this time into the crater, and put a hand out for the necklace.

A flash of images went through Marcus's mind as he looked at her over the dangling necklace. He had only possessed it for a short time, and yet he was loath to let it go. Again, the glittering within the primary jewel distracted him. He could almost feel an electrical current running down his arm, sending fluttering pulses through his heart.

Without being aware, he withdrew his hand, gathering the necklace to his chest.

The woman's eyes tightened again as she watched his reaction. Without another word she strode toward him, looking more closely at the necklace, then into his eyes as if inspecting him for some physical flaw. She spat another bitter comment under her breath in that strange, nonsensical language, shaking her head.

She turned around to look at Justin, then back to Marcus, and then gestured to the murmuring craft idling nearby. After closing her eyes for just a moment, she snapped, "You come."

The words were peremptory. It was not an invitation or a question.

Justin smiled widely, shook his head once as if to clear it, and then moved quickly to the old Camry, popping the trunk and rummaging around inside. Then he moved around the car to the passenger side, forced the back door open and reached in for something, rising with a large gym bag in hand. Marcus recognized what his friend had always called his 'bug-out bag.'

"I'm ready." He said it with a smile that set his bright teeth flashing in the reflecting firelight. His eyes were shining.

Marcus stared at his friend, amazed. "You're *ready*?"

Justin's smile widened. "Hell yeah, I'm ready! Are you crazy? Have you been paying attention to what's going on here? This is some weird-ass shit! You're going to say no? Miss out on all this stuff?" He gestured with one arm to the vehicle, then to the exotic woman who waited for them.

Marcus shook his head. "You have no idea what you're talking about. A man just *died*, for Christ's sake! She *killed* him!" He jerked a thumb at the vehicle. "She killed him with *that* thing! And neither of us even knows what the hell that thing *is*!"

Justin's settled back on his heels, gesturing broadly with his free arm. "Exactly."

Marcus could feel all the pent up anger and confusion rising once more in his throat. "Exactly? *Exactly?* What about your work? What about your contracts? What about Sarah? What about your car? What about *everything*?"

Justin shrugged. "The work'll be there when we come back; *if* I come back. That's what being your own boss is all about. Sarah'll be fine without me, that's the kind of girl I generally end up with." He looked back at the smoking Camry. "My car is old, and ugly, and now dead, so no big loss there. And my closest relative is an uncle who doesn't know I exist!"

Marcus had worked himself up into a froth. "You can't be serious! You have *no* idea who she is, or where she's going! You can't—"

"You too." While the men had been speaking, the woman had moved around to address them both from in front of her flying machine. She was pointing at Marcus, ignoring Justin.

Marcus stared at her, his mouth hanging open, and then shook his head violently. "No! I mean, no way! There is no way I'm going with you! Do you have any idea—"

Something bulged on the woman's shoulder. She was wearing a high, tight jacket, like a bolero made out of a soft, reflective surface. The shoulders of the garment were shiny and rigid. And something like a small arm had just lifted away from the right shoulder. It had a ball on the end that pivoted around like an eye looking for something, and then it settled upon him.

"You too." She repeated, as if she had now made her case.

"Look, I don't know who you are, or where you've gotten all of these nifty movie props, but—"

A red light flared within the orb on her shoulder, and a line struck out, settling upon his forehead.

"You too." This time the words were slow and deliberate.

Marcus was at a loss. Something in his head told him he should feel threatened, but the anger and the fear and the confusion were still there, doing their best to run interference on immediate observation. He shook his head, his brows drawing together toward the floating dot.

The woman shifted her gaze from Marcus's head to the Camry. Without warning, a beam of bright, solid light lanced out from the thing on her shoulder and there was a loud crumpling sound, like a car accident, behind him. He jumped, spinning around, gripping the necklace even tighter, and watched as the Camry seemed to collapse in upon itself, a massive hole punched through the side, taking the back half of the driver's door and the front half of the back door with it.

"Damn!" Justin stared open mouthed at what was left of his car.

"That does not clarify the issue!" Marcus felt as if he was going to drown in the emotions crashing through him. "Blowing up the car does nothing to help!"

"Uh, Marc," Justin hiked the strap of his bag higher up on his shoulder. "Couple things: one, it's not like you've got another option for transportation handy just now; and two, she's pointing it at your head again. Can we just head out, figure everything else out later?"

Marcus looked back at the woman, the glimmering line connecting them again. He opened his mouth to speak, but nothing came out. He had thought he was suffering from shock before, but he now realized, as the cold rose up from his feet and the pressure built behind his eyes, that that had been nothing. As if in a dream, he nodded, forcing his mouth closed. He nodded again, not trusting himself to speak.

Justin nodded as well, turned to the frightening figure with a smile, and started walking toward her. "What we got, sweets?"

She stared at him with those inhuman violet eyes, a snarl building on her lips. With a sudden, jerking move, she turned back to the crater and barked some foul-sounding words as the weapon on her shoulder flashed, sending bolt after bolt into the smoldering wreckage of the Prius. When she was done, there was nothing but twisted metal and glittering droplets of molten glass behind. With a nod, her eyes still glowing, she turned on one heel and marched toward the ship.

Marcus followed, noticing with some half-asleep part of his brain when the red light winked out, the bulge on her shoulder settling back into its hard shell without leaving a sign or blemish behind.

The vehicle looked more menacing as they approached. Hanging above them, the head-like protrusion was about ten feet wide, while the rest of the fuselage was closer to fifteen or twenty. The ramp was smooth, but had no give when they stepped onto it, following the woman up into the ship. They moved through a large, open space with various pieces of equipment fixed to walls and floor. They climbed a steep ship's ladder up into another compartment that reminded Marcus of something out of the Arabian Nights. Shimmering cloth hung from the walls, hiding the full dimensions of the chamber, and pillows and cushions were scattered about in a haphazard manner. It was a swirl of colors and different fabrics, more like a gypsy's wagon than the inside of some strange war plane.

The woman pushed through a heavy curtain of brocade, gesturing for them to follow, and they entered a control area with a single pilot's chair in the center. They found themselves looking down through the gleaming upper surface of what they now realized was the cockpit at the smoking wreckage of two cars littering the roadway.

Justin put down his duffle bag and moved to the window. They could see just as clearly as if they were looking directly down at the scene below. But when he reached out, his hand passed into a hazy field of light and the image distorted around him. He looked back at Marcus, his grin even wider.

"Man, you've got to check this out." Marcus moved up beside his friend and looked out. He saw no glare, no sign of any kind that there was anything between him and the open night air. But when he put his own hand out, he felt a slight tingling, like static electricity, and that distorting effect.

The woman made a hissing noise and gestured for them to back up. By the softly glowing light, Marcus could see that her skin really was a deep purple, adding to the surrealism of the moment. She slid easily into the seat, which was draped with some shaggy fur-bearing hide, and a soft, glowing sphere appeared to hover before her. Behind her and to either side two similar chairs rose out of the floor as if they were rising out of still water, the same neutral color as the deck plating.

Justin sank into the closest chair and yelped as it writhed beneath him. Marcus looked at the remaining chair with distrust. He pushed at it and it gave slightly, like cold clay.

The strange woman barked something and Marcus dropped into his chair. Beneath him he could feel the material shifting and sorting itself out, sinking in some places and rising in others, until he was completely and comfortably supported, his legs stretched out before him, his arms on smooth, perfectly positioned rests.

None of this made him feel any better.

The woman settled back slightly in her chair and leaned forward. She reached out and put her hands into the sphere of light, minute shifts of her fingers stirring dancing motes of dust that glittered, suspended, within the glow. The view outside moved, sliding down and sideways; the burning wrecks slipping out of view.

There was very little sense of motion as they drifted out over the ravine, the old bridge dropping away on their right. Behind them they heard a distant, constant rumbling, but that was the only sign there was an engine of some kind at work.

The view ahead of them shifted again as the nose lifted higher. The horizon dropped away and the clouds swept into view. Marcus's stomach gave an uncomfortable lurch as he realized they were pointing straight up, although he felt no change in the pressure pushing him gently into his seat. The clouds ahead of them surged suddenly, jumping at them in a terribly disorienting fashion. The rumble behind them never shifted, and there was no sense of acceleration within the vehicle itself.

Realization dawned on Marcus just as they pierced the clouds, a panorama of stars opening up before them.

"Wait ... Where are we going?" His voice was shaking, and he didn't care.

"Yeah!" Beside him, this latest surprise just seemed to make Justin even more excited.

"Where are we going!?" Marcus repeated, trying to sit up. There was no belt or other restraint, but something about the way the seat was embracing him kept him from standing, or even moving his legs.

"I said wait! Where are you taking us?" Even as he struggled, he did not miss the sneering smile the woman shot over her shoulder. Marcus saw Justin fiddling with something out of the corner of his eye and turned to stare in wonder as his friend furiously tapped out instructions on his phone.

"What are you *doing*?" He snapped. He was just realizing that he hadn't thought to contact his brother, or Clarissa, or *anyone*.

Justin's smile was wider than it had ever been. "I'm changing my status." His thumbs flew across the screen.

Marcus leaned over to look at his friend's phone, and then reeled back in disgust. "Abducted by *aliens*?"

Justin nodded with glee, but the strange woman glanced back in annoyance, her brows drawing down as she saw the phone. Her eyes closed for a brief moment, and then she was glaring again. She jerked her chin at the device. "Visage Tome?"

Justin thought about it for a second, then laughed and nodded. "Yeah, sure!"

She turned back, shaking her head, and her shoulders tensed for a moment.

Justin's laughter stopped suddenly and he gasped.

"What?" Marcus leaned over to try to see his friend's phone. The screen was an array of somber purples and black.

"It's my automatic death message." Justin's voice was soft. "Everybody's going to think I'm dead."

The star field grew to fill their entire wide field of vision. The moon slid away to the left. Something flashed past on the right, and Marcus had the distinct impression of a massive airplane. He screamed as it disappeared behind them, his fingers sinking into the malleable material of his arm rests as his mind told him they were tearing through the atmosphere, pointing straight up, no matter what his inner ear might have to say on the subject.

A shimmering white object shot past on the right. The moon was gone and they were headed out toward the distant stars. They passed a strange bronze cube that shot a red beam out at them. The beam seemed to pass right through the walls of what he was coming to realize was a spaceship, flashing down the length of the cockpit around them, and he watched as their abductress looked from side to side with sudden tension. The light flared and past, however, and she soon relaxed.

They had been soaring silently for what seemed like an hour, but could have been only a few minutes, when the woman sat up, her seat lifting to do all the work, and turned to smile at them. She held up one finger, a red-painted nail flashing in the dim, sourceless light, and said a few guttural words. She reached out behind her and worked a control on the moving panel, slid back into her seat, and then with the easy grace of a showman, indicated the view ahead.

The star field rippled as if they were looking at it through water. The disturbance grew more agitated, and the stars in the center of the shimmer winked out of existence. The blacked-out area spread as the disturbance flattened, spreading out like a disk around the sphere of disappearing stars. The entire image began to swirl like some cosmic whirlpool.

For the first time, the ship experienced a sense of movement, shaking slightly as the vision ahead of them continued to grow. An occasional streak of blue or red passed them, dropping into the swirl, giving the impression that they were being drawn into the vortex as it continued to grow.

Justin's eyes widened in alarm, and Marcus knew a moment's satisfaction to see the calm finally drain from his friend's face. Then he realized what he was seeing, and he was too terrified to care.

It was a black hole, and they were diving straight for it.

Marcus had failed high school physics, and he didn't know much about black holes, but he was pretty sure they were generally viewed as something to avoid.

This was too much. The fat man, the necklace, balls of electricity, beams of light, strange women and floating ships, death, destruction, threats, kidnapping, and now a black hole?

He screamed with throat-tearing intensity as they seemed to fall into the endless darkness within the colorful smear of swirling stars.

# Chapter 3

Ambassador for the Galactic Council, Khuboda Taurani, looked down at the shape floating in the middle of his hibernation pool. A soft cloud of pink sent fading tendrils out into the crystal waters around the edge. His broad chest heaved in a dramatic sigh as he pulled robes of state over his shoulders.

He took a moment to enjoy how the crisp ivory cloth set off his pearlescent grey skin, reflecting on the sad reality of the moment. Most pleasures in this life were fleeting, and he knew this loss would haunt him in the days ahead. This ceaseless exile from civilization was going to seem interminable without distraction to occupy his mind.

Still, one took one's distractions where they came. The slit of his mouth widened in remembered pleasure. The facial parts of a Kerie were not built for such base displays of satisfaction as smiles, but at times even he could see the enjoyment of such things. After a moment, however, the orbits of his silver orbs quirked in annoyance.

Such diversions were not easily come by so far from the galactic core. He had brought this one with him from his last station, knowing that such entertainments would be few and far between during his new posting. Now, he would be alone until he was able to return, triumphant, to the Council. The sacrifices he made for his family and his race.

With a shrug of heavy shoulders, he turned away. His Eru servant, Iranse, would take care of the mess before he returned from his latest appointment. The brute had had enough practice, after all. He finished fastening his robes and stepped away from the pool. His last post had been on Iwa'Ban, where he and the other Galactic diplomats had been treated with proper respect, their tastes and appetites catered to as was only right and proper. It was one of the most sought-after posts in the Council Diplomatic Corps for just that reason. He sighed again.

This current assignment, on the other hand, was an excellent notch to collect on one's climb upward. If he was able to bring things here to a successful conclusion, the Council would not soon forget his name, and his family would be well along to achieving their deeper goals as well. But the ennui suffered in the process might well come close to killing him. Pulling his robes into line one last time, he wrinkled the olfactory field between his eyes and his mouth and pivoting upon his left hoof, stalked from his inner chambers, through the opulent rooms of the consulate's residential quarters, and out past the two hulking Ntja guards at the door. Moving into the surge of galactic trash that floated through the pressurized halls beyond, he knew that one of the guards had stepped out after him, stomping along at a discreet distance, its beady eyes and fleshy nostrils seeking any signs of danger from the heaving crowd.

*****

The Consulate of the Galactic Council was located in the upper levels of one of the most opulent towers of the city, as befitted the representatives of the most powerful conglomerate of worlds in the known universe. At least, that was how the location had been sold to the Council. In reality, despite the luxurious nature of the location, they were about as far from the control center as they could conceivably be.

The fact that there were no other consulates in the city was a bit troubling. He had done some digging and knew that many of the more prominent races and alliances maintained discreet legations here, often much closer to the control center in what was known as the Red Tower. But the Galactic Council was the only entity with an official residence of record. In a way it made sense, the Council was the de facto ruling body of the entire galaxy. But for some reason, it made him uneasy, here in one of the last independent polities in the galaxy, whose questionable legal status remained central to the question of Council control.

The Council's embassy was located in the heart of the city's western wing, in a tall, elegant tower that, like all the towers here, had been a starship in ages since lost to memory. From the dim, greenish lighting in the corridors, the swirling, grainy pattern of the walls, and the relatively low placement of interface controls, it was clear this tower had once been a Kot'i passenger cruiser, back when that furry, amiable race had ruled its own destiny. It was long and thin, with no bridges connecting it to any other towers for the upper half of its considerable length. In official reports this might appear to set the consulate above the fray, in the lofty heights, as it were. In reality, it just meant that when Taurani had to make the distasteful journey to speak to the creature that nominally ruled here, it took him far longer than he would have liked.

An access port to the spinal lift tube array was not far from the consulate. Although the drop always did dreadful things to his robes, Taurani preferred the swift transportation to the more dignified, but longer, journey of a shuttle. On any civilized planet in the galaxy he would be treated with all the pomp and ceremony of a local ruler, feted and fawned over in a dizzying whirlwind of sycophantic frenzy. Here, he was treated like some diseased outsider. The Council was not revered in Penumbra. And the representative of the Council was looked upon as an interloper, or worse.

The flesh between his mouth and eyes wrinkled again. Let them have their petty victories. Let them play their little games and force him into tramping up and down the local real estate. There would come a time in the not-so-distant-future when things would be set right here, and he would be able to return to the comforts and security of civilization.

Taurani stopped before entering the lift tube and turned to his Ntja guard. The creature was nearly a head taller than him, its mismatched little eyes peering down from either side of the open, snuffling hole of its great nose. The metallic domes of combat and tactical enhancements embedded in its skull emerged through the bruised, puckered flesh of its scalp.

"I'll be going all the way down to the Concourse, I think. I want to taste the mood of the people before joining Virri in his little hovel." He turned back to the tube without waiting for a reply. The guard nodded sharply anyway, moving to follow him with the ease of long practice.

The lift tube was a harrowing, barbaric experience, as always. It was all Taurani could do to keep the panic off his face as the twitching, fitful gravity grabbed a hold of him and pushed him downward at what his brain told him had to be a lethal speed. The gravity-manipulation required for Penumbra's countless thousands of inhabitants to move about, living in the vertically aligned towers but moving through the horizontally situated Concourse that covered the deep core of the planetoid the city rested on, was dizzying.

Coming to an abrupt halt at the designated level, the gravitic field pushed him out, and he shook his robes back into some semblance of order. Heavy footsteps behind him announced the arrival of his guard moments later.

The observation level of the tower was an ornate balcony crafted from one of the immense thruster nozzles that had once pushed the ancient ship through space. A wide opening had been carved into the wall of the nozzle, carpeting and polished handrails added, and a scattering of comfortable-looking chairs and simple tables placed around as a final touch.

Taurani moved up to the railing, his long grey fingers settling down upon the faux-wood surface, and gazed down at the Concourse, two levels below. The Concourse had been constructed around the bases of the many starships whose hulls thrust up into empty space overhead. The ships were joined by countless bridges and transportation conduits up and down their lengths, but here, near the bottom, the world opened up, and the denizens of the outpost could wander free, moving between the ships without having to resort to the bridges above, or expensive personal shuttles or taxis.

The mob that surged and churned beneath him was a veritable rainbow of races, colors, and creeds. Every one of them here against the express wishes of the Council, each one of them a slap in the face to those who would see the galaxy a single, unified expanse of peace, plenty, and happiness for all beings. Those below were violating everything Taurani believed to be most important in existence, and they smiled and laughed while they did it.

A soft hacking sound erupted from the back of the ambassador's throat. It was a Kerie sign of disgust and frustration, and the only response he could think to convey the depth of his disdain for the beings that made this place their home despite all of the advancement and stability the Council had brought to the galaxy in the last thousand years and more.

He continued to scan the crowd, not trying to hold back the sneer that peeled the rigid skin from the fan of baleen lining his mouth. There was no redemption for these beings who had turned their backs on the Council. No reason for him to feel bad for what he knew was coming. A flash of white caught his attention, and his face wrinkled as he focused on one particular being moving sedately through the jostling crowd.

The flowing white garments of a Thien'ha master, offset by the pale green beard frill and pale bald head of a Goagoi Kuak, stood out amid the dull, muted colors of the masses. Thien'ha masters were not uncommon anywhere, their strange credo taking them all over the known galaxy. And although Goagoi Kuak were not known for wandering far from their forest homes, the lure of the Thien'ha path could easily explain its presence. However, the Thien'ha had a bad reputation for bringing disaster and chaos in their wake. Their attempts to witness all of the most tumultuous events of galactic history were well known. It was often hard for the lesser beings of the galaxy to separate the enigmatic monks from the events they chased, and they were seldom welcomed when they arrived in a new location. Taurani scowled.

Behind the Thien'ha master, following with a gait considerably less grace-ful and untroubled, was a Humanoid figure in the dark robes of a Thien'ha Novice. Masters often accepted students, training them and allowing them to follow on the many journeys they made in response to the demands of their strange beliefs. The novice's hood was raised, hiding its race from him. He stared at the two fig-ures moving through the crowd, his pearlescent eyes inscrutable.

He lowered his head, turning away from the mob, and forced a steadying breath. There was a brightening edge to the situation here: the chaos could not endure for very much longer. When his current mission came to fruition, this bas-tion of confusion would succumb to the order and discipline that represented the only path to true, universal harmony.

Taurani's eyes flickered as he accessed the clock function of his nano-im-plants. He was overdue for his meeting with the sniveling amoeba, but by just long enough to make his point. This hellish hole was not worth the time of a high-rank-ing Galactic diplomat, and neither was its nominal leader. He shrugged the robes into place and swept past the silent guard toward the lift tube. They would need to go up several levels to catch a transport linking this tower with the Red Tower that housed the control center. His mouth twisted in distaste at the thought of having to deal with the shiftless slime peddler whose moist bulk currently filled that ragged throne. Still, it would not be much longer. Soon, either Uduta Virri would see the path of sanity before him, or he would be replaced. The pieces were in position, and only the opportunity now remained to be found.

He chuffed in amusement through his brill. Soon this shadow realm, last holdout against Galactic Council rule, would fall.

*****

The control center was located in the center of what had once been a Variyar warship. The brutal lines, the cold, dark metal of its crooked halls, and the crude, if effective, security systems made that clear enough. The reddish tinge to the overhead lighting as one walked the narrow halls was an unnecessary reminder. The Variyar were a rough-edged, unrepentant race, chaffing beneath the mantle of Council rule, as they had since the Council was first founded. Every time Taurani visited the place, he found himself wondering what strange course of events had resulted in some ancient Variyar war leader surrendering his ship to this conglomeration of misfits and hulks.

The broad, studded security doors to the control center were closed when the ambassador and his bodyguard swept around the curved hallway. This in itself was strange, as Virri seldom allowed the doors to be shut. The position of admin-istrator here was constrained with so many rules, customs, and traditions that a certain claustrophobia could not help but result, and the current creature holding the post was even more given to that particular weakness than most.

Taurani expected the doors to sweep open as he approached, as they had always done on those few occasions when they had not been open. Instead, they remained steadfastly closed.

Standing before the mute barrier, the ambassador stared at the burnished steel with wide disbelief as his long fingered-hands wrapped around each other in growing annoyance. Why would the doors be closed in the middle of a normal work session? And why, if closed, would they not open at once for the anointed representative of the Galactic Council?

He cast his glittering eyes all around the frame of the security doors. He had never had cause to look for any sort of mechanism to open them before, or to make his presence known to those inside. And on this ridiculous antique, he would not even recognize one if he found it. The prospect of knocking on the heavy metal, however, seemed ludicrous. For a brief, heated flash he entertained the notion of ordering the Ntja guard to blast the door with his sidearm. But given the Variyar construction, and the innate security systems of the city, the single shot they would get with the weapon would probably not be equal to the task, and he would only be made to look even more foolish.

If there was one thing Khuboda Taurani could not stand, it was being made to look foolish.

He could feel tension rising behind his eyes as the anger began to build. Every indignity, every slight, every hardship he had been forced to endure here on the edge of civilized space, stung in his mind. He began to calculate exactly how many Ntja soldiers the consulate contained, how many heavy weapons were stowed within the holds of his diplomatic shuttle, and what the chances were that, his plans only half fulfilled, he might be able to bring the entire disgusting nest to its knees by sheer brute force…

The hiss of the heavy doors opening stopped him just short of spinning around and ordering his bodyguard to prepare for war. The half-hearted muttering of the many creatures bent over communication consoles, hammering away at data interface controls, and puttering around doing whatever the little cretins who manned the control center day and night might do, was disappointingly mundane as he stepped through the open doors.

The room had been the bridge of this once-formidable warship. It made sense: the command and control stations needed to sail such a mighty vessel might just suffice to house the oversight and mediation forces needed to keep this nasty little city from devouring itself. He had never paid too much attention to the control center, if he was being honest with himself. He had no intention of ruling here when the current regime was dismissed. By the time the smoke had settled and the bodies counted, he would be well on his way to his just and ample rewards. But still, to his untrained eye, nothing about the worn-down, shabby room seemed amiss.

Except that Administrator Uduta Virri was not slouched in the middle of the small reception area beyond the doors, ready to receive him and fawn all over his pressed and shimmering robes. In fact, no one was waiting for him at all. Several of the creatures at the duty stations nearest the door looked up, but there was nothing he could interpret as curiosity or concern on their varied faces. Each bent back to their work without a single sign that they either knew or cared who he was or why he had been kept in the hallway in humiliation.

Virri was not on the high command throne either, looking down at his ranks of pathetic workers. Instead, the fat, hulking form of a Leemuk, its green skin slick with slime, slouched there, staring at him with its weak, widely-space pink eyes. The enormous snaggled teeth clacked together as a swollen tongue snaked out to moisten the wide expanse of its exposed gums.

Disgusting creatures; its presence was just one more indignity he was forced to bear.

He was very nearly ready again to abandon this subtle game and take his chances with violence when a door off to the side hissed open and a pale figure stepped out, hurrying at him.

It was all Taurani could do to keep his eyes steady as the diminutive Iwa'Bantu female approached. So much like the plaything he had left in his chambers.

Her skin was alabaster pale, like all of her race, with a tracery of fine lines, like cracks in fine porcelain, running across it. It made them look like delicate statues that had been roughly handled, and he had always found himself drawn to the effect. Her features were refined, with thin, nearly nonexistent lips beneath a small nose. Her eyes were huge for her face, their ill-defined irises like pale blue stains on white ceramic. It was the only feature about the Iwa'Bantu he found off-putting. Their eyes seemed to radiate weakness and lack of purpose.

The female approaching him, wearing a dark tunic and loose pants that blended in with the almost-uniform of the rest of the control room staff, was Administrator Virri's assistant and deputy, Iphini Bha. It had always been hard for him to read Iwa'Bantu faces, with their perpetually straight mouths and their big, sad eyes. If he had to guess, however, he would have said that Bha looked nervous, skipping between the work stations toward him.

Bha stopped and bowed slightly, her big eyes flicking from side to side. She was holding a metal stylus loosely in her hand, fidgeting with it as she bent low. It was a gratifying moment, as the bow was far deeper than anything Virri would have given him, if the beast had been present.
Taurani's eyes flicked with memory, and he straightened from his own, minimal, nod. "Mistress Bha. Always a pleasure, but I believe my arranged and approved appointment was with Administrator Virri?"

Did her eyes flare at the name? It was so hard to tell. She nodded several times, her dainty hands clutched over her chest the stylus shivering in a way that seemed nervous to him. "Yes, Ambassador, of course." She looked back over the room behind her. "If you would come with me to the administrator's day chamber?" He was sure he caught her glancing at the hulking Leemuk, and he thought he saw the creature avert its tiny eyes.

Something was amiss within the control center, of that he was sure. And there was probably no way he would find out what it was without following Bha deeper into the mess. He wrinkled the patch of skin beneath his eyes and shrugged. Signaling for the Ntja guard to remain by the main door, he turned to follow the deputy back through the tangle of desks and stations at a more stately pace.

When the heavy door had hissed closed behind them, Bha turned to stare at the ambassador with her huge eyes, no expression on her pale, lined face. She was waiting for him to speak.

Taurani took a slow and measured turn about the room. It was cluttered, with items of cloth and paper scattered about in a haphazard manner. Images on the walls showed serene underwater scenes that moved with the living pulse of reality. In the corner was the heavy desk of the administrator, behind which sat the ugly grey tank-like seat that Virri could often be found sleeping in.

The tank was empty.

Taurani kept his demeanor calm as he turned slowly to regard Bha, who had pivoted in place to follow his move through the room. Her face betrayed nothing.

"He's not here." It was not a question. The administrator's habits were well-known to the Ambassador. Taurani had been sent, after all, in part to oversee the creature's downfall. He knew more about Uduta Virri than probably anyone else in this accursed city.

Bha's head gave a slight shake, as if against her will. He made the hacking sound in his throat again. Such gestures were vile to him, and he could not fathom why any denizen of the galaxy, never mind an Iwa'Bantu such as Bha, would allow herself to use them.

"Speak, please. I can't abide such head-bobbing."

Bha swallowed visibly, then straightened. "Administrator Virri is currently away, Ambassador. He is expected back soon, however. I regret that he did not return in time for your appointment."

Taurani stared into the weak, pale eyes. "He's off again on one of his little adventures, and you did not think to inform me, despite my scheduled appointment?" His voice was soft and dangerous, and this time he was sure that Bha's eyes had widened.

She broke eye contact first and moved to the desk, drawing one delicate finger across the surface. "No, I did not. I do apologize."

Taurani almost nodded in satisfaction before he caught himself. "Might I know where he has absconded himself to? When might he return?"

Something occurred to the ambassador that he had been too agitated before to notice. "That Tigan mercenary of his is gone as well." She could normally be found haunting the outer chamber, looking after the questionable well-being of her master.

Bha nodded again, unaware of the effect it was having on the tall ambassador. "Angara Ksaka accompanied the administrator on his current jaunt."

Taurani was well-aware of the effect his lipless, cold expressions had on weaker beings, and he took great pleasure in using that now. "No, Bha, she did not." Yes, those eyes were wider and wider. "Your entirely estimable principal has once again fled his responsibilities here, and your resident wanderer has had to take it upon herself to take to her precious ship and go off to drag him back." His tight features shifted as he saw his barbs strike home. "Tell me, was he so incredibly short sighted as to be wearing the Skorahn when he ran away?"

The string of gems with its enormous central sapphire was the key to the entire city's operation. If the Council found out Virri had left the protection of the city with the Skorahn, and he had not been informed in enough time to dispatch a team of Mnymian mercenaries or Ntja soldiers to try to wrest it from him, his stock would suffer. If any agent of the Council could get their hands on that little piece of jewelry, the entire elaborate structure they had spent so long putting into place would, in a moment, be rendered useless and unnecessary, and this place would fall without so much as a whimper.

"Where did he go?" The words were sharp, even in his own ears, and he cursed himself for not concealing the sudden rush of eagerness.

Bha, for her part, proved more resolute than anticipated. "The administrator is away, Ambassador. Anymore, I cannot say. Angara is with him, as I told you, and I am sure he is quite safe, wherever he might be."

Taurani stared into her eyes. Within the brain behind them lay information that would see him elevated to the loftiest heights of the Council, and perhaps beyond, if only he could coax them from her. But alas, in the here and now that was his sorry lot, there was no way to do that. The best he could do was to intimidate her into giving something away. Anything that might reveal Virri's whereabouts would be invaluable.

"I have every right to know where the administrator fled to, Bha. You know that." He moved toward her, his shoulders hulking forward menacingly. "The diplomatic relationship between your little outpost here and the Council is tenuous at best. You would not wish to damage that bond, and see a Peacemaker fleet appear over your head, now, would you?"

She stared back at him, her huge eyes once again unreadable. A moment of silence stretched on, and she did not move. He tried his heavy stare again, but this time there was no reaction. He might well have been looking at a statue, forgotten in some far off garden.

Without warning, her shoulders slumped and she looked away. When she spoke, there was a break in her voice that soothed his frustrations of the day. "The administrator is gone, Ambassador." She looked small, curling in upon herself. "I don't know where he went. Ksaka followed as soon as we realized he was gone."

His sense of victory fell into cold ash in his mouth at the words. He knew he could trust Bha when she was so obviously reduced. Virri was gone, and the slippery eel would have left no trace of his intended destination. He could be almost anywhere.

Taurani sighed. He folded his long hands against each other and brought them slowly up to his chest as he calmed the tempest rising within his mind. Not only was he not going to be able to assess the advancement of the Council's intentions with the bloated Virri, but the sudden, unforeseen opportunity to see them rushed to a hasty and satisfactory conclusion had been both offered and denied him, almost in a single breath.

It was nearly enough to cause even a seasoned diplomat to scream.

The Ambassador gave Bha another calm look, this time trying to warm it slightly, and inclined his head even deeper than he had when she first greeted him.

"I understand, Mistress Bha. Please accept my apologies for the … forcefulness, of my reaction." He moved to the armored door, which hissed back at his approach. "These are difficult times for us all, and it would be much easier for me to do my job if your administrator were to better maintain a professional schedule. I shall have Iranse make arrangements for a meeting when Virri has returned, and is more inclined to discuss important matters."

The female did not move from her position by the desk, only nodding again in her infuriatingly innocent fashion. The stylus whirring busily away.

As soon as he stepped through the hatch, the door slid shut behind him. The creatures at the stations around him studiously avoided his eyes as he strode toward the main hatch, which was once again closed. At least he understood that, now. Any hint of the administrator's absence would be enough to tip the entire city into paranoid anarchy. Taurani considered himself an enlightened, steady-souled creature, but the thought of that necklace being away from the city for any length of time, while he himself was still stuck in it, was very nearly enough to drive him to thoughts of panic and retreat as well.

The Njta was where he had left it, of course. The big brute stood by the closed door, beady eyes lost in the middle distance, and made no sign of recognition as he walked past. The door opened, thankfully, as soon as he neared, and he strode through without slowing his long-legged pace. Behind him, the bodyguard followed in its customary silence.

So. Uduta Virri was away. Annoyance began to give way to excitement, as further possibilities began to present themselves in his mind.

# Chapter 4

There was nothing beyond the view screens but utter, unrelieved blackness. Marcus slowly released the malleable arms of his chair, barely remembering the tight hold it had taken of him before they dropped into the ... His head rose, and he stared upward. He could not pull his eyes away from the starless expanse that stretched off all around them. Beside him, Justin seemed equally absorbed by the view, and equally unwilling to break the heavy, deathly silence.

Their kidnapper, however, felt no similar restraint. The strange woman pushed herself from her seat and rose before them, the glowing orb of light dispersing behind her. She stretched in a way that would have been quite distracting, if Marcus had not been busy accounting for an entire life left behind, and a physics-defying plunge into what should have left them all dead, their atoms stretched across the solar system.

She turned and looked down at the two silent men, a slight smile on her dark lips. Marcus noted, with some cold part of his brain still functioning despite the shock, that the white teeth peeking out from behind that grin seemed to be inordinately sharp.

After a moment's fluttering blink, the woman looked back down at them with the same smile and spoke a single word. "Thirsty?"

Marcus thought for a moment. His last drink, in the comedy club, watching second-rate comedians to take his mind off his problems while Justin played poker in the high stakes back room, had been several hours and what felt like a lifetime ago. Even so, right about then he thought he would have almost killed for another of those watered down vodka tonics. Somehow he doubted that anything so ordinary was in store, but his throat had gone dry at the thought, and he remembered all the smoke, dust, and terror that had ravaged it in the recent past.

He nodded quickly, looking over to where Justin was making the same gesture with equal energy. There was something about the woman's smile that scratched painfully at the back of his mind, but he knew he couldn't focus on anything much for long at the moment. His eyes drifted back out to the darkness beyond the strange ship. The longer he stared, the more he felt as if he could almost see colors swirling around deep within the empty void. He was shaken by an involuntary shudder as he realized that he could not name any of the colors he thought he might be seeing.

The woman pushed aside a curtain and came back up onto the deck. She was still smiling that disturbing smile, but his eyes were locked on the clear cups she held. Whatever was inside them was clear as well, and as he reached out for the offered vessel, he stopped, eyes narrowing, and looked up at her. Flicking his eyes between hers and the glass, he tilted his head in a silent question.

She paused, her face tight, then blinked, looked down, and spat out, "Water."

If he didn't trust her about some things, he was soon going to starve or die of thirst. While he was torturing himself, though, Justin grabbed for the other glass and tossed the entire contents down his throat in one convulsive throw.

Justin lowered the empty glass with a smile, his good humor returning, and tilted his own head toward their host. "Got any more where that came from?"

She smiled and took the glass while Marcus accepted his own. He sipped. It was cool, and wet, and clear. There was no aftertaste, or anything else he imagined he might experience from a poisoned drink. He took another sip, screwing up his face as he tried to ascertain if he was suffering any numbness in his mouth. There was nothing. His throat felt better already, and with one last glance between Justin and the woman, he tossed the rest of the water down.

She took the glass from him with another smile, and his feeling of unease grew. Rather than take the glasses back behind the curtain, or put them down, she merely took a step back, away from them, her smile growing wider.

Her teeth were definitely pointed.

He turned to ask Justin how he felt, when his stomach clenched as if he had been sucker punched. A sudden, terrible burning swept from his belly outward to the very tips of his fingers and toes at incredible speed. His back arched painfully, slamming him against the soft chair, and he felt himself slowly lowered backward, every muscle in his body immobilized in one massive cramping seizure.

He rolled his eyes wildly, taking in his strange surroundings as fear and anger boiled up in his mind. He found the woman, standing above him, her smile unchanged, looking down. She raised one of the glasses in an unmistakable salute, and he fell back, lifted and dropped by the traitor chair that had held him safely through their entire ascent.

It seemed as if he fell forever, but then there was an impact, a cold, rushing sensation and a crashing sound that filled his ears and his world. He was swallowed by a frigid reality that shocked all other thoughts from his already battered mind.

Water. Where had water come from? The floor behind his chair had been solid when he walked across it not that long ago.

And then there was only darkness.

*****

Angara watched the two Humans fall into the hibernation chambers with a smile she did not try to hide. She felt filthy just having such creatures walk the deck plates of the *Yud'ahm Na'uka*. This had never been a dream job, but it had at least promised legitimacy of a certain kind. Watching over a personage such as the administrator, even a cretin like Uduta Virri, had lent her purpose. It had been a stepping stone to earning herself a place in a society that might come to accept her as more than just a Tigan, and a Tigan outcast at that.

She knew her people were not well-regarded in the more mainstream currents of galactic society. She had once thought that maybe being an exile from such a reviled race would lend her a certain amount of legitimacy. Instead, most of those she encountered assumed that, because the wandering Tigan had cast her out, she must be even lower than they were! It had made her life as difficult as exile was intended to be.

Securing a position as the personal guard and security specialist of the administrator of Penumbra had been the best she could have hoped for. Those wishing to deal with Virri had been forced to put their contempt for her aside if they wanted to get anything done in his domain. It had almost been worth all of the grief he had put her through since she had accepted the position.

She went to put the glasses away. She did not usually carry such nanite cocktails, but Virri had insisted she have some on hand in case he wished to ... liaise ... with any aboriginals he encountered during his many forays away from home. She was glad she had them now, of course. They had not been intended for use with Humans, but she believed they would do the job adequately. She hoped so, anyway.

Returning to the command deck, she crouched down between the two hibernation chambers the *Yud'ahm Na'uka* had brought up behind the Humans while they were distracted by her wormhole jump. She could just make out their outlines beneath the frosted surface of the observation ports. Somewhere within was Uduta Virri's most prized possession. She couldn't believe it. She knew if she returned without the administrator, she might as well not have returned at all. But returning with the Skorahn, she might just be able to salvage something from this whole debacle. And as tempting as putting the damn thing on herself might be, she had seen how miserable it had made him, and had no desire to join him in his suicidal search for distraction and release.

The idea that had struck her beside the crater housing the remains of her former employer had barely been a shadow of a thought then. These creatures had somehow procured the medallion, and the pale one had bonded with it, which should never have been able to happen. And so, as she had tracked down Virri, using her ship to follow the bonded medallion, she had completely misread the situation. A fatal misreading, to her employer, it had turned out.

A twinge of guilt struck her without warning. She had killed Uduta Virri. The administrator had not been a good soul. In fact, he had been reviled by even his own people. But he had given Angara a chance when no else would.

And she had killed him.

She punched the back of the observer's chair in sudden frustration. The *idiot!* As much as she wanted to hate him for having brought this about, she knew it was her own fault. She had allowed him to wander off once again, knowing the kinds of places he went and the kinds of trouble he got himself into. How these Humans had ended up with the Skorahn would be an interesting story, but it would not matter in the end. She had been lazy, assuming the vehicle with the Skorahn had been Virri, and the other whatever local creatures had been giving him trouble. And now Virri was dead at her hands, and only a desperate ploy would allow her to keep her position now.

Looking down again, she shook her head. There was nothing so desperate as trusting a Human.

*****

Marcus came to his senses slowly. The first thing he was aware of was a lack of pain or discomfort. That was followed quickly, however, by the realization that he could not feel anything. His eyes popped open as fear bubbled up within him, only to find that he was staring up at a clear blue sky. Soft white clouds scudded past. Off to one side he could see the lacey tracery of tree branches arching up overhead. It was all very peaceful, and very confusing.

He nervously moved his head from side to side, fearing he was paralyzed and would find the attempt impossible. But his neck moved as it had always done, and he took in the area around him with growing confusion. He was in a small wooded clearing. As he looked around he became aware of the soft susurration of wind through the leaves of the trees overhead. In the distance was a murmur that might have been running water, as if from a brook or stream. It was lovely; and did nothing to dispel his confusion or growing concern.

He could not remember arriving here. He vaguely recalled Justin's old beater Camry tearing down a wooded road, but could not remember where they had been or why he had been driving so fast. And with thoughts of the car, he wondered again why a wealthy young businessman like his friend would have such a wretched car. But that seemed like the least of his problems at the moment.

The feeling that he was being chased erupted in the back of his mind without warning and he leapt up from the soft grass, turning about, crouched down and ready to run, trying to look in every direction at once.

No one was there.

He forced his breathing back under control, stood up a little straighter. Whatever had been chasing him wasn't chasing him anymore. He had gotten away. Or been caught ... He looked around again at the trees all around him. Had he been caught and dragged out into the Connecticut woods?

The panic response was immediate, and he fell, as if trying to escape the trees all around him. The sky above seemed to grow darker, the clouds whisking up and away, and the shadows all around stretched down toward him, dark and menacing.

The air grew thick, and he sucked in great lungfuls, fighting against an ever-rising panic. What the hell...

"Hey!" The voice came from behind him, among the trees, and he turned around, almost losing his balance, to find a young man standing there. Part of his mind registered that the trees around the man were fading away, becoming more insubstantial as he tried to focus on them. But even as everything around the newcomer grew wispy and thin, the young man remained as solid as anything he had ever seen.

"You okay, buddy?" The man approached him, a look of honest concern on his face. A face that was oddly familiar.

Marcus stared at the man as he came closer. Dark hair in a sort of careless, flyaway cut, a strong jaw and straight, Roman nose, and very short mustache and goatee all combined in a look that he felt he should certainly recognize.

"Hey, man, you don't look so good." The man reached out with one hand to help to steady Marcus, but he shied away from the contact.

Which was when he realized that he still could not feel anything. He felt his eyes grow wide and he fell back against a tree. Except that there was no tree. There were no more trees. The darkness that had descended upon the two of them was now complete, and they stood in the middle of a vast, dark, empty space.

"What the hell is going on!" The words came out as a high-pitched plea that he was too nervous and confused to be embarrassed by.

The man held his arms out to his sides, hands open in a calming gesture. "Yeah, I'm pretty sure it's got to be wreaking havoc with your mind, bud. Don't worry. It's all okay." He smiled a lopsided smile that, again, Marcus felt he should recognize but didn't. "Well, I *think* it's all going to be okay, anyway."

Marcus calmed himself, took a deep breath, and straightened. Around him was nothing but darkness, but he seemed to be able to see the young man easily enough. "Who are you? Where am I?"

The man straightened also, and then nodded, his smile fading a little but still there at the edges of his mouth. "Yeah, those are both good questions. Where is a bit hard to tell." He looked around, making a show of taking everything in. "If I had to guess, I'd say we were somewhere in a dark corner of your subconscious."

The words meant nothing. "What the hell is that supposed to mean?"

The man shrugged. "Just my best guess, man." He walked around Marcus, giving him a critical once over. "I'd say you've got bigger problems, if you want my honest opinion."

Marcus looked at him for a moment, and then shook his head. "What the hell is going on?"

The smile returned full force. "Not even remotely curious about my own identity?" The smile slipped as a look of rueful introspection swept briefly across the handsome face. "I can't say I'm entirely thrilled with your lack of focus."

Anger served to burn much of the confusion and fear away. Who the hell did this asshole think he was? "Okay then, who the hell are you?"

"Well, I'm not sure we have to get all pushy about it." The man stepped back, assuming a very dramatic stance with one hand raised to the heavens. Looking upward with angelic innocence, he proclaimed, "I, good sir, am you."

Marcus didn't know what to say. It was insane. But then, he was surrounded by a reality that seemed unable to decide upon its exact shape, and *someone* had dragged him here … wherever here was … or he was hallucinating. That suddenly struck him as a far more likely possibility.

"You're … me." Now that the thought had been planted, the features seemed to fall into place. It wasn't exactly the face he saw in the mirror every morning as he shaved around the carefully maintained look of careless grooming, but it was very close. A little younger, perhaps, maybe a little idealized. But it was there. As if he had a slightly younger, slightly better-looking brother, maybe.

The man's smile widened into a full-blown grin. "Get it?"

Marcus sat down heavily. Instead of hitting the floor, or the ground, or whatever it was he was standing on, it seemed like he had landed on a chair or a bench. He still couldn't feel anything, which was starting to concern him as well. His forearms came to rest on his knees, and he looked down to a ground that seemed like flat, unrelieved blackness.

Without looking up, Marcus muttered, "You're me."

"Well, parts of you, would be my best guess." The voice lowered, and Marcus looked up to see his younger self lowering himself as if into a comfortable chair. There was no chair there, but the man floated on air just as if there was an invisible piece of furniture beneath him. "See, best I can figure things out, you've retreated from a reality that suddenly got far, far too strange for your waking mind." He jerked a thumb up, as if indicating the space above them or a wider world that existed somewhere beyond the bizarre here and now.

Marcus looked up, then back down to the now-familiar face. His mind felt like it had slowed down to an embarrassingly inadequate speed. "What?"

The man in the chair shrugged. "How much do you remember, from before you woke up here?"

Marcus closed his eyes and tried to remember. "We were in Justin's car. We were being … chased?"

The man nodded. "You were! Good job! Anything else?"

A suspicion tickled the back of Marcus's slow mind, and his eyes tightened. "If you're me, shouldn't you know all this?"

The man shook his head, waving the suggestion away with one casual hand. "Hardly. I'm the part of you that thinks without feeling, really. I don't worry about fear, or excitement, or nerves. I just take everything in and try to make sense of it while you're running around inside your own head, screaming to get out."

Marcus shook his head. "So, you're saying I'm insane?"

The answering shrug was less than comforting. "Hard to tell, really. You're in shock, that's for sure. And the shit that's going down right now … well, if you *weren't* in shock, you'd have every right to fear for your sanity, to be honest. And believe me, the idea that you might really be going crazy is not one that fills me with excitement either, old son." The younger version of himself seemed to relax. "But if you remember about being chased and whatnot, the rest can't be that far behind, and so I think we're both going to be okay."

"I still don't understand exactly what's happening here between you and me." Marcus stared at the other face. There was something missing there, and he wasn't sure he liked the cold edge in those eyes.

"Well, given that you weren't exactly the most attentive student back in Psych class, I'm not sure either. I only know what you paid attention to. But if I had to guess, I'd say this is either you on the edge of a full psychotic break from the stresses you just experienced, or you're processing the experiences while your body suffers whatever it is that its suffering at the moment."

That brought Marcus up short. He had not thought through the implications of being trapped in this creation of his own mind, if that was in fact what was happening. He could not feel his body here. Did that mean that his body was somewhere else …? All of the other words he had just heard faded away.

"What's happening to my body?"

The other version of himself shrugged. "Something pretty bad, to be honest." He closed his eyes and tilted his head upward, then continued without turning around, eyes still shut. "A terrible fever." He winced. "Damn, if you could move, I'd say you'd be breaking bones, convulsing." The dark eyes opened again, lowering to look at him. "And there's something very strange going on with our brain." He smiled, and then gestured around them with both hands. "Stranger than this, I mean."

Marcus stood, looking around as if he could find an escape. "What happened? Was it a car accident? Is Justin okay?"

The other man shook his head. "You really don't remember anything else from tonight?" He rose also.

Marcus stared at him for a moment, and then forced his mind to calm down. "I remember the car. I remember an explosion, an accident? We were being chased, and there was an accident? I remember a woman …"

His alter-ego smiled widely at that. "Ah, so that's what we latch onto?

Well, that makes sense. She's quite a looker. And just your type, too, except for the purple skin, pointy teeth, and all. Not to mention she doesn't seem to be too big a fan of Humans."

That brought him up short. "Purple skin?"

And it all came rushing back to him. The chase, the strange weapons, the medallion, the woman and her plane, no helicopter, no …

"Spaceship?"

The other man nodded. "Best guess I've got. Either that, or the most elaborate prank Justin's every played on you. As best I can tell, you've just been abducted by a very attractive, if lavender-skinned and misanthropic, alien."

The panic rose again, but this time arms as hard as iron clenched around his shoulders, and he was shaken into cold stillness. He opened his eyes and stared at identical eyes staring back at him, entirely devoid of compassion.

"You're going to have to calm down, put a lot of what we think we knew behind us, and man up, Marcus. Clearly the world is not entirely as we understood it to be. You are going to have to remember who you are, and what you're capable of, or we're not going to get out of this in one piece. And if you don't make it, I don't make it. And I intend to make it."

Marcus shook his head. "*Aliens? Aliens?*"

The younger face nodded. "Aliens, and lasers, and spaceships, apparently the whole nine yards." The face came closer to his. "And you're going to need to deal with it. Do you understand me?"

A disturbing calm swept up from the depths of his mind. It was too much to deal with. But he was going to have to deal with it. He didn't have a choice. Well, not one he wanted to exercise, at any rate.

He nodded. "Yeah, you're right. I'll have to deal."

The younger version of himself looked into his eyes one more time as if assuring himself of something, then stepped back. "Damn right. You have to remember who you are, Marcus. You're up to this. We're up to this." He looked up, closed his eyes again, and then looked back down. "Whatever she was doing to you, it's almost done. You remember, you're not some lame-ass radio advertising salesman. You were more than that, you *are* more than that. You have to put all the issues with your family aside. You have Justin with you, and you need to watch out for him too. He'll be watching out for you."

Marcus nodded again. He felt calmer than he had since the parking lot of the casino, but owing that calm to this cold, distant part of himself, through this strange, shifting nightmare mirage, was hardly comforting. At the same time, however, it occurred to him that there was a lot in those cold eyes he remembered…

"What if I need—"

A white light blossomed above him, engulfing the darkness around them, and blotted away the world.

*****

Marcus heard a faint humming sound as if from a great distance. He was aware of a terrible, freezing cold, but only intellectually, as if it was happening to someone else. Somewhere nearby, something was humming with a low, continuous buzz. From beneath those sounds and impressions was another sound, a senseless murmuring that rose and fell like the artificial swells of a white noise machine set on 'ocean surf'.

As he focused more on those sounds, a pattern of words began to emerge at the same time the cold became far more than intellectual and a blazing, burning pain blossomed in his head, just behind his eyes. With a gasp, he launched himself upright, hands moving to either side of his head as a grunt forced its way past gritted teeth.

A blanket slipped off his shoulders as he rose and he immediately felt the bite of an even colder chill. He was surrounded by soft, hanging tapestries whose designs were lost in low lighting and subtle needlework. He recognized it nevertheless.

He was in a spaceship. Looking around through clenched eyes as he pulled the blanket back up around him, he found Justin and the strange woman with the purple skin looking at him. His friend's smile was back in full force despite the fact that he looked like he had been through a boxing match, a dark blanket wrapped tightly about himself. The woman looked at him with a blank expression for a moment, and then her own wide smile was back.

Her teeth came to small, fine points.

Her violet eyes were cruel.

"Welcome to the real world, Mr. Wells." The words were clear, without a hint of accent.

His headache got much, much worse.

# Chapter 5

Sitting in a chair that conformed itself entirely to his slightest shift in balance, wrapped in what had to be the warmest blanket he had ever held, and hands wrapped around a mug of something that was, although not coffee, close enough in the present circumstances to offer both warmth and comfort, Marcus Wells stared down into the dark liquid and tried to process what he had just been told.

"Nanites?" The word sounded strange in his own ears, and there was a faint buzzing deep in his inner ear that made him want to open his jaw to relieve the pressure.

"Nanites." The woman nodded. He shook his head. She wasn't 'the woman' anymore. She had introduced herself as Angara Ksaka, although he was still trying to wrap his mind around what she had done to his brain, and hadn't listened too closely to the rest of what she was saying.

"You were under the care of the medical cists until the nanites completed their work. Tiny machines that have—"

"I get it." He waved her off, his headache still nibbling at the edges of his thoughts. He didn't even want to think of the word 'cist' right now. "And so now I understand every word you say? That seems a bit ridiculous."

Justin's smile was wide as he lounged on his own seat, apparently much more comfortable with the shifting furniture than Marcus was. "Any technology, advanced enough, will seem like magic to a—"

"Don't quote Arthur C. Clarke to me, you God damned business major." Marcus looked back to where Angara watched them both. He didn't know why, but he felt like there was a bit less disdain in her voice, a slightly lower level of frustration and annoyance on her face, when she was speaking directly to Justin. "So, I can understand you now, is the thing?"

The woman shrugged, providing scant comfort. "The words will now be those you recognize, for the most part. And I will not have to access my own implants," she tapped her temple, "for the words from your language. Concepts for which there is no parallel in your understanding will find the closest equivalents seamlessly, but there may be some physical discomfort." She traced a vague line from her ear down her neck with one red fingernail.

Her name, when she had introduced herself, had given him that strange inner-ear ache when he had heard it. That word, nanites, had done the same thing. "So, I'll understand you?" He repeated.

Again, that bland shrug that was starting to drive him crazy. "You'll recognize the words. No being will be able to guarantee that you will understand … everything."

Hardly a ringing endorsement. He shook his head, knowing that he was going to have to pick his battles carefully. To cover his discomfort he took another sip of the drink. "Okay, obviously I can understand you well enough, so let's just forget that for now." He didn't feel great knowing that there were millions of tiny alien robots crawling around in his brain interpreting for him. What else might they do?

"So, please go back and explain why you kidnapped us." Those moments in that empty darkness with his younger self were still firmly in his mind. He needed to focus.

"Well, she might have kidnapped you, but she sure as hell didn't kidnap me." Justin's smile was wide, his dark eyes sparkling.

Marcus gave his friend a flat look, and then turned back to the woman. "Why are we here?"

Angara watched the interplay with a sour twist to her lips. When she began to speak again the twist was gone, but the tone remained. "I need your help."

Marcus sat back. Several possibilities had crossed his mind, but this was not one of them. "You need our help?"

She nodded. "I need you to come with me. We won't be gone long; a few weeks at most. Then I can return you."

Justin reached over and smacked Marcus in the shoulder. "*She* needs *us*, man! You get it?"

Marcus's mouth curled in annoyance, but he didn't so much as look at his friend. "You need us to come with you where? To do what?"

Justin's smile slipped, and he sat up as if he was about to take Marcus to task, but Angara shook her head and looked back at Marcus, her back straightening and her head tilted proudly. "I need your assistance in correcting an error I have made." She rose to take the empty glasses, slipped them behind a wall hanging, and returned to her seat. She did all of this without making eye contact.

Marcus nodded to himself. "You made a mistake. What'd you do?"

Justin turned to watch her as well, curious despite himself.

She glanced from one man to the other, and then shrugged, looking away. "I killed my employer."

Justin's jaw dropped and he struggled quickly upright. Marcus nodded. There were things he had noticed back on old State Road 189 that his mind had not been ready to confront at the time. He remembered the pale cast to the man's face, glimpsed as they roared down the highway, and the hints of strange appendages, charred and twisted, around the body in the devastated Prius as it was engulfed in flames at the bottom of a crater.

"The guy that was following us." The words were flat. He might be putting the parts together, but there was still a lot he didn't know. "The guy following us, shooting at us with those balls of lightning, and the lasers; that was your boss?"

Angara nodded, her strange eyes cast down to the rug-strewn floor. "I was tracking him by the Skorahn, that medallion you showed me. He often ran off like this, to indulge himself, and I have had to go after him, get him out of whatever trouble he had stumbled into, and bring him back safely. I thought I was tracking him, anyway. I thought he was running away from locals, or maybe some Galactic agents. Neither were far-fetched, and both have happened in the past."

Marcus heard the capital 'G', and the heavy weight of the term 'agents', but was too interested in the initial line of inquiry to take a detour at the moment. "So, you thought you were swooping in to rescue *him*, then? Because the necklace was in our car, not his?"

She sighed, looking up, and then launched herself out of her seat and began to pace like a caged animal. Her movements were lithe and graceful. "I thought it might make a good object lesson, if I let him hang for a bit before I took out the pursuit."

"But *he* was the pursuit. *We* had the necklace. And you killed *him*, instead." Marcus summed up his conclusions in a flat voice, trying his best to keep any tone of judgment out, for the moment, anyway.

Again, she nodded, moving from one hanging to the next, reaching out to touch the rich weaves as she passed. "Yes. I can only imagine he used the Skorahn as collateral, or something similar, in a game of chance?"

It was Justin's turn to nod. "Yeah. I took him for everything else, so he tossed the necklace into the pot and asked if it would cover his bet."

"And you said yes." She asked the question without turning toward him, already knowing the answer.

"Yeah. I didn't know what it was worth, and everyone else was out, but they were watching, and they all seemed impressed, so I didn't want to seem like a chump. So yeah, I said yes."

"It's the medallion. It can have a strange effect on sentients. And on Humans, apparently." She turned toward them again, her face thoughtful. "He's done this many times before. He usually recovers the Skorahn as soon as he can get the recipient alone."

"He tried, but he shot his taser-thing at Marcus instead of me. Gave me enough time to give him a right cross to the jaw." Justin settled back, reveling in the memory. "Put the bastard right down."

The look she gave him was pitying. "Yes, it would. Rayabels aren't known for their constitutions. Out of curiosity, what did it feel like when you hit him?"

Justin's head jerked slightly at the question, and then he turned thoughtful. "Well, now that you mentioned it, it did feel pretty soft."

"They are what you might call gastropods. Rayabels don't actually even have a head as you would recognize it. Rather, they have a central body from which they might shape any number of pseudopods. Virri's favorite disguise, when he came all the way to Earth, was to don a mask over a sensory-enhanced pseudopod, and cram the rest of his bulk into one of the many designer suits he has had me procure over the years."

Justin looked offended at the suggestion that his right cross had not been as formidable as he had assumed, but Marcus had noticed something stranger about the woman's response. "You don't seem to be that upset that you killed him."

The fact that the woman, or alien, or whatever, had killed her employer without much sign of remorse might hold rather dire implications for the two strange Humans she had just abducted from the middle of nowhere. It did not speak to any particular strength of character, anyway.

She shrugged but her eyes were cast down. "Administrator Uduta Virri was not a creature to claim much in the way of personal loyalty." Her look soured further. "Truth to tell, he was a pig." The term pig gave him that ache below his ear. But as she said it, she seemed sad nonetheless.

"But he was *your* pig." Marcus sat up, the blanket falling forgotten. Justin looked between the two, not entirely sure where the conversation was now headed.

She looked directly into Marcus's eyes, straightening her shoulders. "Uduta Virri employed me in a trusted position when most would have turned me aside. I owed him for that. But he was also an untrustworthy beast, who made my duties, once I earned them, exceedingly difficult. He died through his own recklessness and vice, but mine was the finger on the trigger. I must now secure my own position in the brief time I will have that opportunity, before other forces interfere."

"You called him an administrator. What was he in charge of?" Marcus sensed that this was the true core of where they were headed, and wanted to get there as soon as possible before they went any further. He was also still troubled by her reaction to the death of a being she had known, and killed.

Angara began to speak and then fell silent, her mouth open, before she snapped it shut. Her eyes tightened as she stared at Marcus for a moment, and when she began to speak again, her voice was low and steady.

"Administrator Uduta Virri was the nominal ruler of a social construct that, for lack of a better term, we can call a city. It is a free city, holding no allegiance to any other political entities in the galaxy, and as such, is a crossroads for all beings looking to avoid official entanglements or intrusions. I say nominal ruler because this city is a study in controlled chaos, and no one can rightly be said to rule over much of anything there. But insofar as any creature was the figurehead of the city, it was Virri."

Admittedly, the scope of the world had widened considerably since Marcus had woken up that morning in his dank hotel room at the casino. But as he thought through her words, he realized that they didn't entirely make sense.

"This place is a city? Not a planet, a system, or anything like that?" There was, deep within his mind, a piece of himself, the piece that he would have said was the rational bit only a few hours ago, that was still screaming in denial far down in his back brain, and in shock at the death he had already witnessed that night. The rest of him, however, was coming along nicely, tossing around concepts like planets and systems.

"It is a city that floats freely in space, in a system far from the core of Galactic civilization, orbiting a planet that has been dead for eons." She sighed again and slowly slid back into her chair. "It is an aggregate body consisting of nearly countless starships of all shapes and sizes, from all manner of races and alliances, bonded together and modified into a single gargantuan complex, affixed to an artificial planetoid of unknown origin we refer to as the Relic Core. It is known as Penumbra."

The name brought the unpleasant buzzing to his inner ear again. He shook it off and pushed ahead. "You live in a space station made out of spaceships cemented together?" He looked at Justin with a mean-spirited grin. "Sort of like a space-age shantytown?"

Angara shook her head, her lips pursed in tightly controlled anger. "The ships were joined together ages ago, bonded to an ancient relic that was found floating around the dead planet. It was of no known culture, yet alive with a trickle of power and atmosphere that grew when connected to the first desperate ship to stumble into that system. As new ships were added, the Relic Core's output grew as well. Today it has thousands of added components. For thousands of years there has been almost no fluctuation in output from the core. It has been accepted for longer than I could say, that whatever is contained within that shell, will sustain Penumbra indefinitely. I'm certain those earliest settlers did not take the Relic Core so much for granted, but time has a way of dulling every sentient's vigilance."

"*Almost* no fluctuation?" Justin's words made Marcus jump. His friend, usually at the center of any conversation, had been uncharacteristically quiet, aside from his usual sarcastic jibes. "Seems like you've got a lot riding on this big chunk of mystery. I'd say *any* fluctuation would be a cause for concern."

She glanced at him, then back to Marcus. "The reason for those few fluctuations was well known." She pointed toward his pocket. "The Skorahn is more than just a piece of pretty jewelry. It is the key to Penumbra."

Marcus scowled and pulled the necklace from his pocket, holding it up in the sourceless light. It twisted as he let it dangle, sparkling more than he felt it should. "This is the key to your space city?"

"Not an actual key, precisely. Apparently, it was found by that first ship, and the captain took it as a prize. As long as she possessed it, the relic provided all the power, water, and atmosphere that they needed. When she died, the supplies tailed off. There was great panic until one of her heirs took up the medallion. Ever since then, as long as a living, sentient being has been in possession of the medallion, Penumbra has thrived. During those rare occasions when the owner of the medallion has … passed without an immediate successor, there have been disruptions. It has not happened, however, for a very, very long time."

Justin opened his mouth to ask a question, but Marcus stopped him with a gesture. There were so many questions now, but another line of inquiry had suggested itself, and he needed to follow it before he forgot, in the swirl of mysteries that filled his head. "Atmosphere? One atmosphere for all the different *races*? It's sort of assumed, on Earth, that aliens would need different atmospheres…"

The look Angara gave him was loaded with far more meaning than he had expected. "There is far less diversity, I assure you, than … *Humans* … would believe."

He met her eyes, and was taken by a sudden, shifting set of images. Angara shrugging, nodding, smiling, frowning … In fact, Angara with very nearly a full range of what he would have called expressions of Human emotion. He could only stare at her, as implications slowly occurred to him. But before he could ask another question, Justin jumped into the silence.

"Wait, roll it back for a bit. So, that necklace in Marc's hands, that's the key to your city?"

The dark woman kept her eyes on Marcus for a moment longer before flicking them in Justin's direction. "Correct. When Virri … died … there was a very real danger that Penumbra might have been shaken. But apparently he had lost the Skorahn before he … died." She looked down, pausing, and then back to Marcus. "And apparently, it had already bonded to another."

"Bonded?" Marcus jerked his hand out and away, setting the necklace to swinging. "This thing bonded to *me*? What's that mean?"

That seemed to bring some of the humor back to the woman's eyes. He might not have minded, if it hadn't been aimed at him. "Nothing much. Just that it is now locked onto your vital signs, your well-being."

He was horrified. "Until I *die*?"

That seemed to amuse her even more. "Of course not. We will be able to bond it to another when we get to Penumbra. I only need you to serve long enough to find a suitable candidate."

Justin tilted his head. "What makes someone suitable?"

She shrugged. "Any being with such an affinity to the Skorahn may suffice." She gave Marcus a sneering up and down assessment and shrugged again. "It should not be too difficult."

Marcus looked around the chamber, taking in the hangings on the walls, the rugs on the floor, the constantly shifting furniture, the soft, ambient light; such an odd combination of strange, exotic, and yet somehow familiar elements. His eyes tightened as yet another thought caught up to him.

"What are the people in Penumbra running from?"

That brought her up short. She looked around, trying to see what had prompted the question. "Running from? What makes you think they're running from someone?"

"You said it was for folks looking to avoid entanglements and intrusions." Justin joined in. "If someone's got the power to entangle and intrude, and you're avoiding them … well, on Earth, we'd call that running."

Marcus nodded to his friend. He stood up, stretching. He didn't know when he had stopped being cold, but he guessed it was about the time he found out he was supposed to be pretending to rule over some floating city of misfits, hiding from something big enough, Angara was trying not to tell him about them. "What are the people of Penumbra running from?"

She leaned away from him slightly, her mouth twisting in an expression that was becoming familiar. "No one is running away from them, but it is true, the Galactic Council would rather Penumbra come under their sway; or disappear entirely, to be honest."

"Galactic Council." That sounded pretentious enough to be dangerous. "Who are they, the bad guys?"

Again she surprised him. She shook her head, her brow furrowed. "Not precisely. The Galactic Council is a ruling body that includes representatives from nearly every sentient race in the galaxy."

Justin stood up now too. "Nearly every race? Including Humans?"

This time, when she laughed at Justin instead of him, Marcus found her laugh quite pleasant. "Of course not *Humans*." She shook her head to clear the tears rising up in her lavender eyes. Justin looked nonplussed, and shook his head at Marcus.

"So, a ruling council of everyone but Humans. Sounds pretty enlightened. Very Gene Roddenberry, eh?"

She stopped laughing, looking up at Marcus with the disdain he had come to expect. "You come from one of those nations on Earth where democracy is held in such high regard, yes?"

They looked at each other and nodded. She nodded back, but with a dark, vicious jerk of her head. "The rule of the majority is wonderful, until those in the majority have very different opinions than you do. I do not wish to give you an in depth civics lesson right now. You won't need it for what you will be doing. But suffice it to say that the Council likes to keep tabs on every transaction in the galaxy. They exercise rigid control of almost all facets of life." She stopped and smiled that cold smile again, the one that showed all of her pointed teeth to best effect. "All for the greater good, of course."

Both men stared at her for a moment. When Justin spoke, his words were subdued. "This Penumbra's big enemy is the democratic ruling body of the entire galaxy?"

Angara relaxed back in her seat. "Well, the known galaxy, anyway. And don't allow yourself to get too nostalgic for your Human democracy, either. The concept of everyone getting a say in what everyone is able to do can quickly shift from a dream to a nightmare when the wrong people find themselves in the majority. Believe me, Penumbra exists, no, *flourishes*, precisely *because* of the Galactic Council and their heavy-handed governance. Beneath the weight of the Bureau of Technology and other controlling governmental authorities, innovation and advancement stagnate. With a coalition of the less-enlightened races controlling the council, no matter that they are in the majority, those who do not follow their every decree are punished brutally and without mercy. Without the ability to circumvent Council control when necessary, the galaxy would be drowned in blood. It is why Penumbra exists, and why agents of the Council are forever trying to destroy or undermine it."

Marcus sat back down as the scope of their situation made itself felt. "And you want me to rule this city until you can find a replacement? With the fate of the galaxy on my shoulders, and these agents hunting me down?"

Again the flat expression that denied the warmth of her eyes. "Virri had almost no power at all. You will have even less. And no Council agent ever managed to get close enough to the administrator, in the right circumstances, to do him harm. You will be safe while we find a suitable replacement, and then you will be returned to Earth."

"What if we don't want to go back?" Justin spoke quickly, a strange light in his eyes.

"Don't be an asshole, Justin. We're going back." Marcus dismissed his friend's question with a wave. "We're going back as soon as she lets us."

Justin shook his head, sinking back into his seat, his eyes fixed on Marcus. "No, *I'm* not. What do I have to go back to? For that matter, what do you have to go back to? Clarissa left you, man. You haven't spoken to your father in years, and your brother and sister—" He swallowed quickly and looked away. "They might as well already be gone, too."

The light returned to Justin's eyes and he leaned forward, swept up in his argument. "Think about it, Marc. Aliens? Spaceships? What could be better than this? You can't un-know what we've learned here. Once they replace you, there's no telling where we could go!"

"No." The word was sharp, like a slap to the face, and stopped Justin cold. Both men turned back to the dark woman, who was shaking her head. "There will be no place for … for you beyond Penumbra. And once you have served your purpose to me, there will be no place for you there either."

Marcus's jaw clenched at that. She had been looking at him while she spoke. There would be no place for *him*, she meant. "Why?"

Her eyes shifted. "It is the way of things, Marcus Wells. Your life will be in danger from more than just any agent of the Council the entire time we are in Penumbra. The galaxy is not safe for you. Your rightful place is on Earth, and it is there that I will return you when we are finished with this sad charade."

Marcus nodded, his face bleak. "So, I'll be a figurehead, ruling nothing while chaos swirls all around me, my life in constant jeopardy, and life back on Earth churning on without me." He took a breath. "Hardly seems worth my effort."

"What effort?" Again, her anger reared up, flaring against him with infuriating heat. "All you need do is exist until I find a replacement! Breathe, and all will be well! You will be kept in luxury! You will have everything Penumbra can provide, until it is time for you to be taken home."

Marcus shot Justin a glance. His friend's face was set. He wanted to stay. Justin's business was flourishing with lucrative government contracts that he seldom spoke of in any depth, but he had no family left. He was an only child, his parents had been old when he was born, and both were gone now. And Marcus did not doubt that his friend was following the deeper currents beneath this exotic woman's words. Marcus would not be welcome in this wider galaxy, but she did not seem to be including Justin in that indictment.

"I want more than that. I want money." He shook his head. "Or gold, or whatever. Something that will be worth something when I come back." He straightened. "A lot of something."

Had she been quick to offer him anything, he would have immediately feared for his life. He had seen enough movies to know what to look for, he thought. But she just stared at him. She stared at him for a long time. He started to wonder if he shouldn't try to take back the demand. He could feel prickles of sweat breaking out across his scalp as their locked gazes held, trying to decide how he could break the nerve-wracking moment.

"Fine." She nodded once, sharply, and then looked away with a sneer. "Virri had credit to spare. I'll make sure some of it is freed for your return."

He felt a rush of relief at her words, and forced himself not to expel the breath he had been holding in a relieved sigh. "Good." He tried to smile, but he felt sick to his stomach. "That's ... that's good. That's just fine."

Justin shook his head in disgust and turned back to Angara. "How long before you can find a replacement figurehead?"

Her mouth quirked sideways, lips pursed. "That will depend on how deeply bonded the medallion is. Given that Marcus Wells is Human, I do not imagine the bond can be that deep." She rose with thoughtless grace and moved toward him, taking the necklace in one long-fingered hand. He would not release the chain, which tightened as she drew the jewelry toward her for closer inspection.

Deep within the blue gem he thought he could see movement, as if a distant fog were swirling in a soft wind. Angara inspected the medallion, moving it back and forth against the tension of the chain, her eyes flickering from it to Marcus and back. Her brow furrowed as she continued. Clearly, she was not finding the result she had expected. At last, she released the necklace and settled back in her seat. She was silent for several moments, staring at the jewel.

"Well?" Marcus looked down at the medallion. The movement in the stone seemed to have subsided. "How deep is it?"

She shook her head. "Far deeper than it should be, with a Human."

He had had enough. "What's wrong with Humans?" His anger heated the words more than he had intended, but he didn't care. "And how do you know how deep this frigging thing should go with a Human? How many Humans have been bonded to it before?"

She reared back from his anger, but continued to look at him in disdain.

"No Human has ever bonded with the medallion. Who would—" She shook her head. "I meant no insult." That was so clearly not true it hardly required comment. "It will make finding a replacement slightly more difficult, is all. I had intended to offer the position to Uduta Virri's deputy, Iphini Bha. But an Iwa'Bantu would hardly be a suitable cross-match for a Human." Her eyes grew vague, lost in thought or calculation.

"Why?" This time, as Marcus spoke, he saw Justin nod agreement. There was far more going on here than she was telling them. "Why would this … person … being … deputy … why would she be a bad match?"

Had Marcus been looking anywhere but straight at Angara, he might have missed the look she skimmed his way. But he caught it; evasion and discomfort. Had he doubted the impression, he would have been reassured as she rushed to speak, ignoring his question.

"If any Aijians are in Penumbra, they might do. They accepted alteration long ago to perform their duties. The changes would lend themselves to such a match. Alab Oo'Juto would be an excellent choice, although given the circumstances, I am not certain he would agree." Her words were soft, almost mumbled, and the wash of strange names and sounds, setting the bones of his jaw buzzing, swirled around him in mind-numbing confusion.

"K'hzan Modath would be another possibility, although I doubt he would be willing to serve, even briefly. The Variyar are not given to such positions, and he least of all. Still, he might, just for the insult it would be to the Council, and the spiritual connection would serve, I think."

Marcus slipped the medallion back into his pocket and rose, his hands sweeping out in a sharp gesture. "Enough." She looked up at him, seemingly in shock that he had interrupted her thoughts. "I don't care who replaces me, or why they would be a good candidate. I don't care what kind of connection I might or might not have with these aliens." Several realizations had forced themselves upon him in rapid succession as she recited the strange names. "It's probably been nearly twenty four hours since I last slept." He stomped on the floor. "And I don't mean that forced coma. I'm hungry, I'm thirsty, and I'm exhausted. I'll do what you want, for as long as I have to, and then I want to go home." He tilted his head toward Justin. "And I want him to go home with me."

Justin's jaw tightened at that, but he remained silent.

Angara looked to each of them, and then nodded. "We have a long journey ahead of us. More than enough time for you each to rest after this night's troubles."

She made no gestures, commands, or movements, but the two chairs the men had been sitting on lowered themselves, straightening smoothly like running wax, and were soon two low beds. Angara pushed a couple of pillows on the floor toward them, gesturing to the blankets. "I will have food prepared for you when you awaken."

The men looked at each other, at the beds, and then nodded.

As Marcus's battered mind was drifting off to sleep, his body wrapped in the soft, warm comfort of the incredible blanket, his mind was a senseless jumble of everything that had befallen him since he woke up that morning. He knew he had missed a lot, and failed to follow up on many of the questions that had occurred to him along the way. Whatever his younger self had said in that dream, or vision, or hallucination he had suffered while he was under the influence of the nanites, it was all too much.

As he surrendered his last desperate grasp on consciousness, the image running through his mind was not that of the darkly exotic woman who had captured them, or the spaceship they were riding in, or the strange city toward which they flew. He caught just a glimpse of auburn hair, and a wide smile, and sparkling dark eyes. His last thoughts were of a woman who had cut herself from his life, with good enough reason, only days ago. And so cut the only real tie binding him to the planet of his birth.

# Chapter 6

Iphini Bha sat rigidly on the stool she had had brought into the administrator's office after Ambassador Taurani's last visit. Her antique stylus, the only object from her homeworld she had managed to hold onto, spun deliberately around her fingers. On the walls, the psycho-reactive artwork had shifted from the graceful swirls of color and light they normally projected when she was alone, with jagged crimson flashes splashing through the once-tranquil patterns. Each day Uduta Virri was away, she grew more fearful. The staff of the control center knew that Virri was missing no matter what Bha might say, and with that knowledge came the age-old fear of a disruption in the life support provided by the Relic Core. What if something happened to Virri, wherever he was? If the Skorahn was not secure, they could all be resorting to emergency oxygen very quickly.

Bha, however, had even greater fears. The Council Ambassador had grown more and more insistent upon a private meeting with Virri. She knew the Kerie had to know the administrator was missing. Virri's constant escapes were the worst kept secret in the city, and surely someone at this point had shared the tales with Taurani. His Njta thugs had become far more active around the city in the last few days, and that Eru body servant of his had been poking around in the strangest places.

Bha's body was completely still. Her eyes were fixed on the far wall, not registering the artwork as it continued to chronicle her fear and concern. She cradled the stylus now, forcing herself not to spin it restlessly. If Angara Ksaka could not bring Virri back, the problems that would result would overwhelm the control center, and the Ambassador would be the least of her worries. She had worked with the governance of the city for very nearly all of her adult life, having fled shattered Iwa'Ban immediately after she finished her schooling. This was the only home she had ever known as an adult. She did not want it destroyed because one disgusting Rayabell refused to acknowledge his responsibilities.

The longer Virri was gone, the more likely it was that something truly discouraging was going to happen, and it would be up to her to fix it. She reveled in orchestrating the control center from the shadows, working with the beings that made Penumbra run smoothly despite their inept leader. But without that incompetent lout to shield her from the scrutiny of the city, she was nearly paralyzed with anxiety. She had arrived that morning only to find a discouraging report on Virri's desk outlining a maintenance failure in the executive docking port, the landing bay closest to the control center.

She would need to see that the bay was operational again as soon as possible. Without it, there would be no place for Angara to land and sneak Virri back in when they returned ... *if* they returned. She shook her head, refusing to think of the possibility. This was the first major technical failure to occur since he went missing, but if he was not back soon, it would not be the last.

The soft tone of a communications request insinuated itself into her swirling thoughts. She blinked twice before gracefully turning her head to look at the console on the desk. A personal request would have come through her implants, directly imposing a notification icon upon her field of vision. The fact that this was coming through the console in Virri's private office meant it was either official business, or someone who was not aware that the administrator was still away.

She stared at the glowing ball of light that pulsed gently as it floated above the surface of the desk, and a small image of Ambassador Taurani appeared within the sphere. Bha's pale face quivered, its first sign of emotion in hours of meditative contemplation. The fine lines of her flesh writhed as a frown of distaste warred with a fearful furrowed brow. She had been avoiding the Kerie since his last visit. Aside from not wanting to reveal the administrator's absence, there was something disquieting about the Ambassador's eyes when he regarded her. She felt as if he were sizing her up for some strange, unknown purpose. She knew it was probably the Penumbran distrust of the Council, bred into her after her long tenure in the city. But still, she was left with the discomfited shudder of a prey-animal whenever he spoke to her directly.

The light continued to pulse, and something told her that Taurani was not going to withdraw his request until she answered. She wished Virri had not given the Ambassador the direct link to the office, it made things far more difficult when she wanted to avoid him.

With a soft sigh she reached out and swept her hand through the glowing ball. The viewing field over the desk came alive with a life-sized image of an Eru in Galactic Council livery, his long legs disappearing into the surface of the desk. She had not met the body servant, but she knew an Eru when she saw one, and there was only one employed by the Galactic Council delegation in Penumbra.

The Eru were a race descended from predators only a few hundred years off their homeworld. They stood on two reverse-jointed legs, with the two long arms of a Humanoid, but with an elongated neck that supported a small, vicious-looking head topped with a thatch of coarse black hair. Their tall, muscular bodies were covered with a fine purple fur, and they usually dressed in undyed leathers and hides from their home. Iranse, Taurani's body servant, however, wore a plain pale uniform better suited to his elevated position.

"Deputy Iphini Bha, I trust you are well?" The image of Iranse gave a respectful nod. She was caught off guard by the pleasantry, and the genuine tone of the question. She nodded wordlessly, and he continued without waiting for a reply. "Please wait for the Ambassador."

Of course, Taurani would not have been waiting on the other end of the communication himself. Her nose wrinkled in amused disdain. The wrinkled faded quickly, however, when the image blurred, blending itself into the smooth grey features of the Ambassador. It was always difficult to gauge a Kerie's emotions from its face, with their lack of any nasal feature, a broad expanse of pale, wrinkled flesh sat beneath their two ovoid eyes and above the dramatic, lipless slit of a mouth.

"Deputy Iphini Bha." He gave a cold, shallow nod. "I hope your extra duties do not over-tax you?"

Bha did not even try to respond. She knew a rhetorical formality when she heard one. Her office dealt with diplomatic personnel from across the galaxy, whether they bore a formal title or not. As the lowly assistant to the not-overly-respected administrator, she knew exactly how much this type of creature cared for her well-being. Sure enough, Taurani continued without pause.

"I was wondering if the control center intended to do anything about the

Thien'ha zealot that has been stirring up trouble on the Concourse." The grey head tilted imperiously back to regard her through narrowed eyes.

Bha had been running ragged, juggling the many petitions for official review, the requests for services, and the infrequent complaints from the unofficial diplomats and other beings that filled the corridors of the city. No one had mentioned any Thien'ha that she could remember.

"I do apologize, Ambassador." She used her calming voice, although she knew from experience that he was immune to its effects. "I was unaware of any disturbances along the Concourse. Perhaps you could elaborate?"

Although nominally the control center was responsible for keeping the peace within Penumbra, most of the many factions, delegations, and agencies that divided the populace policed their own areas. The Concourse, being where most of the denizens of the city mingled and mixed, was one of the few areas that fell completely under the remit of the administrator's office, and could be contentious. It occupied most of their time and attention. There had been no reports of any trouble recently, however. Least of all anything about any religious fanatics.

One long-fingered grey hand flipped dismissively in the image, cream-colored robes falling away from the strong, sinewy arm. "A Goagoi Kuak, with some mysterious Humanoid novice." He spit the word 'Humanoid', as of course he might. "They've been stirring up unwarranted anti-Council sentiment, to be honest. I feel quite unsafe, now, wandering the Concourse by myself."

After a lifetime of dealing with touchy diplomatic types, Bha was quite able to school herself to stillness despite the sudden urge to snort. Taurani had not wandered anywhere in Penumbra by himself since his arrival. He was always accompanied by at least one enhanced Ntja bodyguard; and she had never heard of him venturing any closer to the Concourse than the isolated balconies that overlooked the usual press of sentients roaming over the wide spaces below.

Goagoi Kuak were generally quite peaceful unless provoked; a race more known for its scholars and philosophers than for rabble rousing and politics. Still, anything was possible. And Thien'ha could sometimes cause quite a stir with their mere presence. They had a reputation for bringing chaos and disruption with them wherever they went, and often people decided to take matters into their own hands rather than wait, causing the very pandemonium that they feared.

"I will certainly have someone look into that, Ambassador." She bowed her neck, making certain to go deeper than either the ambassador or his servant had gone for her. "I am certain that Administrator Virri would not want you to be discomfited in any way during your time with us."

Taurani's answering grimace was clearly intended to mimic a smile, and revealed the pale expanse of brush that passed for his teeth to full effect. "And when might we expect our esteemed administrator to return, now that you have mentioned him?"

The prints on the walls were awash in jagged blacks and reds, the soft pastels all but erased by her fear and angst. She hated the way this creature made her feel.

"As I have told you, Ambassador, Administrator Virri is away. When he returns—"

"Where is he, you fragile little doll?" The ridges of grey flesh around his glittering eyes tightened in annoyance. "The Council will not be put off forever."

The image lowered its head, the eyes narrowing even more as he stared at her through the viewing field. Time ground to a halt. "You do not know." Again, the pseudo-smile. "Poor Iphini Bha. Always the last to know." The image grew larger as the Ambassador leaned into his own console. "The tides of change are rising, Bha. The time will come, and soon, when you may need to decide who you are loyal to: that boneless animal, or yourself."

The Ambassador's head tilted to the side and the image cut off abruptly.

Iphini stared at the air above the administrator's desk for several heart-beats before she allowed herself the luxury of a sigh. She disciplined her breathing, resting the backs of her long, delicate hands on her knees, allowed her eyelids to slide closed, and forced her mind to let go of the anxiety that speaking to Taurani always caused.

All of her feelings for Virri were shaded with a vague resentment, of course. How could they not be, when his long, unexplained absence caused her so much grief? Her loyalty to her employer, and even to Penumbra itself, was not so great as to demand blind obedience and devotion. She knew her quiet temperament inclined many to take her for granted. She had accepted it as the price of being true to herself. But sometimes, in these darker moments, it was truly difficult to remember why she remained in the city at all.

When she opened her eyes the softer images on the walls had returned. Only hints and ghosts of the jagged emotions that had recently ravaged her peace of mind remained, floating in the background. Generally, Iwa'Bantu did not enjoy psycho-reactive art. Their emotions were too readily accessible by the technology. Unless constant vigilance was maintained, the prints were often far too revelatory for public consumption. She often fantasized about a day when the office could be hers. The first thing she would do would be to send those prints to the recycling center.

Rising gracefully from the stool, Iphini moved to the door. The armored outer door was retracted, leaving only the fragile privacy screen in place. The wave of a hand opened it. Out in the main work area, reports were being received, reaction teams dispatched, and complaints heard, recorded, and filed. Thankfully, it had been relatively peaceful since Virri disappeared this time. She shuddered to think what it would have been like if one of the rare inter-faction conflicts had arisen without a proper administrator present.

She waved a large figure over to her and into a corner. The Leemuk navigated it's obese, pale green bulk through the tight confines of its coworkers with surprising ease. With its tiny, widely set purple eyes and the vast expanse of exposed, glistening teeth, many beings found Leemuks off-putting. Most that Iphini knew, however, were careful, attentive workers and staunchly loyal supporters of Penumbra, which made them a perfect fit for security duties. Their reputation as rather indiscriminate eaters did not hurt, of course. Agha-pa had been the head of security in Penumbra for longer than Iphini had lived in the city. He was not the most proactive leader their small security detail could ask for, but he meant well.

"Have there been any reports concerning trouble in the Concourse with a Thien'ha mystic?" It was not as odd as it sounded, she knew. The Thien'ha were capable of all sorts of strangeness.

The Leemuk cocked its head. Without a visible neck, this was more akin to tilting the amorphous bulk housing its tiny eyes and enormous, toothy maw precariously to one side, then back again. The gaping, lipless hole undulated with disturbing, muscular motions, and her implants translated the sounds into intelligible speech.

"Nothing that I am aware of, mistress." They were also unfailingly polite to their superiors; something that Iphini, in particular, appreciated. "Shall I conduct a more comprehensive scan of the reports?"

She thought about it for a moment. Taurani's discomfiture, if it was even genuine, was really not a top priority for her. She shook her head and gestured for the creature to return to its duty station. "Just flag anything that comes up from now on and let me know, please."

"Yes, mistress."

Agha-pa turned to slouch back to his station, waving her toward the throne at the center of the room. Iphini moved to the raised dais at the rear of the command center, toward the administrator's chair. Once it had been the captain's seat, when this had been the battle bridge of a Variyar warship. She stood behind the heavy piece of furniture, one hand draped across its back, and looked out over the quiet, humming bustle. The efficiency all around owed a great deal to her own efforts. She took pride in that work, as she would take pride in a poem she had written, or a particularly tricky sequence of musical notes she had strung together.

But none of it would mean anything without Virri, and that rankled. Without the Skorahn, the Rayabell would be nothing, and yet, without *him*, she would be even less. It was the central dissatisfaction of her life, and as she got older, it seemed heavier and heavier.

And yet, despite all that, she was desperate for him to return.

One of Agha-pa's workers sat up with a grunt, looking at the throne for his superior. Finding Iphini standing there, he ponderously turned his head over to where the security chief slumped, by the far wall.

"Sir, there's a disturbance in the eastern wing, near the Ring Wall." The Ring Wall was the inner terminus of the Concourse, where it ended and the vast bronze plain at the center of the city began. "Looks like a couple of Nan'Se La from the docks are shaking down a Goagoi Kuak."

Iphini closed her eyes and shook her head. There were not many of the big four-armed Nan'Se La in Penumbra, and most of those worked as manual laborers in the docking bays. They were not known for their intelligence, and often tried to prey on weaker members of the community when given the opportunity.

"Do we have anyone nearby?" Iphini asked. These violent episodes were not common, since the populace generally policed itself, but there were a few roaming patrols, mostly Leemuks, for when things went badly.

"Not near the Ring Wall, Deputy, no." Agha-pa might be lazy, but he knew where his people were at all times. "We can have them there soon, but if the Nan'Se La mean business, it will be too late."

Iphini nodded. They were not common, but if they were not stopped quickly, they were often fatal.

The Leemuk that had addressed her leaned back down to look into the viewing field at his station and then stood back up. "Never mind. The situation has been taken care of."

That was a relief, anyway. "Was it one of ours, or vigilantes?"

The big Leemuk shifted his shoulders back and forth for what passed as a head shake for the big, necklace creatures. "The Goagoi Kuak brought them both down with what looked like a nano-staff, mistress."

That was intriguing. The shape-shifting weapons were ideal for use in Penumbra, where the city's autonomous systems could suppress energy weapons with little warning. They were able to change their shape at the whim of their wielder, making them extremely difficult to use, but absolutely devastating in the hands of a master.

That brought her up short. "What was the Goagoi wearing?"

The Leemuk reared back in confusion. "Mistress?" Then, tilting his head to one side, he leaned back down to look into the field once more. "White robes, mistress. A—" He stood up quickly. "A Thien'ha master?"

She closed her eyes and nodded. That's what she was afraid of. The Thien'ha were not aggressive by nature, but they were utterly without mercy in defense. They had to be, given how they were often received.

It looked like Taurani's fears might not be entirely a fabrication after all. Perhaps if she—

One of the general communications officers jerked upright at her station. A delicate, pale-skinned Humanoid that had a bit of a reputation with the males, she was one of the more emotionally demonstrative inhabitants of the control center. But when she stood up, the frantic pivoting of her head sending her silver hair flying, Iphini could not help the tightening of skin up her spine.

Before she could work herself into a paralytic frenzy of worry, the woman's eyes locked on hers, and the communications officer approached her with a look of undisguised confusion on her pretty face.

"Mistress Bha, communication for you." Her normally-pleasant voice was rough. "It's Ksaka."

Iphini was gripping the back of the command throne with both hands. Ksaka; Virri's personal security officer, bodyguard, and overseer. She had departed in search of the administrator as soon as it had been discovered that it had escaped again. But why was she messaging? Each time in the past, when she had brought Virri back, there had been no direct communication; she had simply dragged the limp sack of depression and incompetence back into the control center, dumped him in his office, and taken the rest of the day off.

The tension in her spine intensified.

"I will accept the message in the administrator's office." She hoped the words sounded as assured as she had tried to make them. The last thing she needed was for the fragile peace of the control center to be shattered by her nervous reaction to the call.

Back in the office, closing both the privacy doors and the armored shutter, Iphini looked in annoyance at the prints, all of them once again showing flashes of violence emerging from the peaceful swirls of color and light. Someday, if the universe was kind, she decided she would not send them to recycling, she would burn them herself.

At the desk, the glowing sphere of light had reappeared as soon as the communications officer routed the message request from the center system to the administrator's private lines. Her anxiety over the viewer when Taurani was on the other end seemed trivial compared to the turbulent fears clawing at her now.

She waved her hand through the sphere and the torso of Angara Ksaka solidified out of the churning mist. Her regal face was stony, her white hair nearly iridescent in the image. But her violet eyes shifted from side to side in a way that Iphini found terribly disturbing, given the bodyguard's usually steady demeanor.

"Iphini, I am on my way back. We will be landing soon." At first, relief washed through the deputy's body. The tension and the fear would be over. The tedium and thanklessness of normal life rose like an idyll in her mind.

She relaxed against the desk, a smile blossoming across her face as the prints all around her blossomed into brighter, richer color. "Where was he?"

Again, the shifting eyes. Some of Iphini's confidence ebbed. "He was on Earth, of course." The image of Angara swallowed, and the deputy's happiness dimmed again. "Iphini, something happened; something very bad."

The tension had returned, this time accompanied by a rush of cold as if someone had opened a door into deepest space. The stylus began to spin. She did not want to ask, but the word emerged anyway. "What?"

"Virri's not with me, Iphini." The shifting eyes steadied, focusing on her. "He's dead."

The room spun. The stylus fell still. The temperature dropped further. She pulled at the collar of her tunic as if she could not breathe. She reached out for the desk to steady herself, in very real danger of falling to the floor.

Uduta Virri was dead. The administrator, the holder of the Skorahn, was no longer among the living.

They were all doomed.

She could hear words, barely, over the roaring of her desperate breath. Were the lights dimming? She felt as if the cold of space was reaching for her; for everyone in Penumbra. The words, mumbling in the distance, were meaningless.

"Bha!" Her name, said like the sharp crack of a whip, penetrated the swirling panic. "Bha, get a hold of yourself! Virri's dead, but I have the Skorahn."

She had the medallion. With that, Iphini steadied herself a little. She took a deep breath. Of course. The station was not dying. The air was fine. Her own life had been thrown into turmoil with the news, but it was not in danger of ending immediately. Somehow, she found that more comforting than she felt she should.

"You have the medallion, but Uduta's dead?" She spoke more to give herself some time, rather than any real need for clarification.

Angara nodded. "He's dead." Her eyes flicked to the side, as if glancing behind her. "The medallion is with me. Everything is going to be fine, I promise."

Iphini lowered herself onto the stool. "How?"

"How what?" The question had an edge to it that she could not understand.

"How did he die?" She clarified, not wanting to anger the fierce woman any more than she already was.

Again, Angara's eyes darted from side to side, but this time Iphini had the distinct impression it was because the woman was avoiding eye contact. "It was an accident. I will tell you all about it when we come in. We will be landing soon. I need you to clear the executive bay for the *Na'uka*."

Iphini blinked. That bay was normally reserved for emergencies or high-ranking shadow diplomats attempting to conceal their comings and goings from Council agents. It was not unusual for Virri to require the bay, especially when on one of his secretive little jaunts. But then, she reminded herself with an involuntary shudder, it was not Virri on the little ship making the decisions.

And then she remembered that the executive bay was not operational, and her body grew very still.

"I am sorry, Angara, but that will not be possible. The bay is out of operation at the moment." She closed her eyes, accessing the current records of the various ports and bays available near the Red Tower. She opened her eyes again with a wince. "The closest docking port I can offer you is the eastern wing common docking bay."

It was a busy bay, serving the primary habitat towers all around the Red Tower. It would be the quickest journey to the center, but it would be through some of the most crowded halls. There would be no disguising the return of the administrator's bodyguard, or her notable lack of a body to guard.

Angara's image seemed to collapse as she put her face into her hands. Her dark skin made it hard to read her expression in the small, misting image, but there was no missing her shoulders as they slumped in defeat.

"Angara, why does it matter? What else is wrong?" The idea that even more could be wrong was enough to put her back on the floor.

Within the image, the bodyguard shook her head. "Forget it. We will be landing very soon now. Secure us a berth in the primary docking bay, and we will be with you as soon as we can."

Something about that did not sound right, and after only a moment, Iphini's eyes widened, then tightened in suspicion. "Angara, who's 'we'?"

The image jumped, and then settled down into total stillness. "When we arrive. I am going now. I have to get the *Na'uka* ready for our arrival."

The image flickered and died without further word. Iphini found herself once again staring at the air above the desk. She focused on the empty space, ignoring the tub-like seat behind the desk, and the shifting prints on the walls.

Uduta Virri was dead. The Skorahn was safe. And Virri's bodyguard was on her way, accompanied by some mysterious entity she would not identify over the standard communication network.

That was a lot to process, but it all revolved around one reality: Virri, the being who had sat upon the powerless command throne of Penumbra, whose very heartbeat had kept every sentient in the city alive, was dead.

She settled down on the stool. She knew she should be preparing for Angara Ksaka's arrival, but she had no idea what she could do in that regard. The last thing she wanted to do now was to face the roomful of curious faces that would greet her if she stepped beyond the confines of the small office.

She folded her hands in her lap and waited, staring at the closed, armored door.

Uduta Virri was dead. Whatever came next, it was going to be more turmoil than she felt capable of dealing with at the moment.

A single tear coursed down her pale, lined face. She was very surprised to discover that she would miss Virri, now that he was gone.

*****

Angara stared through the space that had been occupied by Bha's image a moment before. She had been counting on the executive docking bay to get the Humans, especially the pale one, into the command center without undue attention. Now, they were going to have to parade down half the length of the Variyar warship, after landing in one of the busiest docking ports in the city.

She still could not believe she was bringing Humans to Penumbra. It was not as if she had been offered any better solutions by the uncaring universe, but still, she could not imagine what was going to happen the first time she brought one of these Humans face to face with an Aijian. And may all the powers that be see to it that no Variyar saw them in the corridors before she could get Marcus Wells and Justin Shaw to the control center.

And that thought brought her up short once again. Why was she so sure of a better reception amongst the city's administrators and guardians? She was bringing two Humans into the central command area. Not only that, but one of the Humans actually possessed the Skorahn!

She had contemplated killing Marcus Wells and taking the medallion while he was frozen in the stasis chamber, his mind ravaged by the nanites. Something had stopped her, however. And when she had finally checked the depth of the bond the medallion had built with Marcus Wells, she had been very relieved she had not.

There was something strange about that bond, and she was glad it was not her responsibility to fathom it. Why would a Human bond more deeply than the greasy Rayabell? Why, for that matter, did the Skorahn bond with any creature more deeply than any other? She knew that it happened. It had been one of many things she had learned in her research of the city, its leaders, and the medallion that granted them their station. Of course, there had never been a Human bonded to the Skorahn. There was no baseline to which she could compare her expectations.

And yet, there was no denying Marcus Wells's connection with the jewel.

She shook her head and settled back into her flight chair. She had already decided she would awaken the Humans before she made the emergence into real space. It would terrify Marcus Wells, which was a worthy goal in and of itself. Justin Shaw would, she guessed, find the experience, and the image of Penumbra rising ahead of them, awe-inspiring. She smiled at the thought.

She had not come to the conclusion easily or quickly, but she had decided, contrary to all established knowledge and galactic opinion, that Humans were not quite as bad as she had been led to believe.

# Chapter 7

Once again seated in the smart chairs that had extruded themselves up out of the carpet-covered deck, Marcus and Justin tried to appear relaxed as their kidnapper-cum-hostess explained what was happening.

"The *Yud'ahm Na'uka* has been traveling along a singularity path, a tunnel through higher space, linking two points in our own space. I opened the wormhole—" Marcus had to open his mouth and work his jaw back and forth against the vicious tickle that word had produced beneath his ear. He forced himself to listen again to the description. "—in an instant, the path is created, the wormholes at either end are created as potentialities, and we travel. As we are bound by the laws of our own universe, we must still spend some relatively small amount of time traveling, rather than appearing, in a moment, at the destination."

She was moving her hands through two colorful, shimmering fields that hung suspended in the air before her flight chair. "Our exit wormhole will form as we approach, and we will reenter our own space. I've been told it's quite an experience the first time."

Justin craned his head forward trying to see Angara's profile. "You've been told? You've never done this?"

She shook her head, but didn't look back. "My people live a nomadic life, plying the singularity pathways between systems. Before I could walk I had witnessed hundreds of these moments." She shrugged. "I'm afraid with such familiarity, their beauty has been lost."

Marcus stared at the back of her head. He had only been half listening to her reply. It had been bothering him since almost the very first moment he had seen her. He could forgive himself, he knew, considering everything else his brain was dealing with at the time. But the reminders had been there, constantly refreshed, ever since. And now, staring at her fine white hair, he let his mind wander over the subject.

She had shaken her head. She had nodded. Over the course of their time together, he had seen her smile, frown, shrug, and perform half a dozen other common Human expressions that had made communicating with her far easier than communicating with an alien should be. These gestures had allowed him to grow more comfortable around her despite the unnatural tone of her skin, the exotic shine of her hair, and the frightening sharpness of her teeth. Why would an alien woman, a stranger to Earth from all he could gather, share with him such Human movements and quirks? He knew there were people who attributed the changing aspects of animal faces for Human expressions. He had half worried that he was doing the same before he realized that no, in fact, these various expressions really did mean roughly the same things they would mean for a Human. But how could that be?

He felt certain there was a great deal he was not being told. Her attitude toward Humans, well, at least toward *him*, seemed unqualified and negative. Why that bias, if she had only ever come to Earth to fetch back this scumbag boss of hers? Even assuming that such duties would have exposed her to less-than-desirable individuals, she had to know there was an entire crowded planet of other people, no?

"We will be making our emergence in just a moment." She spoke in the vague tones of a person immersed in important work. She looked up through the view field, then back down to the swirl of colors that hovered before her. "If you watch just below us, there, you will see." She indicated a point just beneath what Marcus assumed was the flightpath of the ship with one long finger.

Putting aside the various worrisome observations that howled for his attention, he sat forward. The chair followed him, adjusting to support him as he watched over her shoulder.

Through the viewing field the unrelieved blackness filled his vision. The sense that he could reach right through the field and into the void was more than a little off-putting. But as Marcus stared, he thought he could see movement for the first time since they had fallen into the black hole above the Earth.

At first it appeared as a swirl of deepest blue against the darkness. He thought it might be his eyes playing tricks on him, but then the blue began to refract into faintly lighter shades. The swirl was spinning, and soon he was sure it was no illusion. The blues continued to divide, and soon they were looking at a vast whirlpool of blues and purples and aquamarine, twisting out of the darkness directly in front of their ship.

They began to fall into the swirl, just as they had fallen into the first hole, and a familiar, unreasoning panic rose up in his throat. He gripped the arms of his chair and the material accepted his fingers, wrapping around them like wet clay. He didn't notice.

The swirling disk of color continued to grow. Without a frame of reference, it was impossible to tell how large it was. Suddenly, it felt as if the ship was rocketing through the darkness toward the swelling shape. It was impossible for Marcus to decide how close they were, but he could not shake the feeling that they were about to strike its surface at incredible speed. Digging into the arms of the chair offered absolutely no relief whatsoever as the material continued to give way beneath his desperate fingers.

"We will be breaking the plane in a moment." Angara looked back at them, her full lips curved in a cruel smile that, for once, did not show her predatory teeth. "Try to relax. It can be a bit disturbing, first time through."

It would have been nice to have had that warning a little sooner, Marcus thought as he closed his eyes and tried to will his body to relax. It was no use. His brain was telling him he was about to crash into an enormous swirling wall, and there was no convincing himself otherwise.

He opened his eyes, figuring that he might as well watch the show, if he was going to suffer through the consequences anyway.

The disk continued to loom, asserting its size violently upon his senses. It was *much* larger than their ship. The colors continued to shatter, remaining within the blue and purple spectrums. He had never known there were so many shades, and under other circumstances, he was fairly certain that he would have found the entire spectacle quite lovely.

As it was, however, it merely added to the terror.

He was searching the center of the churning mess for some sign of a hole or gateway that would allow them to leave the darkness. Although the colors were darker and deeper in the middle, there was no sign of a wormhole like the one they had plunged into before. There was no blackness, no view of a star-speckled sky on the other side; just the spinning colors that had now swollen to fill the entire viewing field before them. The interior of the ship was bathed in cool light; the normal illumination overwhelmed by the luminescent glow from outside.

When they struck the barrier there was no sound, no sense of impact. One moment they were rushing at the azure surface, and then they were through. A billion strange stars blossomed all around them as streamers of sapphire energy tumbled past like spiraling comets. These ribbons flared out ahead, exhausting themselves, leaving fading trails of glittering vapor in their wake.

Justin's gasp was the first sound that registered upon him after their emergence. Looking over, he could see his friend's dark face transformed with childlike delight. His eyes were wide, reflecting the light of those countless strange stars, and his mouth hung open in an innocent smile that showed none of its usual artifice or sarcasm.

"Damn, that was amazing." Justin turned to look at him, and Marcus couldn't help but return the smile.

Marcus nodded. "If I wasn't too busy shitting my pants, I would have wanted to take a picture."

Justin made a face at that, shaking his head. "And you still want to go home?"

That brought Marcus up short, and he looked quickly at the back of Angara's head before returning Justin's gaze. "Not like I have much choice, apparently. So no reason to worry about it."

Justin shook his head, his lip twisted dismissively, and settled back into his chair.

"So, tour guide, what's next on the agenda?" Marcus looked at him, and then sighed. It must be nice, never worrying about anything.

Outside the view screens the sky was an infinity of strange stars, scattered like white sand on black velvet. Again, there was no way to tell how fast they were going, as the stars themselves shifted too slowly to offer any useful frame of reference.

"We are in Penumbra's home system. We will be approaching the planet that anchors the city shortly." She tilted her head, and Marcus thought she was probably closing her eyes again. He had come to realize that she was accessing information when she did that, and he wondered what sort of nanites were crawling around inside her head, to let her do something like that. Would his be able to provide information, if he learned how to use them? And how could he trust such information, coming as it did from a strange soup of alien machines living in his head?

"When we arrive, Penumbra will be on the far side of the planet, so you will be able to watch city-rise before we dock." She turned around, and he saw genuine warmth in her smile. "It is quite a sight, I have to admit." She turned back, settling into her chair in a way that seemed to indicate they had a ways to go. "I think you'll both be impressed."

Marcus eased back, staring out at the slowly sliding arrangement of stars as his mind wandered. He tried to empty his thoughts, to enjoy the moment. There seemed to be a great advantage to Justin's outlook concerning their situation. While he thought of that, he could feel something moving behind his own eyes, taking the situation in, evaluating it, and storing data away for later analysis. He did not think it was the tiny little robots in there, but rather that newly reawakened younger self from his vision.

For years a part of him had known he had taken a wrong turn somewhere along the way. He had purposely gotten himself expelled from the school his father had put so much stock in, and from which his brother and sister had graduated with such high distinction. It had been simple, childish stubbornness, he knew now. He had had no intention of following in his father's footsteps. Even back then, he was determined to follow his own path.

But by seizing the reins and wrenching himself off the beaten track, he feared now, he had lost his way. He had seized control of his life away from the others, it was true, but he had failed to exert corresponding control himself. He had drifted through life ever since, always taking the path of least resistance rather than making a stand on his own. That path had led him from public high school to a state college of no great merit. He had accepted the recommendations and suggestions of others without thinking through their implications.

When he had graduated, he had had no real preparation for a specific career; there was nothing he felt passionate about. He had again declined his father's advice, ignored the efforts of his siblings to offer him help, and drifted off campus like flotsam, being dragged away by the retreating tide, and washed up at a two-bit local radio station selling advertising air time to mom-and-pop businesses and local restaurants that could hardly afford it. He knew radio advertising was nearly useless, who listened to ads anymore when you could just hit a reset button to hear another song? But it had paid decent money, and so he had stayed.

His life had been a grey expanse of meaningless work and empty distractions for as long as he could remember. In fact, other than the time he spent with Justin and a few other friends, only one thing had happened to him in the last ten years that had rippled the boring calm of his life. Clarissa had seen something more in him than others did. She hadn't directed him, hadn't manipulated him. She had been the first person, other than Justin, in a very long time who seemed genuinely interested in what *he* wanted, and where *he* might like to go. His head fell forward at the memory. And he had driven her away with a resolute campaign of indifference and carelessness, not liking the questions she had forced him to ask about his own life and choices.

There was a tightening behind his eyes; that younger self, staring out from the dark recesses of his mind. He could feel its contempt for the choices he had made, or rather not made. And he knew that contempt was his own. He had given up the wheel of his life, and only now, floating God knew how far from it all, did he realize it. It was an uncomfortable feeling, to be shamed by a psychological projection of your younger self.

"Here we are." Angara's voice broke into his cascade of self-pity. Marcus shook himself out of the dark thoughts and leaned forward.

It was only the second planet he had ever seen from space, if you counted the receding orb of Earth as he was being pulled away against his will. There was no doubting the enormous size and scope of the thing floating before them, slowly growing as they approached. And yet, he could not help but feel underwhelmed.

It was a dull, reddish brown ball with few variations in shade or texture to hint at any surface features at all. The sharp line of the terminator sliced off a dark crescent of night in the lower-right hand quadrant. The only movements he could see at all were strange, flickering lights that danced within the darkness.

He didn't know if it was because the sphere out there wasn't Earth, or if there was something more, but it did not carry the same majesty and presence his homeworld had.

"It looks pretty sad, actually." Justin's words were thoughtful. "No clouds, or water, or anything?"

Angara shook her head, sending the cascade of shimmering white hair slinking down over the back of her chair. "It is a dead world; no atmosphere to speak of. Only the endless dust storms and the lightning they generate, illuminating the night-side of the planet."

Marcus got up and moved around the pilot's chair to the viewing field. Even right up against the surface, whatever it was, it seemed to his senses to be a mere hole in the bulkhead, with nothing standing between him and the dead planet floating before him. "Was it always dead?" He thought he could make out vague crescent shapes on the surface below that reminded him of some of the older craters on Earth's moon.

He could hear the shrug in Angara's voice even with his back to her. "There are theories. Nothing left down there now, obviously. But there are scholars who believe the crater patterns are far too regular to indicate the random falling of meteorites."

Marcus cocked his head to one side. He could never remember which word to use for the space rocks that actually made it to Earth. Meteors? Meteoroids? Meteorites? The little bugs in his head clearly decided to translate Angara's word to 'meteorites'. Were they right? Was that knowledge somewhere in his head despite the fact that he could not remember it? Or, rather, did it not much matter, and they just grabbed the first word they could find?

The thoughts brought back the sense of disquiet he had, knowing that everything he heard was being filtered through some system he didn't understand.

Just one more thing to worry about.

The world spun before them as the little ship, dropped lower, preparing to insert itself into the planet's orbit, leaving the advancing terminator behind. The surface slid beneath them as they moved toward the horizon. The system's distant sun was above and behind, its position only noticeable from the illumination far below.

The planet rolled beneath them, the horizon crawling away in the distance as they dropped into a lower orbit. Aside from the slow movement of the planet, there was no sign of the ship's maneuvering.

"You will see the city rise above the horizon in a few moments." Angara's voice was distracted. Marcus glanced back to find her hands moving furiously through the light clouds before her, her eyes flicking and distracted. "We'll be docking in one of the busiest ports in the city, so once you've had your fill of city-rise, I'll need for you both to sit down, or go in back for the landing."

Marcus nodded and turned back to the view. Justin, standing across from him to allow their pilot to see between them, was grinning his stupid schoolboy grin again.

"If you don't smile, I'm going to kick your ass all the way back to Earth,

Marc." The grin widened. "Seriously, if you can't appreciate everything that's happened here, I don't want you to stay."

Clearly, no words of Angara's were going to sway Justin from his decision to abandon their home for good. And just as clearly, he still intended for Marcus to join him in his fantastical exile. He shook his head and went back to searching the horizon for this floating city. He wasn't sure what to expect, other than, given everything else that had happened recently, it was probably going to completely defy expectation.

A sharp glimmer winked at them from the very line of the horizon, and Marcus found himself straightening up despite himself. The flash of light was soon joined by others. Light flashing off distant objects, he figured, although he could not make out any details this far away. He rested his hands against a bulged combing below the image, leaning in until his forehead was nearly lost in the swirling colors of the field.

The occasional gleam resolved itself into a small glittering object that rose above the horizon, twinkling like a thousand stars caged into some strange, mystical lantern. Now, with this sparkling image before them, he had a better frame of reference for their speed. The city, although that word seemed even stranger now as he beheld the thing floating in space, grew at a frightening speed.

As they continued to soar toward the distant object that had to be Penumbra, details began to resolve out of the glimmer. Marcus's first impression was of a flat shape tearing at them out of the night. Tall needles seemed to stick up out of the general mass, stabbing up and down without any sense of planning or organization. Soon, the needles resolved themselves into glittering spires.

As they continued to close, he saw that the city was not spherical at all, but rather U shaped. A sweeping arm reached out on either side, each bristling with towers, embracing a gulf between them that glowed with a cold blue light. A hole set into the material of the planetoid shimmered with deep azure light, and a glittering, meandering ribbon of diamonds floated out and away, reaching down to the planet far below.

The most disconcerting thing about Penumbra, as they continued to close with the floating city, was the jagged, random orientation of the many towers. They slashed out into the darkness in every direction, although the majority of them, oriented above and below the plane of the place, reminded him of pictures he had seen that featured city waterfronts, with a city rising above while its reflection fell away beneath.

As they continued to close, he noted that each tower sparkled with countless lights. Many were oriented along the flanks of the towers, like portholes in a cruise ship. Others, however, followed more esoteric patterns, in circles, spirals, or scattered with no pattern at all. It was as he tried to follow the patterns of these windows that he realized how varied the design of each tower was. Some of them were very similar to each other, but for the most part, there were as many sizes, styles, shapes, and colors as there were towers. He could tell that each was fastened to the massive thing that lurked beneath it all, lending the city its shape and substance. The towers disappeared into a layer of iron skin that seemed to engulf the far aft aspects of each ancient ship.

As they rose up over the city, they could just make out a flat area at the apex of the U, where a semicircle of dull bronze metal, lower than the steel skin, swept around and surrounded a small dome-like structure, the only structure that stood all alone as far as they could see.

"It's a mess." Justin's head swiveled wildly as he tried to take it all in. There were so many different designs, most of them defying any kind of analysis at all. Although the majority was long and thin, giving the appearance of a city Human minds could grasp, others were squat, or bulbous, or organic. Marcus couldn't even begin to imagine the internal layouts of some of the stranger specimens.

"How do you tell which way is up inside those?" Marcus was looking closely at a massive red tower with fewer window ports than most of the others. The construction managed to convey a sense of menace despite being locked into place for God alone knew how many thousands of years.

"Each tower was once an independent starship. They each have their own power and life support runs, as well as gravitic controls. All powered by the Core now, of course, and maintained by their inhabitants, or by the administrator's office. But they all still use their original systems." Her seat began to rise, moving her toward the view screen and shouldering the two Humans back to either side. "Now, if you don't mind, please take your seats as I bring us in."

They could see, now, a flurry of traffic swarming around a scattering of bright rectangles in the armored edge of the city's crust, a few towers over from the tall red one he had been looking at earlier. The rectangle was teeming with small, glittering shapes. The entire thing looked as chaotic as the entrance to an agitated bee hive.

"We're going in there?" Marcus backed in to his seat, which lifted up to accept him and give him a better view as the entire chamber seemed to alter, as if the head of the ship were lowering.

"This is the closest port to the control center." Angara's head bobbed a bit as she spoke, as if by the very motion of her neck she could make the ship weave through traffic that seemed increasingly intent on barring their way. "It also happens to be the main docking bay for this sector of the wing, so always busy."

Marcus was trying to study the other ships as they zipped in and out of his vision. They came in an even more dizzying variety than the towers rising up all around them. Many seemed to follow the basic design concepts of an airplane. Many others, however, defied description. He saw everything from pseudo-jet fighters to floating rocks, spheres, and other shapes.

He did not, however, see anything that looked remotely like the ship in which he currently rode. He thought that might be significant, somehow.

Justin was ducking and weaving beside him, as if watching a car chase in 3-D. Their view dipped, and the broad expanse of the red tower had disappeared off to the side, rising up and away, over the command deck, and beyond the scope of the tilting view screen.

A large red space craft swept in past them, its aggressive moves clearly taking several of the smaller ships by surprise as they skittered out of its way. It was nearly the same shade as the tower overhead, and although much, much smaller, the design was similar enough to suggest a close, if distant, relationship. The brooding menace of the tower was clear in this smaller cousin, whose thick design suggested a belligerence not common among the other craft they had seen.

"Damned Variyar hotshots." Angara spat the words as she swooped down to avoid the other ship's wake, and then back up to resume her own path. "Always convinced they're in a bigger hurry than anyone else."

Marcus watched the big red ship as it swept toward one of the larger openings, came to a hovering stop, and then moved graceful into the dock. The white light emerging from within the building was eclipsed by the crimson bulk of the ship, and then massive blast doors irised closed, shutting out the remainder of the light.

"Hmmm … closing down an entire docking bay. Must be someone important." Angara was bringing them to a much smaller opening. This close in, they were now alone, other ships no longer flitting in front of them, and Marcus felt he could relax a little.

The *Yud'ahm Na'uka* slid into the brightly lit opening, passing through a shimmering field as they did so. A large chamber, the size of a warehouse, opened up around them. Several ships were resting in white cradles. Marcus could feel his mouth fall open as he watched the scene unfolding before him, but he made no effort to close it. He knew that Justin looked just as dumbfounded.

Walking along the floor of the vast hall, most wearing no protective clothing that he could see, was an array of creatures straight out of a child's worst nightmares. They came in all shapes and sizes. Some were tall and lanky, long robes fluttering around their legs, others were squat and fat, staring around belligerently as they stood, arms folded, around a small ship nearly as ugly. Some clearly had recognizable skin of half a hundred shades, while others were covered in hair, or scales, or completely shrouded in environment suits of countless different designs. As he continued to stare out, he noticed that far more of the workers here were Humanoid than he had first seen. Even the enormous, four-armed brutes muscling crates onto floating pallets could have passed for Human, other than that extra set of smaller arms beneath the usual pair.

"It's like a zoo." Justin was up again, standing beside Angara as she brought her ship into a gentle landing upon a cradle that had lit up as they approached. How she had known where to go, or when, he couldn't have said. He assumed, however, that it had something to do with the robots in her head.

"A statement like that, overheard in the wrong quarters, will get you killed, *Human*." She snapped at him, not taking her eyes off her landing. It was the first time she had given Justin a taste of whatever bias she held against the people of Earth. Marcus was honest enough with himself to admit that he enjoyed the reversal.

Justin, however, barely noticed. "You think?" He was grinning, but still standing at the view screen. Marcus got up to join him as he turned to their pilot. "Don't worry sweetheart. I know when to keep my mouth shut."

With a slight shudder, the *Na'uka* settled onto the supports. White vapor shot out from beneath, drifting up to obscure their view for a moment, and then everything was still.

Angara gave a soft sigh, and shook out her hands as if they were cramping. The colored mist through which she seemed to control the ship had faded away. She looked up at the two men, regarding them with her clear, violet eyes.

She seemed to assess them for several minutes, and once again Marcus was sure she was spending far more time, with far less pleasure, looking at him. With a shrug she rose, moving around her chair as it settled down into the floor.

"Come with me. We have to make some quick decisions. This is even busier than I had feared." She pushed aside the hangings and moved back into the chamber that had already played host to so many of Marcus's less pleasant memories. Justin followed eagerly, with no hesitation at all. After a moment, and a last glance out at the menagerie moving around in the docking bay outside, he followed as well.

The lighting had not changed in the cozy interior room. Maddeningly, there was still no source that Marcus could see. Angara was holding up two bundles of cloth, one to each of them. The look on her face brooked no discussion.

"You're going to have to wear these. We're not going to be able to make it to the control center without being seen, and there's no way any of this will work if your first moments in the city feature me having to fight my way through a mob, dragging the two of you in plain view behind me."

Justin took one bundle, and Marcus, after a moment and an impatient shake by the purple-skinned hand holding it out, took the other. They appeared to be heavy robes of some kind; dark, rough fabric with wide, heavy cowls.

"These shouldn't arouse too much suspicion."

Marcus shook his head, looking up from the strange garment. "Suspicion for what? What, exactly, are you trying to hide?"

She looked at him as if he was a total idiot, and again he was shaken to realize that so many facial expressions seemed to carry over between their cultures. When she spoke, it was with the tones one might use to direct a family pet well past its prime.

"That you're Humans, of course."

# Chapter 8

The ramp beneath the outthrust flight deck lowered without a sound, and Angara Ksaka strode down with all the confidence she could muster, looking neither left nor right. She had not anticipated parading through the city with two Humans in tow, but she thought she was carrying it off well enough, all things considered.

Nestled amongst the myriad shocks and fears that continued to numb the Humans, their concern about vacuum was possibly the most irritating. Her explanations of auxiliary gravitic atmosphere fields and the small personal fields built into every article of clothing worn by the air breathers of Penumbra had done little to allay their concerns. In fact, she was not entirely convinced that they had even understood half of what she had said.

Despite her warnings, neither man seemed capable of keeping his head down. Instead, they were twisting this way and that, mooning around them like two farmers off their homeworld for the first time. She smiled at the thought, and then immediately crushed the reaction. They *were* farmers off their pathetic homeworld for the first time, as far as any of the galactics around them might care. And if any sentient nearby discovered which planet they *called* home, all three of them would probably die before Iphini Bha could send help. *If* anyone from the administrator's office would be brave enough to come after them.

"Stop looking around." She muttered, keeping her lips steady. "You need to keep your faces hidden."

She knew the pale one resented this. She could even sympathize with him to a certain extent. But that sympathy only went so far. Yes, she was an unappreciated exile from a despised race, but that was still an eternity from being a *Human*, for the love of all things! Thankfully, Marcus Wells was keeping his resentments to himself for the moment. She figured it was possible that even he had realized the potential for trouble in this new environment.

At the far end of the bay a set of large blast doors were open. She could see the Variyar transport in the primary bay beyond, its dedicated ground crew bustling about the squat, ugly ship. There was only one being in all of Penumbra who could cause such a commotion. Whether he was arriving or departing, her greatest concern at the moment was getting them off the flight deck before he showed up.

She had notified Bha as soon as they had docked. The deputy would be waiting for them at the door to the control center, a pathway clear to the administrator's office. She had had to dodge some uncomfortable questions as they planned, but the timid Iwa'Bantu's normal reserve had made it much easier than it might have been.

Now all she had to do was walk two Humans through the busiest port in the city and all the way up to the control center with no one the wiser.

There was a sudden uproar at the main entrance, off to their left. She had been moving her charges to a small, little-used side door, but even here the crowd was being drawn toward the tumult. She felt a sinking feeling in her gut and glanced at the Variyar ship. A small party of warriors in full dress regalia had emerged through the blast doors, standing stiffly as if waiting to be judged.

She reached back and grabbed the two men by their shoulders, snarling as she realized the dark one had slung his heavy bag beneath the borrowed robe. Neither of them had the faintest idea how much danger they were really in. Both had been busy sneaking glances all around despite her repeated warnings, and were craning their necks to see what the disturbance might be. She tried to pull them against the movement of the crowd, toward the small, unassuming service door, but she knew even as she pulled that it was too late. They were swept along with a tide of sentients, all moving toward the main entrance.

Angara knew what she would see. She could even understand the fascination building in the crowd. In such an enlightened age as this, when violence was publicly shunned by the Galactic Council and the vast majority of its member civilizations, the anachronistic warriors of the Variyar were a rare, fascinating sight. Nearly every galactic culture had put violence so far behind them that even under the heavy hand of the Council, direct rebellion was all but unthinkable.

The Variyar exiles who made Penumbra their home were a distinct exception to that rule.

Angara was not an expert on Variyar history or politics, but she had conducted some rudimentary research into their ruler-in-exile, K'hzan Modath, in the course of her duties to the city. One of the more long-lived races to roam the galaxy, the exiled king and his martial entourage had been ensconced in the city for far longer than Angara had been alive.

Lost in the mists of myth and legend now, the Variyar were said to have once been one of the most powerful races in the galaxy. Second only to the great Enemy, some claimed. And in much more recent history, as the hereditary ruler of that race, K'hzan had been a violent opponent of the disarmament protocols pushed on his people by a Council consolidating its power over the galaxy. When the Council fleet, incorporating the military might of every other major polity to have already succumbed, was finally dispatched to decommission the Variyar navy one way or the other, they found the system defenseless, the majority of complacent denizens left to the mercy of the Council while their king had disappeared with the full might of his fleet, along with those subjects who chose a life in exile over safety beneath the yoke of the Council. It was supposed that he had grown exhausted in the end, fighting both the Council itself and their appeasers among his own race.

No one knew where K'hzan and his fleet had gone. None of Angara's sources had been able to enlighten her. What was common knowledge, however, was that the king had been missing, and then had appeared in Penumbra with no warning or fanfare, and no sign of the fleet he had taken from Variya. There were stories, of course, of adventurers and fools through the years who had sought to track the king's movements when he left the city. Whether motivated by greed, a thirst for vengeance, or simple curiosity, none of those brave enough to follow had ever returned. Eventually, K'hzan Modath and the mystery of his hidden fleet were merely seen as a given, and no further attempts had been made to chase after them. Over time, unbeknownst to any of the self-professed authorities in the city, a large swath of the Red Tower, formerly an ancient Variyar warship, had been secured by agents of the king. He moved into the enclave without delay and had made it his home ever since.

Except that he rarely spent long stretches of time in Penumbra. He was often away, coming and going through the city surrounded by a wave of excited spectators, shielded by the towering warriors of his personal guard. Despite his exile, he had never relinquished the trappings or ceremony of his position.

Sure enough, as she watched, two towering, red-skinned figures pushed out of the crowd, forcing the beings in the doorway back and away. They moved with a strange, fluid grace, the reverse bend in their knees allowing for more freedom of movement, she always assumed, and a lower center of gravity.

More warriors followed, their shimmering armor strange and exotic in a culture where such equipment, outside of the Council enforcers and Peacemakers, was all but unheard of. Their faces were impassive, eyes tight as they surveyed the crowed, sweeping racks of black horn rising above their heads.

Each warrior held a ceremonial blade, burnished copper with glittering crimson gems, in a formal pose that did not waver with each strong step. She had seen this before, but knew how impressive it must appear to the Humans. She even had to admit to a certain appreciation herself. Outside of this unit and their ceremonial regard for their king, such martial displays had been vanishingly rare in living memory.

At the center of the formation, striding onto the flight deck as if he owned it, K'hzan Modath towered over his own, gargantuan sentinels. With a crimson cloak billowing out behind him, the exiled Variyar ruler paid the crowd no heed, moving at his own pace as the warriors around him kept their stations.

The stately group moved through the crowd toward the massive blast doors, and Angara looked to either side to watch the Humans' reaction. Given how much militaristic pomp and ceremony existed on Earth, they could hardly be surprised by the parade-like atmosphere of the event. However, with the Variyar's red skin, gnarled, impassive faces, and twisting tangle of ebon horns sprouting from their skulls, they could not fail to impress.

She knew less about Human mythology than she knew about Variyar history, but she knew about the fabled creatures the Humans called demons; she could even guess at the origin of the image, lost even to galactic scholars in the mists of a bygone age. And she saw, by the widening of their eyes and their open-mouthed incredulity, that the appearance of the Variyar had, indeed, struck a chord.

"What the—" Justin Shaw started, but his voice faded into silence, his arms flopping foolishly by his side.

"Holy shit ..." Marcus, despite his pale flesh, looked very much like his friend in that moment. "What the hell are *they*?"

Angara made no attempt to repress her smile at their reaction. "They are the Variyar; militaristic atavists from the refuse pile of galactic history." She leaned forward to whisper in both their ears. "They *really* don't like Humans."

She had kept her eyes on the king and his entourage as she spoke, and so was looking directly at K'hzan as she said the word 'Humans'. There was no pause in his gait as he swept toward the distant ship, but his head swiveled the moment she finished the word, and his dark, cold eyes pierced the distance that separated them. He was staring straight at her, their eyes locked as if the vast space between them did not exist.

She went cold as she saw his eyes flick to the two figures beside her. There was no expression for her to read on that gnarled, implacable face. But a flickering of something she interpreted as recognition occurred as he looked at the two hooded figures, and her chill grew stronger.

"We need to leave now." She pulled on their shoulders again, pulling them back toward the far corner and the service corridor beyond. She could feel K'hzan's eyes boring into her back, could imagine him growling an order to his guards, and had no trouble envisioning what would happen next. The tension across her shoulders was unbearable as she pushed the Humans to move faster.

When the cry rose up behind her, she stumbled. There was no way the Humans could outrun the Variyar, but she had to try. She refused to give up, this close to her destination. She gathered her strength, shoved with all her might, and surged forward, eyes focused on the small, distant door.

But once again she was struggling against a surging crowd, and quickly she realized that she had misread the situation. She stopped pushing, ignoring the relieved expressions on the Humans' faces, and turned to see what was happening behind her. Her eyes narrowed at the unfolding scene, and she started to push Marcus and Justin backward, once more heading toward the door, away from the procession.

A small group of black-skinned Humanoids had thrown off concealing cloaks and hoods and were brandishing heavy rifles at the tall red honor guard.

She snarled. Mnymians. Most Mnymians made a living as mercenaries, guarding against common criminals and those who most openly flouted Council law. They were also, coincidentally, the mercenaries of choice for the Council itself, when they chose to act outside their own supposed dictates.

The Mnymians, their red hair gleaming under the bright bay lights, were shouting something she could not make out.

She closed her eyes and accessed the communications network, plunging through the levels of security to slam into Iphini Bha's implants.

"Bha! Trouble in the main bay! Mnymians are making a run for Modath!" She tried to push a sense of urgency into her thoughts.

"I see it." Bha's thoughts were icy calm. "I will try to get some Leemuks headed in that direction, but I do not think it will matter."

That was probably true, now that she thought about it. Angara looked back up at the scene unfolding before her. This was not the first time someone had tried to assassinate K'hzan Modath. In fact, it was considered a premium contract few mercenaries would pick up given the results of past attempts.

But how had they gotten this close? They were dressed to appear as common dock workers, which would mean that …

A tall, four-armed overseer glanced over his bulging shoulder at the confrontation, scanned the crowd, and then pushed on through a distant access door. Angara's eyes narrowed, but a sharp report dragged her attention back to the unfolding scene.

One of the Mnymians, growing tired of the shouted threats, shouldered his weapon and fired. There was a jade-green flare of plasma light, and the bolt slashed out at the Variyar. Once such power was unleashed, there was very little hope. No portable field would stand against a plasma blast. One of the guards leapt up, intercepting the shot with his own body. There was a dull cracking sound as the armor absorbed some of the energy, and then the guard was flying silently through the air, over a crouching K'hzan, to tumble bonelessly into a dark heap, streamers of steam rising gracefully up into the recyclers.

The fool. The Mnymians were immediately marked as strangers to Penumbra. Anyone even moderately conversant with the city's inherent defensive systems knew what would happen next. And why the Variyar honor guard carried those long-handled copper blades instead of missile weapons.

She felt her ears pop before the tell-tale tingle across her skin let her know the suppression field had collapsed down over the entire room. The winking indicator lights along the barrels of the assassins' weapons dulled, and the Variyar moved toward them, hefting their polearms with eager looks on their demonic faces.

The Mnymians were game enough, though. They threw their rifles aside after a few failed shots, and each drew long, flexible stringblades that began to whir through the air, filling the chamber with an unpleasant buzzing sound. The crowd surged back, not wanting to be quite that close to the sudden eruption of violence, and the red king's guards started to move more cautiously forward.

"No!" The word erupted across the deck like a thunderclap, and even the advancing guards crouched in place, one looking back for confirmation.

K'hzan Modath leapt over the line of bodyguards, his own polearm glittering, his cloak flaring out behind him, and landed before the assassins in a calm, relaxed pose. His harsh features twisted into a contemptuous sneer, and he spat something she could not hear at the creatures who had dared to attack him.

At some signal she had missed, the Mnymians made their move, leaping at the towering red-skinned giant as one.

The long axe swept around with a hellish whistle, and two of the attackers staggered back, hands to faces as their blood sprayed across the deck plates.

There was no mistaking the cruel smile that crossed K'hzan's crimson features.

"Alright, we need to go." She turned around, her back stiff, and pushed the Humans away from the spectacle. "I have seen this before. The last few will be dead before we even reach the wall."

Marcus and Justin resisted, but she applied some judicious pressure at the base of their necks and they surrendered, wincing at the discomfort. Behind them, a cry rose up from the mob. A more bloodthirsty sound than she was used to hearing outside of the fighting pits.

She looked over her shoulder to see what the Variyar were doing, but the king had disappeared through the blast doors, taking his guardians with him. The bodies of the Mnymian mercenaries were lying where he had left them, bleeding out onto the floor. It would make a nice mess for the Leemuks to clean up when they finally arrived, but then, that was just about the most one could hope to get out of them in a crisis like this, anyway. The blast doors were sliding closed, hiding the shuttle from view.

Her relief at K'hzan's exit was short lived, however, as she turned back to see the security lock on the access door had been engaged. A small light flashed on the panel in the doorframe. They were not going to be able to escape this way. She looked back at the teeming crowd; she did not relish the idea of forcing their way through that mob toward the main access doors into the Concourse.

While she was distracted, her two charges continued to head for the door, unaware of the significance of the winking lights. She sighed, rolling her eyes, and reached out for their shoulders.

And the door slid opened.

Angara blinked. The indicator light had shifted to the steady unlocked signal. Reaching the doorway, the Humans stopped and turned to her, hesitant to enter. The hall beyond was a maintenance corridor, with minimal lighting and no extraneous features. Currently, the lights were all dimmed to standby levels. She had never seen corridor lights do that with an open door.

She looked to either side, and then back out into the docking bay. The crowd was dispersing, many of them milling closer. Moving swiftly, she pushed both of the Humans into the corridor, willing to deal with the illumination issues once they were away from the port.

She had turned to close the door behind them when the lights along the corridor snapped into bright life. She spun around, staring at the Humans, but they were wandering aimlessly, gaping around them. Neither would have recognized the auxiliary controls even if they *had* been near them.

Only their section of corridor was illuminated, which was strange as well. Something was very peculiar here, and she looked at the Humans through narrowed eyes. She would rather not have to deal with eccentric systems while nursemaiding two creatures like this through the chaos.

"Well, we have got some light, and a few minutes' respite, anyway." She took a deep breath. The corridor's strange behavior did not appear life-threatening, so she put it aside for the time being. "We can take these halls up through most of the tower before we have to risk the public access ways for the last leg."

She looked them over to check their appearance and saw the ungainly lump the dark-skinned Human was trying to hide beneath his robes. Her lips tightened in further annoyance.

"Why?" The sour note of her voice was not lost on Justin Shaw.

He avoided her glare and produced the small duffle bag he had been carrying since rescuing it from his wrecked vehicle. It was innocuous enough, although the logos on its side would be unfamiliar to most galactics, and all too familiar to the kind of galactics they were trying to avoid.

"Why?" She said again, folding her arms, her hip cocked to one side in a pose she knew would translate.

The man shrugged, again with that insufferable grin. "Just some stuff from home I'd rather not do without, is all."

She made no effort to hide her annoyance. The sooner she could get them both to the control center, the sooner Bha could take them off her hands for a while. She needed to get to work convincing some poor being to take Uduta Virri's place.

"Come along. We need to get you to the control center before you convince me this is a hopeless cause." She turned to move down the hall, almost not caring if they followed.

But they did. Marcus a bit behind his friend, looking at the open ductwork, wiring, conduits, and cables all strapped to the framework of the walls. He reached out toward an ancillary panel of lights and screens, dark and dead, and nearly jumped out of his robe when the panel came to life.

Angara whirled as a connection tone sounded in the muffled hallway, and her eyes widened in horror as she saw the panel bathing the Human's surprised features in a blue glow.

"This is the control center, who is this? How did you make this connection?" She did not recognize the voice, but it had to be one of Bha's workers.

Marcus's head whipped to look at Justin, then to Angara, then back to the panel. His mouth worked as if he was going to try to respond, and she rushed forward to slap one dark hand over his face.

"Who is this?" The voice sounded annoyed. There was the sound of shuffling and muted speech, and then a new voice.

"If you do not identify yourself, we will dispatch a security team to your location."

It was Iphini Bha. Angara could tell from her tone that the woman was on edge. She was up there somewhere, with no idea what she was waiting for, and was in no mood for unauthorized communications from supposedly dormant service panels.

"Very well," her voice was sharper. Someone who did not know her might have been nervous. Angara just felt sorry for the Iwa'Bantu woman. "I will be dispatching a team to your location immediately."

The panel went dark, and Marcus jumped back. He looked up at Angara, worry on his face. "Are we in trouble?"

She controlled her reaction, annoyed with herself for even being amused. "No more than we already were." She gestured to the panel. "Bha will not be able to get a team down here for a while. She probably will not send one down at all. We do not have that many, and they have got more important things to do than track down an errant connection, especially with that mess behind us." She paused, cocking her head, and then smiled. "But if a giant pale-green monster with wide-set eyes and a mouth like a toothed open sore shows up, run in the other direction."

She gestured for them to continue. They both paused, looking at each other with concern, and then allowed themselves to be ushered forward again. Occasionally, a panel would come to life as they approached, but no more calls came through, and she made sure the Humans stayed clear. The panels dimmed as they passed, and they continued on their way.

The lights overhead continued to act strangely, and something started to niggle at the back of Angara's mind. When they approached the end of a lighted section, the next section down would brighten. As they entered the new segment, the lights in the previous one would dim. This happened several times, Angara growing more and more suspicious, until finally she stopped. There were no systems that behaved this way in the city. The Relic Core produced more than enough energy, and every corridor, when active, was lit all the way down its length. This patch of light, following them like an eager pet, was unsettling.

"Marcus Wells, stay here." She put a hand on his chest to stop Marcus from moving. "Please allow Justin Shaw and myself to continue a few paces?"

A look of panic that would have been comical if she had not already been so frustrated, crossed the pale Human's face. "What? Why?"

She shook her head. "I would just like to test a theory. I assure you, nothing untoward will happen to you."

He shrugged, and before he could voice further objections, she reached out and grabbed his companion, dragging Justin into the next, darkened segment.

That darkness did not recede as they approached, and soon they were walking into the gloom of meager utility lighting. When they were well into the powered-down section she stopped Justin and turned back. Marcus was standing in a pool of light that had not advanced without him.

Angara's eyes narrowed again, deeper suspicions beginning to stir.

She called for Marcus and the man jogged up to them. As he reached their murky position, the lights flared to life, fading away in the segment he had just left. She shook her head and moved off, the light following them as they went.

At the end of the service corridor they came to a ladder rising into a round tube set into the ceiling. She turned to the Humans.

"There are many places in the city where the gravity fields of various towers and other components meet." She pointed up at the ladder. "This is one such place. This particular interface is designed for bipeds and similarly-constructed sentients." She began to climb, and then turned to look down at them. "Do not get disoriented as you reach the center of the tube. The gravity will shift slowly as you continue, until you emerge in the new field, oriented correctly."

She could hear them speaking together as she climbed.

"That doesn't make a lot of sense." Marcus muttered. "Not a very fast way to travel."

"There's probably faster ways, for cargo, emergencies, things like that." She could hear the shrug in Justin's voice. "I get the feeling they've been doing this for a while. I'd say we leave them to it."

Marcus grunted in response, and then started up the ladder.

The narrow tube enclosed her, and she climbed up, moving with the assurance of long practice. As the definitions of up and down shifted gently around her, up became sideways, and she adjusted without thought, following the narrow confines of the passage. Soon she rose up into a wide corridor illuminated in a red-tinged light. The hall was completely unadorned; typical Variyar ship architecture. The Humans emerged behind her and the three of them stood for a moment, catching their breath.

"Not the most inviting place I've ever been in." Marcus looked around, his hands clasped together within the long sleeves of his robes. The hood was falling down from over his face and she reached out to snap it back into place with an exasperated tug. He looked at her, brows lowered, but left the hood where it was.

"Looks a bit like a bunker." Justin reached out and brushed one metal wall with his hand. His hood, too, was slipping off his bald head. But she knew that would be less of an issue, so left it as it was.

"Not surprising. It was a Variyar warship a long, long time ago." She jerked her chin down the hall, and they turned to see that it contained angular jogs as it stretched away from them, each corner heavy with reinforcement. Then she gestured with a thumb at the overhead lights. "You can tell from the corridors, and the lighting. It's meant to replicate the illumination from Variya's sun."

She led them off, whispering for them to keep their heads down. Occasionally, they passed people moving along, heads down, attending to their own business. None of them paid undue attention to the two robed figures pacing at her side.

The corridor eventually swelled into a wide chamber hosting one of the few transit tubes in the tower. She jerked her head at the simple-seeming alcove as they passed. "That is a transit tube. It will take you all the way down to the Concourse if you wish, and alter your gravitic orientation automatically during your journey. That is how most people travel in Penumbra, if they are not resorting to shuttles or other personal craft."

Marcus and Justin stared at the tube as they walked past, and so were not watching the corridor ahead of them when a large being emerged from around one of the armored corners and came to an abrupt halt before Angara.

She felt a chill shiver down her spine as she saw who it was.

There was no mistaking the sleek grey form of an Aijian, hovering in the shimmering hydro-field that kept the creature moist. Its personal gravitics kept its massive marine body afloat, allowing it to move as if it were swimming through the waters of its homeworld. The expressive black eyes took her in and an almost-smile stretched across its beak-like snout. And then her two companions attracted its attention with startled gasps, and the shock of cold shot from her spine to her heart.

The black eyes narrowed. "Angara Ksaka." Her implants translated his voice into a pleasant baritone, although the sounds of his native language were squeaking and buzzing just beneath. "This is a pleasant surprise."

Angara gave a shallow bow. "Warder Alab Oo'juto, I could say the same." She glanced back at the two Humans, and saw with relief that their hoods were safely in place. "I actually have a great deal to discuss with you, if you would allow me to call upon you later today?"

The immense being floating before them seemed to nod its neckless, bullet head. Its eyes however, continued to return to the shrouded forms behind her. "That will be pleasant, I have no doubt." He looked back at her. "Tell me, is there any word of Administrator Virri? I come from the control center, and I must say that Iphini Bha was less than forthcoming. I hope that Uduta has not gotten himself into a difficulty?"

She pushed the guilt down and forced a smile onto her face. She hoped it was not as sickly as it felt. "You know *him*, Warder."

She reached back and dragged the two Humans forward, pushing them past the Aijian. "If you'll excuse us, Warder Oo'juto, the deputy needed to speak to these two as soon as possible."

Again, the warder dipped its head in a bow. "Of course. Duty first, as in all things." There was the typical Aijian nip of sarcasm in the translated tone, but she ignored it with a smile.

"I shall look forward to seeing you again soon." She bowed, and began to move around the creature's bulk.

"And I you." He replied as she walked past. "And may time embrace your two companions within its waters."

She almost tripped. She had not thought to school the Humans on even the most basic of galactic greetings. Her throat tightened and her stomach clenched, but Marcus stepped forward and bowed deeply, making some sort of sweeping, circular gesture with a hand still concealed within the sleeve of his robe.

Oo'jutu reared back at this, then his head shifted slightly to the side, and then his smile returned. The sharp faces of the Aijians seemed built for smiling, which made it very hard to tell when they were genuinely happy, or concealing some other emotion behind the expression.

With a flick of his flat tail, the warder shot down the corridor, around the corner, and was gone.

"Holy shit!" Marcus reached out to a near wall for support, his eyes wide with disbelief. "That was a God damned dolphin!"

Justin stood stiff and unmoving, his eyes fixed on the corner behind them. He shook his head in stunned disbelief. "It sure looked like it."

He turned his dark eyes to Angara. "Well? Was that a dolphin? And if so … *What the hell?*"

She could feel her shoulders slumping. There was so much they did not know, it was hard to decide what to tell them and when. And she was nearly shaking, knowing they were so close to their final destination, when she could be relieved of at least a small measure of this burden. She looked up and down the corridor. Things seemed to be quiet for the moment.

She looked at them both, and shrugged. "What you know of as dolphins are, in fact, Aijians, like Warder Alab Oo'juto." She nodded back down the narrow corridor. "They've got a—"

Marcus put a hand up with a sour look on his face. "Don't tell me. They've got a low opinion of Humans."

She nodded, her head tilted to one side. "With more right than most, I might say."

She saw him think about it for a moment, then have the decency to blush. "Why do they stay on Earth?"

She had avoided several topics with the Humans as they traveled, and this would open several of those up she would rather not have alone, in the middle of a corridor where any sentient could, any moment, stumble upon them.

She shook her head. "We need to get moving. Iphini will be thinking that something has gone wrong."

It was clear they both had more questions. Oo'juto's appearance could not have been more poorly timed. And meanwhile, as she shepherded these creatures toward Bha, what was the Aijian thinking? Had he seen something that might alert him to the true identities of her robed charges?     No one in Penumbra would be more likely to see through her little ruse, or be more offended by it.

"We need to get out of the corridors." She started to walk, turning to call over her shoulder. "We need to get out of the corridors *now*, in case he decides to come back."

She maintained a pace that was hardly conducive to leisurely conversation, and the two Humans hurried after her, clearly deciding they would rather not be abandoned for the sake of petulant questioning.

The blast doors that could be dropped to seal off the control center were open, and she quickly gestured for the two Humans to precede her in. They stopped as they entered the quietly bustling room, took in the banks of communications stations, the viewing fields showing reports, images of various areas of the city, and scrolling information panels that took up most of the walls. Several of the stations were currently dedicated to tracking what was occurring down in the docking bay. She nodded to Agha-pa as he rose from the command throne, looking at her with a look she recognized as suspicion in his small, pink eyes.

Iphini Bha was waiting just inside the doorway, the pallor of her skin beneath the stark black lines adding to the impression of terrified near-panic that moved just behind her eyes. Angara hoped she was only interpreting the Iwa'Bantu's expression that way because she knew what was really happening. In fact, even *Bha* didn't know what was *really* happening. So she probably was not panicking. She was probably nervous; or maybe frustrated at being kept in the dark. Or maybe, Angara realized, she was mourning Uduta Virri.

Bha gestured for them to follow her, the ever-present stylus glittering dully in one hand, and led the three of them through the room, past lines of curious faces of various colors and shapes, and into the back office of the administrator.

As the door closed behind Justin, the last to enter, the pale-faced female spun on them, unmistakable anger flaring in her eyes. She took in a gusting breath, about to say something undoubtedly acerbic, when she came up short, staring at Marcus as he reached up for his hood.

Angara lunged for him, words of warning crashing together in an incoherent jumble.

The hood came down, Marcus looked around the room with curious eyes.

And Iphini Bha screamed in pure terror.

# Chapter 9

The strange woman Angara had called Iphini Bha fell over backward, tripping on a small stool and catching herself on a large desk-like piece of furniture in the corner. Some metal pen-like object flew from her hands. She was screaming the whole way, her blanched skin writhing with lines that looked like fine cracks. Her eyes, a strange pale blue, were wide with terror.

"No!" Angara reached out with one hand, trying to catch the frail-seeming woman. But she slapped the offered hand aside even as she fell, her feet scrambling for purchase. Soon she was braced behind the desk, crouched down staring at Marcus with those odd, alien eyes.

Marcus staggered back, not knowing quite what to make of this reaction. The high-pitched shrieks of the pale woman disoriented him even more than he had been. He was in a chamber that looked very much like a small conference room, with a table down the middle surrounded by strange constructions that must have been chairs. The large desk dominated one end, and there seemed to be some kind of tub or trough behind it.

At first he thought the walls had been decorated with mundane, if abstract, paintings. They had appeared to be gentle studies in pastel clouds when he first saw them, before the wailing began. He had lost interest in the artwork after the woman had her fit, but now, trying to put a little distance between them, he saw that the paintings were moving. They were shifting within the frames, the colors churning together, changing as he watched. And it wasn't uniform, either. Those closer to the distraught woman were now dominated with jagged red slashes and splashes of black, while those at his end of the room remained somewhat peaceful; although the images were changing there as well.

He thought he could see a face emerging from the swirl of colors; a face he thought he should know. And then he realized that he *did* recognize it. It was a face that had been haunting him since before they had left for their little getaway weekend to the backwoods of Connecticut.

Clarissa.

It was still abstract, with the colors blending with light and shadow, but she was in there. It was a less-than-calming effect, all things considered.

He was staring in wonder at the nearest painting, the anxiety of an alien woman less pressing than it had been a moment before. He was vaguely aware, however, of Justin moving toward the woman, open hands outstretched. He turned to watch. If she shrieked at *him*, she should have a similarly heart-warming reaction to Justin as well. It would do his soul good to see someone else shrieked at, after the way Angara had been treating him.

But as the hood slid away from Justin's bald, dark head, the woman, her eyes fixed on Marcus, barely registered him. She flicked a glance in his direction and then went back to staring at Marcus as if afraid he was going to leap across the room and try to eat her.

"Iphini, calm down!" Angara was standing on the opposite side of the big desk, her hands flat on the surface. "Everything is fine! I promise."

The woman looked to Angara, then back to Marcus, her eyes still wild.

"Fine? *Fine*?!?" The huge eyes narrowed, and she pointed one long finger at him. "Did he kill him? *Did he kill Virri?*"

"What?" Angara looked genuinely confused for a moment, and then put up her hands again. "No! Iphini, honestly, they didn't kill Virri! They had nothing to do with it!"

The pale-skinned woman deflated somewhat at that. Her eyes flicked from Marcus to the dark-skinned woman with sad, wide eyes. "How did it happen, Angara? How did Virri die?"

The bodyguard's eyes darted away. There was embarrassment there, but sadness as well. Marcus watched, fascinated. It was easy to forget that he was here because of the death of another person. Any reminder, especially involving the administrator's bodyguard, was compelling.

"I can't talk about it now, Iphini. There was an accident." She looked back at the smaller woman. "I promise, I'll tell you everything. Right now, we need to address the difficulties at hand. But you have my word: they had nothing to do with it."

"They?" That seemed to stop the woman. She looked confused, and then turned to Justin, her eyes narrowed further, and her face twisted once more into horror. "Oh no. *Another one*? He's *another one*?!? You brought two *Humans* to Penumbra!?!"

That brought a little satisfaction. Although, even in the moment, Marcus had the presence of mind to wonder why the woman hadn't realized there were two Humans in the room the moment Justin's hood fell, revealing his eyes.

"Iphini, you've got to calm down, or we're all dead." Angara's voice was quiet, but there was an edge of steel in it that Marcus heard loud and clear through the bugs in his head.

The porcelain-skinned woman's face screwed up at that, her eyes narrowed, and she stood a little taller. "What is that supposed to mean?" She looked back at Marcus and Justin, then her eyes widened. "No."

The word carried such clear disbelief, Marcus desperately wanted to know what she thought was happening, and why it was so terrible.

Angara nodded. "Yes, but you have to listen to me."

The woman shook her head, and again, Marcus had to wonder about the universality of gestures in the wider galaxy. Iphini Bha was definitely giving an emphatic 'no' with her entire body.

But Angara was equally as forceful. "Iphini, we have no choice. And you have to listen." She fetched the pen from the floor and gave it to the strange little woman who took it absentmindedly.

Bha looked from Marcus to Justin again, her lip twisted as if she had tasted something rotten. "A Human? You're going to trust a *Human*?"

"That's enough!" Marcus stepped toward them, trying not to feel terrible when the slighter woman shied away. "What the hell's so bad about being Human?"

That seemed to strike Bha as hilarious despite her shocked and terrified state, and she gave a bark of high pitched noise that he could, with a squint, call a laugh.

When she turned back to Angara, the little woman's outrage was clear. "You *cannot* mean to place a Human as administrator of Penumbra. The city won't stand for it!"

Angara shook her head. "Not permanently, I promise. But you have to understand, Uduta Virri *gave* them the Skorahn! It is bonded to this Human more deeply than I have ever heard or seen it bonded to anyone before!"

Again with the shaking of the pale, bald head. "Virri would have never given that medallion away. He knew what it was worth."

"It was worth a lifetime of luxury and sloth, and to a Rayabell like Virri, that was a great treasure indeed." Angara agreed. "But he gave it away all the time, and you know it. It was one of his standard ploys, knowing that primitives would sense its worth without understanding why. He used it as collateral for half a hundred ruses, and every time he did, he would get it back with equal facility." She jerked her head at Marcus. "Until now."

Marcus was getting sick of seeing the blue expanse of this woman's eyes. "That one?" Bha dropped to her knees behind the desk, letting her head fall into her long-fingered hands. "Why did it have to be *that* one?"

"Okay, that's it!" Marcus slapped the table with the flat of his hand and both women stopped, turning to look at him. "What's so bad about *me*, eh? How come he keeps getting a pass?" He jerked his thumb at his dark-skinned friend. Justin, for his part, looked just as confused and curious.

But if he thought he was going to get his questions answered just then, he was mistaken. "There would be riots throughout the towers, Ksaka, and you know it." Bha flung a gesture at Marcus. "No one will stand for it." Her expressive eyes rolled. "And what about Taurani? It wouldn't matter what ancient treaties and agreements keep them off our backs for now. If the Council knew there were Humans here, never mind one in charge of the city, they would send everything they have to destroy us!"

Angara sunk into one of the chairs, her shoulders sagging, with a nod. "I'm not saying it's going to be easy, Iphini." Her violet eyes were pleading, shadowed by the fall of her white hair. "I'm saying we don't have a choice."

The bodyguard turned to Marcus and gestured him forward. "You need to see the Skorahn. Maybe then you'll understand why it has to be this way."

Marcus moved forward, pulling the medallion out from the neck of his robe. He had taken to wearing it as a necklace on the *Yud'ahm Na'uka*. It seemed proper.

Iphini Bha watched him approach as if she was seeing a monster stalk toward her through a jungle. She peered at the medallion as he took it off and held it out for her to see. A ghostly image was floating within the central stone. It had been forming since before Angara had performed her little test back on the ship. Now it seemed to float even closer to the surface. It looked like a letter or a symbol of some kind, but of a design that he didn't recognize.

She didn't appear to be able to read it either, but its very presence seemed to frighten to her, and she backed away. The little woman, supposedly the deputy to the man … thing … alien that had commanded the entire city, looked up at him in awe.

"It cannot be." Her voice was low and soft. Her grip on the pen tightened.

Angara nodded. "It is. It is bonded more closely to him than it has been to anyone from the records I have found in my time here."

Iphini Bha's face went from frightened to despondent. "Then there really is no hope for us." Her words were bleak. "We will all either die as the city shuts down around us, or we will die when the Council decides we are more trouble than we are worth."

Angara shook her head and reached across the desk to take the woman's hands. "No, Iphini. Marcus Wells will only be administrator for a very brief time. We can find another more suitable being to replace him." She looked back to him and her face was pleading. "He wants to leave. Do you not want to return to your home, Marcus Wells?"

He nodded without thinking, ignoring Justin's face. "I do."

That set Bha into another fit of laughter. "He wants to *return* to Earth? To *Earth*?"

"Iphini, please, you have to relax and believe me." Angara leaned down again. "Marcus Wells will be leaving here. He will be surrendering the Skorahn. We need only find a suitable replacement."

The laughter trailed off, much to Marcus's relief. And Bha stood, still wary, still keeping an eye on him as if he might attack at any second. And still, he noticed with a bitter twist to his mouth, not tracking Justin at all. But now her eyes were thoughtful, and her lips pursed in an unmistakable expression of reflection.

"It could be something genetic. A match might require some amount of compatibility." She flexed up on her toes, and then lowered herself down again. "An Aijian?"

Angara nodded. "That was what I was thinking. Alab Oo'juto is here. He would make an excellent candidate."

Bha snorted. "He will not thank you. You know what Virri and his predecessors did to the reputation of this office." She shot another look at Marcus, but this time it seemed to be shaded more with distaste and less with fear. "And he will not thank you, even if he can see the value, for any gift that comes from the hand of a Human."

"Wait." Justin raised a hand before Marcus could spit a comment back. "What kind of possible link could extraterrestrial wannabe dolphins have with Humans?"

Angara sighed. "The Aijians are not *wannabe dolphins*. All creatures you call dolphins are Aijians. Any who serve on Earth have been … genetically modified to carry the codes and markers for what your scientists believe is 'Earth' DNA, so as not to arouse suspicion."

"But … *why*?" Justin was shaking his head, and Marcus did the same. "Why would an alien race want to be genetically altered to go to Earth? What is there to gain?"

Angara and Iphini shared a look, and then both turned to the Humans. "You would not understand that level of racial focus." Iphini's words were probably more hurtful in their matter-of-fact delivery than if she had been trying to insult them.

"The racial commitment to purpose shared by nearly all Aijians is ancient. They have been on Earth for almost as long as you have." Angara seemed to be speaking more on the subject than she ever had, and that made Marcus suspicious.

Iphini turned back to Angara. "What if Oo'juto refuses to serve? It is a distinct possibility."

Angara sighed. "I know. I am still trying to think of alternatives. I had thought, maybe K'hzan Modath?"

That brought a bark of laughter from Bha, and the bodyguard bowed her head with a nod. "Although it might do the Council some good to have their noses tweaked in such a fashion, I fear they would make quicker work of us with K'hzan at the helm than if we had these Humans announce to the galaxy their intention to burn the entire thing down!"

Angara looked disturbed by that, and Iphini Bha stopped laughing, an embarrassed look crossing her porcelain features. "I'm sorry." She shot the two Humans another fearful look, as if she might have given them an idea.

Marcus shook his head and fell into one of the chairs. It molded itself to his body, almost bringing him jumping right out again. It wasn't as quick or as complete as the furniture on the *Yud'ahm Na'uka*, but it was comfortable almost instantly. He had no interest in comfort at the moment, however.

"Listen, if you guys know the *real* story, and you're *still* concerned about us being Human, how do you think you're going to sell this to the rest of the city?" He didn't like the idea of being thrust out into a galaxy of hostile aliens who hated him for no reason at all.

"I was thinking we would keep you hidden, actually." Angara had the manners to look uncomfortable. "If we were to keep you isolated, keep knowledge of your actual origin a secret, we should be able to hold things together until a suitable replacement can be arranged."

"If Oo'juto declines, we will most likely have to send a request to Omiaye and hope another Aijian can be found who will be more amenable."

"That's not entirely true. There are countless Children here, many of them will share enough of a link, I believe." Angara looked distinctly distressed at having made the suggestion.

The suggestion upset Iphini as well. "No Child has been an administrator in the history of Penumbra."

Angara tilted her head to one side. "Maybe there's a reason for that." She looked at Marcus and he felt his skin grow warm under her gaze. "There's never been an administrator as deeply bonded to the medallion as him, as far as I can tell."

"Who the hell are the Children?" Marcus snapped, sensing the capitalization. "And what is a Child?"

"It would be easier if it was this one." Iphini Bha gestured at Justin, who looked as uncomfortable as Marcus now. "Change his eye color, keep his head shaved, shave the face? There would be very little problem with that."

Angara nodded. "I know. I had thought that. He did not bond with the medallion, however. The pale one did. And so he is the being with which we must now deal."

"Wait," Justin raised a hand. "What's this all about now? Change my eye color? Keep my head shaved?" He slid one hand across his smooth dark scalp as he settled into a seat. "That's the plan, by the way. But why would it matter?"

Another frustrating gaze passed between the two women, and Iphini Bha answered. "With your midnight skin tone you look very much like a Mnymian, a race familiar throughout the civilized galaxy."

"We saw those in the docking bay from afar, if you will recall. Although they have bright red hair and completely white, featureless eyes." Angara included. "Both easily addressed. Alas, it does not matter. The Skorahn bonded to Marcus Wells."

"Dude, someday you are going to owe me so bad!" Justin snarled.

"Yeah, that's fine." Marcus launched himself out of the seat and began to pace. Not caring at all when Iphini Bha jerked back behind the desk, raising a marbled hand to her mouth. "Hide me in a closet for all I care. The sooner you get me out of here the better. I've only dealt with you two, and it's already been too much."

The pent-up frustration had pushed him to the breaking point. His pacing became more and more erratic. He could not honestly have said if he was going closer and closer to the desk to serve his sudden need for motion, or because it was making Iphini Bha more and more uncomfortable. "I don't care why you hate Humans, or what you think I did, or why he," he jerked a thumb at his grinning friend, "will make such a great … Nya-mumbo-jumbo, and so a better Human being."

"Not, actually, a—" Bha began, but he cut her off.

"Just find a replacement as soon as you can so I can go home. I'm only going to be able to stay under lock and key for so long, before I go insane." The threat struck home with Iphini Bha for sure. And the effect was entirely ruined as he moved to settle his back at last against the wall.

It was not the wall he was standing before, but the secure door. A door, furthermore, that should only open at the express desire of a duly-delegated executive of the city.

As he moved toward it, the door opened smoothly, dropping him on his ass just outside, into the bustle of the outer office.

All of the movement and commotion died away as the menagerie serving the many stations stopped their work to turn and stare. The array of creatures gaping at him would have been impressive under different circumstances.

He almost expected it when the first scream echoed off the low ceiling of the bunker-like room. When others joined the chorus, he couldn't stop himself from nodding with a sigh.

Several beings rushed past him and out through the massive blast doors, their cries fading into the distance down the bending corridor outside.

Iphini Bha and Angara rushed out after him, lifted him up by his arms, and dragged him back into the office.

"Everything is alright, everyone!" Bha's voice was far more commanding than he would have expected. "This is not what it appears to be. Everything will be set to rights soon enough." They had Marcus settled back in a chair, where he could start to realize that his back hurt from his unanticipated fall. "Please, go back to your duties, and I will let you all know exactly what is happening as soon as the situation allows. But I promise you, all is well."

"Where's Administrator Virri?!" One of the creatures shouted the question. Marcus saw that it was the big hulking green brute sitting in the fancy chair on the low stage.

"Please," Bha was begging now. That wasn't a good sign. "Go back to your duties, and I will explain everything in due time."

Before anymore comments could be launched, Bha jumped back into the office and waved the door closed behind her.

"Well, we could have done without that." Marcus couldn't help the small smile on his face. These two women had been speaking about him as if he wasn't even in the room since he had arrived. It was nice to see they didn't know everything.

Of course, his own safety might very well be in jeopardy now …

Angara and the smaller woman stood staring at the closed door, their breathing heavy, their eyes wide.

"Maybe they'll stay quiet." Angara didn't sound like she thought that was likely.

"No. Several ran off down the corridor in a panic. There will be no hiding them now." Bha shot Justin and Marcus a poisonous look.

"Okay," Justin pushed himself up from his chair, hands raised in surrender. "This is insane. Why in the name of all that's holy on God's green earth are you people so against Humans? We haven't even made it off our own planet! I mean, sure, we can generally screw things up pretty good when we've got a mind to, but we haven't even had a *chance* to mess around with your corner of the galaxy yet. What gives?"

Marcus nodded. "You've been treating us like animals since you forced us onto your ship." He waved away the look Justin shot him. "And now, between this air-raid siren and the freak show out in the office there?" He gestured first to Bha and then to the closed door. "I'm not going another step until you tell me what the hell's going on."

Bha and Angara exchanged a worried look. By the writhing of their expressions and the twitching of their eyes, it was clear they were trying to decide how much to tell the two Humans, and who would have to do the talking. The silent battle ended with Bha collapsing onto the little stool by the door and the tall bodyguard sighing in frustration.

Angara rounded on Marcus and Justin with iron in her eyes. Her fists rested upon her narrow hips, and her lips curled into a half-snarl that set them both back into their chairs.

"The Humans on Earth are not the only Humans in the galaxy." She held up a hand to silence their rush of questions at that. "There are small, vicious, nomadic splinter fleets that wander the galaxy, sewing violence and death wherever they go." Her eyes burned as she continued. "The Humans left roaming at large are not beings you would want to associate with, trust me. They are a barbaric, malicious race of killers trying to resurrect a past they cannot possibly understand through unspeakable acts of horror."

"What did they splinter from?" Justin was as angry as his friend now.

Marcus's eyes narrowed. "What kind of past? Where'd these splinter fleets come from? How far back are you talking?"

"Not far enough." Bha spat the words, then shook her head as Angara gestured for her to take over.

With a sigh, the dark woman finished. "You will not be well-received. That's really all you need to know."

Justin and Marcus looked at each other, then back to Angara. She would not meet their eyes.

"It is a truth you must accept." She said it with authority, but Marcus had the distinct impression that this was even more an evasion than it seemed. "Suffice it to say that Humans are nearly universally reviled, and our work now will be much, much more difficult because of that last little stunt."

Marcus wanted to object to that. He hadn't consciously asked the door to open and drop him into the outer office! But he was so close now to so many of the mysteries that had plagued him since Angara Ksaka had whisked them away.

"I assume this splintering happened a long, long time ago?" He shook his head. "How long ago, that you folks *still* hold such a grudge? And Justin's right: what did they split *from*? Where are those Humans?"

Angara's eyes rose to meet his, and tightened as she looked at him. "I understand your anger; I am more likely to empathize with you than any other being in Penumbra. But the truths you seek do not exist. They are myths and legends now, woven into the very fabric of the galactic society you will have to contend with."

It was Justin's turn to shake his head. "Bullshit. This makes no sense. We're going to be damned for something someone did *thousands* of years ago that obviously has nothing to do with those of us who grew up on Earth?"

Again the women shared a hooded glance, and then looked away. Angara cleared her throat, and moved to the desk. "Well, do not forget that those feral Humans are still a threat today." She glanced at Iphini Bha and then continued. "There are many, even here in Penumbra, who live with the scars of their attentions. As for the deeper, more general animosity you will experience, I am afraid I am not qualified to speak to that. It will have to wait for another day. We need to get the two of you situated, and try to consolidate our position with the command staff before fear and rumors carry us all away."

Bha nodded, standing. "Our task will be much harder now. We will need to move quickly if we are to have any hope at all." She moved to the desk and two spheres of colored mist rose up from the surface. She stuck her hands into the light and began to twist them about.

"We will need to schedule a full public audience. It is the only way we can hope to curtail the pressure that will be building against us."

Angara looked back to the Humans. "We will get you to suitable quarters, and then make the preparations for the public audience."

Marcus felt his heart beating faster. He was great with small groups, but he had never been overly comfortable in front of a large crowd. He was terrified to think of what might be at stake for both of them this time around.

He shook his head. "I don't get it. What if they find out there's a Human in charge? What's the worst that could happen?"

The look Angara gave him was icy cold. "The resulting panic could cause a mass exodus from the city, destabilizing everything and throwing all of Penumbra into a spiral of chaos and destruction. But before that, there are many in the city whose violent natures are not nearly so suppressed as galactic society would like to believe. They could well kill you both out of hand long before the city itself perishes."

He swallowed, unable to take his eyes from hers, and nodded. "We'll do what we have to do."

Bha looked up. "You will do better than that, *Human*." She shot a sour look at Angara. "All of our fates are tied to yours, now."

The bodyguard looked like she wanted to deny this, but then her proud shoulders slipped, and she only nodded.

He hadn't thought it was possible, but that made Marcus feel even worse.

# Chapter 10

Menials bustled about the Central Council Chamber, cleaning the various chair-like pedestals designed for the manifold shapes and sizes of the delegates that would shortly be sitting there. Iphini Bha watched them from the dais, her mind numb. The vast majority of the galaxy did not employ sentients in menial positions, using the latest technologies to create a raft of mechanical servitors that were better suited, cheaper, and faster. Sadly, this was just another thing about living in Penumbra. Without the infrastructure needed to build and maintain an army of automatons, it often felt like she was living in some strange, twisted museum.

She sagged against the raised podium. Due to its unique place in the galaxy, ironically, it just so happened that Penumbra was replete with sentients willing to fulfill these menial tasks. In her mind, it was one of the many shortcomings to being the one location where these misfits and eccentrics could run from the central control of the Galactic Council.

It was all well and good for scholars, philosophers, and exiled bureaucrats to discuss the importance of individual initiative and the power of self-determination. It was quite another for the beings that followed their rhetoric out to the very edges of civilized space with no concrete plan for how they were going to support themselves. And so many of them ended up like these small, fur-covered Kot'i and their big, slick-skinned Tsiikis companions, shuffling around, preparing the chamber for those great thinkers, when and if they deigned to attend.

That made the uneasiness in her stomach surge again, and she backed into one of the chairs lining the rear of the dais. No one was paying any attention to her anyway. She was just the deputy, right?

Word had flashed through the city as soon as the pale Human had fallen out of the office. Rushed official announcements had been made of Administrator Virri's death and the appointment of a new administrator to be introduced at this open session. But rumors had outpaced the proclamations, and the people of Penumbra knew something was terribly wrong. Savage, ridiculous rumors that the new administrator might actually be *Human* were the wildest tales being told, but they also had the benefit, she thought with a sour twist to her mouth, of being entirely true.

One of the massive doors to the chamber slammed open and Ambassador Taurani came sweeping in. His personal servant, the Eru Iranse, and two Ntja guards followed, taking up positions on either side of the door.

Taurani's glittering eyes flashed above the pale cream of his robes, his smooth gray complexion shiny beneath the bright lights. It was almost impossible to read the hard, immobile lines of a Kerie face, but something about the glimmer in the ambassador's eyes suggested the heat of terrible anger.

Iphini stood, pulling her tunic straight as she forced herself up out of her despondent crouch. She forced herself to pocket the stylus. No need to give him any additional proof of her discomfort. She had been hoping to avoid this. Part of Angara Ksaka's plan, if it could be called a plan, had been to isolate the Humans until the moment of the announcement, hoping that the Penumbran taste for drama and intrigue would carry them all through the initial reaction to the nightmarish revelation.

She should have known Taurani was not going to wait on anyone else's timeline.

"Deputy Iphini Bha." Taurani's voice was a rolling boulder, driving timid menials out of his way. There was no doubting the towering fury of his anger.

"Deny these rumors, Bha." The words were an open challenge as the ambassador swept down to the edge of the dais and glared up at her, his hands folded in the sleeves of his robe. "Tell me Virri did not bring a Human back to the city to replace him."

That shocked her. Taurani's intelligence network in Penumbra was excellent. How could he not know that Virri was dead?

She shook her head, looking from one corner of the chamber to the other for rescue. The menials continued to prepare the room, ignoring the brewing confrontation. And aside from the crawling peasants, the hall was empty.

Looking down at the stern Kerie, Iphini cleared her throat. "There was an accident. Uduta Virri is dead, Ambassador."

The silver orbs narrowed. "Dead." His voice had dropped down to a low mutter as the grey flesh around his eyes tightened with suspicion. "*What kind of accident?*"

Iphini cast about again, but the room remained stubbornly empty; no one would be coming to save her. "He was visiting a feral planet. There was an altercation with the locals." She looked away; lying was not among her strengths, she knew. "He died during the incident."

"And what of Angara Ksaka? Does she not draw a handsome salary from your treasury to keep just such things from happening?" His lipless mouth was rigid, and yet seemed to clearly indicate a sneer.

"Ambassador, if you would like to take up questions of security with the new administrator, I can make an appointment for you at a later date." She did not know where the courage was coming from. She was quaking on the inside, but had had enough of Taurani. Standing up to him was the only way she might get him to leave.

But he stopped her with one raised hand. "I could not possibly convey to you how little I care for your new administrator, or how he, she, or it came to power. What I truly want to know, Deputy, is what truth is there behind the rumors?" The eyes flared. "Has a Human been brought to Penumbra?"

Iphini swallowed. She had no faith in Angara's plan, nor in the creatures she had brought into the city. She had a healthy, rational fear and distrust of Humans, more perhaps than most. Her homeworld, Iwa'Ban, had been nearly destroyed by a feral Human incursion when she was very young. She had grown up amidst the devastation wrought by creatures just like those that now breathed Penumbran air. She would not defend them.

And yet she knew that the Galactic Council wanted nothing more than the complete capitulation and annexation of Penumbra, or its destruction if that proved easier. The grey creature before her would be the instrument of that destruction, if he could.

The Iwa'Bantu were generally a quiet and reserved people, but at that moment all she wanted to do was scream.

"All will be revealed when—"

"No!" Taurani swept a hand down sharply. "You have no idea what your little cabal has done, Bha! The Galactic Council will not stand for a Human taking the reins of power in Penumbra! Do you understand how thin the thread is from which you all hang? The Council's tolerance is not infinite, and it has been stretched to the breaking point. No clever blanket of threadbare old treaties will save you when they hear that you have allowed a Human to rise to power here." He stepped closer, craning his neck to look up at her. "And it will not be the Council crowing for your blood, you little porcelain fool. Not a sentient being in the galaxy will countenance a Human ruling Penumbra. *They will be begging* the Council to destroy you!"

She wanted to cringe back behind the podium, but forced herself to stillness. She could not argue with a single word, and she hated him for that.

"You should know, better than any other in this city, the kind of madness being courted here, Bha." Now his voice was almost reasonable, fanning her anger with condescension. "No being wants a return to the chaos you are courting." He stepped back, his hands returning to the deep sleeves. "It won't be tolerated, and I think you know that."

She tried to conjure up some response, but the words stuck in her throat. She saw the shattered remains of the cities of Iwa'Ban in her mind: the devastated landscapes. She blinked at him, silent.

"I don't believe I've had the pleasure?" The tone of voice was strong and even, but something about it tightened the flesh of her back. Her narrowing eyes twitched to the open door.

Marcus Wells stood there, wearing a version of the standard administrator's uniform tailored to his Human frame. His facial hair had been neatly trimmed, the hair on his head smoothed back, and his dark eyes glittered as he looked around the chamber.

A confusing rush of feelings filled Iphini's chest. Presented with such a target, there was almost no way Taurani was going to continue his assault on *her*. On the other hand, she would never feel comfortable in the same room as a Human, no matter how large the room or the circumstances of his appearance.

She saw that the workers in the hall had all ceased their work, standing still, seeming to stare anywhere but at the Human in their midst. Of course, none of them had ever seen a Human before. She saw fear in many of their faces, but curiosity and fascination as well. She was not alone as she struggled with the emotions crashing through her mind.

There was no denying, however, the effect the pale Human's appearance had on Ambassador Taurani.

The ambassador whirled, his robes swirling, to confront the newcomer. The immobile face jerked back in surprise as he regarded the being standing before him, the familiar black and white uniform registering immediately. A diplomat of Taurani's experience would have no problem interpreting the Human's facial expression. Marcus Wells looked supremely unimpressed.

The Human strode down the wide steps into the bowl of the chamber, his empty hand outstretched in a common welcoming gesture from Earth. Taurani watched the approach, waving his huge Ntja guards back, but made no move to meet the Human. When he was standing directly in front of the Ambassador, the

Kerie regarded the hand with a slight curl of his lipless mouth and an expressive tilt of his smooth head.

The Human allowed his hand to hang there for only a moment before he smoothly withdrew it with a little smile of his own. He swept past the Ambassador, looking up at Iphini with a nod she barely managed to return. Then he spun on one heel and rested up against the edge of the dais with every sign of comfortable ownership.

"It was hard as hell getting any of the shuttles to bring me without an escort, let me tell you." He smiled in a way that was clearly intended to disarm, but had quite the opposite effect on Iphini and the Ambassador. "You must be Khuboda Taurani." His tone was dismissive, and she almost smiled as she watched its impact on the representative of the Galactic Council. The Human could be almost amusing when he was aiming that sharp wit at someone else. "Come for the big speech? You're a little early."

Taurani regarded the shorter man with empty, glittering eyes that could mean nothing to a Human fresh from Earth. Iphini, however, could see the dangerous hatred rising there.

"And you must be the Human that features so prominently in the gossip running rampant throughout the city." Taurani took a step back and folded his hands into his sleeves once again. His eyes flashed as they surveyed the Human. "Not quite so terrifying as one might have imagined."

Marcus Wells was facing away from her now, but she could hear the smile in his voice. "Oh, I try to keep that side hidden for first impressions. Wouldn't want to scare away the locals quite yet, would we, Khuboda?"

It was a terrible breach of etiquette, but Iphini again felt her reserve toward the Human thawing just a little.

The patch of flesh at the center of Taurani's face twitched. She imagined that if he had had a more Humanoid facial structure, he might have sniffed.

"I look forward to watching you work." The ambassador turned away, then stopped and looked over his shoulder. "Your designation is Marcus Wells, I believe?"

"That's my name." Again, she could hear the smile. It must have grated on the diplomat's nerves, judging from how he stiffened.

Taurani grudged him a nod. "Yes, I eagerly look forward to seeing how you fare, Human." He raised one elegant hand. "Be careful, however. Apparently, your new position carries greater risks than any of us had anticipated."

He stared pointedly toward Iphini in a gesture she could not understand, and then turned away, stalking up the stairs and out the door, the lanky Eru and the towering Ntja swept up in his wake.

As the door boomed closed, the Human turned to smile up at her. There was a tightness in the corners of his eyes, however, that seemed to belay the confidence of the expression.

"Is there somewhere nearby we could wait until the meeting?"

She had the thought that he might be more distressed by his run-in with Taurani than he had appeared.

She gave him a quick nod and descended from the dais by a short set of steps on the side. She gave a quick series of instructions to the small Kot'i female in charge of the menials and gestured for Marcus Wells to follow her through a small door in the rear of the chamber.

He followed very closely behind her. She was not surprised to find that, despite the minor warming she had experienced, his proximity set the flesh between her shoulder blades crawling once more.

*****

Marcus's heart was beating thunderously in his chest. The tall alien with the glittering metal eyes had clearly not been a fan. He had always hated bullies, and he had recognized the type as soon as he'd seen the way the ambassador had been speaking to Iphini Bha; the fragile little thing had obviously been terrified. Although, with her wide, liquid eyes it was often hard to tell. She almost always looked either frightened or surprised.

He had not spoken with any other aliens since the unfortunate incident at the door of the administrator's office three days ago. It had actually been more than three days ago, according to his watch. But there had been three quiet, dark sleep cycles on the station, and he had gathered that the day measured by the inhabitants of Penumbra was longer than the standard twenty-four hours he was used to by almost two full hours.

They had brought him to a lavish set of rooms that would have been suitable for a king. Justin had stayed with him for a while, but he had his own quarters, apparently almost as opulent, and had gone to them not long after. He hadn't seen his friend since; one reason he felt so isolated.

He had spent much of that first day discovering the ins and outs of his living space. The furniture was of a more permanent nature, rather than the extruded seats, beds, and whatnot aboard Angara's ship. It had taken him over an hour, in what he finally identified as the bathroom, to coax actual water into the cleaning stall. Apparently, the galactics, coming in such a wild variety of shapes and sizes and values of cleanliness, were accustomed to using something called, as far as the little creatures in his head could tell him, an ablution field. The tingling field passed over his body and eradicated dirt, sweat, and microbes. It did the job, he had to admit, but nothing could compare to the pure animal pleasure of a shower with water.

His food and drink was made to order, but communicating his tastes to those in charge of their preparation was not easy. He had taken to eating a great deal of breads and well-done meats. His greatest frustration on that front, however, had been the complete inability of the Red Tower kitchens to recreate anything remotely resembling his one vice and mainstay: Mountain Dew.

Once he had exhausted the excitement of discovering the various mundane aspects of his rooms, he had settled down in the cool, dark workspace they had provided him and began to learn how to access information from the city's records. He had begun by looking through anything he could find with Uduta Virri's name attached. The tentacled creep hadn't done much, as far as he had been able to find. Marcus had some ideas, but he knew he needed to learn a lot more about how the city ran before he tried to implement anything. If Angara would even let him.

A great deal of his time had been spent trying to learn as much about his new home as he could. He studied the mosaic of alliances and agreements that made up the social contracts of Penumbra, the various corporate relationships, the manufacturing and service industries, and even a few research groups, where he could make any sense at all out of their work. He couldn't even begin to make sense of most of the research. What the hell was 'time dilation'? What would a 'singularity dampener' do? There was so much to learn, and the relationships and alliances were so labyrinthine, that he could barely wrap his mind around the basics.

He had eventually turned his attention to the puzzle of Humanity and their place in this wider galaxy. He had found plenty of information on the feral splinter fleets Angara and Iphini Bha had mentioned. But other than a persistent, vague current of hatred and fear running throughout every type of record he could access, from historical accounts to current reports, there were no actual mentions of the Humans of Earth, or indeed any Humans beyond the feral nomads.

It had almost driven him mad, and had been the final impetus needed to drive him from his quarters and to wandering the zig-zagging halls of the Red Tower. He had braved the averted glances and muttered commentary until Angara had found him and ushered him back to his rooms.

Angara had visited him every day after that, instructing him in his duties and telling him about life in Penumbra. Every attempt to brace her on the subject of Humans had been met with stubborn silence, but otherwise she had been quite accommodating. She had coached him on what was to be expected at today's ceremony, and how to behave around the suspicious denizens of this wider galaxy. She had provided him with several sets of the uniform he now wore as well as other, more comfortable clothing that had been placed in the storage areas of his suite. His trouble there was that he didn't understand yet if those were casual day outfits, lounging clothes, or what he was supposed to sleep in.

But the enforced solitude had gotten to him, and he had eventually rebelled again, leaving his quarters early to make his way to the Central Council Chamber; to stretch his legs as much as to scout out the venue for his first public speech.

One of the few people Angara had warned him about was the Council's representative to the city of Penumbra, Khuboda Taurani. So he had recognized the tall, grey figure pestering Iphini Bha as soon as he came into the hall. He knew the ambassador was an enemy to what he was slowly coming to think of as 'his side', insofar as he had a side in a galaxy as hostile to him as this appeared to be. Watching the way Taurani had been treating Iphini, he had decided a little of his frustration could be vented in that direction.

It had not seemed to put much of a dent in Taurani's confidence, however.

"That guy's a prick, eh?" He tried to say it with a smile, but he knew it was more of a scowl. Iphini Bha had led him to a small room behind the main chamber, clearly intended as a preparation area.

There were several comfortable-looking chairs of various shapes and sizes, and a circular niche in one long wall with a couple of softly-glowing colored dots on the wall beside it. Everything looked much less squat and utilitarian than what he had come to expect in the Red Tower, and the light had a soft, golden quality that set it apart from the light provided in his new home.

"Ambassador Taurani is an important, powerful entity. Even here, in Penumbra, he has a great deal of force at his disposal, and can call upon a great deal more if provoked." She was not looking at him, but had relaxed enough to settle onto one of the big seats. It shifted beneath her to accommodate the particulars of her size and shape, but she remained balanced on the edge, her back straight.

He wandered to the wall niche. A soft glow grew within the recess, but it did not resolve itself into any sort of clear image. He moved to wave his hand within the light, but nothing happened.

"You need to indicate what you wish to see." Iphini's voice was still distant, but at least she was paying attention.

"I'd like to know what's happening out there." He pointed to the wall separating them from the hall. "People should be showing up soon, right? It would be nice to see what we had waiting for us."

Iphini Bha nodded and looked at the wall opposite. It disappeared. Marcus stumbled away from the opening, his mouth falling open. Before he could fall, he steadied himself against one of the room's chairs and looked more carefully at the chamber outside.

If he focused, he could just make out the details of the wall that had disappeared. Ripples in the scene beyond indicated corners, the doorframe through which they had entered this smaller chamber, and the door itself. Somehow, all of these things were still there, they had just become transparent.

He straightened, smiling at the invisible wall in admiration. If this room was, indeed, meant for people preparing to address the hall beyond, this was a great way for them to gauge their audience. He turned back to Bha.

"That's pretty impressive." He nodded to the bustling activity outside. "Someone thought of everything, I guess."

She frowned, still not looking at him. "Hardly everything." She slumped back down into the seat, not so much relaxing as giving in to an exhaustion that was plain even on her marbled, exotic face. From a pocket she pulled out her fancy pen, but did not seem to have the strength to fiddle with it, as she usually did when she was nervous.

Marcus found himself feeling guilty for making Iphini Bha's life more difficult. He moved away from her and toward the transparent wall, folding his arms over his chest. The workers had left, and a small but steady flow of creatures was replacing them. He recognized several types from the docking port, and was curious to note how many Humanoids there were in the growing crowd. None of them had his coloration, to be sure, but the differences seemed, for the most part, entirely superficial.

He saw a small delegation of small, orange-skinned men and women with short-cropped black hair. Another group came in; with pale white skin and flowing, glossy white hair that reminded him of Angara Ksaka's. If it had not been for their flashing dark eyes, he might have taken them for albinos from Earth. In the midst of this group was a tall being of far more alien appearance. Its face was like a mottled brown flesh mask stretched over a long skull with a broad plate covering the lower face. High cheekbones underscored the deep pits that housed yellow eyes glowing with reflected light.

Without turning away, Marcus nodded to this newest group. "A lot of the people here seem like … well … people …?" He trailed off, feeling foolish. He had never understood those who judged people on their color or nationality, but it was a lot harder to do when the differences were so much more noticeable.

Bha's voice was hard, and he knew she had not missed his fumble. She glanced out into the hall with a sour look. "Children."

That brought him back around, eyes narrowing. He had been puzzling over that phrase since his first day in the city. "What does that mean?"

She looked at him, her eyes dull, and then jerked her chin back at the wall. "Those you find most intriguing share a common genetic heritage. They are similar in many ways, are they not? They are often referred to as 'Children', although they would not thank you for addressing them as such."

He looked back. He saw that the white-skinned arrivals all seemed to be inordinately attractive. They clearly differed from the tall, brown-skinned monster, but they all walked with a proud, easy gait that spoke volumes for their self-esteem. He nodded. "Yeah, I see it, I guess." He turned back to her. "They almost look Human."

She barked one of her humorless laughs. "Suggest that to any of them, especially a Subbotine there, and you would quickly find that no, they are not."

He went back to staring. He felt like a voyeur, but he could not turn away. "But you call them 'Children'."

"You need to prepare for your introduction, Marcus Wells." She stood and moved to stand near him. "The room will soon be full." She stared out, her wide eyes shining. "I have not seen such a crowd in all my time in the city. Administrator Uduta Virri seldom called general meetings, and even when he did, attendance was ... sparse."

Marcus continued to watch as the menagerie filed in through the many doors in the back of the room.

Beside him he felt Iphini Bha stiffen, and looked out at the chamber, trying to see what had caused this new tension. A pair of beings had entered from one of the smaller side doors. The shorter of the two wore elaborate white robes that reminded him vaguely of the disguises Angara had forced upon him and Justin when they had first arrived. A pale green snout emerged from the hood, bordered by an ivory beard of braids or tendrils. This figure walked with the assistance of a pale, metallic staff. One step behind it came a taller Humanoid in very dark robes of a similar cut. He couldn't make out much detail within the shadows of the hood, but the face looked Human enough, with some sort of markings scattered beneath the eyes and over the nose.

"Who are they?" He jerked his chin at the newcomers.

"Thien'ha." She answered stiffly. "Let us be glad that Ambassador Taurani chose not to stay. For some reason, he seems to find their presence objectionable."

Marcus smiled. He found himself more positively inclined toward any beings that annoyed Taurani. Thoughts of the ambassador brought with them darker considerations, and the smile faded.

For the first time, trying to take his mind off what was about to happen, he looked out at the chamber itself. Between its white coloring and the tall pillars that lined the walls it reminded him of some piece of classical architecture from Earth's distant past.

"Where are we now?" He asked without turning to Bha. "What kind of ship was this?"

She tilted her head as she gazed up at the pillars melding into the distant, vaulted ceiling. "It belonged to the Mhatrong." She raised a delicate finger to point to the tall alien standing with the pale-skinned Humanoids. "Thousands of years ago there were far more of them, and they traveled on such ships to quench their thirst for knowledge. Even today most of them are philosophers and truth-seekers. This ship was the furthest they ever got from their home planet, Te'Jeonah."

He watched the frightening creature as it found a seat amidst its shorter companions. It didn't look like a philosopher. More like a nightmare.

He let his mind wander; trying to remember the last time he had performed before such a hostile crowd. He had avoided such obligations as often as he could, and on those few rare occasions when he had needed to talk to a large group, it had happened spontaneously. Here, he had plenty of time to brood.

His mind was turning down darker paths when he noticed a new group coming through the central doors. Something about the man leading the little entourage struck him as familiar. Most of the creatures were within his rapidly-expanding idea of 'normal', with two arms and two legs, a head above a torso, that sort of thing. Many of them seemed to be what Bha would call 'Children', too, among the more alien offerings. But his eyes went back to the creature leading the parade, and he nearly choked.

Justin looked nothing like himself, dressed in the flowing tunic and loose pants of a galactic. There was something decidedly odd about his face that Marcus could not make out. But as he concentrated on his friend, something about the wall warped, the view zoomed in on Justin, and it was suddenly as if he were standing right in front of his oldest friend.

The neatly-trimmed goatee had been dyed red, but that was not the strangest change.

Justin's eyes were entirely white.

Somewhere, Justin had managed to find himself contacts, or something similar, that would make him look like the black-skinned galactic Iphini Bha had assumed him to be when they had first met. And under this guise, he seemed to be doing quite well for himself.

"Justin Shaw has adjusted to Penumbra, it seems." Bha dipped her head toward the distant party, taking seats near the back. "He looks like a true Mnymian now, and clearly his new companions feel likewise."

Marcus wandered if the sour chill he felt might be jealousy. He had been isolated in his opulent rooms for days, and Justin had clearly been making himself right at home in their new, outlandish surroundings. With a sigh, he shrugged. Better one of them be happy, anyway, as long as they were trapped here.

And they *were* trapped here, he knew. Once again, his tendency to allow himself to float along had left him at the mercy of a current that clearly had no regard for his own desires.

A small door to the rear of their room hissed open and Angara Ksaka stepped in. She was wearing a more formal-appearing version of her flying jacket, sweeping to her knees and belted at her narrow waist. Her white hair had been braided into something that looked a lot like a crown. Her boots snapped sharply on the hard, stone-like floor.

"Are you prepared?" She stalked passed him and stood at the wall, watching the milling crowd. She whirled, the tails of her coat flaring, and glared at him. "Remember, you are just taking the position until a suitable candidate can be found." She jerked a thumb over her shoulder. "They just care that a beating heart sits beneath the Skorahn. They want to know that you are not a blood-thirsty killer, that you're not going to cause difficulties to the many folk who come here to conduct business unmolested."

Marcus nodded, although she was doing nothing for his confidence. "I understand." He looked at his feet. Black boots, maybe some kind of leather? The uniform aspect of his clothing reminded him more of his family than he would have liked while trying to marshal his thoughts for the speech.

"But it will be easier if they feel comfortable with me in the office, yes?" He looked up at Angara. He was not the only one who had been elevated by their current situation. From bodyguard to king-maker with a single pull of the trigger. If he was being honest with himself, he had lost a bit of sleep at that thought.

"Just don't get … intricate." She looked sour and nervous, stepping back to check his appearance. "Half of the beings out there are only here to see a Human in the flesh. There are thousands of years of expectations on the line. Please try not to meet any of them."

"That would be easier if I knew more about what they're expecting." He muttered.

The three of them watched as a last rush filled the remaining seats in the large room. Something Iphini Bha had said earlier came back to him now that Angara had arrived.

"Iphini mentioned that Virri seldom called this kind of meeting." He wasn't sure how to broach the subject without giving the wrong impression. The last thing he wanted to do moments before his big debut was to start another fight with the purple-skinned woman.

Angara nodded, her face closing up.

"Well, I wouldn't have thought he would have had *any* meetings like this, the way you talk about him." He gestured out to the crowd through the invisible wall. "If all they really care about is my beating heart, and Virri didn't care at all for the job himself, why would he have *any* meetings? In fact, from what you've said, the position of administrator is almost entirely symbolic. Why would *anyone* have a meeting like this?"

The two females looked past him to share a glance, and then turned back to the wall. Angara shrugged. "The city runs itself, for the most part. Corporate conglomerates, racial alliances, and powerful individuals all form the moving parts of a society in constant flux. The office of the administrator is there to ease the jagged edges where those parts meet. The office has a great deal of discretionary power, actually, but it has been a very long time since anyone exercised it. The city was really started, thousands of your years ago, as the Galactic Council was forming at the tail end of the last great war. The purpose of the city has always been to offer a place for beings to come together without fear of incurring the wrath of those who strive for dominance in the wider galaxy."

Marcus thought about that for a second. "So, it isn't necessarily an empty position, then? I mean, the administrator has some power?"

Angara looked at him sharply. "You are a cipher, Marcus Wells. You are a place saver, and nothing more. Penumbra's citizens have far more to *lose* here than you have to *gain* by seeking to rise above the moment."

"Still," he wouldn't give up. "The city is important for a series of very specific reasons. And the office of administrator seems to be one from which those reasons could be well-served." He looked to her with a small grin. "It seems to me, anyway."

"The people of Penumbra have grown used to conducting their own affairs." Iphini Bha's voice was distant. "There is no need for any one being to insert themselves into the process and endanger the entire construct." The cool blue eyes fell on him. "Such efforts would not be well-received."

She was afraid of something. He nodded; Taurani. The shadow of the Galactic Council reached even into these hidden chambers, in a floating city that apparently existed solely as a refuge from their influence.

It was something he would need to remember. Khuboda Taurani had seemed like nothing more than an insufferable prig, but a far larger, more dangerous entity crouched behind him, ready to pounce.

Well, he would just have to make sure he didn't give anyone any reason to pounce. And yet, as he had that thought, a tight smile twisted at the corner of his lips.

"Well, if it's time, I think maybe we should get this over with? I've got more sleeping I have to do in my bed built for ten." He looked from one woman to the other, a professional, confident smile in place, and he gestured to the wall. "It will be easier to go through the door if I can see it."

Iphini looked to Angara, who looked through narrowing eyes at Marcus. "Do not wander from our intended path, Human." She spat the word, and it sent a chill up his neck. He didn't like the tone or the sensation, but he nodded.

Iphini Bha waved her hand and the wall solidified before them.

Marcus took a deep breath, straightened his tunic, and turned to the two alien women. "Well, wish me luck, ladies!"

Before either could respond, he stepped forward, the door slid opened at his approach, and he entered the now-silent Central Council Chamber.

# Chapter 11

The low, rumbling rush of countless conversations hissed into silence as the door opened. Even so, the nanites in his brain gave him a sharp pain as they tried to translate every sound into something he could understand before the blessed silence descended. He winced, but the pain faded even as he became aware of it, leaving him clear-headed and focused.

The kaleidoscopic range of sizes, colors, and textures seated before him seemed much more daunting without an invisible wall to hide behind, but he tightened his smile and skipped up the short flight of stairs to the dais and the podium at its forward edge. As he walked, his eyes scanned the room, smiling to any face that seemed remotely receptive, nodding to those with a more grave aspect.

He found Justin and his associates and his smile widened. Let him hide behind his contact lenses for now. Marcus was going to redefine what this crowd of alien creatures expected of a Human, whether Angara approved or not.

As he came up to the podium, he wondered how loud he was going to have to be. He could see nothing that resembled a microphone, of course. These people appeared to carry everything they needed with them as tiny implants in their heads. He shrugged. He'd speak as loudly as it seemed necessary, and trust the room and the various galactic technologies to do the rest.

He cleared his throat, smiling again, and almost coughed as he saw the tall, long-necked, purple-furred creature that had accompanied Taurani earlier slip into the room and stand near the back. So, the Council's ambassador would be represented after all, hm? Well, word of what passed here would have reached him eventually anyway. Better to be able to see the snakes than to have them hiding in the shadows.

"Welcome, everyone." He had decided early on to keep things generic. He gave them his best smile, and nodded. "I know you all have important duties to attend to, so I will attempt to keep this brief for today."

As he finished his welcoming statement, another of the doors in the rear opened and a giant figure stepped through. It was the red-skinned demon they had seen in the docking bay. Everything Angara had told them about K'hzan Modath fled from his mind as he stared into the gnarled face, its red flesh and sweeping black horns leering at him from deep within the mists of race memory. The red king was not alone, accompanied by several of his guards, who quickly pushed a small party of brown-furred, white-faced creatures from their low chairs. The chairs immediately rose to accommodate the much larger aliens, who settled in with blank faces, staring at him in a way that he could interpret only as a challenge.

He coughed into one raised hand and quirked an eyebrow at Justin. His friend looked back, then turned to face forward again, his white eyes round.

"Ah," he tried to rally his thoughts. "Ah, yes." His smile reemerged. "My name is Marcus Wells, and I am, indeed, a Human from Earth."

He was braced for almost anything. He had expected an explosion of denials or threats. Angara and Iphini Bha had him so wound up, if weapons had been drawn he wouldn't have been completely surprised; although they had assured him he would be safe through his speech. Of course now that he thought of it, the fact that they had made that stipulation, and not mentioned what might happen after his speech, had been less than comforting.

What he had *not* anticipated, was total silence.

The room was completely still. Countless eyes stared at him. Some were hostile, some were open, some were idle. Most, however, were completely inscrutable, in faces whose alien structures he could not begin to decipher.

"I … well, I … I just wanted to let everyone know, I'm not a monster." He raised his hands out to his sides with a big smile.

More silence.

He could see Justin looking around him in alarm. It made sense, when he thought about it. How often did diplomatic efforts on Earth go completely wrong because of cultural differences in tenor and humor? And the gulf between Americans and Russians was nothing compared to the gulf between a Human being and some of the things he saw out there staring back at him now.

There was a fluttering in his gut that forced its way up his throat and into the back of his mouth. It carried with it the sour tang of fear.

He watched as the big demonic creature settled deeper into his chair, his twisted face unreadable.

He was going to throw up.

It started as a vague itching behind his eyes. His first thought was that the tiny robots in his mind were rebelling. He thought he could almost feel them struggling to break free. He looked to either side. There were citizens of Penumbra seated right up to the edge of the dais. There in the front row he saw the two creatures in their mystic-like robes, the short green one in white watching him with an encouraging smile, the taller figure in black with flat, narrow eyes. He glanced behind him. The door had closed, but he could feel Angara Ksaka and Iphini Bha staring at him through the one-way transparent wall.

He felt his gorge rising up, following the trail blazed by his first rush of fear and failure.

Then the feelings in his brain twisted somehow. There was a strange clicking in his mind, as if footsteps on a bare stage. The itching grew worse, his body stiffening with the discomfort.

Then it ended. There was a sense of peace and confidence. And of someone else looking out from behind his eyes.

He knew what had happened immediately. He remembered the image of his younger self threatening him within a dark world constructed in his own mind, back on Angara's ship. That calm, clear voice was rising now, assessing the room with cold precision. For a moment, fear surged again in that part of him that was falling away. What if this wasn't some mild psychotic break at all? What if this was a construct of the tiny robots filling his mind? It didn't matter, though, because the consciousness that thought of itself as Marcus Wells, who had made a living for over ten years writing inane radio ads for a small local station, who had let every major decision in his adult life wash past him, easing him along the path of least resistance, was only a passenger now in his own head.

His eyes scanned the room again, but this time with a foreign, cold regard. He saw much more than he had. He saw doubts, fears, and disbelief. And somehow, as he saw all that, he felt certain he could pull strings that would yank those emotions in whatever direction he wished. He saw facial expressions that, defying reasonable expectation, were far closer to Human equivalents than they should be. And he knew that this version of himself, the man he would have been had he seized the reigns of his life years before and not left himself to the mercy of expediency, could read those faces far better than the man he had become.

He felt a single hand rise as if to calm a grumbling crowd. Eyes glittered in the room as they followed the hand, and then dropped back to his face. He felt himself smile a reassuring, gentle smile. Feeling the cold behind that smile, it was strangely terrifying. He didn't know what this suppressed part of his mind intended, but it frightened him.

"We are entering a difficult time, Penumbrians." Was that even a word? They didn't seem to mind. "Not only have we lost Administrator Uduta Virri to a terrible accident, but we live in a time shared with those who see no value in your contributions to the galaxy. They see no value in you or your efforts, and they have the power, if they decide to do so, to destroy us all."

Within his own head it was hard to tell, but he thought his voice had gained a depth and a richness that he could not have achieved on his own. The silence of the room now seemed less ominous, and more laden with anticipation. But anticipating what? This deeply-buried part of his psyche had no more information than *he* had. And yet, through the same observations, seemed to have gathered far more knowledge than his waking mind.

"Penumbra serves an indispensable purpose in the galaxy. It is a place for beings of good conscience and self-determination to forge their own destiny, regardless of what others might say." He took a breath, and he saw that many of the creatures before him were leaning forward in their shifting chairs. "Especially, I might add, those who live lives of pampered luxury, existing off the bounty of others in the comfort of their palaces far, far away."

Many in the room were shifting. Eyes were skittering to the tall alien standing in the back; Taurani's servant and spy. There could be no doubt who Marcus was trying to call to mind.

"Now, these beings look to the freedom and opportunity you enjoy here as a threat to their ordered universe. They seek to undermine you at every turn, to influence that which they cannot outright dominate. Nothing has stood between you and these benighted fools save for ancient treaties and agreements coated in the dust of ages and neglect, and a succession of beings who looked to the city of Penumbra as nothing more than a source of wealth and comfort."

He felt his hand dive into the neck of his tunic. What was he going to do next? There was a surreal pleasure to this experience, watching himself work a crowd with the ability and ease of a veteran politician. There was a dreamlike sense of disconnection, however, watching this new self maneuver through the maze of intergalactic politics. When he pulled out the amulet, even *he* was surprised.

He found the Thien'ha again in the front row, and watched the tall Humanoid's eyes widen in surprise. The green-furred snout, however, gave nothing away.

"You have all heard that a Human has replaced Uduta Virri." The medallion sparkled as it dangled from his hand. "No doubt your emotions have run the gamut since." He held up his other hand again, as if for begging for quiet from the silent room. "I will address my own place in these events soon, but first, I believe it would serve us all well to remember from whence we come.

"I have no doubt many of you were friends of Uduta Virri." Marcus felt a slight twist curl his lip, and felt the beings in the room respond. "I have no doubt many of you were friendly with Virri's business practices." The curl blossomed into a smile, and he saw many answering smiles start to peak out from the crowd. His own smile vanished more quickly than it had appeared, and he saw those mirroring expressions fold in upon themselves. His brow furrowed, and he leaned forward.

"Rest assured, Virri would have presided over the final destruction or annexation of Penumbra." Many heads reared back at this, and Marcus found himself hoping that he could back the statement up. "The Council moves more blatantly than ever before. Under the protection of plausible deniability, they have sent agents against the administrator more than once. And others as well, I dare say." Here, he cast a quick glance at K'hzan. He leaned over the podium even further, fingers gripping the smooth material tightly. "Who's to say this accident that has swept us all along in its wake wasn't engineered by them, hm?"

Marcus caught the purple-furred Eru jerk at that. It was buried, however, by the sudden surge of sound from the crowd. Marcus did not believe the Galactic Council had anything to do with Virri's death, but it was clear that the beings in the chamber were more than ready to believe exactly that. In the muttered moments of doubt, he replaced the necklace. It seemed none of the creatures in the room would have noticed had it not been for the Thien'ha, both of whom watched him with intent eyes.

"Even if they had nothing to do with *that*, is there any sentient here today that doubts the grasping reach of the Council? They would have moved against a weakling like Virri sooner or later, and everything around us would have been lost." He shook his head, a strong, rigid smile blooming over his face. "This accident, failed assassination or honest mishap, was a gift, my friends. What Penumbra needs now is true leadership, not the stewardship of a lazy, egotistical hedonist."

Many of the attendees were on their feet now; or on what passed for feet in the various lifeforms present. There was shouting, and in the buffeting chaos of sound, the nanites struggled painfully to provide a hundred conflicting translations.

But that part of him that had taken charge seemed unaffected. Marcus raised his hands for quiet, and received it. The silence rippled through the crowd, reaching the outer edges where Justin sat, wide-eyed, and where the huge red-skinned giant watched with implacable calm. The Thien'ha had not changed their expressions since the beginning, staring at him with unnerving intensity.

"You have no doubt been told that a replacement will be sought immediately for the position of administrator, and that is true." He nodded at the dark, suspicious looks he received from several quarters. "I do not intend to remain in this position any longer than necessary. Even now efforts are underway to find a leader that will be able to secure your safety for many generations to come. A true leader, able to guide you into a future where the Council knows full well that it is not welcome in Penumbra!"

No one cheered at that, but he could tell many of them wanted to. There was only one thing holding them back now, and he was dying to see how this new version of himself intended to deal with that concern.

"And so finally we come to me; a minor cog in the wheels that fate has now set into motion." He rested one elbow on the podium, assuming a far more casual pose. "My Humanity is the single greatest bone of contention to be contemplated in this moment of grave historical significance. I beg of you, do not lose the galaxy for the sake of some ancient fear." He stood up straighter. "I am no legion, I am no fleet. I am no great threat come back from the mists of time, no matter what you may believe of my nature or my inclinations." Damn, he had put a lot together, sitting there inside his skull!

"I am one being, seeking to do the best in a bad situation, just like many of you." He pointed out into the crowd. "I am no more dangerous than a Subbotine with memories of greatness." The white-skinned Humanoids seemed to rankle at that, but the beings around them smiled and smirked. "I am no more of a threat than a single Namanu, contemplating the engines of the universe." The orange skinned beings smiled themselves, clearly possessing a healthier sense of humor. "I am far less perilous than a single Variyar, lost in remembered glories." There were far fewer smiles at that, although the red-skinned demons remained still and silent.

"The reality is that I am only one sentient among tens of thousands." He shrugged. "You have my word that I will step down as soon as a suitable replacement for these dark times is found. I will return to Earth quietly, never to return, and you will be in far better hands than the tentacles with which Virri encircled you in the past."

The room was quiet again, and he leaned back over the podium. "You need to prepare. You need a leader that will *help* you to prepare. The galaxy as you have known it is dissolving around you, and only with effort and commitment will this bastion of freedom remain." He felt his shoulders shrugging in a cavalier twitch. "You do not have to allow me this freedom, of course. You can demand that I remain in my quarters until the Skorahn can be presented to my successor. That is within the rights of the citizenry of Penumbra as I understand them." Again, leaning over the podium. "But please just think of this: would you rather have the only Human within thousands of light years brooding in solitary confinement, setting his mind to all sorts of dark and forbidden thoughts, or would you rather have that mind turned toward your own wellbeing and that of the city?"

Marcus felt himself straighten to a position that his father might have even been willing to refer to as attention.

"I leave myself in your hands, citizens of Penumbra." His voice hesitated. He cocked his head, and raised a hand. "No, I'm sorry. I leave myself in your hands, fellow Penumbrians." He felt his head tilt back, his chin rising defiantly. "For I have come to see your struggle as my own. Many of you did not even realize your way of life was in jeopardy, but I am proud to now share your danger. This city is a beacon of hope and freedom in a galaxy regimented and controlled by the Council. I am proud to call it my home, no matter how brief my time among you will be."

Had the crowd been Humans, there would have been a rousing, roaring shout of approval. Marcus had no doubt about it. But they were not Humans. They were as far from Humans as you could apparently get in the galaxy. And yet still he felt there was the intention of a rousing shout. As many of the creatures in the room stood to look up at him in silence, there was a bond of emotion that tied them together that had not been there before.

Whatever caused these people to hate and fear Humans, Marcus had somehow mitigated that, at least for the moment. He had redirected their animosity at the Council. He didn't know how much of what he said had been truth, and what had been somewhere between an educated guess and outright manipulative lies. But it had struck a chord, and for the time being anyway, enough of these people believed in him that he need not fear for his safety. At least for the moment.

Justin stood with the rest of his new friends, his eyes still wide. The red-skinned warriors stood silently and filed out without a backward glance. Among Bha's 'Children' there was a wide range of responses. From the doubtful sneers of the albinos to the warm smiles of the orange-skinned workers, it was clear each had seen him through their own lenses.

Standing in the midst of the others and yet seemingly alone, the two Thien'ha were the only people he could see that did not seem to have been effected in any way. The smaller, green-furred figure in the white robes watched him for a moment, and the lips beneath the snout curled in something a Human would consider a smile. The orange-tinged-face beneath the dark hood watched him with cold eyes that seemed to have passed judgment on him before they had ever met. The two of them turned at some silent signal and wove their way through the standing crowd to disappear through another small side door.

The fur reminded Marcus of the Eru, and he scanned the back wall for Taurani's towering servant. There was no sign of the beast, of course. As soon as the tenor of the crowd had clearly turned in favor of the Human spouting anti-Council rhetoric, he would have made his escape to set his master's ears to burning. Something to worry about later, though. Right now, Marcus just wanted to bask in the success of the moment.

Somehow, without any outward voting or debate, the assembly seemed to have agreed to his request. None of the slime-green Administrative guards had come forward to escort him back to his rooms. Their little tiny brain robots had probably talked to each other and agreed to give him just enough rope to hang himself. But for now that was enough. He would worry about the amount of rope later; for now, it was nice to have some at all.

He could feel the consciousness residing in his mind sliding back into the shadows. There was that clicking sensation again, and slowly control of his body returned, as if he was waking up from a restful nap. As he came back to himself he turned at the waist to regard the wide, opaque wall behind him.

The smile he gave the women hiding there was all his.

*****

Angara and Iphini Bha stood frozen in the preparation room. Beyond the transparent wall, the citizens of Penumbra were milling about, discussing what they had just seen, flowing steadily toward the doors. Marcus was still standing at the podium, his stance confident and relaxed, and watched them go.

"Well that was … unanticipated." Angara folded her arms before her, following the retreating band of Subbotines and their Mhatrong companion. The Subbotines would not be among Marcus Wells's proponents after this meeting.

She had expected more trouble from them than from *any* of the other Children, to be honest. But she had not dared hope that any of their ilk would look kindly upon the first Human they had seen in their lives. The fact that many seemed willing to take Marcus at his word was reassuring at the same time it was … alarming. If enough of the Children were willing to accept Humans back into galactic society, what might the wrong Human be able to accomplish?

"We shall see how it all falls out, now that they have seen him." Iphini Bha had not been willing to extend Marcus Wells the benefit of any doubt since his first moments in the control center. Angara hoped she would stay constant long enough for them to find a replacement.

Iphini Bha turned to her, wide blue eyes haunted, and Angara realized the deputy administrator had a lot more on her mind than bigotry against the Human. "Taurani will not be pleased with this speech." She swallowed, stylus wobbling back and forth across her knuckles. "Virri always said that they left us alone because we were just ineffectual enough that destroying us was not worth their trouble." The eyes moved up to find Angara's own. "Do you think he can do what he said? Could Marcus Wells rally the people of Penumbra against the Council?" The confusion of emotions behind her eyes seemed to include equal parts hope and … jealousy?

Angara shook her head and looked back out at the chamber beyond. She had not slept well since her return to Penumbra, seeing the last moments of Uduta Virri's life over and over again whenever she closed her eyes. She had been living a nightmare since the moment she realized the vehicle she had saved had held Humans, not the Rayabell she was sworn to protect.

But what if Marcus Wells was right? What if Virri had been a danger to the city in the long-term? If, through the mistake that haunted her nights, she had inadvertently given her home a new lease on its existence; would those nightmares one day lessen?

Suddenly she realized she had a whole new reason to hope that Marcus Wells was correct in his assessment, and in his sense of hope for the city.

But that made her eyes narrow again, and she stared at the back of Wells's head. Had it come to this? Was her only hope in the hands of a *Human*? Thousands of years of fear and distrust gave the thought a deeper sense of terror than anything she had ever felt before. What if she was wrong about him? What if every sentiment ascribed to the Humans of Earth proved well-founded after all?

"I do not know if he can do it, Iphini," she said at last. "But do not fall into a false argument. Marcus Wells was not chosen because we felt he was the right being for the work at hand. He was forced upon us by circumstance." She shrugged, looking down at the pale creature beside her. "We need to watch him closely. If he can pull the city together in his time here, if he is right about Taurani and the Council and their plans for Penumbra, then this might all work out for the best."

She turned back to watch as Marcus nodded to his retreating friend. "If we are wrong, and he becomes a threat to the city before he can be replaced…" She shrugged. "Then he will be far from the first administrator to die in office."

She sighed, looking away. He would not even be the first administrator she had killed.

# Chapter 12

Ambassador Khuboda Taurani sat stiff and upright in the soft plushness of his grooming chair. His latest companion, acquired against all hopes from a passing courier carrying dispatches from the galactic core, crouched at his feet, massaging the tension from the long muscles of his legs with bowed head. The black traceries that ran across the porcelain skin were pleasant reminders of the damned deputy and her stubborn lack of vision.

"He as much as accused you of murder, Ambassador." The indignation in Iranse's voice was clear to anyone familiar with Eru intonation. The purple fur was raised along his shoulders and neck. If the Human had been in the Ambassador's chamber at that moment, nothing would have stopped the servant from crushing his windpipe.

Taurani could appreciate loyalty like that, but now was not the time for direct confrontation.

"Well, he's not far wrong." He stared into the viewing sphere before him at the dead planet spinning below. The twisting path of glittering water vapor that curled up from the planet below, the lifeline of the city the inhabitants called the Diamond Road, was visible as a shimmering line across one corner of his vision. "Of course, he's got the specifics incorrect, but it is not as if we do not have the vitae of innocents splashed upon us, my friend."

Iranse's head reared back slightly on his long neck, his pale red eyes blinking. "Ambassador, you can't be—"

"Silence, Iranse." Taurani snapped at his servant. The Eru was loyal to a fault, but lacked anything resembling an imagination. "These fools have forgotten why the Council was first brought into existence, and why we have striven to expand its power ever since."

With one foot he pushed the Iwa'Bantu maid back and rose, wiping the imaging sphere away with an abrupt gesture. "We could not have wished for a better outcome than this, truly. A Human sitting upon the command throne of Penumbra is exactly what we need to galvanize those systems who have been vacillating against direct action here." He waved one long arm as he spun about for Iranse to drape a fresh set of robes over his shoulders. "There are still those on the Council that revere the ancient treaties, but their legal application has faded into insignificance. Nothing but bureaucratic inertia keeps the city safe now, and with the addition of a Human into the mix, that inertia can be broken with a little judicious application of force from the right angle."

With a slight nod of his head as he accessed his nanite-implants, a shimmering mirror surface appeared on the wall before him. He turned to appreciate the hang of his robes, turning from one grave, dignified pose to the next. He had accepted this assignment knowing the winds of change were churning. When Penumbra fell under the sway of the Council at last, it would be his name attached to the relevant treaties, his image appearing in the histories.

Thousands of years ago the Kerie had been instrumental in transforming the Grand Alliance into the Great Council, shifting the bulk of galactic power from those few most powerful polities and coalitions to the far more numerous civilized systems that had been kept as client states to the mighty for far too long.

Since then, however, his people's power had become diluted by the very size of their own creation. The Galactic Council was a convoluted nightmare of factions, blocs, and cabals with so many contradicting mandates and goals that it was nearly impossible to get anything done. The ancient powers, such as the Children, the Aijians, and others, had been brought into line over the course of millennia; and even the last, the barbarian Variyar, had fallen in the end. The countless smaller systems whose alliances wielded the true power had nothing to distract them from each other now, and the process that had assured the down-trodden races and systems could flourish on the galactic stage followed its natural progression, and the Council continued to balkanize as the relationships that tied the polities together were no longer seen as essential.

It was time for the Kerie to take their place amidst the great races of galactic history and clear the flotsam created by the Council once and for all. By destroying the most visible symbol of defiance standing before the ruling body, he would both strengthen his own race's position and create the illusion that the Kerie were toiling away in the best interests of the Council.

"And how is your own little project? I trust things proceed apace?"

His servant smiled slyly. "It is, Ambassador. She has—"

"I need to speak with Admiral Ochiag, Iranse." It would never do for the creature to become too familiar. "Please see if you can establish the connection for me." He felt no need to look at the tall Eru, and instead moved to the little Iwa'Bantu serving girl.

A swift backhand propelled her toward his private quarters. "Clean the sleeping pool, girl. Make sure the water is crystal before I'm done with the admiral."

With a soft sound that might have been a sigh, might have been a sob, the creature scuttled off to see to the pool. He shook his head. The fiction that every race was equal had been beneficial when the Variyar and their ilk had held sway; but now that they had all been defanged, these lesser races would need to be put back in their places.

"Still with a taste for the Iwa'Bantu, I see." The rough voice grumbled from behind him.

Taurani forced his facial muscles into the unfamiliar exercise of an ex-pression recognized as a smile by most of the debased races of the galaxy, then turned around.

Floating within the imaging field was a face that only a blind Ntja brood-mare could love. Admiral Ochiag was an old soldier; the coarse, wrinkled brown flesh of an Ntja male all but occluded by the metallic domes of cranial enhance-ment lobes. The wet nasal hole in the center of the face, rimmed with a purple flare, split the ugly visage and swelled to the bucktoothed mouth holding the sog-gy remnants of a brown cylinder, burning at the end. The Ntja upper class often ingested these tubes of rotting vegetable matter by burning one end and inhaling the fumes. It was a foul habit they had learned from illicit observation files from Earth, and one that did nothing to endear the creatures to their fellow power bro-kers on the Council.

"Admiral Ochiag," Taurani dipped his head in acknowledgement. He glanced over his shoulder at the door through which the serving girl had just ex-ited. "Have you ever served on Iwa'Ban? The plentiful supply of such servants is an excellent balm to an otherwise tedious posting."

The big head floating within the swirling cloud shook, sparks flaring from the end of the soggy roll. "Ntja tastes don't generally run in that direction." The head scanned the rest of the room, nodding to Iranse, standing straight nearby. "Iranse. Still lapping up after your master's indiscretions?"

Taurani tensed. One mistake made when he was a young low-level diplomat, and the dogs in the military services would never let him live it down. The Eru, however, stared with cold, loyal eyes at the admiral's image, his purple fur flat.

Ochiag shrugged. "What do you want, Taurani? I think I've got that damned Variyar cornered. My scout vessels have found a system that could be harboring the bulk of his fleet. I have preparations I should be making."

Taurani bared his baleen in a wide, bristly grin. "Things in Penumbra have taken a turn, Admiral." One should always be courteous when possible. That way, when the daggers came out, one had preserved the element of surprise. "It is possible that I may be able to eliminate the automatic defenses sooner than the Council's timeline required." His smile gained a more genuine edge despite himself. "I may be able to offer you a target that would make leaving your fruitless chase for another day worthwhile." Most of the Peacekeeper fleets had been chasing K'hzan Modath's main strength for decades with little to show for it, led on the merry chase by a chortling red king. Undoubtedly, Ochiag's most recent findings would prove equally as fruitless.

The beady, watery eyes narrowed. The Council fleet was seldom called to action nowadays, except to police the more bumptious systems or hunt for feral Humans. The Variyar ghost fleet was the elusive prize they all dreamed of. Taurani was suggesting a very big promise with his off-hand remark.

"Pray tell." The admiral removed the tube from his mouth with blunt, stubby fingers. An unspoken warning flowed beneath the words. Ochiag was under no obligation to maintain this connection, and could sever it in a moment without reprimand or repercussion.

"The Administrator of Penumbra, a particularly odious Rayabell designated Uduta Virri, has somehow done us the service of moving on to the next plane." The smile grew a jot brighter again.

Ochiag's eyes narrowed to shadowed slits. "I was under the impression that Virri was the Council's creature?"

Taurani gave as close to a flippant shrug as he ever allowed himself. "A poor tool at best. His passing has nullified some minor schemes, but it offers something much greater in the personage of his replacement." A diplomat as talented as he always knew what his expression conveyed. Now, he allowed it to speak volumes about his own sense of satisfaction.

"I will not play your hunt and seek games, Taurani." Ochiag placed the nasty roll of paper back in his mouth and shifted it from side to side. "If you do not offer some incentive for me to maintain this connection, I will indulge my growing impulse to end this little dialogue without any of the diplomatic niceties you find so appealing."

"They have replaced Virri with a Human." That was only half of his momentous news, but he held the remainder for a moment to keep the admiral dangling despite his protestations.

He did not believe he had ever seen an Ntja's eyes so round and wide before. "A Human?" The wet mouth twisted into a sneer to make any professional consul proud. "Why would they do that? Where did they even find one capable of rational thought?"

Taurani allowed his cheek ridges to rise, revealing the full expanse of the baleen bristles. "Earth." The second bit of information, and he watched it sink home with glittering eyes.

The image of the admiral jolted upright, and this time Taurani was sure he had never seen Ntja eyes that big.

"A Human from *Earth*?" He spluttered, and the burning roll fell out of his mouth unnoticed. "How? How did a Human get *off* Earth in the first place?"

Taurani shrugged. "The administrator's bodyguard, apparently. You know it happens from time to time. With help, it's more than possible."

Ochiag snarled. "A Tigan, if I remember correctly?"

"Indeed. An outcast, for whatever that is worth."

"Trust a Tigan to stumble into something so monumentally thoughtless." The Ntja paused for a moment, and then coughed. He began to speak before he had completely recovered. "Wait, did you say they *replaced* that venial little worm with this *Human*? They gave a Human their precious medallion?"

"Apparently so. From what I gather, they were not given a real choice in the matter, and are only making the best of a very strange situation."

The tiny eyes narrowed again. The flesh around them tightened, puckering around the bronze and steel domes. "And why would this lure me away from my current mission, Ambassador?"

Ah, that part of the negotiation where the price was decided. His favorite portion of the proceedings. "Chaos, as a military commander of your vast experience knows, is replete with opportunity for the focused mind. As these fools scramble to find a replacement for their pet Human, breaches will appear within their command structure; breaches we will be able to exploit."

"No Human will relinquish that kind of control." The big head shook violently. "They are even greater fools if they believe this creature will simply step down for another candidate."

Taurani shrugged. He did not care if the Human Marcus Wells stepped down voluntarily or not. "That is not our concern. The Humans of Earth are far different creatures than the feral splinter clans you have dealt with in the past. There is no telling what he might do, or what they may have offered him. Regardless, there will be a moment in time when their medallion is vulnerable. I have been insinuating several vectors into their command staff. When the moment comes, amidst the chaos and the confusion, the Skorahn will be mine, and I will possess it long enough to disable Penumbra's automatic defenses. You will be able to land your troops and take control of the city without having to contend with the quantum core of the city."

The mysterious Relic Core of Penumbra had proven itself capable of defending the city more than once in the lifetime of the Council. Entire expeditionary fleets had been lost, and no records existed that could definitively say how. This threat, as much as the old treaties, assured Council meddling in the affairs of the city was kept to a minimum.

The possibilities inherent in the loss of those defenses dawned in the Ntja admiral's eyes.

"Your Peacemakers will have control of the city before anyone is the wiser. The annexation will be a fait accompli." Taurani raised his hands from his sides in a slow gesture of inevitability.

"And you will reap the master's share of the glory." It was a muttered statement of fact, rather than a question or an argument.

Taurani inclined his head. "I will, of course, be assuming the greatest share of risk, until the moment of our ascendancy arrives. The delegation has a small guard force, of course, but my Ntja are not furnished with the weapons and equipment the Peacemakers will carry. I can push Penumbra deeper into chaos with a few judicious applications of violence, as well as the agents I have been fostering throughout the city. If your fleet were to be nearby, able to take full advantage of any opening I can create, she will fall before the cretins even know there is any danger. I do have one other minor incentive I might offer."

The admiral's tiny eyes narrowed further, and Taurani wondered how he could see anything at all. "What?"

"As you know, Penumbra is known for its technological innovations. It has come to my attention that several conglomerates here have been working on projects that have come to the Council's attention. I might see clear that one such little bauble find its way to your waiting claws before I secure it for official dispatch, if you were near enough to receive it."

Was it possible for those eyes to narrow further? Apparently it was. "What kind of bauble is on offer?"

Taurani shrugged with all the understated elegance of a lifetime of diplomacy. "I will not go over the specifics here, but let us just say that it will be very difficult to flee from you, if the device works as intended."

Ochiag's eyes wandered in thought. The big head jerked once in a single, spasmodic nod. "The fleet will be nearby when you give the signal. Do you have an estimate of the time you will require?"

Taurani folded his hands into the sleeves of his robes as he inclined his head, deeper than at the beginning of the conversation. "I cannot know, of course. It will not be overly long. By the time you are in the vicinity, the city should be ripe. I will, of course, keep you apprised of any changes in the situation."

The ugly face in the image returned his nod. "Do so."

The image faded before Taurani could dismiss it, and he sneered. A minor point to the admiral, then. No matter, the histories would care nothing for the thug who ferried the troopers to Penumbra. Only the hero who contrived the city's fall would matter to posterity.

Staring at the empty view field he ran over the conversation again in his mind. The Council would not begrudge Ochiag the prize he had offered. They had sent him to secure several technical marvels, but the admiral was high in the Council's esteem, and would doubtless put the machine to good use. It was not as if he was giving the barbarian the plum, after all. The time dilation technology, upon which so much of the Council's future plans rested, would still be safe.

He only needed to secure these technologies from the consortia that had developed them, and the Council's work would be done. They had little hope in his plans for subjugating the entire city, which would make it all the sweeter when he reported his success.

His mouth tightened as it always did at moments like these. Why was it that so much innovation was to be found here, at the edges of civilized space, while the Core worlds had not made any significant discoveries in centuries? What about this horrible little trap spurred the creatures who called it home to heights the Council could no longer aspire to?

It was almost enough to make him want to spit.

He turned toward his chamber. "Iranse, leave me. I would like some time alone with my newest servant." He glided to the door with an extra bounce in his step. "Life expectancy is so short when one takes them from their homes." He turned, a warning glitter in his eyes. "Arrange to have several more smuggled into the city, if you could? I fear I will be in sore need of distraction in the coming days."

The little Iwa'Bantu girl was wading in the pool, her robes floating around her thighs, as he entered. She was waving an atomizer wand over the water, leaning down to make sure it brushed every inch of the surface.

His rigid smile faded, an unnatural expression worn only as a communications tool. The gleam in his bright, metallic eyes, however, was entirely genuine.

*****

"Let me see if I understand you." The tall, dark-skinned man was sitting with a group of beings of various colors, shapes, and sizes, all of them relaxing in a private niche at the back of the exclusive lounge, sipping various liquids or inhaling multi-colored clouds of gas from jeweled emitters. "There are no actual commerce laws in Penumbra?"

A pale, splay-headed Matabess clacked its beak, big green eyes flaring. "Well, as such, the only actual laws in the city are those that will stop any citizen from directly interfering with any other citizen." It held up one spatulate finger. "However, there are countless conventions and traditions that, if not properly adhered to, will result in a being's exclusion from the active community."

"What's a Mnymian care for business, anyway?" This was from a Leemuk with port authority collar flashes. "Aren't you lot usually more interested in the arenas, or personal security?" The toothy maw gaped wide as the slimy creature shot a cloud of pink gas into its mouth.

The black-skinned man shrugged, tossing back a mouthful of clear liquid. "I'm a bit of a maverick, to be honest." He shifted forward, one elbow resting on the table. "Diversity is the hallmark of any sane being's portfolio, wouldn't you agree?"

The creatures around the low table shared in various iterations of a laugh.

"But honestly, there is no controlling legal authority for goods or services?" His tone was aggressively casual, and his companions seemed willing to accept it at its offered value.

"No." The Matabess repeated. "As long as your reputation is sound, you will be able to work whatever dealings you have contrived for as long as you can find partners to join you."

"Forgive me if I speak out of turn," a short Kot'i muttered, a large mug of some smoking beverage held in its two small furry hands. "But is there perhaps a deal in the offing that we might be interested in?"

The black man smiled, his teeth gleaming from within his deep red goatee. "There may well be, friend. You'll have to let me test the waters first. But if I encounter any opportunities," he held his glass up to the rest of them. "You will be the first sentients to know."

"Enough of this business talk!" A white-skinned Subbotine pouted. "You promised us an interesting evening." She smiled an entirely different kind of smile, sidling around to sit beside the Mnymian. "I've heard very intriguing stories of your people. Many speak very highly of your ... stamina?"

The big black man coughed, his grin slipping just a little. Several of the females sitting around the table laughed, and this time it was the males and the aliens of indeterminate gender that looked annoyed. The Mnymian's white eyes widened, but then he smiled again.

"Plenty of time for experimentation later. I've heard some things myself, that I'd be interested to see put to the test." The laughter was more evenly distributed this time.

"We should take what we can for the time being, business and pleasure both." The Leemuk muttered. "There's no telling how much longer we have before it'll all be over."

"That's rather nihilistic for a Leemuk, isn't it?" The Kot'i said, sipping on its drink. "Aren't you people better known as pragmatists than philosophers? You sound like a Mhatrong floating in drink."

The sleek green creature shrugged, its amorphous shoulders slumping up around its nearly-non-existent neck and then receding. "Nothing is for certain when a Human holds the Skorahn."

A shiver of fear and agreement seemed to sweep around the circle. The Leemuk's enormous wet mouth worked soundlessly for a moment, and then he continued. "I have a cousin that works in the administrator's office that saw the creature. She said he was crazed, right out of the old tales."

The white-skinned woman shook her head, her pale hair rippling in the lounge's soft light. "I was there at his investiture. Everything you've heard is the truth. The beast was a violent, warmongering savage. The sooner we are rid of him, the safer we will *all* be."

"I don't know." The Kot'i shrugged with far less drama than a Leemuk could ever manage. "I was there as well. A lot of what Marcus Wells said made sense to me."

"I heard he called for the Galactic Council's overthrow." This from a petite Tsiiki whose lightly colored cephalic lobes and high voice marked her as female. "I heard it means war if he stays."

"Nonsense," the Kot'i said. "He was warning us of the inevitable, is all. Anyone who doesn't realize the council is out for our life's blood is living in a fool's dream."

"His presence here could mean war nonetheless." The Leemuk grunted, squeezing the last gas from the emitter. "There's no way the council will countenance a Human on the command throne of Penumbra. It would call into question too many of their policies and positions."

The Matabess snorted, clacking its beak again. "There can be no doubt the creature is a monster, however. It cannot be allowed to remain any longer than necessary."

The black-skinned Mnymian shifted uncomfortably. "I don't know, as well. He didn't seem like a monster to me."

"No more monsters than any other genocidal, apocalyptic force of ravening hunger, no." The Subbotine spat, her attractive features twisting with a bone-deep hatred. "Look into the eye of a voracious singularity and find more compassion than in a Human heart."

"Well, that seems excessive." The Mnymian muttered. "They can't all—"

Every other creature around the table was staring at him; his voice faded off into silence. Most returned to their drinks and gasses, but the tone of the group was far heavier than it had been.

The Leemuk shifted its bulk, its tiny eyes sliding to the Subbotine and then away. "There is another certainty. The Children will not allow him to stay in power a moment longer than he must."

The pale woman snorted, her eyes burning. Her back was stiff, her arms folded. "I would not be surprised if some enterprising Diakk solves the problem for us." She looked over at the black-skinned man with a wrinkle marring her petite nose. "Or some brave Mnymian."

"The Children do not speak with a single voice." The Kot'i asserted. "There are many who refuse to judge this Human based on nothing more than ancient tales and rumors."

"Tales and rumors?" The Tsiiki scoffed. "The evidence is there for anyone aberrant enough to seek it out! Earth is a cesspit, exactly what Humans deserve. And any Child that would stand to breathe the same air as a Human has something wrong with their head, their heart, or their soul."

The Mnymian stared at her for a moment, then shook his head and stood. "Well, my friends, I believe that is my cue for the evening." He dropped several coins of Council specie on the table. "Last round's on me." He edged past his companions, some of them nodding their thanks or farewells, others looking quickly away. The Subbotine remained icy cold.

The lounge was still crowded despite the hour. He began to move through the mob with a distracted air.

She figured that was why he had not noticed her. She moved up beside him from where she had been sitting alone, nursing a drink, a hooded cloak pulled up over her white hair.

"Running with an interesting crowd these days."

Justin Shaw spun around at the sound of her voice, and looked sour when he found her approaching him from the shadows.

"Angara." He nodded sharply and then continued on his way. "Shouldn't you be getting your beauty sleep, so that you're bright eyed and bushy tailed for another bout of king-making in the morning?"

"You think I'm beautiful?" She asked lightly, and he shot her a look. Sitting next to a Subbotine for the night had clearly served him his fill of egotistical compliment fishing. She snorted. "I needed to speak with you."

He nodded, not looking back as he navigated his way out of the lounge and onto the bustling Concourse. "You could have reached me by comms at any time. Or left a message in my rooms."

"You have not been spending a lot of time in your rooms, Justin Shaw. And you have not been responding to comms either, from what I hear." She quickened her pace to keep up, her long legs more than equal to the task.

"Whatever." He looked around for a moment, and then moved off toward a shuttle port. "What do you want? I'm tired. I need to get some sleep."

"I'd imagine the interface lenses must get irritating after a while." She pulled up even with him and reached out for his shoulder, spinning him to a halt. "And the beard ... how often must you apply the dye?"

"Angara, talk, or I'm leaving." He looked around with a furtive air. "You won't be doing either of us any favors if the wrong people see us together."

"Marcus needs you, Justin. He's had several levies since the first, and each one is proving harder and harder."

He nodded, and she thought there might be just a touch of guilt haunting his eyes. "I know. I've heard."

"Support for those early proposals has not solidified. The tradition of petitioning he seeks to restart will not work without the good will of the citizens." She looked away. "And we lose that more and more every day. It seems like the rumors spread like weeds, growing more violent and implausible every day."

"They're coming from Taurani's office." He muttered, almost as if he was ashamed to admit it. "I've tracked more than enough of them to his agents to tell you that." He looked up at her and planted a rigid finger in the center of her chest. "*And* you should have done that too. He *needs* me? He's got me! He needs you and Bha to be working at your best! Why do you think I'm doing all of this?" He gestured with his wide-sleeved tunic, indicating his galactic garb. "If he needs *more* from me, maybe he should come himself!"

She grabbed his finger and applied just enough pressure to bring a wince to his dark face. He pulled his hand away and snorted. "I heard him plain as day up on that stage. He doesn't need me. You just don't know which Marcus you're dealing with. That wasn't my friend you got up there. That was his brother, hell, that was his *father* up there. He might think he needs me, but he's going to do fine on his own, now that he's decided to run down a new path."

The words made no sense to her, and so she dismissed them with a shake of her head. "He needs his friend, Justin Shaw. None of us can give him what you can: a feeling of normalcy."

That made the black man laugh, and the sound rolled through the crowd around them, drawing unwanted attention, but he scarcely seemed to care now. "Normal? You *kidnapped* us! In a *spaceship*! There's *nothing* normal about any of this!"

That confused her. "I thought you wanted to be here? I thought you had planned to stay..."

He nodded his head. "Yeah, it's exciting, I won't deny that." He pulled out a wallet and waved it in front of her. "And thanks to my bugout bag, I had some gold, was able to parlay that into a nice small pile of specie, and I've got several transactions in the works now. I'll have a network up and running just in time for you to kick us both out, but I don't care." He shook his head with frustration, looking away again. "Listen: I've still got Marc's back. I'm watching out for him, and his interests, every day. If he really needs me, I'll be here. Tell him that. But I saw the way he looked at me during that first gather, levy, whatever you called it, and I heard the words. He doesn't need me near him right now, trust me. When he used to get like this, he always did much better on his own."

He started to turn away, and then stopped, looking at her with his colorless, sparkling eyes. "Tell me one thing, and I'll stop by to see him."

She nodded eagerly, but felt a crawling sense of suspicion shift in her mind.

"What?"

He turned back to face her, looking to either side, then leveling a weighted stare directly into her eyes. "Who are the Children? Every time I try to bring it up, all I get are hostile looks and the cold shoulder."

She blinked. She and Bha had decided to keep certain things from Justin Shaw and Marcus Wells, and she still believed that to be the best course. But she also believed, despite what Justin said, that Marcus needed his friend beside him if his foolish scheme had any hope of success. But given the crowd to which he seemed to have gravitated, it was no wonder they wanted nothing to do with a conversation about the Children.

"They are not called merely 'Children'. The more common term is Children of Man, and it is a term used to refer to a group of Humanoid races that share a common ancestry stretching back into the mists of ancient time." She kept her face calm, willing it to reveal nothing.

"Common ancestry," he repeated. "You mean *Human* ancestry?"

She shook her head. "Not exactly."

He blew out a breath in an exasperated hiss. "Just the same old shit with you, eh? The truth, or Marc can do without any handholding from me."

She could feel her nostrils flare as she tried to control her reaction. Why did this Human have to be so infuriating? She blinked, and met his gaze with flat eyes. "The Children of Man share many genetic markers with Humans. They are differentiated by color, morphic type, intellectual capacity, and other traits. Typically, they hold a more negative-than-average view of Humans."

His brow furrowed as he puzzled this out. "So, they are at least part Human?"

She shook her head. "No part that any of them would admit to. Justin, that is all I can say. Please, leave it alone."

His lips pursed within the red beard. "So, let me guess … Subbotines are Children of Man?"

She nodded. "Some of the most emphatically anti-Human, yes."

"And the Namanu, the," he indicated himself, "the Mnymians? The Diakk?"

She nodded, folding her arms and dipping her head. She wanted nothing more now than for him to leave with a promise to visit Marcus.

"And you."

That brought her up short. Her eyes narrowed and her head lifted. He was smiling. "Your people … the Tigan? They're Children of Man too, right?"

She wanted to spit at him. Any reminder of her people irritated wounds that had never healed, that were still open and painful after all this time. She forced herself to nod with a sharp jerk, her mouth set into a firm, thin line.

And he smiled. His smile caught her completely off guard with its warmth. He had clearly gotten more out of her answer than she had intended to give.

"Don't worry, Angara." He patted her gently with one dark hand. "I'll go talk to him. We'll all make it through this together." He nodded one last time and turned away to move toward the shuttle port.

She watched him go, nonplussed.

When he turned around, his old grin firmly in place, her eyes tightened.

"And when it's through, we'll see what we shall see."

Before she could respond, he was lost in the crowd.

# Chapter 13

Marcus sat in one of the comfortable chairs in the preparation room, swiveling it back and forth morosely as he watched the vision field in the wall niche. He had attuned it to an exterior view of the large docking port at the base of the Red Tower, and watched as ship after ship slid from the docking stations and sped away.

The citizens of Penumbra were fleeing.

He had been singularly incapable of recapturing that burning rhetoric that had carried him through the first meeting. The cold, analytical part of himself that he had taken to seeing as his younger alter-ego had remained silent. Sometimes he felt that presence lurking behind his eyes, watching silently as everything fell apart, but it had been weeks since that first meeting, and nothing he did had arrested the slide toward failure he now saw unfolding before him.

Iphini Bha sat nearby, her wide blue eyes unfocused as she accessed information through her nanites. She shook her head as if clearing it of daydreams and pivoted it toward him on the long neck to regard him from across the room. "Shall we open the wall?"

They had entered through the side corridor, rather than through the council chamber. The mutters and dark looks had gotten progressively worse, and he had been spending less time near crowds as things in the city continued to deteriorate. He had started to avoid the lift tubes, instead falling back on the administrator's shuttle from the executive docking bay. It now took more than half an hour to get from his office to the damned chamber, but at least he didn't have to deal with the rising hostility and suspicion.

He looked down with a snort. He still wore his watch. The artificial day of the enclosed city was just over two hours longer than a twenty-four hour day back on Earth, but it wasn't broken down into any smaller increments he had been able to make sense of. Still, if he started his stopwatch when he first woke up, it gave him a sense of where he was over the course of the work 'day', which lasted just about fourteen hours.

"Administrator?" Bha repeated, waving at the pale wall.

Marcus hated when she called him that. He tried to remind himself that any attempt to read meaning in subtle changes in tone or inflection were depending on the nano-bugs in his head, but it was Human nature, and he thought he was getting pretty good at it. And Iphini Bha definitely sounded insincere whenever she used his title.

He nodded. "Sure. Might as well see what's waiting for us today."

He didn't wait for her to do it. As he said the words he looked at the wall with one upturned eyebrow. The wall became transparent at once, and the deputy snorted through her delicate nose, her eyes shifting back to that inward stare.

He had been making steady improvements in his work with the medallion they called the Skorahn, anyway. He was almost never surprised by doors opening for him, lights coming on as he approached or going out as he left a room. Everyone, especially Bha, still seemed surprised at the level of control he was gaining over his environment, but he didn't much care. His work with the delicate necklace was the only thing he had been doing that had met with *any* success at all.

He had tried to get in touch with Justin several times, but his friend seemed to be quite busy with some project of his own. He had spent days trying to dig deeper into the anti-Human prejudice he found still clinging to his treatment from most of the denizens of Penumbra, but again, with no success. The bias seemed to be so deep, coming from so far back in time, that any actual events that might have triggered it were not to be found. It was an assumed value in almost anything he came across. Humans were evil, dangerous, and vile. It was a truism, and explaining why didn't seem to be overly important to any of the sources he had found so far.

A sharp knock from the room's rear door made him jump to his feet. He hadn't heard anyone knock on a door since he had first arrived. He shot Bha a glance, but she shrugged, standing slowly, watching the door with a strange look on her marbled face.

Marcus moved to the door and waved it open.

Justin stood on the other side in his galactic finery. It was unsettling to see those blank white eyes where the expressive dark irises used to be, and the bright orange-red beard was jarring. But it was still his friend, and the only Human within God alone knew how far.

"Where the hell have you been?" Marcus snapped, abandoning the calm he had promised himself he would exhibit when this moment finally came.

Justin blinked, his smile fading. Then he shrugged, strange eyes narrowing, and he folded his arms. "What the hell do you care? I figured you'd be far too busy changing the galaxy."

Justin pushed past him and went into the room. "Look, I'm sorry I haven't been by. You looked like you were dealing with things just fine on your own." He shot him a look. "Last time, you were hardly yourself. I haven't heard you sound like that in years." He shrugged again, turning to the wall and watching as the multiform citizens of Penumbra took their seats. There were markedly fewer of them than there had been at the first gathering.

"What?" Marcus turned away from the door and let it slide shut behind him. "What the hell are you talking about?"

Justin didn't turn around. "You know what I'm talking about. You could have been channeling your father up there with that speech." He shot his friend a sidelong glance. "You were never much fun to hang out with back then, when you were dancing to your father's tune. You know that, right? I much prefer the Marcus Wells that is his own man, not his father's stooge. Alex and Liz always did better at that role anyway."

Marcus remembered those years, long ago. His father's expectations had always been high. And living in a military family, in *his* military family in particular, there were certain things that were expected of Colonel Wells's offspring. Meanwhile, he had watched his childhood friend, attending the much more relaxed local public school, growing up at a far more normal pace, and having a lot more fun. It had all led to the cataclysmic battle that had essentially ended his relationship with his father and begun what now seemed like a long succession of easy, expedient choices. He had won a great victory, and then immediately surrendered the trophy.

Standing up to his father that day had been the last real stand he'd ever made.

Marcus sat down, desperation and fear threatening to choke him.

"Something's wrong, Justin." He muttered the words quietly, shooting a quick glance at Iphini Bha, who pretended to be gazing out the translucent wall. His friend looked down at him, his mouth still tight, his strange eyes inscrutable. Marcus tapped on his temple. "Something's wrong up here."

With his irises completely occluded by the white lenses, it was impossible to tell where Justin was looking. Somehow, however, he managed to convey a dramatic rolling of his eyes.

"What does that even mean?"

Marcus sat back. "Something happened back on Angara's ship, when she first gave us that nano-drink? I had a ... well, some kind of hallucination, I think; or an episode." He shook his head as the words failed him. "I saw something."

Justin laughed and dropped into another chair. "I saw something too, Marc. I saw all kinds of screwed up shit! Our brains were being deep-fried as the little buggers were changing all sorts of things up there! It was just a delusion. No big deal. You're fine now, I'm sure."

Marcus shook his head again. "No, I'm not. It's happened since then, too. I feel like someone is looking out through my eyes, making observations and conclusions without me."

Justin's white eyes narrowed. "Someone like *who*?" He finally looked concerned. "You mean, something to do with the nanite-enhancements?"

Marcus leaned forward, elbows on knees, and settled his forehead into his palms. "No. I don't think so, anyway." He looked up, meeting his friend's strange gaze. "It's me. But it's ... a different version of me. It's me from back then," he titled his head, feeling sheepish after Justin's initial attack. "From back when I was more ..." He groped for words.

Justin found them. "Back when you were daddy's good little soldier?" He nodded. "Yeah, I told you, that's exactly what you sounded like."

"But that wasn't *me*!" Marcus insisted. "It was different, I wasn't in charge of my own body!"

Justin shook his head, waving one hand dismissively. "The stress we've both been subjected to is ridiculous, Marc. Hell, we're living in a city in space, filled with monsters who hate us. And if that's not enough, it all seems ready to fall apart around our ears."

His friend spun to face him. "It's you, Marc. It's all those parts of yourself you tried to disown years ago. Your brain is playing some sort of weird mind game on you, and that makes sense." He reached out and grasped Marcus's shoulder quickly before sitting back. "It's all you, man. You're going to be fine."

Marcus was not convinced, but it felt good just having spoken of it. He nodded, not wanting to spend this brief moment with his friend fighting about his own psychosis.

An awkward silence stretched on for a moment, and then Marcus cleared his throat. "So, thanks for coming by." He waved at his friend's outfit. "You look like you're doing well."

Justin grinned, looking down at his colorful tunic. "Not bad." He shrugged. "Folks are folks. Find out what one person wants, but can't get, go find it, tie it to what another person wants, but can't get. Usually, within three or four removes, you've made several people happy, and if you're not an idiot, you've made a nice profit."

Marcus got up, shaking his head. Justin would always land on his feet, no matter where he landed. "Well, good for you, anyway." He moved to the wall and looked out. The two figures in their robes, one black and one white, were in their customary places. They had become one of the few constants in these meetings; them, and the steady decrease in other attendees.

"I assume you hear things, in all that running around you've been doing?"

Justin came up beside him, nodding. "Yeah. One of the main reasons I started."

"Well, that and it's in your blood." Marcus smiled, and then indicated the two Thien'ha with his chin. "Learn anything about them?"

Justin peered through the wall at the two figures for a moment, and then shrugged. "Not that much, I'm afraid. They wander around a lot. I haven't had a lot of luck digging into their religion, or philosophy, or whatever. Those things seem a lot more jumbled up here than back home. I think their particular area of interest and belief is in moments of transition and testing. The concept of cycles, and beginnings and endings, figures prominently in what I *have* been able to find. So they show up during periods of upheaval and difficulty. Gives them sort of a storm-crow reputation, you know what I mean?"

"Pretty standard stuff, I guess." Marcus nodded. "Do they cause the upheaval, or are they there to help people?"

"The Thien'ha do not help or hinder." Iphini Bha said from her chair, her eyes fixed on her pen. "Their order believes that entropy is a trial, provided by the universe to test all creatures. They worship the larger cycles of life, the spheres within which sentience travels in its progress through the ages. Thien'ha, in particular those of the Hoabin discipline, seek to observe these transitional moments to see what they may reveal about the sentient condition."

Marcus shared a glance with Justin, and then looked back at his usually-reticent deputy. "Are they common? You seem very familiar with their beliefs."

She shrugged, staring down at her hands. "The Thien'ha are masters of dealing with pain and loss. An initiate into their mysteries is said not to experience the cruel buffets of fate. There was a time I craved such a thing."

Marcus looked at Justin again, and his friend raised an eyebrow, turning to look back to the larger chamber beyond. "Well, from everything I've heard, they've come to the right place for some upheaval."

They watched the sparse crowd for a moment in silence when Marcus said, "Ambassador Taurani has not yet made his appearance." Bile rose in his throat at the thought.

Justin's smile at that seemed a little out of place. "Taurani comes to your little shindigs?"

Marcus nodded sourly. "Never missed a one. He sits right up front, with that long-necked freak of an assistant standing behind him, gets up just as I start to talk, denounces me in the name of the Galactic Council, and then storms out." He smiled wryly. "It's one of the few points of normalcy in my schedule, lately."

Justin shook his head. "I don't get it. I don't get how the Council could have *any* power in a society like this. Why do these people even care what he thinks?"

Marcus looked back at Iphini. "Any enlightenment you can offer? What's the Galactic Council all about? I feel like I've been running or hiding from them since I first met Angara, but I've had other things on my mind. Angara seems to think they're the bad guys. Are they evil?" His mouth twisted. "That last one sort of answers itself, considering they've chosen Taurani as their envoy here."

Iphini Bha looked up at him with unblinking eyes, then looked away. "Ambassador Khuboda Taurani is a well-respected, powerful servant of the Council. They are not evil, their concern is for all beings in the galaxy. It is a view easily confused with callous disregard for the minority."

Justin snorted. "We've heard that kind of bullshit before. How do they do that, by keeping them in chains where they can be safely contained? Human history's got a few examples of groups that had similar goals."

Bha rose up, her huge bald head swinging back and forth. "No! The Council controls the larger polities, stewarding the resources of the galaxy so that they can be best used for the betterment of all. And do *not* compare the Council with anything you debased beasts have grunted into existence back on your pathetic little prison-planet!"

Marcus's eyes widened. She had never shown such heat before. Justin's eyes narrowed. "Makes me wonder why you'd be working against them, Iphini. If they're so great, why help Churchill here to stick a thumb in their eye?" He jerked a thumb in Marcus's direction.

Iphini stared at the black-skinned man for a moment then turned away. "I do not work for or against them. I merely state a reality. The Council manages the resources of the galaxy. Most beneath their rule are entirely content with things as they stand."

Justin looked incredulous. "So, every race in the galaxy lets this Council dictate everything? How does something like that happen?"

She shrugged, but Marcus had the impression she was getting uncomfortable. He waved a hand, frustrated. "It is all ancient history now, anyway. The Galactic Council has ruled since before Jesus wore knickers, from what I've been able to find." Seeing Bha continue to squirm, Marcus felt a stirring of pity. He turned to his friend to change the subject. "So, what sorts of wheelings and dealings are you bringing to bear as you build your little trade empire?"

But Justin's curiosity was piqued, and he wasn't about to set things aside as readily as Marcus often did. He continued to stare at the small alien woman. "No, I'm confused. How does a galaxy-spanning empire like you describe form and maintain its power for thousands of years? Someone would have risen up, surely?"

"Why would anyone throw away ages of peace and prosperity only to dominate others? What do you think we are, *Humans*?" She spat back at him. "Every race in the galaxy has an equal say in the governing of the Council. And meeting together, they agree on every aspect of Galactic life."

"So, there's no powerful nation, or planet, or whatever, ruling over the weaker ones?" His skepticism was obvious to Marcus.

"Each race, or system, receives a single vote. There are more aggressive races, to be sure. The Variyar come to mind. But their single vote is overwhelmed by the smaller, more enlightened polities."

"And so the Variyar just let themselves be outvoted? To their own loss?" He shook his head.

"I would not expect a *Human* to understand the concept of the greater good." She spat back at him, moving to the door. "Administrator, if you've no further need of me?"

"Wait!" Marcus had conducted one session without Iphini behind him, and it had been a disaster. "He'll shut up. We're done with that topic." He turned to Justin, who was still fuming. "We're done, right?"

His friend shrugged, his mouth a tight line. "Whatever, man."

She stood by the door, looked from one man to the other, and then nodded. "Very well. It is almost time to begin, anyway." She gestured toward the transparent wall, and as Marcus turned to look, he nearly jumped. The room beyond was almost full, holding far more creatures than it had since his first session. There seemed to be an energy whispering through the crowd that had not been there before.

"There's a lot of people out there." He muttered under his breath. "They seem a lot more engaged than usual."

Justin smiled. "I might have had a word with a few of my friends. This session should go a little smoother than the last few. I've also got it on good authority that Ambassador Taurani might be delayed today."

His friend stepped up beside him and slapped him on the back. "Go be your best self, Marc." His smile was wide. "Don't worry about where it's coming from. If we're going to both get out of this in one piece, you're going to have to get over it and just do the job."

*****

Marcus found himself once again behind the podium in the grand chamber of the ancient Mhatrong. The crowd was restless, and he felt the old nerves rising again. Maybe, if he got so worked up he was going to vomit, that old version of himself would resurface again?

He actually contemplated bending behind the podium and jamming a finger down his throat. The thought made him smile, and he felt something loosen in his chest. He could do this. Also, without Taurani glaring at him, he thought he might actually be able to get through the entire meeting without sweating through his tunic.

In a few brief moments that sped past, Marcus opened the assembly and reiterated his intention to step down as soon as a replacement could be found. He also offered a quick report upon the business of the city as proof that a Human in the command throne had not brought immediate Armageddon down upon Penumbra. He then carefully made his case for solidarity against the Galactic Council. Over the past few sessions, these moments had been met with a smattering of catcalls and dark looks. This time, much like the first session, there was silence, and he saw several heads nodding along with his words.

Marcus cleared his throat after he finished formally opening the session. He cast his eyes over the sentients arrayed in the first few rows. They appeared to be waiting for something.

He cleared his throat again, and then, gripping the podium with both hands, looked out over the waiting crowd. He tried to push all the sincerity he felt for his newfound crusade out over them, to bring them to his side.

"Tradition confers upon me the power now to offer any being a hearing who wishes to beg for the assistance of the city. This tradition has not been exercised in a very long time, but please believe that I extend the offer now with only the most genuine hope in my heart that we might work together to fully realize the dream that first established Penumbra in the lost and distant past." He looked around, hoping for any sign that anyone might come forward this time, to help him take the next step. "Is there any sentient here who might benefit from the power of Penumbra?"

An expectant silence settled down over the chamber. It was as it had been every other time he had extended this offer. The room was still, eyes sliding quietly from side to side as everyone waited to see if someone would stand.

Marcus closed his eyes, his head lowered. He was almost relieved. He wasn't entirely sure what he would do if someone *did* step up at this point.

And then he heard someone cough. Looking up, he saw a man making his slow way toward the dais, a wary look on his jaundiced face.

The man was a Diakk, yet another of the Children. Marcus had seen several Diakks in his wanderings since coming to Penumbra, but had learned almost nothing about them. The hooded figure accompanying the Thien'ha master was a Diakk, he believed, but that was the only one he remembered seeing on a regular basis.

The markings or scales on this man's face ran between his eyes and down his nose, and then reemerged on his chin, similar to Marcus's goatee. His hands were curling in upon themselves, and he looked as if he thought the crowd was going to rush him from behind.

Marcus dismissed the podium with a thought. He hadn't even known he could do that! He looked down at the dais at his feet, his brow wrinkled, and the surface of the raised platform shifted, carrying him down with it, to create a sort of semi-circular bench that would allow him to sit at floor level.

He waved to one arm of the curving seat with what he hoped was a reassuring smile. "Please, join me." Now that he actually had a supplicant before him, he had no idea how to proceed.

The pale-skinned man nodded, looking to either side, and then lowered himself to the hard surface. He perched on the very edge of the seat, looking like he might bolt at any moment.

Marcus had to remind himself that Humans had a terrible reputation here in the wider galaxy. This man was not seeing a mild-mannered salesman sitting before him, or even the administrator of the city. He was probably seeing some horrible monster that might be expected to cut him down without a moment's thought.

Not for the first time, Marcus cursed the barrier that separated him from everyone else who lived here. How was he supposed to do this job, even briefly, when he was hated and feared by the very people he wanted to help?

But that was for another time. Right now, he needed to treat this man with respect, and see that he didn't run away at the first opportunity.
"What's your name?" He tried to sound natural, feeling anything but.

The Diakk man looked at him through eyes that twitched to narrow slits.

"I am Copic Fa'Orin." His voice was soft. There was something going on in those eyes, however, that put some steel into his spine, and he sat up straighter.

Marcus nodded encouragingly. He started to reach out his hand, but thought better of it as Copic Fa'Orin flinched away. "I am honored to meet you, Copic Fa'Orin." He inclined his head slowly, trying to avoid sharp movements. "What can Penumbra do to help you?"

Again, the man cast a quick glance behind him, shoulders hunched. When he spoke next, his voice was so soft Marcus could barely make out the words.

"My son is very sick." Saying it seemed to give the man strength, and he straightened again. "My son is ill. I cannot secure his treatment alone." He looked directly at Marcus for the first time, his dark eyes flashing. "I need your help."

Marcus pursed his lips. This was exactly the kind of thing he had been hoping for, except he had no idea how he might be able to help this man. He gestured for the Diakk to continue, hoping that something would come to him, or that that cold, calculating part of his mind would reemerge.

Copic Fa'Orin took a deep breath. His eyes slid away from Marcus's face and seemed to be focused somewhere else. "My son suffers from a rare genetic disorder indigenous to Varra, our homeworld. There is only one known remedy, but my petitions to the local Council legates were all rejected." His mouth twisted with a bitter snarl. "There are too many Diakk on Varra, it appears, and the treatment, in short supply, was needed for citizens of less well-represented stock." The fire in his eyes built, and his fists clenched. "I was told, to my face, that my boy represented excess population, and thus vital resources could not be *wasted* … wasted, for his benefit."

A cold pit opened up in Marcus's gut. He could not even begin to imagine the horror this man had experienced. But at the same time, he didn't know what he was supposed to do about it. He had intended to defy the Council, yes. But he had no power to force them to do anything, either.

The Diakk man must have seen that in his face, because he shook his head and continued. "There is a consortium operating out of Penumbra with the necessary equipment to treat my son, but I cannot pay their fees. Without those credits, they do not have the power allocation to prepare the therapy."

The man's words faded away, but Marcus continued to stare at him, his brain refusing to provide a solution. He needed time to think. He needed to stall long enough for something to come to his mind. He could sense this opportunity slipping away, and he could not let that happen.

"Which consortium has such facilities, Copic Fa'Orin?" He tried a smile and a self-deprecating shrug. "I'm new around here. I wasn't aware of such advanced work being conducted in the city."

"It is a consortium of Namanu, Administrator. The Sama Collective, working along the left wing of the city." Both the Red Tower and the Mhatrong survey ship that housed the Central Council Chamber were located within the right wing of Penumbra. He had no familiarity with the left wing at all.

Marcus nodded. Something about the name had struck a chord in the back of his mind. He thought, if only he could stall for a little longer, he might be able to build on that note. "And the Sama Collective demands credits for the procedure?" He heard someone in the vast hall cough and looked up quickly. He had almost forgotten there was a crowd watching the two of them. The weight on his shoulders pressed down even harder.

The man looked down at his intertwined hands. Marcus saw there were plates or markings on their backs, like those on the man's face. "We have tried to come to an agreement, but it is ultimately the power allocation. This treatment will fall beyond their current provision agreement, and so they will need to compensate another party for the use of their power."

The Sama Collective. The more he repeated it in his mind, the more he felt he should know where he had seen it before. He had done some extensive research in his quarters of the major players within the city. He also saw countless reports cross the big desk in the administrator's office every day.

Marcus nodded, settling back into the low bench as his hands fell to rest on his thighs. He had it. The Sama Collective had been requesting preferred trading status with the administrator's office since before Marcus's arrival. He knew that many of the business consortia in the city contested with each other for preferential status. It had been one of the primary sources of Uduta Virri's additional incomes. He remembered, now, seeing the Sama Collective on one of those reports.

But his office had no way to provide more power. The power inexplicably provided by the Relic Core of Penumbra was vast, and more than enough for the basic needs of its citizens. But many of the collectives, enclaves, and conglomerates needed more, and those needs were negotiated among the citizens themselves.

His eyes narrowed. He remembered another syndicate that had been requesting an expansion of facilities. Territory was finite in Penumbra; there had been no more ships added to the unwieldy mix for over a thousand years. Much like the power allocation, such agreements were concluded primarily by the parties directly involved, under the auspices of his office. Bribes for quick or advantageous conclusions had been another revenue stream for the unlamented former administrator.

He tried to remember why that particular group had suddenly come to mind. There had been more in their file. Their portfolio on offer was public knowledge. Something in that file … He looked up, his eyes flashing, his teeth gleaming.

Marcus shot off the bench and wagged a finger at Copic Fa'Orin. "Wait a moment, sir."

He hoped back up onto the upper level of the dais and waved to the small door in the back. Iphini Bha came through, looking uncomfortable, glancing from side to side. The entire hall hushed as the citizens of Penumbra watched the events unfold.

"Iphini, am I right in remembering that there was a Kot'i consortium, the Kopi'Ba, or something, looking to establish themselves in one of the lower towers of the right wing?" She nodded, her brows coming down. "And part of their portfolio on offer was an excess energy allotment?" Again, she nodded. He saw her eyes turn speculative. She had been paying careful attention through the transparent wall.

Marcus smiled and began to pace, throwing a quick, thankful glance at the wall, figuring Justin was probably still there, watching.

"And am I remembering correctly that a Matabessi delegation, newly established on the Concourse of the right wing, has been applying for trade concessions through our office?"

The pale little woman nodded again. "The Kesatuan Manufactorum." Her eyes began to gleam, caught up in the excitement of the moment as her mind began to put the pieces together. "They are said to have territory in excess of their current needs."

Marcus snapped his fingers and spun toward the low bench, where the pale Diakk man looked up at him in confusion. "It's really very simple." It was, in a way, but most puzzles were simple when all the pieces had already come together. And if there was one thing the administrator's office had in plenty, it was puzzle pieces.

"The administrator's office of Penumbra will grant trade concessions to the Kesatuan Manufactorum in exchange for the extra territory of their current facility. We will also reach out to the Sama Collective, offering preferred status." A flickering light appeared within Fa'Orin's eyes. "The territory will be granted to the Kopi'Ba in exchange for their excess energy allocation." He wanted to raise his arms in a final flourish, but he controlled himself. "And this allocation, along with the aforementioned preferred status, should be more than sufficient to allow the Sama to perform the procedure your son requires to grant him a long and healthy life, Copic Fa'Orin."

Marcus finished, almost panting with his excitement and exertion, looking down at the father expectantly.

Copic Fa'Orin, his eyes widening, looked up at him in growing disbelief. He had come believing that only a miracle could save his son, and through some creative bureaucratic wrangling, Marcus had delivered that miracle.

The pale man stumbled to his feet, reaching up with both of his hands, and grasped Marcus's. He felt awkward, with the man below him, looking up with such gratitude. "You have saved my son's life, Administrator." The weight and conviction behind the words hit him like a punch to the gut, and he wanted to shake his head. He hadn't done anything; it was all sleight of hand. But at the same time, it was exactly the kind of thing he had *wanted* to do.

Low murmurs rippled through the hall, and Marcus could not help but feel a rush of warmth as he realized he had done it.

"Congratulations, Administrator." The sour tone of the words was like cold water across his back. Marcus looked down to find that Ambassador Taurani had arrived at last. The pale gray flesh set off the ivory robes in a mildly-distasteful way, and the glittering metallic orbs of the Kerie's eyes seemed to bore into his mind. The rigid flesh of the creature's face was not overly expressive. Nevertheless, there was no doubting the disgust radiating from the tall, regal form.

"Congratulations." He repeated, and Marcus was alarmed by the note of sincerity in the voice. "The machines and processes of these consortia will now be used to save a child. I am truly glad that the Diakk boy will live." He turned to address the crowd, rising in their places to better see the confrontation. "But if you believe this moment to be an indictment of the wisdom of the Galactic Council, you are most sorely mistaken!

"We live in a galaxy with finite resources." It was clear he was speaking to the chamber full of sentients watching intently and with an eye toward the rumors that would push his words far beyond the walls of the chamber. "Those resources must be marshaled in a way that is fair and equitable to all. And who will decide that distribution? Will these decisions of life and death fall to those pure chance has granted with the most resources? The most wealth? Would you trust these decisions in the hands of those in authority here, that gained their authority through nothing but blind luck?"

He whirled around, addressing the entire room with a dramatic flourish. "The Galactic Council hears all pleas, and weighs all lives. The Council speaks with the collective voice of every race and system in the galaxy. And the Council will not stand by to watch as the weak are ignored and crushed beneath the weight of the mighty." Those eyes turned like weapon turrets toward Marcus. "We will not abide such wanton, indiscriminate evil to be perpetuated on citizens of the wider galaxy."

"How dare you!" The father spun on the ambassador, jabbing a finger at the creature's chest. Two Ntja guards lumbered down an aisle toward them both, and Marcus hopped down and ran to the Diakk man, pulling him back by a shoulder. He shot a look at Iphini, still up on the dais, but she gave a sharp shake of her head. She would be no help against the ambassador.

"We're merely doing the best we can with what the galaxy has handed us, Ambassador. This man's son is dying, and now he will live." Marcus was trying to sound reasonable, but a combination of anger and fear colored his words.

Taurani scoffed, puffing air through his baleen, and put his long hands on his hips. He surveyed the crowd around him, and Marcus saw an echo of something in those metallic eyes. The ambassador felt the uncertainty of the moment as well.

"You have done a fine thing here today, saving the life of this innocent child. But know this: such petty disregard for the greater good may well succeed in a dissipated microcosm like this, for a time at least. But to think that such behavior could be sustainable throughout civilized space is a farce of epic proportions. The Council guards the well-being of *every* race, no matter where they might be, or what their circumstances. In the end, the life of this child will not matter to the galaxy at large, or to the Council."

The ambassador swept up the aisle and away, and Marcus found himself sharply expelling a breath he had had no idea he was holding.

Between them, Marcus and Iphini reassured Copic Fa'Orin that his son was safe, and then dismissed the crowd. It was obvious they all had a great deal to think about as they wandered away, many looking back to the dais where the Iwa'Bantu woman, the Diakk man, and the Human stood together, talking quietly.

Justin had slipped through the small door and made his way out with the rest of the crowd, but not before tipping an imaginary hat to Marcus, and promising that he would stay in touch.

Iphini had gone back to gather their things in the preparation room, while Marcus had used the medallion to dismiss the seat on the apron of the dais and raise the podium back into place. As he waited for her, sitting on the edge of the platform, he thought back to the moment when he had seen the fear in Taurani's eyes.

The Ambassador knew what Marcus had done. Taurani had seen the Council's grasp called into question. He had seen their influence, and the sanctity of their cause, brought into doubt. Marcus couldn't help but smile at the thought. He liked the idea of Taurani feeling uncomfortable.

Then his smile slipped. If the Council envoy really was getting scared, what might he do next?

When Iphini Bha emerged to escort him back to the Red Tower, Marcus's brow was furrowed and his smile was gone.

# Chapter 14

The halls of the tower that had once been a Mhatrong generation ship were wide, with evenly-spaced support columns of a polished material that reminded Iphini Bha of the ancient stone temples of Iwa'Ban. She paced beside Marcus Wells in silence, the confrontation between the Human and Ambassador Taurani churning through her mind.

Marcus Wells was also silent as they paced down the well-lit corridor to the Administrative docking port.

She had not expected that the Human would be so versed in the various factions and entities struggling within Penumbra. He had clearly put his hours of imprisonment to good use. The way he had traced the needs and assets of the necessary consortia to bring the Diakk man's son treatment had been most artful.

And yet, Taurani's argument had hit deeply as well. If it had not been for the Council, it was doubtful Iwa'Ban would have been able to recover from the attack that had nearly destroyed it. The attack by a *Human* fleet, she remembered bitterly. The resources that had dragged her homeworld back from the brink of annihilation had been allocated to them undoubtedly at the expense of other worlds and peoples.

She felt her brows draw down as she struggled with the conflicted thoughts.

"Wait." Marcus stopped, touching her shoulder lightly. "I don't want to go back yet."

She looked at him wordlessly. There was a great deal for her to do back in the control center. The last thing she wanted to do was spend more time with this confusing, frustrating Human.

"I want to go *somewhere*, to do something, *see* something *different*." He fingered the medallion hanging around his neck. She noticed that that floating lines over the central gemstone had become clearer. She could not decipher anything legible there, but they were certainly more defined. "I'm going insane, cooped up in that apartment. I need to get out of my comfort zone a little bit." He smiled at her with one of his lopsided expressions. "As comfortable as I've been, anyway."

She continued to stare at him. She had no idea what he was talking about. Different?

Marcus shook his head. "What's the oldest section of the city? Where are the first ships that landed here?"

She thought for a moment. "There have been several periods of disruption in the city's history. The earliest records were lost, or erased, millennia ago. But by conventional agreement, a ship we call Sanctum is considered to be the oldest location in the city. You probably saw it upon your approach. It lies in the middle of the Bronze Plain, at the center of the city."

He smiled. "That sounds exactly like the kind of place I'd like to go!" The smile faded slightly. "Could you take me there?"

She fought back a sigh. Why could he not find his own way by now? But she had been forced to do much worse for Virri. Of course, Virri had not been a

*Human.*

"Briefly." She forced an edge of firmness into her voice. "There are still duties we both need to perform today."

A light kindled in his eyes, and she forced down the moment of responding warmth it caused. She gestured forward. "We must still take the shuttle. There is no other route."

He nodded and moved off down the corridor with a lighter step than he had had since leaving the Council Chamber.

They had not gone far when two figures stepped from a lift tube alcove, robes swirling about them; the Thein'ha. Although they had attended every levy, she had not seen them outside the walls of the chamber.

The shorter figure in white robes, its soft green jaw fringe swaying back and forth, nodded to Marcus with a slight smile on its muzzle. The taller figure in black was a woman, and Iphini saw now that she was a Diakk, recognizing the black splash of markings across her cheeks and around her thin, set lips. She did not nod, but stared at Marcus with cold, dark eyes.

The pair had moved past them before the Human could react to their presence. He followed their passage with a craning neck. They moved off down the corridor and were soon lost at an intersection in the distance.

"Why do I feel like those two are following me?" He mused aloud, but did not seem overly concerned.

Iphini sniffed. "The Thien'ha have no particular interest in Humans, or in the leadership of the city. I would not expect that they care anymore for you than for any other being in Penumbra."

He didn't seem to agree, but let it go.

The Administrative shuttle was a small, utilitarian craft that might have fit ten additional beings if they were friendly. Iphini interfaced with the autopilot and requested passage to Sanctum at the fastest safe speed. She settled down into a seat that rose up to embrace her, and closed her eyes as she accessed her working files. Maybe he would leave her alone to get some work done while they were in transit, anyway.

Apparently it was not to be.

"Damn!" he breathed the word.

She opened her eyes to see him standing in front of a viewing field on the left flank of the shuttle. A quick glance showed her the exterior of the Mhatrong generation ship floating away behind them, as the shuttle moved off into the thicket of up-thrust ships.

Most of the ships were cylindrical, reaching up above them and glittering in the cold light of vacuum. A causeway bridging two towers sailed overhead, throwing a stark shadow across the shuttle before passing off into their wake.

She tried to see the view through the Human's eyes. It resembled countless cities she had seen, including several forbidden images from Earth. But she had to admit that the wide variety of shapes and colors, with the graceful spans connecting them in a dizzying, crisscrossed pattern, gave Penumbra a beauty all its own. She also knew that to many beings, the diversity of the jumble of ships was even more beautiful for what it represented: the history and efforts of countless races coming together in a common cause.

Something about that thought narrowed her eyes. It sounded very much like something the Council might tout as a great success. And yet, the Council and the city were forever at odds.

She had never really cared about that side of the city's spirit. She had come here looking for a new life, not running from her old one. But she knew many who had more than a passing nostalgia for that image of Penumbra.

"How goes the search?" Marcus Wells continued to look out the view field, his tone nonchalant.

She frowned. Her thoughts had been far away. "I'm sorry?"

He shrugged, still not looking at her. "The search for my replacement? I know you two haven't given up. That's where Angara's been spending most of her time recently, isn't it? Working with that dolphin, or looking for another one like him?"

Her answer was reflexive, without thought. "Warder Oo'juto is an Aijian, not a dolphin."

She could not see his face, but she knew he was smiling from his tone. "Same thing, though, right? Anyway, any luck with the Warder?"

In truth, she was not sure. Angara Ksaka was supposed to have been pursuing those negotiations vigorously, considering this entire foolish enterprise had been entirely her plan. But she had not seen the Tigan outcast for days. She tried a shrug of her own, trying to make her voice as indifferent as his. "She is continuing to work with Oo'juto." He had not turned them down flat, which was a good sign. But then, neither had he embraced their suggestion, either. His initial reaction seemed to have been closer to Iphini's own than to Angara's.

Marcus nodded, looking over his shoulder at her. He did, indeed, have a little smile on his face. "Well, as long as she's not dragging her feet." He turned back to where the city passed below them through the viewing field, and his voice turned wistful. "I could get used to this, if you don't get me out of here soon."

It was meant to be a joke, she assumed. But the thought sent a shiver down her back. What if the Human didn't want to leave? Exactly how much power did the Skorahn afford him, above and beyond what they knew to expect? It would have been hard enough to oust Uduta Virri if they had wanted to, and it appeared now that he had not even been marginally attuned to the medallion.

The old discomforts arose again. She could not believe she was in a shuttle, alone, with a *Human*. No one needed to tell *her* about Humans. She did not need a history book to remind her what they were capable of. She only needed to close her eyes and remember the scars stretching across the surface of Iwa'Ban. In fact, since Marcus Wells and his friend and been dragged into her office, she did not even need to do that. The old dreams had come back with a vengeance, and every night as she slept, she wandered the ravaged cities and burnt plains of her homeworld.

"Where is Sanctum?" Marcus Wells turned to look down at her, breaking unknowing, into her dark reverie. "Right or left wing? Top or bottom?"

He had spent a great deal of time familiarizing himself with the city, but the new administrator occasionally showed his ignorance in the strangest ways. "Not top or bottom. We refer to the right and left wing, correct, oriented by looking out over the Furnace and the Gulf. The portions of the city pointing 'up' or 'down' from the Relic Core are designated as the high city and the low city, using the planet below as a reference."

He nodded, his eyes fading out of focus as he committed the information to memory. Sometimes he was obviously frustrated when he made such an error, but he never acted hurt or annoyed when she corrected him, only grateful for the help. It was another thing that differentiated him from his predecessor.

His smile returned as his eyes concentrated on her once more. "So, where is Sanctum? Left or right? High or low?"

For a moment, she almost smiled back. Then, with a chill, recoiled from the moment, retreating into the cool professionalism that might keep him at a distance. "Sanctum is located upon the very center of the Relic Core, overlooking the Gulf."

He nodded. "Makes sense. You're landing on some strange artifact, you land on the top; or, at least the top as dictated by the artifact's current orientation. Whose ship was it?"

She shook her head, settling back into the seat. "No one knows. It doesn't follow any of the standard patterns of known species. Its origins obviously stretch before the Great War, but no race has ever successfully claimed it as their own. It has become as close to public property as Penumbra gets, really. Sanctum and the Concourse."

He nodded and moved back to the viewing field. Beneath them, the raised surface of the Concourse fell away as the Ring Wall passed below, revealing a dark, pitted surface. Ahead of them crouched a squat bronze structure, all alone on the dark bronze-colored field.

"Is that it?" He asked, and she nodded. "It's not connected to anything else?"

She rose to stand beside him. "It is not. The only way to reach Sanctum is by shuttle or walking across the Bronze Plain with protective gear."

He made a buzzing noise with his mouth and turned back to the view below. Sanctum rose up to meet them, lights flashing into brilliant dots of illumination at their approach. It had been a long, low-slung ship; the forward section was a huge swollen dome of paned crystal several stories tall.

The shuttle had chosen a primary docking port, and as they sailed in through the wide bay, the chamber snapped into bright life to receive them.

As the shuttle settled into a landing cradle, the wide side door opened automatically, and she moved down the integrated stairway. "The observation hall is this way," she gestured at two massive blast doors off to their right. "That is probably as close to 'new' and 'different' as Penumbra can come."

The burnished material of the ship gave the corridors a heavy sense of ancient times. The architecture was soft and flowing, with very few straight lines or right angles anywhere to be seen. The lights snapped on at their approach with an alacrity she had come to expect from her experiences escorting Marcus Wells. The Skorahn had never served Uduta Virri so well, but it seemed very eager to please its new, Human owner. It made her vaguely uneasy when she thought about it.

Current thinking in Penumbra agreed that the observation hall was probably the bridge of the ancient ship; a vast oval space, a terraced floor oriented toward the vast array of crystalline windows, actual openings into space rather than viewing fields or screens. The enormous panels began high overhead and reached down to the lowest level far below them, and to either side more than half way around the space. The bronze surface of the Relic Core could be seen stretching out around them, and then abruptly diving down into the Gulf beyond. The wings of the city swept out past them to the right and left, vaguely lit by the fiery sapphire illumination of the power source, known as the Furnace, far below.

Marcus Wells was speechless as he moved out into the middle of the wide space, staring out over the void above them. He moved past the small, silent islands that had probably been the various command stations of the ancient ship. The entire thing looked more like a temple or some other sacred place now, but with a little imagination, one could easily see a living, breathing command bridge stretching out around them.

The Human stood staring out into space for some time, and then turned to her, a slight smile twisting his lips upward. "Yeah, this is exactly the kind of place I meant." He looked around. His eyes found the recessed area known as the Alcove. Everyone noticed it eventually.

The most popular theories concerning Sanctum focused on the interface between the material of the ancient ship and the surface of the Relic Core. The massive opening in the ship's decking might once have been an airlock or docking connection point, using energy fields to keep the vacuum out. But when the ship had first landed, it had been pressed up against the surface of the Core, in the only place on the entire artifact where there was an identifiable point of entrance. The dark features of Sanctum gave way, in a circular hole, to the eroded bronze of the Relic Core itself. The two surfaces existed here side by side. Within the center of the revealed section the metallic surface formed a ramp heading down into a depression that ended in a broad, featureless wall of smooth, glassy blackness.

Marcus nodded at the wall. "Is that what I think it is?"

Iphini followed his eyes. "An entrance to the Relic Core? Most think so."

He peered down into the shadows. "There are no wires, or cables, or anything. How does power move from the core into the ship?" He looked back up at her. "Or any of the other parts of the city, for that matter?"

She frowned. She had almost no idea how Penumbra worked. No one did. She had only been to Sanctum a handful of times, escorting Virri on one of his disgusting little jaunts. And yet for some reason, she was loath to answer the Human. It felt too much like offering assistance to the enemy. She was going to have to control these reactions, she knew, if she wanted to last until they convinced someone to replace him.

She looked down at him, forcing herself to meet his dark gaze. "The best guess is through mere contact with the surface. There is very little understanding as to how it actually works, however."

He looked skeptical. "Water? Air? It all just passes through contact? And where does it come from? It's not like those sorts of things can be easy to come by up here. And they can't just pass through solid metal."

She looked at him with flat eyes, and then gave a slight shake of her head. "There are reservoirs beneath the surface that we have access to. In fact, the crust of the Core is honeycombed with passages and storage chambers, all of which are supplied with air and water. The creators of Penumbra simply tapped into those areas for the needed substances. As for the energy, merely contacting the material of the Core, whether you choose to believe it or not, appears to be enough."

He nodded with a shrug, and turned back to the door, his head tilting curiously to the side. "How do you get in?"

She moved away. "You don't. At least, no one ever has."

The Human navigated his way down the steep ramp to stand before the high, lustrous sable wall. After a moment's hesitation, he put his hand upon the material as if communing with the ancient Relic. His head was cocked to one side as if he were listening to something only he could hear, and again she felt a little unnerved, seeing a Human in this place, behaving in such a way.

He looked back to her. "Why hasn't anyone tried to force it?"

She laughed. "In all the thousands of years, you think no sentient has lost their patience? Many attempts have been made." She pointed to dark splotches that marked the edges of the starship's floor around the black expanse. "No one has ever been able to claim any greater success than damage to Sanctum." She nodded back to the black wall. "They have not so much as blemished the Relic Core itself."

Marcus turned back to the wall, spreading both hands out, splayed across the shimmering surface. He stood that way for a very long time.

"Wow." The word was low, almost inaudible, and sent a frightened shiver down Iphini's back nonetheless.

Marcus Wells was somber when he finally turned away from the wall and made his careful way back up to her. He stood one last time in the center of the chamber, looking out over the Gulf, and then nodded to Iphini that he was ready to leave.

He was quiet as he followed her through the corridors, which fell into dark silence behind them as they passed. Back in the shuttle, he stood at the forward viewing field, one forearm resting on the bulkhead, head resting on his arm. He no longer paid any attention to the dizzying kaleidoscopic skyline as it slid below them.

Her disquiet grew.

*****

Marcus watched the improbable cityscape below without really seeing it. He was normally fascinated by the Escheresque geography, reaching out in all directions with no concession to such mundane qualities as up or down. But his hands still tingled with the remembered sensations of the smooth black wall, and he could still hear the soft, nearly inaudible whispers that had called to him in the ancient observation hall.

It was clear from the way Iphini had been acting that she didn't feel quite the same sense of awe the place had instilled in him. And he was fairly sure that the sounds, if they weren't hallucinations, were not reaching her either.

What they might mean, however, he couldn't figure. Coming off his seeming victory with the Diakk and his son, and then the confrontation with Taurani, he had been frazzled enough as it was. He had just wanted to distract himself for a little while. He had succeeded in that, for sure. The ancient ship and its observation hall, and the doorway into the Relic Core, whatever it was, opened up whole new vistas of mystery and confusion.

The shuttle slid silently into the executive docking port, and the big blast door snapped shut behind them. Iphini was waiting at the hatch as it opened, and led the way down and to the access door across the cold room.

"I shall take my leave here, Administrator, if you don't mind." She didn't turn to look at him as she moved through the door. He could not get a handle on the pale, hairless little woman. He had dated girls he would have categorized as running hot and cold, but Iphini Bha would have out played every one of them at that game.

"Certainly." He tried to be gracious, bowing slightly in her direction in the off chance that she could see him in her peripheral vision. "Thank you for taking me to Sanctum."

She nodded, glancing over her shoulder, her face blank. "Of course."

The corridor behind Iphini was well-lit despite the slightly ruddy cast to the illumination. It stretched away following that strange zig-zag pattern that all the halls in the Red Tower shared. He had been told it was a defensive measure, making boarding actions more difficult. And as each corner loomed up, heavy and reinforced with studded metal, he believed it.

Even with the heavy, metal architecture, however, shadows were not a common occurrence in the well-lit halls of what had once been a premier warship of a very warlike people.

But there was a strange shadow against the wall behind his reluctant deputy. It was incongruous, there in the well-lit passageway. His brows fell as he scanned the stretch, looking for something that might be blocking the direction-less light. There was nothing, and yet the shadow seemed to grow darker as he watched. If he focused on it, it faded away, but from the periphery of his vision, it was a brooding, physical presence.

Iphini Bha realized that he was not speaking, standing behind her staring off down the hall, and turned with an annoyed expression. The fine black lines that divided her pale features into small, irregular sections often made it hard to read her, but those big blue eyes made it a lot easier to tell when she was irritated.

"What—" She began, but cut off abruptly as his eyes widened in sudden fear.

The shadow leapt off the wall without warning and swirled down the corridor toward them. It moved like a swarm of insects, undulating through the air in an erratic pattern that seemed to fill the hall, but left no doubt as to its ultimate target: Iphini and her boss.

Marcus grabbed the girl's arm and tried to pull her with him down the hall, but she yanked away from him, her own eyes narrowing in fury, and stumbled backward. Backward into the rippling shadow.

As he felt her slip from his grasp, Marcus began to fall himself, away from her. He set his arms swinging in a pinwheel as he struggled to keep his feet beneath him, carrying him farther down the hall. He fetched up hard against one of the reinforced corners, the back of his head ringing against the steel, and watched in mounting horror as the shadow swept down over Iphini Bha.

And flowed right past her. As harmless as smoke, the cloud divided, puffed around the Iwa'Bantu woman and set her clothes rippling as if a stiff breeze had blown past.

Whatever it was, it cared nothing for Iphini. It continued to move directly at Marcus.

Iphini's eyes widened as she saw the shadowy form sweep around her, and felt her clothing ruffle in the ethereal wind. Her mouth opened, moving with the slow, deliberate pacing of a nightmare, and screamed a single word that meant nothing to him in his panic.

"Nanites!"

Marcus staggered backward, grasping at the wall behind him, and tried to flee. He tripped over his own feet, spinning and staggering several steps toward his rooms before falling to his knees on the hard, rubber-like floor. He flipped over, seeing the cloud rearing up above him, and raised one hand as if shielding himself from the bright light of the sun.

The cloud descended.

There was an explosion of heat over his chest and a bright, blinding light flooded the corridor. An electrical crackling sound exploded in his ears, and he tasted ash on his tongue.

Opening his eyes, the first thing Marcus saw was that the hallway was empty. There was no cloud of darkness engulfing him, hovering over him, or fleeing down the corridor. Iphini stood, her blue eyes wide, staring at him.

Marcus looked down at himself as he sat up. He was lying in the middle of a dark, amorphous stain. His tunic and trousers were dark, a layer of fine ash coating his entire body. He reached one gritty hand up to his face and drew a finger down over his cheek. It came away smudged with ash as well.

"What the hell." He muttered the words, and then spat gray gobbets onto the floor as the harsh, acrid taste registered. "What the *hell*!"

Iphini Bha took a couple tentative steps forward, staring at the fine layer of ash that had settled across him. "Offensive nanites. They're … they're illegal, even here." She looked up, casting a glance up and down the hall. "They can be programmed for a particular genetic code, and then they attack, tearing the target apart at a cellular level … there's almost no defense."

The heavy warmth on his chest was still there, and he looked down to find the medallion glowing with a single, unwavering spark deep within its sapphire depths. The lines floating within were sharper than they had ever been, and he started at the familiar surge of near-recognition.

The sharp slaps of running feet brought his head back up, and Iphini spun quickly in place, crouching as if ready to flee. Marcus scrambled up, brushing his hands across his chest and thighs. The dust cascaded into little drifts at his feet.

Two figures came running down the corridor, tearing around a corner not far away. One figure wore fluttering white robes, the other in flowing black: the Thien'ha.

The two figures fetched up in front of Iphini. The female Diakk in the black robes looked annoyed, her nose wrinkling beneath the scattering of markings. Beside her, the pale green fur of the creature in the white robe was luminous in the red-tinged corridor lighting, the white fringe of tendrils that swept up either side of its jawline and into the hood swayed with its slight panting. It seemed to be smiling. Clutched in one furry hand, a dull metal rod absorbed the light.

Marcus felt his eyes narrow, his nostrils flaring, as a snarl began to twist his lips. He pushed Iphini Bha roughly behind him, thrusting himself into the path of the two robed figures, and put one hand up to stop them from coming any further.

"We've got the situation well in hand, thank you." He kept his tone even, but suspicion tightened his chest. "Please move along."

The woman scowled at him, but the smaller creature rested a long-fingered hand on her elbow. His serene expression was a marked contrast to her glare.

"We heard the yelling and ran, Administrator. That is all." He smiled, tiny, sharp-looking teeth glinting from his muzzle. "Please forgive our intrusion. We will, indeed, be on our way."

"Thank you for your concern, revered Hoabin."

Marcus looked around to find Iphini Bha bowing to the furry creature. The figure in the white robe returned her bow, dipping even lower and waving its arms out to either side, which brought the rod whipping around in an impressive little spin. When it stood, the smile was still in place, and a twinkle in its eyes seemed to mock Marcus. It added fuel to his already smoldering anger.

"Please, little sister, no need. We merely heard your cries and thought to help." Marcus could not take his eyes off the little creature's delicate-seeming hands. With each word, one or the other waved about in a hypnotic pattern, the staff passing to the idle hand with each shift of intonation. Tiny black claws extended out from where a Human's nails would be, and each finger seemed to have one too many knuckles.

"Bullshit." Marcus spat the word and shook his head to clear the fog from his thoughts. "You've been shadowing me since I showed up here. You two haven't missed a council session, but you don't talk. All you do is watch." He jerked a thumb at the dust on the floor behind him. "Until now."

"Surely you don't mean to suggest—" The Diakk woman's face was twisted as it battled to convey both amusement and insult.

"Sihn, what have I told you about your temper?" The smaller figure smiled again, head tilted to the side, as he reached a long, thin arm out to block the black-robed woman. He looked back up at Marcus, and this time the eyes seemed to temper the grinning muzzle with a touch of sadness. "Administrator, again, I apologize. Sihn Ve'Yan is young in the ways of the Thien'ha, and has not yet reached the emotional equanimity of an old campaigner like myself." He touched his chest wryly with one delicate hand.

Marcus continued to scowl at both of them. He brushed one palm against a thigh and held it up to show the dust. "You just happened to show up now? How the hell do I know this wasn't your doing? I should throw you in jail until I can figure out what happened here, just on general principal!" He turned to his deputy, her wide, concerned eyes not registering. "Do we have a jail? We have to have a jail, right?"

The small furry creature dipped its head again. "Please, Administrator. Understand, we only wanted to help."

Iphini muttered, "No, we don't."

The Thien'ha master continued over her. "We want only good things for you here, Marcus Wells." His eyes shifted up to his acolyte's. "We should go now, however. I can see you are upset by what transpired here." He bowed low. "I am grateful you are well. May your efforts here in Penumbra be fruitful."

He jerked his head down the hall the way they had come and after holding her smoldering glare a moment longer, the Diakk woman, Sihn Ve'Yan, spun around and followed.

Iphini Bha was shaking her head when Marcus turned back to her, his face still burning.

"What?" He snapped.

"This was not the work of the Thien'ha, Marcus Wells." She gestured down to the fine powder on the floor. "The Thien'ha never take a hand in events. They observe, that is all. Sending a cloud of assassin nanobots is not something they would do."

His eyes narrowed. "And every one of them is a paragon of virtue, right? Didn't they just say they came here to help? How's that square with your faith in them? There has never been a single one who has wavered from this ideal path you're so impressed with?"

She shook her head. "I don't believe so, no."

He was breathing heavily, only now coming to understand the threat he had been under, and the miraculous deliverance that had saved him. He looked down again at the medallion. The marks there were clearly a symbol of some kind, although still too vague to read. It was warm to the touch, as well. Whatever had happened, it was the Skorahn that had saved him. He had no doubt about it.

"I don't suppose the medallion ever behaved like that for Virri either, eh?" His eyes drifted back down the corridor, but the mystics were long gone.

"No." She shook her head, her voice low, as she stared at the gem.

"Whoever was controlling the cloud ..." He brushed more dust off his chest. "Would they have needed to be close?" He jerked his head down the corridor. "Say, right around the corner?"

She shook her head again, eyes rising from the Skorahn. "No. These nanobots could have been programmed hours or days ago. They could have been left here, or they could have moved here on their own, knowing that you would be returning to your quarters at some point. There is no reason to suspect the Thein'ha due merely to their proximity to the attack."

He was calming down, but his anger and fear were settling into a hopeless, heavy feeling that he did not like at all. He wanted to talk to Justin, or Angara Ksaka, at least.

"Could you see if Angara would meet me in my quarters at her convenience?" He felt the world going vague around him, as if parts of his brain were shutting down. He didn't even think to worry if it was the nanites in his brain this time. Without waiting for a reply or noticing Iphini's nod, he moved off down the corridor toward his quarters.

They were lavish and spacious, decorated in pleasing, neutral greens and blues, with the reinforced armor of their initial intended function hidden by sweeping decorative columns and draperies. A central living area featured two wide couches with matching tables between them and an advanced viewing field system that could turn the central area into a massive screen capable of showing him almost anything.

His bed chamber, beyond, featured a huge circular bed that could have been most intriguing at some other time in his life. Lately, however, the foam mattress had known only hard sleep, often with him collapsing onto it fully dressed, when his marathon study sessions finally wore him out.

He collapsed into a chair softer than a cloud and looked blandly at a series of glasses arrayed on the table beside him. Each held a yellow-green liquid, each slightly different from the others. He knew before tasting them that none of them would be what he wanted.

The world of the galactics might have all manner of advances and miracles, and their culinary efforts had to be appreciated, but no matter how hard they tried, and what kind of assistance he tried to give them, they could not recreate the magic of Mountain Dew.

# Chapter 15

The roaring of the crowd around them was nearly deafening. And yet Justin sat, his arms folded over the table before him, lost in thought. He had been begging for her to take him to an arena match for ages, but now that he was here, all he could do was brood over the events of the past few days. She tried not to be annoyed. She did not share her people's affinity for the blood sports of the arena. It was one of the few instances where her own opinions and those of the Galactic Council coincided.

The Council frowned on any show of aggression or violence, and had been most diligent in stamping out all of the various ritualized forms of competitive combat throughout civilized space. There were few races or systems now with the fortitude to brave the Council's displeasure on the subject. The Tigan nomad fleets were already looked upon as shiftless vagabonds, so no one was surprised they enjoyed such diversions. And here, in Penumbra, where to defy the Council was a laudable reason unto itself, the arenas were among the most popular distractions of the city.

Most of the fighting pits in Penumbra were located in the same massive tower, a converted liquid hauler that had been welded into the Relic Core millennia ago. Each of the massive tanks had been transformed into a sporting arena that could be configured for a limitless array of contests. For generations, however, the majority of the arenas had remained fighting pits for the violent contests that brought so many tourists to this city on the edge of nowhere. Each arena featured specialized venues, from aquatic to arboreal. She had chosen the most traditional arena for Justin's introduction to the sport, so they now looked down at a flat surface liberally covered in fine dust or sand, the better to absorb an errant splash of blood or bile.

Still, she hated the fights. Combat was not some frivolous pastime, but something to be taken most seriously. It was something she had dedicated her life to, and she knew she was not unskilled in that pursuit. She hated to see it relegated to a casual pursuit for unrefined dilettantes. On some level she understood the need for a sort of pressure release valve in society for those individuals who were perhaps more aggressive than might be wished, both among the participants in these contests and in the myriad creatures inhabiting the stands. But she had never thought of combat as a game, and she did not like to see it treated as such.

But Justin had been dying to see something of the local scene. It apparently reminded him of similar events back on Earth, which did not surprise her. They had made these arrangements a while ago, and she had almost forgotten until her implants had reminded her upon waking that morning.

Things had been tense since the attempt on Marcus's life. Angara had been forced to slow down her search for a replacement administrator. She was spending a lot more time with Marcus lately, and found herself, at odd times of the day, wondering how Justin might feel about that. More to the point, she was not sure why she was even thinking about how he felt about it.

They had gone to see Marcus together twice since the attack. Justin had had a hard time understanding what a threat the pile of inert dust in the hall had actually represented. At first he could not envision the layer of grit as an assassination attempt, but she had calmly explained to him what a nanobot attack was, and eventually he had understood all too well. The attack had not only been aimed at the new administrator, it had been aimed by a person with access to the Human DNA codes needed to program such an event. She shook her head, staring at the play of light and shadow on Justin's hands as they lay tangled before him.

Both of the Humans seemed to have finally sensed the galaxy's pathos against their kind. It should have been impossible for them to miss it, the more Marcus tried to fit in. She found herself wondering how Justin felt about abandoning his friend to this acclimation by assuming the identity of a Mnymian himself. She thought she had caught a vague edge of guilt every now and then, when he was off his guard. Since the attempt on Marcus's life, he had seemed far more on edge. She felt like maybe he was finally realizing they were going to have to leave someday; someday soon.

She did not enjoy the emotions that thought brought to the surface.

She had no idea what had been in the bag he had dragged with him all the way from Earth, but whatever it had been, he had been able to parlay it into quite an impressive network of associations in Penumbra. She could see he was good with people, if she was going to be honest with herself. There were very few groups he was unable to insinuate himself into, given time and credits. And credits he had in plenty now, from his many business dealings throughout the city. She did not know the particulars about any of them, but she had done enough digging to learn that he was fairly highly regarded in some very interesting circles.

Despite his rise to relative prominence, she could not imagine that he would stay here with his friend in such obvious danger ... could he?

Another bone-shaking roar rattled the table, and her eyes slid up of their own accord to look into the arena. Justin's position and influence had secured them a private box above the fighting chamber, giving him and his friends an excellent view of the impending carnage. But he had made these arrangements a while ago, long before the attack on Marcus had wrenched his entire life sideways. He did not seem to care where he was now, or what the crowd was shouting about.

While his party had taken their places around the table by the edge of the balcony, the arena below had hosted a series of bouts and practice matches. The fighting styles varied wildly, the contestants were good journeyman fighters but lacked the polish and showmanship of the true veterans. She had expected him to be interested, but he had merely shrugged, saying he had seen better back on Earth. It certainly had not been interesting enough to take his mind off his current troubles.

But as the crowd's bellowing went on and on, he finally looked up from the table, following her eyes down toward the gritty surface of the fighting pit far below. His breath caught in his throat and a vague smile inched over his features.

The arena had been abandoned by the earlier combatants. What they had seen before had been nothing more than the opening acts, meant to keep folks interested while the true connoisseurs arrived fashionably late and made their ways to the private boxes. But now, as the lights around them dimmed, a single figure had stepped from one of the dark metal gates onto the sand, announcing that the true entertainments were about to begin, and was now basking in the crowd's accolades. He was turning slowly, four arms extended, flourishing four glittering blades that whirled and spun, each independent of the others.

She raised one eyebrow in appreciation; a Nan'Se La. The four-armed race had been bred for just such spectacles, but few of the sad creatures ever truly mastered the slightly smaller, lower pair of arms that had been grafted onto their Humanoid frames in the dim recesses of the past. Most of the poor beings were unskilled day laborers, scattered across the galaxy and with no planet of their own.

Occasionally, however, a Nan'Se La rose beyond those limitations and reached the vaunted heights the monsters who had created them had intended. The specimen moving out on the sand now was clearly one of those.

Justin watched, the glaring white false lenses flashing wide. The pit fighter was wearing an open long coat of gleaming black micro-armor that looked like metal but rippled like cloth, fluttering behind him like a performer's cloak. Contrasting with the creature's sea green skin, it gave the impression of a massive shadow moving across the sands, four blades spinning around the periphery in an amazing show of dexterity and skill.

He carried himself like a veteran pit fighter, but Angara recognized him from far more mundane pursuits. His name was Nett'to Ha; a supervisor in the vast docking bay situated closest to the Red Tower.

"What the hell is *that*?" Justin could not take his eyes off the preening fighter.

Angara smiled at his distracted enthusiasm. It was probably for the best, considering there was little they could do for Marcus at the moment.

"That is a Nan'Se La." She accepted a drink slid to her by one of the Subbotine women who seemed to follow Justin everywhere he went. She took the drink with a smile she knew did not make it to her eyes. She had never met a Subbotine she liked. "You may have seen one or two down in the port when we first arrived; I can't remember."

He shook his head. "I don't remember. Do they all ..." He waved his hands about to indicate the warrior's flashing limbs.

Angara shrugged. "I don't know. I would imagine, if you want to get the most out of a crowd like this, you would want to use every asset your creators gave you."

"That's Nett'to Ha." The Subbotine said with a breathy smile on her pasty face as she leaned into their conversation. She brushed her silken white hair off her shoulder with careful artifice. "He's only been fighting in the pits for a few weeks." Her eyes flashed at Justin, and then slid slyly over Angara's face, tightening for the Tigan bodyguard. "He hasn't got anything nice to say about the disgusting Human in the administrator's throne, I'll tell you that for nothing. And he hasn't lost a bout yet."

"He's about to." A small Kot'i muttered. The little furry creature was one of Angara's favorites among Justin's usual crew. His name was Elam, and he had almost as little patience for the Subbotines as she did. "They've just announced a change in schedule." One furry hand waved a colorful sheet of shifting images. "The fight card for tonight now has him up against the king."

A murmur ran around the table. Most of Justin's associates were leaning forward now, looking down at the arena with building anticipation.

Angara felt her stomach drop slightly. She looked over at Justin, wondering if she would be able to convince him to go. He missed her concerned glance completely, staring at the Nan'Se La fighter. He probably had not heard the Kot'i's comment, and would not have understood if he had. She leaned in to look more closely at his eyes. The false lenses were quite good. And they were high above the sands in a private box …

The crowd, whose raucous cries had been thunderous before, were deafening now as a giant stepped out onto the sand. Angara was not watching the arena, however, but Justin, to gauge his reaction. She recognized the new arrival immediately, but then she had dealt with him countless times before in her work for the administrator's office. It was doubtful, in fact, if anyone in the room could fail to recognize the most famous, or infamous, inhabitant of the city.

Justin's white eyes widened. He had recognized the new warrior. He must have remembered the battle in the docking port as well, because the dark skinned Human settled back behind the balcony railing, his eyebrows lowering in concern.

K'hzan Modath was a formidable figure in his full-body fighting suit. The shifting plates were held in place with gravitic bonds similar to the systems that connected the control surfaces of **the Yud'ahm Na'uka to the hull of the ship. The plates floated over a suit of** shimmering mail, giving the red-skinned giant the appearance of an avenging god from some primitive pantheon. He held a dark bronze staff in his left hand, more like a badge of office than a weapon. The base of the staff swelled out to a formidable looking knob, while at the top the substance of the shaft flared out to embrace an oblong gem that glowed with a sullen, crimson power.

"Oh, damn." Justin swallowed, growing more uncomfortable as he watched the exiled Variyar ruler walk calmly around the periphery of the arena.

There were no showy displays of skill here. K'hzan did not spin his staff, or leap and jump in an acrobatic exhibition. Instead, he stalked around the wide circle with the calm gait of a ruler surveying his lands.

Nett'to the Nan'Se La looked somehow diminished, sharing the sand with the red king. Even though they were nearly of a size, with the four-armed alien perhaps the taller of the two by a hair, just by his nonchalant attitude, the Variyar showed himself to be the master here. And there was no hiding the sudden wash of surprise and fear that spread across the armor-like plates of Nett'to's face.

Angara knew that the Nan'Se La had lost before the first blow had been struck.

Although she did not enjoy watching the arena combats, social pressures and the requirements of babysitting Uduta Virri for as long as she had meant that she had sat through more than her fair share. She explained the preliminaries to Justin Shaw as below on the sand the two combatants were brought together by a robed Leemuk judge who checked the weapons with his glistening hands, making sure none were sharpened or charged, and then sent the fighters to their corners.

"So, if the weapons aren't sharpened, that means it's pretty safe, right?" Justin's brow was furrowed as the reality of what he was about to see dawned on him. She appreciated that small show of concern, at least.

"Well, the combats are structured so that deaths are …" she looked at him from the corner of her eye. "Deaths are uncommon." She shrugged, looking back down again. "There is plenty of blood for the crowd to lap up, never fear."

"Not when the king is fighting." The Subbotine, hanging off Justin's other shoulder, simpered. "That huge club of his breaks bones and sends his opponents flying." She cuddled closer. "It's quite a show."

Angara knew that Justin had been spending a lot of time with several females since his arrival. She had found the thought vaguely off-putting, despite the fact that they had all been Children. But tonight he seemed to hardly notice the girl ... what was her name ... Fiearra?

"Means the wagers will be pretty thin on the ground." Elam's words were bitter as the little furry creature leaned heavily onto the railing. "Profits dry up when K'hzan takes the sands." He opened one little hand as if dropping coins over the edge. "Great show, no credits."

Justin turned around. "They don't take wagers when he's in the match?"

Elam looked at the disguised Human as if he had sprouted a second head. "They'll take anybody's money. But who would give it to them under the circumstances? The odds are so one sided you'd need to give them a fortune to make anything betting with the king, and you'd have to be a fool to bet against him. And when there's a change of schedule like this? All wagers are rendered void and must be resubmitted." One small shoulder rose in a shrug. "Only an idiot would do so."

Justin nodded absentmindedly, turning back to the scene below, and Angara felt a sudden rush of nerves. "Don't think about it, Justin Shaw. I don't know where your credits have come from, but you don't have enough to risk on this."

He smiled at her and she felt a little of the tightness ease. "Don't worry. I'm not an idiot."

Down below, the judge had clapped his hands with a wet slapping sound and moved away from the two fighters, watching them both with intent, wide-set eyes.

Angara could see at once that her initial thoughts had been correct. K'hzan Modath walked tall, circling his Nan'Se La opponent, who had lowered his considerable height into a fighter's crouch. He was moving with quick, skittering steps, feinting first one way and then another, the blades spinning like propellers on primitive aircraft.

"He's not really interested in giving a good show, is he?" Justin nodded at the fight. "He just looks pissed off."

Angara nodded. "K'hzan Modath does not often fight, but when he does, he does a workman's job of it."

Elam snorted, turning away to pick up a drink. "He only fights when he feels he has a reason, or he hasn't been able to sneak away for some time."

"He hasn't left Penumbra since the new administrator's first meeting." The Leemuk, Skrish, put in with a quick glance at Angara. The group had not objected to her joining them after Justin convinced her it would not jeopardize his identity. But they did not often speak of Marcus Wells in her presence, and when they did, it was either passive aggressive barbs from the Subbotines, or incidental comments like Skrish's. "He's not the Human's biggest fan."

Elam snorted again. "The depth of this group can't be underestimated."

Justin was not paying attention to the others, however. He watched the giant red demon stalking the four-armed fighter without apparent concern for his own safety, and leaned away from the Subbotine and back toward Angara. "I don't get it. If they don't make any money, and he doesn't give a good show, why do the owners of the arenas indulge him?"

Her eyes narrowed. "The king? Why do they indulge the *king*?" She waved a hand down in the direction of the arena. "Have you *seen* him? *You* tell him no!"

"Besides," Elam muttered. "There's definitely a market for the tall, brooding, blunt-object type." He nodded his head at the moist-eyed girl, Fiearra.

Justin chuckled at that, and Angara was glad to hear it. Then her gladness stopped her short. The fact that she cared did not sit well with her, and she went back to watching the fight unfold, hoping the issue would slip from her mind.

The Nan'Se La had become skittish, unnerved with K'hzan's relentless, unreadable pursuit. He kept shooting hooded glances into the stands, but no help was forthcoming from that quarter. He was dancing around the periphery of the arena, all four hands rising to urge the crowd to greater vocal efforts. Judging from the hooting and the catcalls, however, the rising attitude of the audience was starting to turn against him.

The spinning four armed dervish pivoted on one planted foot in mid-twist, and one long blade, shining dully in the light, curved in at K'hzan's left calf with a howling war cry. Just the kind of ridiculous grandstanding that brought a tired, dismissive snarl to her face at these fights.

K'hzan, possibly warned by the howl, perhaps reading his opponent's body language, or perhaps just by chance, took a casual step to the side and the blade whisked past. The other blades came in, flashing toward the red king's legs as the other fighter continued to spin. The next two blows missed as well, and the final blow, with the creature's other long blade, clanged off the dark staff with a dull, heavy sound.

At no time did K'hzan Modath look as if he was exerting himself in the slightest.

When the staff suddenly spun up and around in a lazy arc, Angara almost missed it. The movement seemed idle, unconcerned with the rest of the activity in the pit. And yet the gem-sporting head of the big weapon, moving casually, just happened to sail through a piece of air that Nett'to, the undefeated Nan'Se La warrior, had moved into a split second before.

The weighted staff crashed into the elongated rib cage between the two left arms. There was the distinct, wet-crack sound of bones breaking, and Nett'to was flying through the air.

Nett'to's grunt echoed off the arena walls as he came rolling up onto his knees with a dizzying motion. The young warrior leapt back up to his feet and continued to move in his careful circle. He was crouching in a lopsided stance now, favoring his wounded side. He had dropped one of his smaller blades, as well. He no longer spun the weapons in grand arcs, but held each loosely in a practiced grip. The heavy, sea-green face was immobile as he watched K'hzan from deep within the shadowed pits of his eyes.

"You don't have to be a show-off to give a good show." Fiearra said with a smile that was directed at Justin, but caught Angara in its peripheral heat.

The bitch.

K'hzan continued to move with the same slow, unhurried pace. The staff was now in his other hand, and he moved obliquely with Nett'to, angled away from him even as every step somehow brought them closer together.

The four-armed fighter growled again, and then barked, lunging at his foe in a sharp, jerky motion, arms wide, before withdrawing. The heavy-featured face was not easy to read, but the desperation in his voice and his posture was clear. As was a growing sense of fear.

K'hzan did not rise to the wordless challenge, and instead continued to move toward his prey with slow inevitability.

It was almost a blessing when the big brute lunged forward with abandon, his patience at an end and his four arms blurring as they moved, lights glittering from the dull blades.

And it was a resounding anticlimax when K'hzan thrust his staff forward, the gnarled top striking the malformed chest with another crack. Nett'to stopped in his tracks, his arms falling to his sides, and stood, swaying gently, looking at the big red demon with what almost seemed to be mild annoyance.

With a slow, graceful motion, he began to fall. Before the big body could drop, however, the red king's massive staff came up and around again, catching his opponent on the side of the head with enough force to snap the creature's neck. The body did fall this time, jerking spasmodically to the sand where its erratic movements slowed, and then stopped completely.

Around Justin's table, his friends and associates seemed to run the gamut from elated and entertained to shocked. Elam shook his head and looked across the table at Angara.

"He usually takes a little longer, at least. That was hardly fitting for the main event of the evening."

Skrish shrugged his sloping shoulders. A massive tongue lolled out and moistened the snaggled teeth and exposed field of gum. "His work is usually not so … final, however."

A suspicion had begun to build in the back of Angara's mind. Memories of the attack they had witnessed in the docking bay came back, as well as her thought that the Mnymian assassins could not have been working alone.

Below them, K'hzan was taking a victory stroll around the arena as a Tsiiki and a Namanu dragged Nett'to's corpse out through a small service entrance. The red-skinned beast walked with a business-like gait that gave no acknowledgement of the crowd screaming themselves hoarse above him. His gleaming black horns shone dully in the overhead light, and the gem at the head of his massive staff had started to glow.

Justin was staring down at the Variyar warrior king, a slight furrow between his eyes. Angara could not tell what the Human was thinking, but she thought there was an uncharacteristic dullness behind the white lenses.

"Perhaps we should leave, if you have seen enough?" She tilted her head toward the exit to the box. "It is late, and I am certain you have empires to expand in the morning."

He smiled faintly, but his eyes remained on the sand below. He nodded. "Yeah, I guess."

When K'hzan Modath stopped suddenly in his progress, Angara noticed at once. The rest of the crowd, their howls and cries winding down, faded even more quickly into silence as the armored warrior paused.

Below them, K'hzan's prominent nose wrinkled as the craggy features drew back in a sneer, as if he had smelled something foul. The glittering dark eyes drifted upward and began to scan the very top levels, raking across the private boxes.

Angara felt something cold drop into her stomach, and was moved with a sudden need to leave the fighting pit and get as far from this tower as possible. She reached out for Justin's arm, meaning to pull him from his chair, when the last voices fell away, and silence reigned within the confines of the arena.

She did not want to look down, but forced herself. Below, K'hzan was glaring upward.

The dark eyes glittered in the gnarled face. There was no doubt in her mind that, even at this great distance, the red king was staring straight up into their box, directly at Justin.

"I smell you, coward!" The words echoed up from the sand, and most of the Human's acquaintances sidled away from him, not knowing what was happening, but sensing the target of the Variyar's displeasure. She smirked when the Subbotine, Fiearra, backed away, and a spiteful little voice in her head hoped that Justin had seen the pale bitch flinch.

"Justin, we need to go." She pulled on his arm again, but he was still and stiff, unmoving as he stared down into the demon's eyes.

"I smell you, coward! And I call you out from among those with whom you seek to hide!" The snarling voice echoed up from the pit, filling the air around them.

"What's he mean?" Skrish turned to Nomen, one of the quiet, thoughtful Namanu that had been instrumental in helping Justin build his network in the city.

The Namanu shook his head, looking around as if there might be some being with a sign proclaiming them a vile coward somewhere in the box.

"Justin, honestly, we need to go." She pulled him more forcefully, and he came slowly off his seat, still looking down as if he could not tear his eyes away.

"Your stench fills this vast chamber, *Human*!" K'hzan punched the heavy club up into the air, straight toward Justin, and the coldness in her gut froze into a jagged chunk of ice at the word.

In the box, Justin's companions were looking around more frantically, still not understanding.

"Did you think your pathetic disguise could hide your true nature, thewless worm?" The staff lowered, and the dark eyes burned. "I challenge you, Human, here and now. You wish to watch me fight? You wish for me to dance for your pleasure? Come down onto the sand and dance with me, if you are worthy of your heritage." The thick lips pulled back in a sneer, revealing jagged teeth. "Let us see the cut of your valor, and the color of your blood."

Justin finally pulled his eyes away from the scene on the sand and turned to Angara, his white eyes desperate. "What the hell's he talking about?"

Around them, light had finally dawned on the Human's companions, and they were rising all around the table, their faces a jumble of emotions. The Subbotine, in particular, looked horrified, as if Justin had become some horrible, diseased wretch before her eyes.

"Justin, we need to leave." She pulled him toward the door. This time, he came willingly, his body limp.

"But, what was he talking about?" Receiving the full weight of K'hzan's attention had unnerved him, and he was not even thinking about the blow to his disguise.

As she pulled him away from the railing, the Variyar bellowed louder from beneath them. "Run, worm! You contaminate the very air with your presence!" The voice changed, becoming less directed, and she imagined the big creature addressing the audience as they made their escape. "I will not share air with such a wretch! It contaminates the substance of the city with the tread of its craven feet!"

Angara pushed Justin out into the narrow connecting hall. This high up in the venue, the corridors were narrow to accommodate the larger boxes. He turned to the stairs, but she pulled him around and behind her, dragging him in the opposite direction.

"There's a small docking port at the top of the tank. We'll call for an Administrative shuttle." She tightened her eyes and scanned through the options and frequencies to make the request.

"I don't understand." Justin muttered. He was coming out of his daze, and had probably realized that all of his careful work had been unraveled with the Variyar king's denunciation. "What's that asshole got against *me*?"

Angara shook her head, although she knew he probably was not paying any attention to her as she led them up into the close confines of the service access conduits. "It's not you. It's Humans."

"Of course it's Humans." Justin nearly spat the words. "Let me guess, we somehow offended his ancestors as well?"

That almost brought a smile to her face. "You might say that."

For some reason, he left that alone, which she found alarming. "But how did he know about me? How did he know I was Human?"

The cold returned. How *did* K'hzan know about Justin? "I'm not sure. There are tales of a deep connection between Variyar and Humans that stretch back before recorded history. If you are inclined to give credence to such stories, he could most likely sniff you out of a large crowd without much effort."

They came to the plain service hatch and she ushered him through, looking behind to be certain they had not been followed. A shuttle from the administrator's office was already waiting for them in the small docking bay, and she gestured for him to board before entering herself. She moved immediately to the controls and sat in the stiff, still seat. No self-respecting Tigan would ever allow an automatic system to fly a ship she was in.

"Well that was … odd." His voice was distracted, and she took her eyes from the viewing field long enough to cast a quick glance back at him. He seemed far less troubled than she would have been herself, in his position. He stared through the viewing fields at the tall ships passing by around them, his eyes lost in thought.

"Have you no concern for your safety or your enterprises, now that K'hzan has stripped you of your Mnymian mask?" She made sure to keep away from regular shuttle traffic as she brought them down toward an out of the way docking station on the Concourse.

"Hmm," he grunted. "Not really. I'm sure I can come up with something. He's not that familiar to most in the city, from what I gather. I can play on that. I'll be fine." And he sounded as if he truly believed that.

For some reason, it bothered her. "Some of your companions seemed most distraught. The Subbotine, Fiearra? Appeared upset at the thought that you might be Human." Damn! Now, why had she said that? She jerked the controls of the shuttle around harder than anticipated, and their viewing fields veered wildly, although the inertial compensators of the shuttle prevented any of the force of the turn from getting to them.

She did not like the sound of the short chuckle from behind her. "Angara! I'm shocked, really. Jealousy does not become a warrior woman such as your-self."

The coldness that had gripped her in the arena had faded, and was now replaced with a burning heat that threatened to rob her of all discipline. She want-ed nothing more than to deny the charge, but knew that any attempts to do so would make her look only more envious. Her lips tightened and her teeth ground together behind them. She was most certainly *not* jealous!

"Meh," he continued, oblivious of her inner turmoil. "Fiearra's been getting a little boring, lately, to tell you the truth."

She shot another look back at him, but he was still lost, watching the con-toured surface of the Concourse rising up to meet them. The notch in the dark skin between his eyes deepened. "Most of the Subbotines I've met haven't seemed too deep, now that I think about it."

She turned back to bring them into the bay. She could feel a smile pulling at her lips, and tamped it down with an angry surge. She had no idea why his words should cause such a reaction, but it unnerved her all the same.

# Chapter 16

Marcus looked across the table to where Iphini Bha sat demurely sipping at a clear liquid that might have been water for all he knew. He had grown weary of taking his meals in his quarters, and the sense of being under siege day and night had only grown since the attack, or whatever it was, in the halls. It had been well over a month, according to his old watch, since the incident, and Bha and Angara had watched over him like over-sensitive mother hens ever since. He was starting to feel like a trapped animal.

The close confines had done nothing positive for his working relationship with his nominal assistant, either. Bha seemed more and more frustrated and upset, but refused to share with him any possible reasons for her strained temperament. He felt as if every effort he made to put her at ease was being undermined by some invisible force he could not puzzle out.

And so, refusing to be put off any longer, he had ordered her to take him someplace nice to eat; alone. It had felt awkward, and oddly inappropriate when he had made the decision, but he knew that many of the morals that dictated behavior on Earth were as much strangers here as he was. There was no romantic component to his desire to sit down with his assistant and share a meal; nevertheless, he felt as uncomfortable as he had on his first date.

Iphini Bha had been taken aback by his suggestion, but had eventually relented. She suggested several grand establishments that had seemed too much, even for him, and they had settled on a small place that promised excellent views. His position had assured them a nice table in a quiet corner despite the obvious discomfort of the frog-eyed Matabessi servers. The viewing field over their table looked out over the Gulf between the wings of the city, and the glittering thread that spiraled out from somewhere beneath them and down to the desolate planet rotating far below.

He watched the gleaming, twisting beam with genuine awe. He had come to take many amazing things for granted since they had first arrived in Penumbra, but the city still found ways to surprise him. Bha had told him that the ribbon he was seeing was called the Diamond Road. Apparently, it was the source of the city's water, siphoned up from somewhere beneath the surface of the planet and into the Relic Core, where it was processed and divided among the countless reservoirs of the city. How it was processed and divided Iphini Bha could not tell him; just another mystery that the people of the city lived with every day.

"I was surprised Angara Ksaka allowed you out." Bha was not meeting his eyes, the pencil-like object she always had with her spinning idly in one marbled hand. "She has been quite adamant that you need to be sequestered until she can convince Warder Oo'juto to assume the … your … to become the administrator."

That put a bit of a damper on his mood again. The dolphin with the bad attitude, Marcus refused to think of it as anything else, had apparently been slow to agree to any kind of assumption of power. Days could go by and no one would even mention those efforts to him, and he would as often as not forget that this situation, that he was finally coming to accept as his new normal, was only temporary. When it was brought up, though, it took him right out of whatever he was doing at the moment, and threatened to plunge him into a depression he was only now coming to identify.

Marcus sipped at his drink. It was a tart, citrusy juice, reminding him a little of orange juice with a strange, watermelon-like aftertaste. It wasn't Mountain Dew, but it was as close as he'd yet come. He shrugged. "I didn't give her much choice. She's been wanting an evening free herself. I knew she had arranged to take Justin to those fighting pits tonight, so I told her I was going out." He smiled at the memory. "She was mad enough to spit, but when I told her I'd bring you along, she gave in."

Bha nodded, looking down at the plate of multi-colored vegetative fronds. "Lucky me." The words were flat, even though the translators in his head.

That set Marcus back into a tailspin. He had spent a large part of nearly every day with Iphini Bha for months now, and he thought they had come to a decent working relationship. She seemed to understand instinctively what he was trying to do, and had often assisted him in ways he didn't even know to ask for. And yet, there was still some darkness under the surface he never seemed able to penetrate.

He looked down at his own plate. Their technology meant that if he could describe it, the chefs working in the small back room kitchen could recreate it. The problem was, he found his memory for most of the foods he had enjoyed was often less than equal to the task. His plate was now home to a brown lump of protein that looked less like a steak fresh off the grill and more like a steak fresh out of the business end of a dog.

Overall, the evening was not shaping up to be the refreshing outing he had planned.

He tried another conversational sally. "We haven't heard much from Taurani since I peed in his porridge, working the deal with Copic Fa'Orin for his son."

Marcus liked to sprinkle his conversations with little colloquialisms from time to time. It made him feel better about the near-constant low-grade earache his own implants gave him.

Bha looked up, then away, the fracture-like lines on her pale face standing out more starkly than normal. "His guards have been active in the Concourse. There have been threats against some of the associates of your conglomerates. Nothing actionable, so I did not think to bring it to your attention. I assume he awaits word from the Council, before he does anything more drastic."

That didn't sound good. "Drastic?" The coalitions he had been able to make since that first breakthrough were only now starting to make their influence felt in the city. He had assumed Taurani's silence meant the gangly grey freak was powerless to stop him. If there was some way for the Council's bag man to stick his foot into things now, it could make a real mess.

She looked up at him, and there was an edge of pity in her wide eyes that he found mildly insulting. "Ambassador Taurani will not leave things as they are. Your work with the Diakk man, and with all the others since, has been a direct challenge to everything the Galactic Council stands for." She shook her head, looking back down. "They will not let it stand without response."

Well, that was just great. He wished Bha had told him about the Ntja making nuisances of themselves in the lower levels of the city, but he could not really fault her. Their working relationship had improved immensely, but there was still something hanging, unspoken, between them.

"Iphini, can I ask you a question?" He wasn't looking at her as he spoke. The conversation had been a touch stilted all night, as he had tried to avoid anything that might upset his delicate-seeming assistant. If it was going to be uncomfortable, however, he figured he might as well dive right in and talk about what was really on his mind.

She nodded, her own eyes downcast as well.

"What, exactly, do you have against me?" The words came quickly. They had been building for weeks, and he had only avoided asking them for fear of damaging the carefully-crafted rapport that had made his work possible. But that silence had not banished his awareness of her subtle reactions. If there was going to be this wall between them, he might as well know what it was.

Her slender shoulders lifted in mute deflection. "I have nothing against you, Marcus Wells." Her voice was flat. "I have found many of your goals laudable, if your methods were ... opaque." She turned to look out the viewing field at the glittering bridge to the barren surface far below. "There are many that do not understand you, but then, there is little enough understanding to be had between any two species, is there not?"

He had not anticipated that. He knew something was there between them, some shadow that haunted her at odd moments in their work. But with her words, even if they sounded forced, he found himself unwilling to make an asshole of himself by pushing the issue.

"Well, thanks for that, anyway." He summoned up a smile. "I couldn't have done what little I have without your help. That's for sure."

She looked up at him, her huge eyes confused. "Little? You have done a great deal. Violence throughout the city is down, and many more have come forward to be helped by your networks since you arranged to save the son of Copic Fa'Orin." She paused, her eyes shifting, and she looked back down to the spinning pen that was never far from her, especially when she was nervous. "It has been an honor to be a part of such work."

His smile became more genuine. "Well, like I said, I couldn't have done it without you."

She shrugged, her eyes sliding back up to look through the field and out into space. "I would be able to assist you more, truth to tell, with the executive codes. But I have been honored to do what I have done."

That caught him off guard. "Executive codes?"

"There are systems you can call upon, for both research and reaction, that will not respond to the deputy to the administrator." Again, the gentle shrug. "It has always been that way. It is only that until now, very little has actually been attempted."

"What kinds of systems?" So much within the administrator's office happened almost without his conscious thought, as the systems seemed to sense his needs and desires and strove to provide what he needed, that he often found himself taking the city's systems for granted. Until a moment like the assassination attempt, of course. Then they were enormous, violent, and terrifying mysteries.

She paused, and he could not shake the sudden feeling that she was more uncomfortable than usual. She seemed to be thinking better of her earlier comment. "Mostly data retrieval and organization. Some communications functions." She hunched her shoulders slightly in an oddly diminishing way, shaking her head. "It is nothing I cannot work around, to be honest."

He felt awful, wanting nothing more than to make Bha feel better. He shook his head and reached across the table, gently taking one of her hands in his. "No, Iphini! Is it something I can release? If there's something I can do to give you access to those systems, why wouldn't I? You should have asked me sooner! Of course I want to help you! You've been a huge help to *me*!"

She looked up at him, her blue eyes wide, her hand rigid beneath his. "You would give me that kind of access?"

Something in the back of his mind seemed to jerk at her tone, but he had learned not to depend too much on reading into people's tone of voice since arriving in Penumbra. The nano-tech in his brain did an amazing job of translating all aspects of communication, including the vertigo-inducing experience of reading written text and the maddening buzz of vernacular phraseology. But he still could not bring himself to trust the actual sound of someone's voice, when he found himself in an uncomfortable spot.

Before he could stop himself, he nodded, his smile firmly in place. "Of course!"

She smiled at him; a shy expression that emphasized her big, wide eyes and smooth, hairless features.

His own smile grew warmer. He thought he just might be sensing a thaw in that dark shadow between them.

*****

Marcus had convinced Iphini Bha to take a stroll with him through the Concourse on their return journey to the Red Tower, sending the small Administrative shuttle back under its own guidance. It was late, and so traffic beneath the city's artificial skin was thin. Still, a dizzying array of creatures moved among the enormous tower-footings and independent buildings. There were no Ntja present, and he thought he detected at least a small change in the general attitude toward him as they walked, side by side, through the crowds.

Iphini Bha was obviously nervous, her gaze darting back and forth as if expecting an attack at any moment. But Marcus had a good feeling about the night. He had been working tirelessly to create more networks that led back to the administrator's office, that would allow him to exercise more influence on many of the consortiums that called the city home, and thus help those in need who came to Penumbra, like Copic Fa'Orin, as a last resort.

He thought of the Diakk man and his son, Copic Fa'Elic, often. If it had not been for Fa'Orin, he doubted if any of what he had accomplished since would have been possible. People's concerns about Council reprisals had been stemmed by that first success, and he had found himself emboldened by his confrontation with the ambassador in the council chamber afterward, believing he had somehow scored a victory, even one as minor as saving a single boy, over the old politico.

Bha's stories of Ntja interference and her certainty that Taurani still had a play to make worried him more than he would let on, but with each passing day, it would be harder for the slimy, lipless toad to derail his work.

The two of them had arrived unmolested at the base of the Red Tower and taken a lift tube up through the primary habitation deck. He still hated the strange jogs in the hall that kept him from seeing more than a hundred feet in front of him at a time, and questioned, once again, the Variyar design philosophy that dictated the strange layout. It made the simple task of moving to and from his suite the most anxious part of every day. Iphini Bha had stationed Leemuk security guards from his own office to guard the approaches to his apartments, and although he wouldn't have wanted to admit it, the sight of the big green blobs with their wide, creepy, snaggle-toothed smiles always reassured him.

As they stepped out into the quiet, empty lift tube annex, he felt something cold drop in his gut.

"Where's the guard?" He moved toward the hall, wishing he had a weapon. Everyone, from Bha to Justin to Angara, had told him that an administrator going armed would send exactly the wrong message to the people of Penumbra. They had said it would make him look weak and fearful at a time when he needed to project just the opposite. He had argued that there had to be something small he could carry, if for no other reason than to make himself feel better. But Bha had countered that the Skorahn had taken care of him before, it could be assumed it would continue to do so.

Of course, that made the thought of giving it up as soon as they could convince the dolphin to take it even less appealing, but he had not told them that. He assumed they knew.

Still, it would have been nice to have a gun in his hands as he inched down the hallway now. Even the little pistol from Justin's glove compartment would have made him feel like he could do something about his own fate.

"He is probably relieving himself." Bha muttered from beside the tube. She had not moved any further into the alcove.

Marcus was not familiar with the bathroom habits of the Leemuk, but thought it would have seemed relatively unprofessional for a sentry of any sentient species to wander away from their post like this, especially if Taurani's goons had been making noises as Bha had said.

"Well, why don't I just scoot back up to my apartments, then, Iphini. You go home. I'll see you tomorrow." He put a brave face on it, but he had every intention of sprinting as soon as the girl was around a corner.

She surprised him by shaking her head. "No, I will see you to your door as I promised Angara Ksaka."

He tried to smile at her, but felt it twist sickeningly on his face.

Together they moved down the hall, slowing as they reached each offset jink in the path, gazing around the shallow corners, and then moving on into the next segment of corridor. There was no sign of the Leemuk guard anyway along their route.

As they passed the tight juncture where the nano-attack had taken place, Marcus felt a cold shiver run up his back and into his scalp. He knew that, in some way, he was still not processing the reality that someone was angry enough to want to kill him. The method of attack was exotic and strange enough that it still had not registered with the buried, instinctual level of his brain.

Still, though, as they moved past that now-familiar twist, a similar twist pulled at his gut, and the cold fingers of fear pushing through his hair became more insistent.

By the time they approached the last section of hall before his rooms, he was jumping at every imaginary sound, ready to tear off down the corridor at the first sign of danger. He cursed Bha's presence, keeping him moving at such a sedate pace when his hammering heart counseled that he spring as fast as he could for the safety of his apartment.

There would be another Leemuk at his door. Or there should be, anyway. But as they made their way through the final twist in the corridor, Marcus's hand raised to greet his stalwart defender, the rigid, official smile slid off his face.

There was no one standing before his door. There was, however, someone in the hall. A body was slumped on the textured flooring before the big double doors to his rooms. Wrapped in a dark cloak, he could not make out any details, but it didn't seem bulky enough to be a Leemuk.

Marcus reached back and pushed Iphini Bha behind the corner. She slapped his hands away, however, and moved back around to glare at him, then past him to the door. Her big eyes fell to the shape in front of the door and her expression darkened.

Before he could stop her, she moved past him and to the prone figure. Her eyes flicked back and forth from one pinched end of the hall segment to the other, walking with a strange-yet-graceful, sideways gait. Marcus hurried to catch up.

As they drew near, he saw that it was not a single figure by the door, but two; one significantly larger than the other. His mind skittered away from the smaller figure, focusing on the man-sized shape as if in self-defense.

The body was draped in a cowled robe, hood pulled up over the face. As Iphini moved around them, one hand over her mouth, he forced himself to kneel beside the larger body, checking first for any sign of blood on the floor. There was none, but he felt no better for that.

With one shaking hand he reached out and pulled the rough fabric of the hood away from the figure's head. As the cloth fell away, he realized that he had known what he would see the moment he had seen the shapes.

The pale, bloodless face of Copic Fa'Orin stared into the middle distance before him, unseeing. The black marks stood out in stark contrast to his pale features. The expression the Diakk man wore seemed to hover, frozen, somewhere between surprise and terror. His identity made it sickeningly clear who the smaller bundle would be.

Something in Marcus's chest tightened, and then snapped with an audible click that shook his body. He fell away, catching himself on one palm against the rough floor.

As he caught himself, a blazing green bolt of energy flashed through the space he had just vacated. The energy struck the wall before him and reduced a large section of it into a flash of steam, fire, and fine particulate matter.

He remembered the color and the vibrancy of the bolt from his first moments within Penumbra, when he had seen the strange beings he now knew as Mnymians make their abortive assassination attempt on the red king. Someone had just fired a plasma weapon at him.

"Run!" Iphini Bha dragged him to his feet and pushed him toward the doors to his apartments. She was right behind him as another bolt flashed into the wall, and he shied away, turning from the door. The shot had come from behind them, from the reinforced corner there.

He had just a moment of lucidity to curse the insanity of the Variyar's anti-boarding action layout. He *knew* it had made no sense!

A hulking figure stomped around the corner, brandishing a large rifle-like weapon. Whatever it was had donned a robe similar to the one that had covered Copic Fa'Orin and his son, and the face was hidden by the shadows of the cowl. It was big, whatever it was. Maybe a Leemuk, or even one of those four-armed bastards from the flight deck.

Or an Ntja dog. The thought struck him without warning, and he knew, with iron clarity, that it would be true. Another figure pushed around the corner, brandishing another plasma gun.

There was nowhere for them to hide in the long hall, and there was no way they could stumble to his door in time.

The figure nearest them raised its weapon before the dark shadows of its hood, taking careful aim directly at Marcus. Looking down the siphon-like tube of the plasma gun's discharge mouth, the opening seemed to swell and he grew dizzy, feeling as if he might fall into the gaping opening and be lost forever.

A flash filled the corridor, and Marcus's ears both popped painfully. He flinched, thinking his attacker must have fired, and jittering after-images danced across his eyelids as he staggered back, reaching blindly behind him for the door to his rooms.

There was a puzzled grunt, and he realized that he was still alive. Forcing his eyes opened, he gazed through tightened lids at the creatures who had come to kill him. Both of them stood still, looking down with heads cocked beneath their concealing hoods. They were shaking the weapons with frustrated, brutish force, stabbing them repeatedly down at Marcus and Iphini Bha.

The weapons would not fire.

"Suppression field!" Bha muttered the words under her breath as if she could not believe what was happening.

Marcus looked aside at her as he pushed the door to this rooms open. "What?" He waved her past him into the foyer.

"They activated a suppression field!" She moved in a daze to his door, staring back at the two robed figures in the corridor.

"Who did? How?" He had seen the field deployed by the city after the shootout on the flight deck, but how could it have known there was trouble in front of his door so soon?

Iphini Bha was staring at his chest, and he looked down. He should have thought of it first. The Skorahn was glowing a faint cobalt, and when he reached up hesitantly to take it in his hand, it was warm to the touch.

It had saved his life again.

There was a slurred growl, and then the two attackers were charging down the hall at them, huge dull blades in their hands.

"They've thought of everything, I guess." Marcus muttered, backing away deeper into his room. These creatures were huge, the robes doing nothing to hide the size of them as they ran.

He suddenly realized that there was most likely little defense to be had in his rooms. It wasn't like there were weapons in there, after all. There were several exits, of course. Angara would never have allowed her prize possession to be kept in a death trap with only one entrance. Maybe if they closed and locked the doors, the assassins would take long enough breaking through, and then searching the rooms, that he and Iphini Bha could make their escape out one of the other entrances and get to the control center, where they would be able to close those enormous blast doors behind them.

Marcus was lost in thought, trying to push the doors vaguely closed in his panic, when a white blur exploded from his left, into the chest of the lead attacker. In a fluttering white robe, a small, spindly figure was spinning and dipping, forming a barrier of stiff arms and legs that brought the two enormous attackers up short. There was a long length of silvered piping weaving through the patterns, while a wizened old head with a fringe of pale green fur, grinning like a child, seemed to settle into the center of the chaos as the metal staff struck elbows, knees, and heads with equal abandon.

The second monster bowled into the first, pushing it through the small defender's guard, and Marcus thought he saw a flash of slick teeth in a dark muzzle as the first creature, still off balance from its partners shove, realized it was through. Beady, dark eyes locked onto his as his mysterious defender looked back, chagrined.

And then a black-robed shape dove into the fray, meeting the descending blade with slapping strike with an open palm. Those tiny eyes widened in the shadows, and soon the beast was fighting for its life as the newcomer tore into it, fists and feet flashing in the red-tinged light.

Marcus found it incongruous that he was in the middle of a huge, technologically advanced city hanging in space untold light years from Earth, watching three or four different alien species all fight with sticks, swords, and fists for the honor of killing him, or letting him live, hopefully, depending on the outcome.

The second assailant began to force the little defender back toward the near wall, a flurry of blows ringing off the whistling staff, forcing its wielder into a series of defensive forms that stopped it from doing anything more dangerous than an occasional, flashing attack at an elbow or flank. Even when these blows struck home, they seemed to have little effect on the brutish attacker.

Nearer to the door, the taller defender in the black robes was more hard-pressed. It had made no attacks since its initial appearance, and was instead concentrating on weaving a steady, blurring defense that managed to keep the attacker at bay. In fact, as Marcus stood there gaping, he realized that this figure wasn't even trying to attack, but was only fighting a holding action, keeping the brute from advancing any further.

"Close the door!" Iphini Bha was screaming at him, but he couldn't bring himself to close out these strangers who had rushed to his aid. He knew it was the Thien'ha and his acolyte, of course, but he had no idea why they were fighting for him like this. Still, he could not close the doors when someone was fighting such a desperate struggle in his defense.

Desperately, Marcus began casting about him for something he might use as a weapon. There was nothing, of course. But his eyes did alight on a large vase whose cool blue colors had caught his eye in the Concourse. Without a second thought, he lunged for the vessel, grabbing it and pivoting back to the desperate fight outside. He had no idea what he intended to do with it, but thought he might throw it at one of the attackers to distract it, hopefully creating an opening for one of the Thien'ha to shift back onto the offensive.

He spun back into the door just in time to see the end of the fight.

The little mystic, obviously tired of the battle, brought his staff up in a dizzying arc that crashed down upon his opponent's head. The tall figure stumbled back, staggered by the blow, and the staff snapped around toward its chest. The long dull-metal bar blurred as it flew, and Marcus's eyes widened as he watched the thing flatten and elongate, a broad blade appearing at the top just as it struck the attacker.

The blade slashed through the robe and into the flesh beneath, while the weight of the weapon itself, with the momentum of the powerful swing, dashed it back down the hall where it landed in a still pile, one clawed hand thrust lifelessly out of the bundled fabric.

Marcus had no idea what he had seen, but before he could even ask Bha what was happening, the little mystic had whirled around to face the final opponent. The taller mystic was still holding the last brute at bay with an impressive display of unarmed skill, neither of the combatants appearing capable of striking a telling blow. But Marcus realized that the Thien'ha wasn't *trying* to strike. She was holding the big monster for her master, keeping it occupied while he removed his own opponent.

The small, light-furred creature brought the pole-weapon around again, not pausing in its continuous, graceful movements, and thrust it at the last assailant's broad back. The big alien never even saw its danger. The pole blurred again as it stabbed forward, the blade now shifting and lengthening again into a flat spearhead that took the robed attacker in the center of the back.

The spearhead exploded out from the figure's chest in a spray of dark fluid. The large sword swayed slightly as the thing's arms jerked to a halt, shaking. The head bowed, shadows swallowing the glimpse of bone and glint of eye, as it looked down at the gleaming blade that now stood out from its flesh. With a soft sigh, the monster collapsed forward, the blade sliding out as it fell.

Marcus stared at the body, lying very near the Diakk man and child, his mouth hanging open in dumbfounded confusion. The two Thien'ha consulted briefly with each other, and then came into his apartments. The small, furry creature, what Iphini Bha had called a Goagoi, wrapped in gleaming white robes, was pushing the female Diakk apprentice before him.

"You will need to close this door, please." The short alien bowed slightly to Marcus, indicating the door with a gesture from his weapon, which had once again returned to the shape of a short metal rod. "There will be no more attacks for the present, but that is no reason to abandon prudence at such a time."

"How—" Marcus cleared his throat. "How do you know? That there won't be more attacks, I mean?" He moved to close the door all the same.

"Because he killed the other two dogs before we got to these two." The Diakk woman spat the words, anger clear in her flashing dark eyes. The black design that spread out beneath her eyes writhed with repressed fury. She cast one last glance behind her at the bodies littering the floor as the door closed.

"What have you done?" Iphini Bha pushed past Marcus to address the mystics, both of whom turned to look at her with bland eyes. "Thien'ha never take a hand in the events they observe! What kind of Thien'ha *are* you?"

"Not very good ones." The Diakk apprentice muttered. She was clearly unhappy, and would not meet Bha's eyes.

"We follow our conscience, Deputy Administrator." The small, green-furred mystic spoke clearly, the rod falling back to rest on his shoulder. "We follow the path of the Thien'ha as we understand it. Our path *is* often that of observers, set to watching the trials and tribulations of the galaxy as it contends with the great Entropy." He shrugged, and his little muzzle twisted into a bright smile. "Sometimes, however, we like to give it a little nudge."

Iphini Bha shook her head. Marcus thought her reaction was bordering on rude and boorish, all things considered.

"Well, thank you, anyway." He moved vaguely into the receiving room. The shock was wearing off, and he could not forget the glimpse of Copic Fa'Orin's face beneath the matted hood.

"It was Taurani." There was a burning taste in his throat. "It had to be."

"There are few Ntja in the city that do not serve the Council, that is true." The smaller Thien'ha confirmed. He moved to one of the couches and hopped up onto the cushions. "It seems a safe assumption that the Ambassador has decided to act at last."

"Why?" Iphini Bha had collapsed into one of the smaller chairs, her eyes wide and staring at nothing. "Why now?"

Marcus looked up at the Thien'ha again, and started as he realized that the young Diakk woman was staring at him with a clearly hostile glare.

"What?" The loss, danger, and anger were swirling through his mind, and the last thing he wanted to do at the moment was deal with another baleful look by some alien who knew nothing about him.

The girl said nothing, her lips tightening, but her master chuckled. "Sihn Ve'Yan blames you for my poor choices, I'm afraid, Administrator. Do not take it personally."

She flicked her cold glance from the little alien and back to Marcus. She did not deny his claim.

"Nonetheless, I believe you should be safe, now." The mystic hopped off the couch and moved to the door. "I would perhaps stay in for the night, and see that your security is tighter from now on." A sad shadow passed over the furry face. "You will find your Leemuk guards in a service room down the hall, I'm afraid. The Ntja are not known for their gentle natures."

Marcus was looking at the rod again. He couldn't take his eyes off of it, remembering the way it had flashed and blurred and changed shape in the middle of the battle. Without realizing it, he was looking down into the Thien'ha's face.

The Goagoi's eyes were deep vermillion pools, and they seemed to bore into his own as the creature stared up at him. "Do not render my actions this day futile, Administrator Marcus Wells. Take care as you navigate the waters before you."

The door hissed quietly closed behind them, leaving Marcus staring after them with a wrinkled brow.

"I must return to the control center." Iphini Bha pushed passed him. "I will see that the corridor is cleared, and the bodies returned to their people."

Marcus grabbed her by the shoulder, heedless of her sudden, jerked response. "I want the Ntja studied. There has to be some sign of where they came from. If we can link them to Taurani, I want him imprisoned before he can cause any further harm."

Her eyes, always overlarge to his mind, widened even further. "He is an ambassador, Marcus Wells! The only one in the city! You cannot seize him, it is against all convention!"

Marcus shook his head. "If he's responsible for this, I don't care. We'll *build* a jail if we have to, but if I can pin this on him, he's going down."

She shook her head, opening her mouth to respond, when the lighting in the room shifted darker for a moment, and then brightened again. An alarm sounded throughout his rooms, and Angara's voice echoed through the chamber.

"Marcus, are you in your rooms?" Her voice was sharp and full of concern.

"How the hell does she always know what's happening?" He shook his head, and then looked up, for lack of any other focal point. "I am, Angara. We're okay. But—"

"You need to get to the control center at once, Marcus." Her voice was crisp and full of command.

"Well, I was going to stay in for the night—"

"You must go to the control center immediately. I will meet you there." She paused for a breath, as if gathering her thoughts, and her next words sent a chill down his spine. "Everything has changed, Marcus. Everything has changed."

# Chapter 17

Angara Ksaka paced back and forth within the administrator's office. The prints on the walls reflected landscapes of jagged reds and blacks against stark grey backgrounds of senseless, swirling chaos.

She had always hated psycho-reactive art.

Where was Marcus Wells? She had returned to her quarters after parting ways with Justin in the primary Concourse flight deck, frustrated and annoyed with herself, only to find one of her clandestine agents waiting for her.

The Namanu's report was not good.

She had been rushing to the control center, trying to contact Marcus Wells, when she learned of the latest attempt on his life, and the death of the Diakk man and his son. She knew what that would mean for the Human's initiatives, and with what she had learned from her Namanu friend, she knew that their time was nearly up.

Penumbra was not a safe city. It had never *been* a safe city. She knew that, and had known it since before deciding to make it her home in exile. Still, from the office of the administrator she had assisted in making the city as safe as possible. Such concerted incidents of violence were nearly unheard of, and had triggered a cascading sense of terror in the city that was even now rippling out from the Red Tower to the surrounding sectors.

She knew Taurani was behind the whole thing, and the rumors her operative had brought her provided all the circumstantial evidence she would need to convince Marcus Wells. And that was before the Ntja thugs had been killed outside of his apartments.

The door behind her whisked open and Marcus hurried into the office, Iphini Bha behind him. Her perennially-wide eyes seemed dull with shock, and she moved with a slow, almost dream-like gait.

"What's happening?" The Human looked haggard, his hair wild and his eyes hard. "It's already been less than the best day ever, Angara."

Behind him, the control center was filled with the quiet, rushing sound of whispered conversation. There had been no further attacks or acts of violence, but everyone in the room could sense the potential in the air. And if the rumors she carried with her had not spread to the office's workers, it would only be a matter of time.

She put her arms up to calm him, but Marcus was already lurching past her and collapsing into the chair behind the desk. "It's got to be that bastard, Angara. It's got to be." His eyes, while hard, were haunted. "That poor kid." He muttered the words, and she was alarmed to hear the despair leaking into his voice.

"I do not anticipate the situation will be improving in the near future, Marcus." She took a deep breath. They were only rumors, but with everything else that had happened, her heart told her they were true. "A fleet has been dispatched by the Council. They are coming here to remove you."

That brought him up short. His head whipped up. "What?"

Iphini Bha sank into one of the seats by the long table. Her eyes were lowered, staring at the floor, her shoulders slumped. She held her ancient stylus loosely in limp fingers.

Angara looked back at Marcus. "It must be Taurani, but it no longer matters. If they have truly dispatched a fleet, they must feel that combining the symbolism of Penumbra with a Human administrator poses too much of a threat to their authority." She tried to give him a smile, but it would not come. "You are a victim of your success, Marcus. If you had just stayed quietly in this office until we could replace you, they would probably have not felt the need."

Marcus shook his head. "I don't understand. What do they hope to accomplish? Are they going to attack us? Are they going to destroy the city?"

Iphini shook her head, her eyes still locked on the floor. "They could never approach the city with its defenses active. But no one will follow you with a Council fleet hanging over their heads, Marcus Wells. By their very presence, they will freeze your initiatives." She looked up, and her eyes seemed strange, flat and dead. "Your work here is done."

"What about all of those ancient treaties and agreements that kept them at bay?" His words dripped sarcasm, but with an edge of desperation as well. He was shaking his head, looking from her to Bha and back again. "Don't they have to honor their own pacts?"

"No Human had ever set foot within the halls of Penumbra, Marcus." She needed him to understand before he did something drastic and endangered them all. "Having a Human sitting on the command throne of the city was obviously too much."

The door buzzed and opened, and Justin Shaw swept in. He was still wearing his Mnymian disguise, his fashionable clothing impeccable. "They've sent a damn fleet after us?"

She should have known that if her network had picked up the whispers, Justin would not be far behind.

She nodded. "I believe a fairly large armada will arrive within the next few days, with the intention of 'protecting' subjects of the Council from the Human who has seized control here." She shrugged. "It is a time-honored script they have used in the past. In some ways, we may have provided them with just the excuse they needed to come in and end Penumbran independence."

"What kind of fleet is it?" He looked at Iphini, then back to Angara. "I thought the Council was some kind of civilian coalition government. They have their own fleet?"

She nodded. "Their silk glove is very fine, but the Council has ruled with the iron fist that hid within for over ages. Do you think they forced K'hzan Modath from his position as king of the Variyar with parliamentary tricks and harsh words?"

Justin looked blankly at her for a moment, and then turned to Marcus. "What are you going to do? Are you okay?"

Marcus smiled bleakly. "What am I going to do? What the hell can I do?" He shook his head and turned to Angara, his smile faltering. "What the hell can we do?"

She knew this moment was coming. She had mentioned it before, but she had seen how the Human processed information under stress. "The city has more than ample defenses to deal with a standard-sized fleet incursion. There have been efforts in the past to force compliance and annexation, and Penumbra has always responded with sufficient force to quell the attempts."

"She defends herself." Iphini Bha said. She was now staring at Marcus's chest, and Angara agreed, pointing to the Skorahn.

"So long as the amulet is possessed by a bonded administrator, the systems of the Relic Core will engage any enemy foolish enough to approach us." She swallowed, not wanting to voice her true fears. But there was nothing else to say, and Marcus needed to know how dire she feared their situation truly was. "I do not think Taurani would have moved against us if he did not believe he had sufficient force to carry out his will."

Marcus and Justin looked at each other. Fear showed clearly on the administrator's face, while his Human friend, despite the milky lenses, looked more like he was trying to puzzle out the answer to a particularly difficult riddle.

"You think they're going to attack?" Marcus seemed incredulous, but she could see what he was trying to say.

"I do not." She nodded toward the quiet Iwa'Bantu deputy. "I agree with Iphini. The presence of a large Council fleet will create an environment of fear and oppression that will only serve to advance Taurani's efforts in the city."

Justin seemed to agree. "So, they'll be here mainly to back up the Ambassador's play. Most folks won't want to draw their attention, and while everyone's running for cover, Taurani will make his move with the forces he already has in the city." His mouth twisted. "Whatever that's going to be."

"I want to see the defenses." Marcus rose, moving around the desk. "You said they've been used in the past. How long ago, though? Do we know they even still work?"

Iphini Bha looked offended. "Penumbra takes care of itself. The automatic repair and maintenance of the city's physical plant should be accepted as a given no matter how long ago the systems had been used." She looked bitter, and Angara wondered exactly what was going through the girl's mind. "It's saved your life on more than one occasion."

That did not seem to assuage Marcus's concerns, however. "I want to see them with my own eyes. I want Angara to help me understand how they work, and what we can expect from them."

"I need to find Warder Oo'Juto." She looked away from Marcus, not wanting to watch her words hit home. "If we can convince the Aijian to take command before the fleet arrives, we may be able to persuade them to return to Council space. This new threat might convince him to submit."

Justin looked skeptical, and Marcus shook his head. "If they're ready to make their move, and they're convinced the time is right to the point that they've planned a strong military response, I doubt they're going to back down even if the dolphin's floating over the throne when they show up."

He looked to Iphini for support, and she shrugged. "I cannot know the Ambassador's intentions. I do not believe they mean to destroy the city, however."

Marcus moved toward the door. "Doesn't matter." The door flashed open at his approach and he turned to address them. "I want to look at these defenses, and have them explained to me. If I have to find them by myself, it's probably going to take a while."

Iphini Bha looked up with those strange, hollow eyes. "I know nothing about the workings of the weapon systems. You will need to bring one of the security officers, so they may as well lead you as well."

Marcus looked behind him and surveyed the office, pointing out a large Leemuk leaning over another officer's shoulder. "Agha-pa can take me. He must know all about that sort of thing, right?"

The chief of security looked up at hearing his name, his wide, grotesque dentition making it look as if he was grinning at some private joke, his tiny moist eyes questioning.

"Very well." She moved out past him.

"I don't think you should be leaving the control center, Marcus." Angara put her hand up. "But if you insist, I want you to have more security if you're going to be moving around the city." She folded her arms over her chest. "Taurani is going to make another move soon, and when he realizes that his attempt at your apartments did not succeed, he will be working even harder." She desperately wanted him to understand his current danger.

His smile was grim and wan, but at least he could summon one. "Nonsense. It's the middle of the night. But I won't say no to some extra company. Justin?"

The dark skinned man nodded grimly, and it seemed to her as if Marcus's answering smile was a little wider.

"And knowing the Thien'ha, they'll probably show up at some point as well. After their work tonight, might be I trust them more than half of the sentients you've got on your staff."

She had heard about the Thien'ha and their battle at Marcus's rooms. It was very strange behavior for their kind, but things were coming to a head, and she was going to have to trust someone eventually. Truly, if Angara could not be there for the administrator, there were few beings she would rather stand in for her than a roused Thien'ha. They seldom took a direct hand in events, but when backed into a corner, their response was usually definitive.

"No!" Iphini's objection caught them all off guard, and Angara whirled to stare at her questioningly. The girl shrank back, almost as if she had surprised herself. She shook her head almost convulsively, raising one hand as if to ward them all off. "Fine. Deal with the Thien'ha if you feel you must. I do not trust them."

There were many who did not trust the strange mystics. The silent, mysterious observers had watched too many horrific moments in galactic history without raising a finger to assist the victims for most sentients' taste. Angara assumed there must have been some on Iphini's homeworld when the Humans had attacked.

Still, her reaction struck a false note that stuck with Angara for a long time after Marcus, Justin, and the Leemuk officer left to tour the defensive batteries of the city.

\*\*\*\*\*

"We may as well begin with the defenses of the Red Tower." Agha-pa's voice was rough and raspy as he waddled ahead of Marcus away from the control center toward the old ship's prow. "The city's system basically ties all of the point defense weaponry of the towers together into a single network. Enough of the original ships that make up the city were either military in origin or had rudimentary defenses, that it presents a formidable array of weaponry to attackers, no matter what their orientation."

Marcus nodded as he skip-stepped to keep up. "What about an attack from beneath? There weren't as many towers oriented toward the planet." In truth, he had been in awe of the massive city as they approached, and barely remembered what it looked like. But he was fairly sure there were fewer towers along Penumbra's underside.

The Leemuk shrugged, an interesting phenomenon to view from behind, as the creature had no neck to speak of. "There are energy sinks scattered throughout the more sparsely-occupied sections of the Relic Core's surface. We have records of them performing the roles of both close-in defenses and offensive emitter arrays in times of attack."

"Records, because the city hasn't been attacked in living memory?" Marcus was still trying to come to grips with the scale of time they were dealing with. It seemed like everything he heard about had happened thousands of years ago, except that no one here measured time in Earth years, of course, and so he had a hard time keeping track of the relative scope of galactic history.

"That is correct." Agha-pa stopped beside a lift tube. "We can head to the top of the Tower. There are several batteries that cover this quadrant of the city's skyline spread across what was once the dorsal surface of the old Variyar warship, but most are concentrated toward the bow, which is now the top of the Tower, of course."

Marcus truly believed he would never get used to traveling within the lift tubes of Penumbra, even if the aliens let him live here for the rest of his life. The disorienting rush of air, the blur of the tube's walls rushing by, and the flattening of any sounds within all combined to make him feel as if he was getting pushed through some sewer pipe at high speeds.

The tube deposited them in a small chamber that seemed stark even by the standards of the Red Tower. Something about the room made him feel that it had been abandoned for longer than he wanted to think. The three of them moved out into the small room, the air of abandonment clearly affecting each of them. Agha-pa reached out to unlock the door before them when it popped with an audible click at Marcus's approach. The Leemuk turned to look at him, the two moist eyes questioning. Then his gaze fell to the glowing medallion, and the little eyes widened as wide as they were able within their tight, glistening sockets.

"Thank you." The security chief muttered, turning back to the door. A noise in the shadows behind them brought him whirling about, cursing that in the rush and confusion he had still not acquired a weapon. Justin's hand plunged into a deep pocket in his tunic, scanning the shadows for threats. Marcus reached out behind him for Agha-pa, thinking that the security chief had to have some kind of weapon about him, when he saw the two figures emerging from the shadows.

Visions of Copic Fa'Orin's dead body, his son draped across his still form, flashed through his mind. He thought he caught the distinct stench of Ntja on the stale air of the abandoned chamber. He crouched down, his hands low as he turned, every intention of taking one of the big bastards with him before he died.

He was not ashamed of his audible sigh of relief as he recognized the short figure in the white robes stepping into the light, a taller figure in black striding along beside it. The little master pushed back his hood to reveal his grinning muzzle and gleaming red eyes. Marcus noticed that his apprentice did not push her own cowl back, but stared at him balefully from within its shadows. He took a suspicious sniff of the air and sensed only the stale, recycled atmosphere of the Tower's empty service regions.

Marcus smiled, some of the tension draining from his back and shoulders as he saw them. "Thank God." It was strange, deriving this much comfort from two beings who had been enigmatic strangers to him only hours before, but he could not deny it. The smile turned wry as he realized that, until that night, he hadn't even known their names. Khet Nhan, the little master, had come to Penumbra in search of some vague truth he refused to explain, while the novice, Sihn Ve'Yan, had followed her former master out of a sense of obligation that he sensed, from their limited contact, she was now regretting.

He looked for the fascinating staff weapon Nhan had wielded against the Ntja, and his eyes narrowed as he realized the little creature's hands were empty. "Where's the ..." He waved his hands about, trying to convey the blurring, trans- forming shape of the weapon. "Where's your staff ... thing ...?"

Khet Nhan's smile widened and he rubbed his paw-hands together in childlike glee, and then tapped at something hanging from his belt. It was a metal rod, made from the same material as the staff, hanging from an elaborately woven sheath.

"Never fear, Marcus Wells." The master's voice was much deeper than Marcus had at first expected, given the furry little creatures diminutive stature. "The nano-staff is never far from my hands."

Agha-pa stared at the rod in wonder, but shook it off and turned back to the door. "We should continue, before word of our objective reaches unfriendly ears."

Khet Nhan nodded and gestured for them to continue. Marcus and the big Leemuk moved through the door. Justin stared at the smaller alien, his white eyes wide, and the Thien'ha nodded amiably as he passed on through the door, followed by the surly apprentice.

The standard, rosy-tinged lighting of the Red Tower gave way to dim shad- ow as they moved forward. The narrow corridor was a challenge for the Leemuk, who had to sidle sideways whenever a bundle of pipes or cables narrowed the passage. An uncomfortable crawling sensation began to work its way up Marcus's back as they moved deeper into the shadows, with the bulk of the Leemuk ahead of him and the soft sounds of the mystics following up behind. He found himself wishing that Justin had entered at his side.

Eventually, the corridor opened out into a large work area, with a series of viewing field recesses lining a far wall. Each was dark, deactivated, but paired with a work station below it. Several lights blinked in what he assumed was some kind of standby pattern at each station.

But as Marcus approached, they each winked to life, the viewing fields filling with roiling clouds and then settling to show images from the outer hull of the Tower. He saw low, sleek shapes nestled into armored recesses, several visible within each field. As he focused on a work station he saw the colors of the various lights and telltales winking from a confusing pattern of colors and shapes into a steadily gleaming row of green indicators. His feelings of growing claustrophobia lurched into the foreground of his thoughts as he realized that somehow, the room was reading his mind, transforming itself into a legible pattern.

Agha-pa's little eyes drew together in what must have been a confused expression as the stations reconfigured themselves. He couldn't be certain, but he felt that Khet Nhan and Sihn Ve'yan were looking at him strangely as well.

"How do we get them to work?" Marcus wondered out loud, his eyes locked on the nearest viewing field with an anticipatory smile.

As he watched, one of the sleek shapes in the image rose out of its covert and began to pivot back and forth, snouts extending out of the metal as if the thing was searching for some hostile prey. He wanted to laugh, as he felt in control of *something* for the first time in days.

He narrowed his eyes, focused his thoughts, and the rest of the shapes rose as well, all of them pirouetting around, scanning the skies above the Tower. He could see other towers around them, none reaching quite the height of the Red Tower. From up here they more resembled the ships they had been in antiquity rather than the repurposed structures of their current lives. As he focused on one of the distant shapes, the vision field obliged by bringing it leaping into closer view.

He saw gleaming metallic domes dotting the bow of the new tower. As he concentrated, small rings flashed into being around each protrusion, with data streaming beside each. Somehow, through the uncomfortable buzzing just beneath his ear, he knew they were energy projectors, capable of spitting out a hail of nearly-solid light to break up incoming ordnance in their slice of the sky.

He turned back from the viewing field. "So, what happens where the towers weren't first warships, or lacked defenses?"

Agha-pa was looking out a viewing field at the end of the row and turned around. Somehow, despite the enormous, glistening teeth and the tiny eyes set into the slick green flesh, he managed to look nervous. "I don't know. The records are sparse, to be honest." He shrugged his massive shoulders. "The city has never been successfully attacked, so the coverage it has must be sufficient?"

"Perhaps our records are a bit more substantial than the official reports of the city?" Khet Nhan smiled politically, his paws rubbing together again. "I believe, from what I have gathered, that there are more than sufficient point defense batteries, the purposes of which were manifold, but now serve to defend Penumbra from an attack originating overhead. Batteries were added to those towers deemed insufficiently protected. We also believe that there is an inherent capability of the Relic Core itself to defend the city, should the need arise. The records speak of at least one instance when the city was called upon to do that. The details are scant, but there can be no doubt that the Core rose up in its own defense."

Marcus shook his head, his mouth twisted. "Forgive me if that's not quite enough for me. I think—"

"Master." The word cracked across the confined space like a whip. They all turned to the dark-robed acolyte. "You should address him as Master."

Marcus stared at her. The hostility in her eyes was undeniable, and he suddenly doubted his instinct to trust the Thien'ha with his safety. Killing those damned Ntja would have been an easy way to earn his trust; and cheap, too, if the reports of the Ntja's value as agents were true.

"Please, Sihn, there is no need to stand on ceremony." Khet Nhan's smiled sent the fine green beard fringe writhing. "I am no being's master here save maybe yours, and even that only by courtesy, it would seem." It was a mild rebuke, but the fires in the girl's eyes guttered, and she looked down as if she had been slapped.

The tension in the room ratcheted up another notch, and the two Humans and the Leemuk exchanged uncomfortable glances before the small Thien'ha master clapped those small hands and gestured back to the viewing fields. "Regardless, I believe we can trust in the defenses of the city. Others can be sent to reassure you of their status, Administrator, but I think there will be more pressing concerns for you to pursue in the days ahead."

Marcus stared out the viewing field at the massive batteries and then turned back to the little alien. "And what would you suggest I pursue?"

The big red eyes blinked, and the smile faded. "Your efforts here are noble, Marcus Wells. The potential of this city is great, if it were to be realized. The concerns of its many, disparate citizens must be harnessed and pointed in the same direction."

Justin nodded. "Sounds like we're getting sent home either way, Marc. If you can lock down some of your ideas before the fish takes over, could be some of the good we've tried to do here will stick after we're gone."

Khet Nhan nodded, while Agha-pa looked between them as if he could not follow the conversation. Marcus smiled a grim little grin as he thought of the big Leemuk's nanites trying to translate 'fish' in context.

Marcus turned toward the chief of security. "I want at least five towers manually checked in each quadrant. The rest can be reviewed remotely, but by morning I want a report on all of the defenses," he looked sideways at the little mystic, then back to the giant green monster. "I want reassurance that everything is in working order."

"Yes sir." The Leemuk's bulbous head dipped, his small eyes blinking rapidly. "I will see to it personally."

"No." Marcus shook his head, looking back through the view screen. "I want you to go back to the control center. We need to get in front of Taurani. See that any of our initiative partners have security, and run up a schedule that will see as many of those who have proven willing to work with us will be as protected as we can make them." He closed his eyes, shaking his head. All of the time he had spent in his quarters studying the city could now pay dividends, if only he did not let his newfound appreciation for the scope of the work ahead crush him into immobility.

He turned back to the room, meeting each creature's gaze. "We're going to need to recruit more security personnel. The office of the administrator has never been configured to provide active security for the entire city. I think we're going to need to think in those terms from now on."

Khet Nhan's furry head bobbed up and down encouragingly while his acolyte's lips tightened. The Leemuk's eyes had shrunken into the massive head even deeper, and Justin looked lost in thought.

"I might have to give this all up soon, but Justin's right. There's a chance to do something worthwhile here, and I mean to do the best I can to see that it doesn't fall apart the minute we have to leave."

# Chapter 18

Ambassador Khuboda Taurani floated in the shallow pool, his wide eyes closed to glittering slits as the salty water lapped all around him. His thin, lipless mouth had settled into a contented slash that did service with the Kerie as a smile.

He could not have foreseen, when he first heard that a Human had stumbled into the administrator's throne, how much easier this was going to make achieving his ultimate goals for this filthy backwater.

Marcus Wells had faltered from error to error. The Human had been most obliging in his lack of guile and his reflexive response to every cut and thrust. The city was on the verge of collapse now, and he had barely had to stir himself from his consular apartments for a gratifying stretch of days.

"Ambassador." The growling word sliced through the peaceful calm, but he rigidly refused to allow his body to jerk upright in the water.

"Yes, Iranse?" His Eru servant had been instrumental in directing the breakdown of the city's morale. His Ntja guards made excellent shock troopers, but they tended to behave more as a blunt weapon, and required a bit of a controlling hand to ensure their most effective use in a sensitive operation like this.

Iranse, however, had been indispensable.

"Another consortium has refused the Human's offer of protection. Most of the independent interests have now turned him down, and are barricading themselves in their offices, awaiting the end." The tall purple creature stood respectfully ten paces away from the pool, hands folded over his belly and red eyes downcast.

"Excellent." Marcus Wells's move to offer protection to those syndicates that had opted to work with him in the past had been one of the few decent ideas the foolish Human had had. Luckily, the Ntja had managed to beat his fledgling security forces to the punch in several key locations, and the resulting massacres had done wonders to convince the rest that the administrator's office would be incapable of protecting them.

"The entire city is all but shut down." The Eru were a naturally-subservient people, and thus it was hard to judge from Iranse's tone of voice, but it appeared he was quite pleased with the Ambassador's work. "By the time Admiral Ochiag arrives, they will have lost the last vestiges of unity they might have possessed."

Taurani tightened his mouth but decided to allow his servant this moment of unseemly exultation. He finally sat up and drifted to the smooth edge of the pool, his hands flowing back and forth in the warm water. "I do not suppose you've any Iwa'Bantu tucked away somewhere against such a celebratory moment?"

He asked, knowing that he had wrung the last moments of amusement from the final plaything available to him in the city days ago, after Iranse had reported the successful completion of the mission that had seen to the Diakk troublemaker and his whelp .

"Ah…" Iranse cleared his throat, obviously at a loss. "Well, no, sir. Aside from the deputy…"

That brought the smile back to Taurani's tight mouth. The Iwa'Bantu were gentle and quiet, and almost never voluntarily ventured from their home planet of Iwa'Ban. It was intriguing that this female should have wandered so far on her own. But there would be plenty of time to pursue those intriguing thoughts when he had secured control of this nest of vermin once and for all.

The Ambassador shook his head as he emerged from the pool. "Let's allow poor Iphini Bha these last moments of calm while we can afford to be magnanimous." The servant rushed to a stand by the wall and brought forward the soft robes Taurani preferred when relaxing. "I think we are entering the last stages of our plan, my friend. Is everything in readiness?"

His massive servant's incongruously small head dipped in acknowledgement. "Everything is in place, sir. When the admiral arrives, you will be in full possession of the city. I have seen to the last elements personally."

"Never underestimate the impact of the fear of imminent death, Iranse." He smoothed the robes over his well-formed body with a nod of approval. "Such terror is an essential tool in any good diplomat's arsenal. By the time the fleet arrives, there will be little more for the admiral to do than to show the Council's flag, round up a few undesirables, and head back to the galactic core with nothing more to show for his time and effort than a trophy prisoner or two." The tight smile stretched from one side of his face to the other. "The glory will belong almost entirely to the Kerie, and our important work can begin."

*****

Marcus sat behind the big desk in the administrator's office. He was exhausted. He had gotten almost no sleep since the latest attempt on his life. Each time he closed his eyes, the pale, still form of Copic Fa'Elic, the innocent Diakk boy he had tried so hard to save, was waiting there to stare at him with blank, accusing eyes.

Iphini Bha was silent at the table, going over reports in the silence of her own mind, the ancient stylus spinning in her fingers.

On the wall, the images hung silent in their frames, their dull tones reflecting a lack of hope and conviction that he found disheartening, knowing they were picking up on his own thoughts. He thought he could see hints and suggestions of a face lost somewhere in the somber shadows, Clarissa looking out at him through sad, lost eyes. But her image in the framed pieces had faded more and more with each passing day. Lately, he could hardly see her at all.

There was a jagged, violent disturbance in the background of some of the images that he found confusing, but there was enough going wrong now that almost any negative reflection would have made sense.

The halls and pathways of the city were empty. The citizens had withdrawn behind barricaded doors, venturing out only when necessary, and then only in numbers, and heavily armed. There was no denying the sense of impending doom that hung over the entire place. It was as if the people of Penumbra were holding their breath, waiting for the Council to come and finally end their independence once and for all.

It did not help that every attempt he had made to forge his loose alliance of corporations, consortiums, and syndicates into a more cohesive whole had come to nothing. The massacres at the two Namanu factories had not helped in that regard, of course.

What made things even worse was that Taurani, for he had no doubt the damned Kerie bastard was behind the whole thing, had managed to avoid leaving even a single piece of damning evidence behind. The independent-minded citizens of Penumbra would rather live in this constant fear than have him descend upon the Council Ambassador's residence without proof.

And that, of course, presupposed he had the ability to attack Taurani's gang of thugs. Despite his mandate to expand the city's security forces, he was losing guards every day, and there were precious few recruits stepping forward to take their places.

By the time the damned fleet arrived, he'd be holed up in the control center with Justin, Angara, and Iphini Bha. The city *better* be able to defend itself, at that point.

"What I don't understand, Iphini," he began hesitantly. His deputy had been acting more and more distant over the past few days. "If the city is so capable of defending itself, why is everyone afraid?"

She turned to look at him, her face a mask of stillness and despair, the pencil-like rod pausing in mid-spin. "The Council's reach is long, Marcus Wells. Most of those here in the city have already fled from them once." She looked away. "They are not likely to stand up to them now."

He still didn't understand. "But with the defenses up, how can they get to us? Taurani's got his thugs, yes, but how many can he have? Twenty? Thirty? Against a whole city?"

"Agha-pa fears that he may have far more than that. We have no way of tracking arrivals in the city. It's one of its many attractions for those seeking refuge. Agha-pa is afraid that Taurani has been bringing Ntja in for quite a while, before we even knew to watch for them."

That sent a cold shiver down Marcus's back. "How many does he think they have?"

She shrugged and turned away from him. "There is no way to know. It could easily be hundreds."

Hundreds of violent thugs against a city already suffocating under a blanket of fear. It was not a thought liable to make sleep any easier.

As things had continued to collapse, he had begun to look forward to Angara's long-sought successor making his appearance. As much as it still disturbed him on some deep level to be replaced by a dolphin, he was afraid he might be ready to leave.

The door slid open and Justin and Angara came through. He hadn't seen Justin in days, but it was his bodyguard that caught his undivided attention. She was brusque as she came into the room, and her intense, distracted energy swept through the psycho-reactive images like a tidal wave of primary colors and hard, blocky shapes. Justin, moving behind her, looked directly at him, his pale eyes wide and sympathetic.

"Warder Oo'Juto is on his way." She moved to stand before his desk. "A scout ship has just returned. The Council fleet will be emerging into the system in a matter of hours. Oo'Juto was reluctant, but he understands our desperation. He has worked with the Council in the past, of course, in his capacity as Warder of Earth. Hopefully that will carry some weight with the admiral of the fleet when they arrive."

"I think we might want to make a quick exit before this all goes down,

Marc." Justin shook his head. "Even if things are as peaceful as we're hoping, there's a lot of folks here who're going to be looking for someone to blame for the disruption of the status quo." He shrugged. "You know we're going to be the number one target. It's not like we've scored any major PR achievements as far as the reputation of Humans around here is concerned."

Marcus found that a bit disingenuous, spoken as it was from behind concealing contact lenses, a dyed beard, and a galactic wardrobe. But there was too much occurring, too quickly, for him to indulge in petty sniping now.

"You think this will do it?" There had been a time when Marcus had taken great pride in never leaving any job unfinished, but that had been a long time ago. "If you're convinced the dolphin's taking over will spare these people, I'll go. But if you think Taurani and his bulldogs are going to continue to make trouble…"

Iphini Bha stood abruptly and moved to a far corner. The art nearest her altered subtly, something dark swirling in the background.

"I don't think anything is going to deter Taurani now, Marcus." Angara paced behind the long table. "But Oo'Juto will be able to talk to him. The transition will be less painful." She shrugged, looking at him through a fall of white hair, her violet eyes glittering within her dark, purple-tinged face. "Perhaps something can be salvaged from your work here."

"And all I have to do is run away to even find out." Marcus felt something inside his chest give way. His shoulders slumped; he slid back into the seat.

The low murmur of conversation out in the control center faded suddenly to a hushed quiet. Marcus knew that the Thein'ha were watching the door, and had no doubt that anyone moving into the room outside did so only with their permission. Nevertheless, a chill chased itself down his back as he turned to look at the door, his heart beating painfully against his ribs.

The door slid open, and a massive gray shape floated through.

Marcus had seen the giant creatures Angara called Aijians a few times around the city. They floated along on some kind of anti-gravity system that must have been related to the variable control surfaces grav-locked to the hull of Angara's ship. They were surrounded with a shimmering field of water that softened the lines of their body and caused them to glisten under light.

No matter how graceful or stately they might seem, he only saw them as giant dolphins swimming through thin air.

The fact that these creatures were, in fact, responsible for keeping mankind locked on Earth for God alone knew how long bothered him on more levels than he cared to admit. The fact that no one seemed willing or able to explain the crime that had relegated Humans to their distant prison in the dim, lost past of the galaxy only made things worse.

He had always liked dolphins; who didn't? He remembered a visit he had once paid to a small local aquarium in Clearwater, Florida. He had stared at the dolphins swimming around in their pools for hours, and had daydreamed about diving in with them.

And those little bastards must have been staring right back at him the entire time, laughing behind their slab-nosed faces.

He understood, vaguely, that Aijian DNA had been altered in some way to bring it into some cosmic norm with all of the other denizens of Earth. He even understood, on some level, that this alteration made them more likely to successfully replace him if he stepped down from his office. He looked down at the Skorahn. It gleamed brighter than the office's subdued lighting could account for. He wondered if he would be more comfortable giving it up to someone other than an alien who had overseen the incarceration of his entire species.

"This is the Human to whom you have granted the power of the administrator?" The voice seemed to speak directly into his mind, with undertones of high-pitched trillings just out of his range of hearing. A quick glance at Justin showed his friend wincing in reaction.

Angara nodded, stepping forward. "Please accept my gratitude for your acceptance of this burden, Warder Alab Oo'Juto." She moved around the table to stand between Marcus and the dolphin.

The alien waved one shimmering flipper in an alarmingly Human gesture of dismissal. "Please do not refer to me by this title. Warder am I no longer." The long head twisted to look again at Marcus, and he found himself having to concentrate hard to maintain contact with those deep, black eyes. He wondered what the creature was thinking. Did it harbor residual opinions from its own time on Earth? Was it laughing at him too?

"I will take the Skorahn now, Human." The squeaking beneath the voice grated even more, and Marcus shied back, one hand rising to the necklace that had caused all of this trouble; that had brought him so far from home.

From the corner of his eye he caught Iphini Bha spin around, glaring at the door as Khet Nhan and his acolyte came in, moving off to the side. Marcus's eyes narrowed as he saw the paintings behind his deputy spike with sudden, jagged violence.

"I think perhaps we should revisit this decision, Marcus Wells." The high-pitched voice of the Thien'ha master caught him by surprise. The little Guagoi had taken part in no policy discussions since being brought into his confidence after the death of the Diakk Copics. This was the first time he had spoken up in such a way.

"The Skorahn represents a great potentiality of power." The small, delicate-seeming hands almost clutched at the jewel dangling below Marcus's fist. "Entropy is drawn to it like filings to a magnet." The crimson eyes locked on his. "It should not be surrendered lightly."

"No one is surrendering anything *lightly*!" Angara barked, stepping toward the little creature. Nhan's eyes never wavered from Marcus's.

"What is this?" The bulk of Oo'Juto spun gracefully to bring its baleful eyes swinging over to Angara. "Does this creature have a place here in our deliberation?" The voice in his head was getting shrill again, and he saw Justin reach back to brace himself against the far wall. "I have no need of this draw on my attention and resources, *exile*."

Marcus saw Angara's eyes widen in shocked surprise. Despite the lack of tone as Oo'Juto's meaning sliced directly into his head, the contempt he had piled into that last word was clear. Tensions rose, and some clinical part of his mind watched with vague curiosity as the artwork on the walls erupted in sparking images of blood and violence.

The Thien'ha bristled at the word as well, and Marcus thought he was going to rush the dolphin floating before them all, little hand clasping at the metal cylinder hanging from his waist. The Diakk girl, Ve'Yan, placed a hand on her master's shoulder to restrain him. Having seen him in action, though, Marcus hardly felt that one hand would be sufficient, should he decide the dolphin needed to be taken down a peg.

"Please!" Angara shouted, her hands flying out like blades in a violent sweeping gesture that claimed the center of the room. "We have discussed this. There is *no* other choice! Our only chance to get the Council to leave Penumbra alone is to have an established Galactic at the helm when they arrive. We cannot have a Human on the administrator's throne if we want any chance at peace!"

A heavy stillness settled upon the room, and Marcus felt the breaking sensation in his chest intensify. If there was no other way, how could he bring these people down with him, no matter the reason for their bigotry against Humanity?

It had been a very long time since he had made any difficult decision. It had been an even longer time since he had made such a decision wisely.

With eerily still fingers he lifted the Skorahn over his head. With a quick look he quieted Khet Nhan and extended his arm toward Alab Oo'Juto. The sapphire jewel spun from the glittering necklace in his hand, light sparking off its surfaces from an unknowable source.

An unseen force began to pull at the necklace, and the chain slipped through fingers gone suddenly numb as whatever mastery over gravity Oo'Juto possessed seized the medallion and drew it gracefully through the air.

As the last length of chain slipped through his fingers, something deep within Marcus went dark, and he was suddenly very, very tired. The lights seemed to dim in the room, and sounds became muted, as if his ears were filled with water.

The entire room seemed suspended in that slow, painful moment. Everything was still but the medallion floating toward the big Aijian, whose inhuman smile seemed to steam with arrogance.

A warning bell sounded from behind the dolphin as lights began to flash out in the control room. Someone shouted something about an Alpha Lock override. Marcus turned, as if moving through thick water, to look at Iphini Bha.

She stood, still as a statue, against the wall. Her eyes were closed, her face tight and focused.

His stomach imploded within his belly.

A shriek echoed across the office, and a massive explosion erupted out in the control center. Everyone in the office dropped slightly into tense crouches, whirling toward the door. With a flick of his tail, Oo'Juto spun in place, somehow registering wounded dignity and outrage.

Smoke bellowed through the low-ceilinged center as Marcus's people scrambled for cover. A blast of green plasma flashed past and shattered a bank of processing nodes, sending arcs of energy from their viewing fields to ground themselves in walls, ceiling, and floor.

There was a great deal of shouting in the outer room, much of it by guttural voices that were hardly intelligible, even to the nanites living in his brain.

A shape barreled past Marcus and flew through the space between him and Oo'Juto. One pale arm, fine black lines crisscrossing the skin in a delicate tracery, flashed up and grabbed the medallion where it floated, forgotten, in the air.

Iphini Bha scrambled behind the big administrator's desk, crouching down there, her wide eyes terrified, and yet an unholy light flashed from behind them as her face twitched, fear, terror, and vindication warring violently across her flesh.

Two big shapes emerged through the fog, their dog-like faces masked with armored rebreather units, their tiny pig-eyes glaring from within globular vision modules.

Ntja. They wore the brown uniforms of their Council allegiance. One held a rifle in its hands while the other was wielding a heavy, vicious looking sword-like weapon that dripped with pale, viscous fluid he was almost sure had to be the blood of one of his people. Another such weapon hung from the belt of the rifle-dog.

Even a suppression field was not going to stop the Ntja.

Within the office, it seemed like everyone was screaming. Justin held something small and dark in his right hand, white eyes flashing back and forth in his dark face. Angara's shoulder weapons were deployed as she settled low, a blade in either hand. The two Thien'ha had moved away from the door, Nhan's nano-staff a long-bladed spear in his hands. In the center, gently holding his position with slow waves of his flippers, swam Oo'Juto.

The Aijian focused on the doorway and an old blast door began to descend. Marcus cursed himself for forgetting the security door.

With a flick of the staff, Nhan's spear shimmered and became something that looked more like a long rifle. Iridescent blue energy flashed out and took the rifle-wielding Ntja in the chest, blowing him back out through the door and into the fog. Before the dog with the sword could respond, another blast sent him after his companion. By the time Marcus looked back at the little master, the spear had returned, gleaming dully.

It looked like they would be safe in the office, anyway. Marcus was hardly sure he understood the benefit of that if the Ntja held the control center outside, but at the moment, having a blast door between him and the hulking, canine shock troops seemed like a fine idea. They could puzzle out the rest later.

The door ground to a halt.

In the corner, still crouched behind the desk, Iphini Bha, her eyes wild, was shaking the medallion at the door, screaming incoherently, spittle flying from her open mouth.

The blast door began to shake violently. One quiet corner of his mind was fascinated to watch his deputy trying to wrestle the control of the Skorahn manually, when so much had come to him without a second thought. It gave him just a moment of superiority, welling through the mind-numbing sensations of betrayal and confusion that dominated his mental landscape.

Oo'Juto began to shake as he continued to focus his gravity manipulation on the door. Iphini Bha shrieked again, and the door surged upward, sliding into the ceiling recess that had hidden it. The standard door was thrust against the wall as well, and the way was open for the forces moving toward them through the smoke.

A single tall figure was revealed as the doors swung away. Khuboda Taurani, wearing tight-fitting trousers and a loose shirt that was more conducive to action than his standard diplomat's robes, held an enormous gun cradled casually in his arms.

The alien's rigid gray face was not prone to smiles; the thin, lipless mouth perhaps incapable of the expression. Nevertheless, those inscrutable metallic eyes glittered with malicious amusement as he stepped through the swirling smoke, obviously enjoying the drama of the moment.

"I might be of some assistance here, I believe." The Kerie diplomat's mouth widened in what had to be some version of a smile, and he raised the lead-colored weapon in his arms.

Everyone in the office shrank away from the bright flash of crimson light. Marcus knew the bolt could have been meant for any of them, and his mind made a lightning-quick calculation as to his own odds, coming up alarmingly low, when an ear-piercing, deafening shriek echoed off the thick walls and a cascade of warm water rushed across the floor.

The bolt of energy, whatever it was, struck Alab Oo'Juto in the side, the weapon unaffected by the suppression field. The water on that side flashed to a super-heated steam as flesh and bone buckled and ruptured, throwing the big gray body violently against the back wall, which partially buckled beneath its weight. Justin's eyes were wide as he disappeared behind the shattered, leaking bulk.

The Aijian diplomat's body shuddered on the sodden floor, blood and water flying in large, dark droplets across the room's other occupants. Marcus felt the warmth running down his face and started to shake as adrenaline coursed through his system.

Taurani sauntered into the room, flanked by two enormous Ntja soldiers brandishing guns even bigger and more menacing than his.

The Council's Ambassador to Penumbra looked down at the still-twitching body and gave an eloquent shrug. "Well, what else can you expect, when you run with vermin, you're bound to get dirty."

By the wall, Angara was helping a stunned Justin to stand, while everyone else stared at the ambassador in varying states of outrage and fear.

"Deputy Bha, I believe there is a further responsibility for you to fulfill?" He turned to stare at Marcus with those alien, glittering eyes. One long-fingered hand flicked out toward the desk, unfolding in a clear demand.

"Bha? Why?" Angara's voice was choked with rage and confusion.

Iphini Bha picked her way around the desk and held out the medallion. She walked with an unsteady gait, but forced her shoulders back, her chin lifted high.

"You would have a *Human* rule in Penumbra. A Human?" She almost screamed the word, although she refused to meet Marcus's eyes. "And even worse, you would allow him to strengthen the administrator's hold over the city? Over your vaunted free city?"

The deputy dropped the Skorahn into the waiting hand. "I don't care one single speck of dust for your city or your freedom." She turned at Marcus at last, and those wide, pale-blue eyes were filled with hatred. "But I won't let a Human hold power over anything for a moment more than I must."

Marcus stared at her. They had worked together for months. Probably close to a year, if he took the time to do the math. They had laughed together, shared meals, and even spoken about their hopes for the city with each other. Something about those memories scratched at his mind now, though, and he remembered, vaguely, how she would always avoid speaking of her home planet, and of her past.

Had she always hated him? Had she always hated him because he was a Human?

Taurani raised the medallion and watched it spin beneath his grasping hand. It glittered as it turned, sending azure shards of light flashing across the walls. Was it Marcus's imagination, or was it in fact duller than it had when it had been his? The ambassador let the heavy rifle drop with a sopping flop onto the floor as if he no longer had a need of its direct, blatant threat.

"Humans. Am I correct, Iphini Bha?" Taurani held his empty hand toward the Thien'ha, to stave off any rash actions. "And thus the wheel continues to turn, does it not, Master Nhan?"

The Thien'ha master crouched lower, his fine teeth gleaming in a hate-filled grimace. Behind him, Sihn Ve'Yan still held his shoulder, and it was clear she was restraining him from moving against the diplomat.

"You, of all beings here, should have known how this ended, Master Nhan." Taurani flicked his empty hand and the Ntja soldiers moved further into the room, covering them all with their enormous rifles. "The Humans have ever tainted every cycle in which they moved with violence and hatred. It is really a shame that so many citizens of Penumbra were taken in by these villains." He moved again to stand over the now-still body of the Aijian. "So sad that so much had to be lost, because you all forgot your history."

He spun dramatically to point to Marcus, who had a very hard time not daring the Ntja weapons by launching himself at the tall, gray-skinned bastard. "Humans destroy everything they touch. You all knew this long before this Marcus Wells and his pathetic friend soiled the corridors of your little city. It is truly an important lesson, and one that will be well-learned by those who survive the aftermath of this current treachery."

The thin mouth stretched again, and the noseless face seemed to twitch, trying to smile. He raised his empty hand at his soldiers. "How unfortunate that you all had to die to underscore the experience."

Khet Nhan yanked his shoulder from his acolyte's grasp and lunged across the room. The metal staff lengthened as he swung it in a whistling arc, and Taurani shrank away from the blow, clutching the medallion to his chest as he stumbled back, slipping on the slick flooring.

But the staff had not been aimed at Taurani. A blade materialized from the rounded butt of the staff and took one of the Ntja soldiers in the throat, slicing without apparent difficulty through the armored gorget of his rebreather. The beast dropped his sword and clutched at the wound with clumsy, grasping fingers, falling to his knees as a thick, dark fluid sheeted down his chest.

"Out, now!" Nhan spun, the staff shortening again to allow him to come up against the wall, just beside the door.

Angara shoved Justin forward, past Taurani and toward the open door. Her shoulder weapons rose out of their sheathing and sent two weak blasts into the remaining Ntja guard. The two bolts struck the soldier in the chest and knocked him over backward, out into the control center. The telltales across the small barrels winked and went out before the dog soldiers fell, and the dark-skinned woman grunted.

"Suppression field!" The knives glittered in her hands as she reached one arm around Marcus and forced him through the door. Behind them, Nhan and

Ve'Yan followed as Taurani bellowed in anger, and Iphini Bha cowered away from Ambassador and mystics alike.

Out in the control center, the suppression field that had stopped Angara's weapons had rendered the massive guns of the Ntja useless as well, and they were hefting their heavy blades, ready to bar the fugitives from the hall beyond.

Marcus saw Agha-pa's body slumped against a wall, his green skin pale, a pool of viscous fluid pooling around him. The head of security was still, his big hands firmly grasping the neck of a dead Ntja shock trooper. The other control center workers were either still on the floor or huddled against the far wall, behind the administrator's throne.

There were five giant Ntja standing between the door and the small group, their brown uniforms blending into the smoke. Marcus began to lose the slight, new-kindled hope he had felt as they ran from the office.

Somehow, in the confusion, he had forgotten for a moment the violence of that night in front of his apartments.

Khet Nhan flew past him like a pale streak, his light-green fur bristling, teeth set, and dull staff flashing through the air. The staff blurred as it spun, first a spear, then a long-bladed sword, then a metallic, chain-like whip that lashed out, taking a soldier in the throat and stripping it of armor, leather, and flesh with one vicious pull.

Sihn Ve'Yan leapt by and took one of the big warriors in the gut with a cruel kick, spinning past and reaching behind her with a slap that seemed casual, but nevertheless sent the beast tumbling backward into a bank of observation stations.

There were only two standing when Angara pushed past Marcus, shoving the still-dazed Justin into his arms. Her knives flashed as she danced into the melee. She moved with a grace that belayed her deadly intent, and despite the shrieking ambassador standing in the doorway to the inner office, soon the last heavy body fell to the deck.

"You fools! You have no idea what you are doing!" Taurani was wearing the medallion now, hefting his massive gun in both hands again.

Marcus saw the small lights on Angara's shoulder-mounted weapons flash back to life just before the big cannon in Taurani's arms barked.

"Down!" He shouted, his throat raw from panic, smoke, and fear.

Angara dropped without hesitation. Ve'Yan, however, stood up straighter as if she doubted the warning. Nhan dropped, his legs sweeping around to strike his acolyte behind the knees, knocking her to the deck.

The blast flashed out into the corridor, its roar accompanied by the deep-throated cries of Ntja panic. More soldiers were pouring in from side chambers and work spaces deeper within the control center.

Knowing the suppression field seemed to be wavering, Angara took a chance and turned to send two bolts back toward the Ambassador, who ducked into the office as the small, thin privacy door was smashed by their energy.

"Run!" She screamed, pushing Ve'Yan ahead of her.

They ran. Khet Nhan stood by the door, waiting for Marcus to hurry past, Justin's arm hoisted roughly over his shoulder. As they came out into the corridor, littered with fallen Ntja, he watched as Nhan brought his staff around, the tip reshaping itself into a glittering, slender spike that he sent sliding through the control panel of the big blast doors.

Marcus's mind flashed back to the effortless control he had had over the city's systems only moments ago. Within the control center, Ntja were moving toward them, raising their big weapons to burn them down. The Thien'ha's attack on the door's controls seemed to have had no effect, and he imagined that he could see the dark, squinting eyes of the alien warriors coming to kill him, standing there like a swaying statue, unable to move. When the door flashed down just as he had imagined, he jerked away in surprise.

Nhan did not seem to be surprised, however, and pulled him, Justin in tow, down the zig-zagging corridors to the nearest lift tubes.

The corridor was littered with dead Ntja. Some had been the victims of the big blast from Taurani's wild shot. Others had died to the blades and blasters of his allies.

Behind them, within the control center, the only place he had felt truly at home since he arrived in Penumbra, the shouts and cries of countless enemies echoed dully from behind the blast door.

As they fled down the corridor, he found himself wondering what sorts of images the psychoactive artworks were reflecting now.

# Chapter 19

She felt as if the pounding of blood in her ears would drown out every other sound in the world. They were crouched in a service conduit at the very bottom of the Red Tower, in the defunct engineering spaces of the old ship. Ntja soldiers had pursued them back through the Tower, destroying several ancient lift tubes in the process. But through her own efforts and the work of the two Thien'ha, they had lost their last pursuers some time ago.

Until the damned Skorahn unlocked the security systems for Taurani and the traitor Iphini Bha. Then there would be no hiding; no matter where they ran.

"I still think we need to be further from the Tower." Justin was looking ragged, his clothing stained with sweat and his dark skin slick. "Even if they can't get the security feeds working, the first thing they're going to do is a sweep of their own damned building."

"It's not their damned building." Marcus Wells sat, his back against a metal bulkhead, his breath heaving. "None of this is theirs." He struck the wall behind him with an elbow, his mouth twisted in bitter anger.
Khet Nhan and his acolyte stood quietly nearby, watching their back trail for trouble.

"I can't believe she did it." Marcus was staring at the pipes and cabling lining the far wall, but seeing nothing. His eyes slid up to hers, the pain in them clear. "Why would she help him?"

Angara stared down at the Human she had put on the administrator's throne. There was no way she could have foreseen the way things would turn out when she forced the two Humans onto her ship back on Earth, but the guilt that pressed down upon her at his expression hurt no less for all that.

"Her planet was nearly destroyed by Humans when she was only a child—" She looked away. She had worked with both Marcus and Justin for too long now to speak of the old prejudices and fears with any seriousness. She knew no one had told the two Humans about the ancient past. If it had been anyone's responsibility, it would have been hers, and she just could not bring herself to start that conversation, no matter how many times she tried.

Justin stood up, staring at her. Whatever it was growing between them twisted painfully, and she found she could not meet his eyes. "I've had enough of the cryptic 'it's because you're Human' shit you've all been piling onto us since before you got us onto that damned ship of yours." The words were hot, and she looked up to see Khet Nhan staring at her as if waiting for some momentous revelation.

Damned Thien'ha. She had always hated that about them; that blank stare they all seemed to gain when they thought they were about to watch something interesting happen.

She shook her head and forced her eyes to lock with the dark skinned Human's. "There is more history than you can possibly know at work here, Justin. I promise you, I will tell you everything. But we need to get away from here before we can worry about any of that."

"You have a ship." Sihn Ve'Yan said in her low voice. "We need to get there, and get out of the city before the Kerie gains full control of the Relic Core."

The fact that Taurani was having such a hard time finding them and directing his damned thugs in their pursuit had confused Angara all through the flight toward the Concourse. Marcus had been able to exercise control over nearly all of the city's systems almost immediately upon arriving. The Ntja, however, seemed to be constantly running into slamming doors that refused to open for them, suppression fields that shut down their weapons, and areas of corridor that were suddenly plunged into darkness with no warning at all.

Marcus had been distracted the entire time, and she found herself wondering if he might not, through the abnormally deep bond with the Skorahn, be manipulating their environment despite being separated from the medallion. He had denied it, and the despondent cast to his features seemed to radiate helplessness even now. But she could not completely shake the feeling that things were going better for them than they had any right to expect.

"There's no way we'll be able to get to the *Yud'ahm Na'uka* without having to fight through an army of Ntja." She frowned. "And we are hardly in possession of a force that would make such a fight survivable, never mind viable."

"Perhaps if we could draw the guards away?" Khet Nhan had settled the small rod of his nano-staff back onto his belt, and his small hands were curled around each other in a calm, thoughtful pose. "Truly, Ambassador Taurani cannot have an endless supply of these creatures at his disposal? You would have known if there had been so many."

Marcus looked sheepish, pushing himself up along the wall back to a standing position. "They could have been sneaking them into the city forever. There are tens of thousands of sentients living in Penumbra. Taurani could easily hide hundreds of those ugly pug nosed bastards among them and we would never know about it." His mouth twisted bitterly. "And if Iphini was helping him, God alone knows how many they might have. They don't have to worry about the defenses now. They'll be able to land as many marines as they need as soon as the fleet arrives."

"Nevertheless," the little mystic's voice was calm. He raised a single finger, gently pressing his point home. "If we can somehow direct the attention of those currently in pursuit away from the docking bay long enough for us to make it to your ship, we will have a greater chance of escape than if we face them all directly."

She shook her head. There was so much they didn't know. "Even if I can get the Na'uka out of the bay, we'll be working against the city's defenses. We can't assume Taurani won't get those guns working by the time we engineer a distraction, make our way around the city, prep my ship, and take off." Her voice dropped. The truth of their situation was painful to contemplate.

"And even so, we cannot stay here, we will be found or starve. We must venture forth and hope for the best. Even a blind Ntja will stumble upon us eventually." The big red eyes blinked, and Angara could not look away. "I see no reason we should not try our best with what the universe has provided. We gain nothing by surrender."

Ve'Yan's face looked pinched as she turned away. Angara had to admit, the little master seemed to be taking a far more direct hand in events than any Thien'ha she had ever met. They were famous for watching unpleasantness unfold. To the best of her knowledge, they never took part.

"I think I might be able to arrange something." Justin cleared his throat.

Angara waited for him to continue, but he seemed unwilling. "Justin, if you have something to offer, I can't think of a better time."

He coughed again, looked quickly at Marcus, and then spoke in hurried tones as if afraid of being interrupted. "My consortia are still functional. I should be able to summon up some assistance, maybe create a scene to pull the guards away from the main docking bay long enough for us to get to the ship?"

Marcus smiled wanly and shook his head. "What, are you afraid I'll be mad that you were having better luck than me?" He reached out and patted his friend on the shoulder. "You were always better with people than I was." He tilted his head to the mystics, and then Angara herself. "No reason that shouldn't still be true even when those people are small and furry, green, or purple."

"You think they'll be able to stage something big enough to matter?" Angara did not want to rest their plans on shifting ground. And if the motley group of fools and grifters with which Justin had been associating were unable to put something big enough together, she did not relish the thought of being caught by a platoon of Ntja halfway to the ship.

The dark-skinned man nodded. "I think so. I'll need to sneak off and talk to them in person, though."

"We don't want to take any chance that Taurani discovers our preparations." Angara nodded. "Maybe we should split up. We'll make some noise moving off in the opposite direction, you gather what assistance you can, and we will meet back at my ship."

Justin's smile was just a touch wild, and she felt more nervous than she wanted to admit. His voice was firm, however, as he moved toward the entrance to the small alcove, patting Marcus on the shoulder as he passed. "Set your implants for two hours, Earth time?"

She saw the wisdom in that. The city's systems, should Taurani succeed in wrestling them back under his control, would not see the pattern of Earth time as anything significant with such a small sampling, until they were safely away. If they *managed* to get safely away. She closed her eyes and activated her implants for a two Earth-hour countdown.

"Done. Do you want to take either of the Thien'ha with you?" She looked from the small Goagoi and his Diakk acolyte. Neither of them seemed eager to leave with the Human.

"I think I can make better time if I'm alone," Justin said from the door. "K'hzan's accusations didn't really get much traction. Most people still see me as just another mercenary Mnymian." He winked one of his milk-pale eyes. "I should be fine on my own."

She nodded. She felt the unnerving impulse to say something more without having the first clue what it might be. She paused, hoping something would come to her, or the feeling would go away. In the end, she just nodded again, and said, "Good luck."

He smiled as if he could see right into her brain and flipped her a casual salute. "You too. You guys have the hard job. I'm just running."

And he was gone.

She had to take a moment to think, trying to ignore the small symbols floating high in her peripheral vision, counting down the time they all had before their last chance expired.

"Perhaps if we were to head to the near reservoir?" Ve'Yan murmured the suggestion, no more shocking for the softness of her words. The girl had not taken an active part in their efforts from the beginning, from what Angara could see. "If we make some noise in that direction, any pursuit will be heading the wrong way when the Human's distraction, whatever it might be, occurs."

The Goagoi nodded at his young assistant. "They will be trying to convince the populace that we are mad. If they were truly trying to protect the city from such ruthless terrorists, they would have to station some of their force to protect the water." His small teeth gleamed in a cruel smile. "They probably will not send their best, however, knowing that we are not really terrorists, and so are not likely to attack there."

The prospect of slaughtering some of Taurani's second-string thugs did not appeal to Angara, but it would make creating the proper level of havoc easier.

"We *should* be able to make it there, do some damage, and return to the docking bay with just enough time to spare if Justin is able to come through on his end." They were all standing, and looked to her for instructions now. "We should make our way through the service ducts and into the Concourse—"

"Wait!" Marcus held up a hand. "I thought we were trying to *avoid* crowds!"

She closed her eyes with a forbearing sigh. Before she could speak, however, Nhan stepped forward.

"There is a series of arteries carved into the topmost layer of the Relic Core, just beneath the lowest level of the Concourse. It will be one of the last places the Ambassador is able to secure control. We can take one of the small service trams toward the Gulf and arrive at the reservoir with none of his people the wiser."

Angara opened her eyes to glare at the little furry menace. "How do you know so much about Penumbra, Master Nhan?"

His answering smile was maddening. "We are Thien'ha, Mistress Ksaka. There is little we do not learn."

Ve'Yan's mirroring smile almost caused a brawl, but Angara wrestled her impulse back under control and shook her head, waving them to the door. "Well, then, by all means. Why don't the two of you lead the way. Marcus and I will see to it that we're not followed."

They moved toward a set of rickety-looking iron stairs leading into the last levels of the Red Tower, and to a gravitic interface that would deposit them into the lowest levels of the Concourse. She had never ridden in a service tram before, but she had heard stories.

They were said to make lift tubes appear sedate by comparison.

*****

Marcus slogged along the narrow corridor, his feet on autopilot, his mind dull with shock. It was almost laughable, if he thought about it: shock was nearly a perennial condition for him since he had emerged from that damned casino in what seemed like another lifetime.

The walls of the passageway were a dull bronze color that reminded him of the door Iphini Bha had shown him in the ancient starship they called Sanctum. He was walking through what they called the Relic Core, he knew. And yet, even finally having skimmed beneath the surface of that mystery was not enough to bring him out of his gray despair.

"This should bring us to one of the observation points above the reservoir." Angara spoke low, dropping the words over her shoulder as they moved down the dimly-lit passage. "We should have a few moments before the Core can drop a field down on the area." He cocked his head to one side as one of the mini shoulder turrets emerged from her heavy coat, small lights gleaming along its barrel.

"Although I have a small capacity for ranged havoc, my reach is not great." Khet Nhan spoke up from the front of the column. "And Ve'Yan will be of no assistance. Should we not seek some way to fall upon them in close proximity, so as to maximize our full potential for havoc?"

Angara pushed a frustrated breath through her nose. "Let's get to the observation point first and see what Taurani's stationed here. If there are too many of them to take out from a distance, we'll get closer."

"We don't have all day." Marcus could almost hear the ticking of the timer slashing away the minutes before Justin's distraction would force their hand. "I'm not sure what we gain by getting embroiled in a running battle here."

"I mean to spill blood, Human." Ve'Yan spat the comment at him without turning around. "If we are abandoning our principals here, I will reap my share of the deaths that will result. We have plenty of time."

Marcus shook his head, but at the back of the line no one could see him. Sihn Ve'Yan was a mystery to him, noticeable despite the flood of mysteries in which he was currently drowning. He was still trying to understand anything that identified as a monk to his nanite implants and yet fought like those two, and seemed more than willing to continue fighting. This wasn't their war, and in quiet moments over the last few hours he had wondered why they were still standing with him.

On the other hand, he had no doubt that he and Justin, and probably Angara, would all be dead at Ambassador Taurani's gray hands if it had not been for the Thien'ha.

Ahead of them a strange, shimmering light threw ribbons of luminescence onto the ceiling of the corridor. The temperature of the air seemed to drop with each step, and the nature of the sounds he was hearing changed subtly, becoming heavier and more distant at the same time.

The corridor opened up before them into an oval-shaped room with a wide opening along one wall. The reflected light was shining through the breach and filling the small chamber with bright, wavering streamers. The four of them moved to the opening. The bottom sill came up to Marcus's hip, so even the Go-agoi could look out comfortably.

Marcus had made a conscious decision not to anticipate anything particular when Angara was throwing the word 'reservoir' around. Images had come into his mind anyway, of course, and much to his surprise, in many ways, they had proven closer to the truth than his past experiences in Penumbra had led him to expect.

The reservoir chamber was an immense underground lake, the far shores

hidden in murky darkness. His mind balked at any attempt to guess how much water must have been down there, but he knew that the lake could have swallowed
many, many football fields without a trace. The ceiling did not arch dramatically
overhead, but was a low, brooding, bronze presence dappled with reflected light
dancing and swirling as an array of telltales twinkled in recesses overhead.

The mundane expectations, however, ended with a glowing blue funnel
almost hidden in the darkness off to his right, where a constant flood of water
gushed down into the reservoir, sending slow, heavy waves lapping out into the
darkness. He recognized the color of the funnel from his dinner with Iphini Bha.
Here was the resting place of the Diamond Road that drew moisture from the
planet below to support the city.

"Is that all the water there is?" Nhan muttered the question as if he didn't
want to break into the silence of the moment. It seemed like a lot of water to Marcus, but the little mystic apparently did not agree.

"There are many such distribution pools around the city." Angara's answer
was nearly as soft as Nhan's. Something about the peaceful air of the place had
even affected her. "This is less than a hundredth part of the total water available
to the city at any given moment."

"Enough with the water." Ve'Yan's mood had not settled. She pointed with
a steady finger down to the left, where a bronze shelf pushed out into the lake.
There were lights on the little peninsula, and shapes could be seen moving about.
Without any frame of reference it was hard to tell, but it seemed to Marcus that
they were quite large shapes.

"I see five." Angara was squinting, probably calling up some more of her
implant abilities, he guessed. "Not too many, if we surprise them."
"Well, they do not appear to be aware of our presence here." Nhan turned away
from the scene. "But the range is far too great for my staff, I'm afraid. And time is
of the essence, as you will recall."

Angara was looking down at the Ntja detachment hungrily. Marcus heard
the slow, ponderous crashing of the mental clock again, and nudged her elbow.
"We don't have enough time, Angara. We need to get back so Justin's not hanging
in the breeze."

She looked at him, the soft blue glow flashing in her eyes, and then she
blinked and nodded. "You're right."

They turned away, Nhan seeming to be even more relieved than the others, when they saw that Ve'Yan was moving toward a far doorway, hidden in the
shadows to their left.

"Ve'Yan, where are you going?" Nhan's voice was sharp.

She didn't even turn around as she disappeared into the darkened hall.
"Obligations were made to be broken. I believe that is the essence of today's lesson?"

Marcus couldn't believe it. He whirled on the little Thien'ha master. "We
don't have time for this! We need to go!"

Nhan nodded with a jerking motion that set the fine pale green fur fringing
his jaw waving. "I will bring her back."

He jogged into the corridor after his acolyte, but they could hear the slapping of her shoes as she began to run, and he knew there was no way the little
creature was going to be able to outrun the bigger, younger Diakk.

"Angara, we need to do something." He begged her, and watched as her calculating, violet eyes narrowed. She shook her head, white hair waving with her frustration. "We either leave them here, or we help them." She focused on his face. "It's up to you, Marcus. You want to leave them here? Or do you want to try to eliminate the five below, and then go back to the docking bay?"

He wanted to leave them. It was almost out of his mouth before he could think about his response. But Khet Nhan and Ve'Yan had been by his side almost constantly since things had turned violent. They had endangered themselves more than once in his defense. And there was something about the little Goagoi that made him loath to leave him behind.

But the weight of their schedule pressed sorely on the back of his mind.

He felt like collapsing as he spat. "We can't—"

The words were hardly out of his mouth and Angara was running past him, down the darkened corridor and to the shore below. He still wasn't even sure what he had been about to say. He wanted to ask for a weapon of some kind. He would be less than useless in a fight against the giant dog-faced aliens, especially at any distance.

Still, he couldn't let these people face such a danger to get him safely out of Penumbra without at least sharing in the risks.

With a muttered curse, he ran down the halls after his three protectors.

The corridor was empty as he ran. Soon he was sucking wind, his lungs burning painfully. Exercise had not been much of a focus since coming here, and he felt it now. He slowed to a jog, and then, sooner than he would have liked to admit, to a cautious, pained walk.

There was no sign of his companions.

The corridor swelled again into a larger chamber, with a wide door at one end, when he heard the first signs that he was catching up. The whirring detonation of Angara's shoulder weapon, remembered from that Connecticut roadside so long ago, echoed out over the water with a muffled crunching sound. It happened twice more, with the high-pitched blast of Khet Nhan's staff flaring out beneath it.

Deep screams bellowed over the water, throwing back flat echoes. There was some splashing as several heavy objects fell into the reservoir. That wouldn't do the water quality any good, he thought with a guilty, grim laugh.

Coming out onto the shelf he saw that three Ntja had abandoned their heavy rifles and were charging up the bronze shelf with their brutal falchions in hand. One seemed to be limping, favoring a squat leg. The two remaining soldiers were missing entirely.

Angara's weapons had retracted back into her coat, and Nhan's staff had reshaped itself into a long, glittering spear with a broad cross-piece. He howled with unseemly glee as he lowered the weapon beneath the lead Ntja's guard and plunged it through his belly. The cross-guard caught the alien and stopped his forward progress. The spear blurred into a wide-bladed ax that erupted from the side of the howling beast. The mystic swung the big weapon over his head and buried it in the soldier's other side, cutting him nearly in two. The thing slumped to the slick ground without a sound and didn't move again.

Angara was holding her own against the wounded Ntja, her blades flashing, weaving a fence of glittering steel that defeated the clumsy sword at every attack. As Nhan's opponent slumped down, Angara's was distracted by his falling companion and turned in disbelief to the grinning little fur ball now rushing at him with what appeared to be a giant string of metal cylinders, each connected to the next with heavy, bladed chain.

One thin, simple knife slid up behind a metallic bubo on the monster's neck and into its brain while it was distracted.

It took a moment for Marcus to find Ve'Yan's place in the battle, as she had allowed her attacker to press her back up against the cavern wall, where the blue light from the tunnel and the overhead telltales was dimmest. At first he was afraid that she had met her match, rushing down here to her death. But soon enough he realized that she was only playing with the soldier. The monster never had a chance.

She did not fight with knives or guns or blades, but rather used her body as a weapon more lethal than any of those. She reminded him of some martial arts expert on a movie or demonstration. Her blows were precise and almost lazy in appearance. She lashed out with bladed hands, booted feet, and once, he swore, with her own forehead. The staggered Ntja reeled from hit to hit, his blocks and parries always a moment too late, and coming slower with each injury.

Marcus was no expert on unarmed combat, but he was certain that she could have ended it several times before she did, finally, bury one stiffened hand up into its neck and set it toppling over backward to slide into the water.

When she turned back to the rest of them, Ve'Yan's pale face was shining with a childish grin, and the black markings on her skin writhed with barely-suppressed laughter.

Marcus's feelings for the girl had run the gamut from grateful to frustrated to annoyed since he had met her. He was furious now. "Do you have any idea what you could have cost us, running down here on your own?" He left the shelter of the small chamber and stepped out onto the shelf.

She stood up straighter, her smile unwavering, to meet his charge.

The Ntja that came around the corner caught them all by surprise; not the least Marcus himself. There were three of them, coming out of the shadows behind Ve'Yan at a heavy trot, hefting their cleavers in eager hands.

Marcus tried to shout a warning, but something in his eyes must have conveyed to her the danger before he could draw breath. Ve'Yan whirled, eyes flat, smile gone, and crouched down to face the new threat. A big blade came whistling down in a vicious overhead cut that would have surely dashed her to the metal ground. But her palm struck the sword as it fell, knocking it out of line, and it buried itself in the material of the Relic Core with a dull clang as she moved aside.

Nhan and Angara were upon them before the other two could work their way around the first, and in a moment they were all on the ground, joining the others in death.

The three fighters were panting, looking around them at the carnage they had wrought without satisfaction. Ve'Yan looked angry, Angara tired, and Nhan's alien face was unreadable in the soft gloom.

"We need to go now!" Marcus waved back toward the door.

Angara nodded, and Khet Nhan as well. He swung his staff in a flat arc down and away from them, and it blurred, shedding blood and brains, and then resolved itself into the short rod that he tucked back into his belt.

Ve'Yan, however, did not move.

Angara and Marcus were halfway to the entrance chamber before they realized that they were alone. Turning back, they saw the small Thien'ha master standing before his student, little hands on hips, head cocked to one side.

Ve'Yan's eyes flickered to Marcus and then back to her master. "This is wrong, Master." She jerked her head toward him, and Marcus felt again the anger of being separated out for reasons he did not understand. "I thought we were coming to Penumbra to see the reemergence of Humans. Then you told me you wished to warn them of the cycle. Then you wished to see them safely out of the city." She shook her head violently. "Each step you have taken has dragged me farther away from the path you had taught me to follow."

Nhan nodded, but he did not speak. Instead, he turned to look out over the water, his little eyes glittering in the reflected light.

Ve'Yan was not finished, however. "We take no part, you told me. We observe the cycles of the universe. We record those cycles. We study the nature of time and events. But we take no part." Her voice sounded almost as if it was breaking now, and Marcus could feel his anger ebbing as he realized how wrenching the girl had found this situation. "Do we not follow the Hoabin path of Thien'ha any longer, master?"

Nhan nodded again, but still did not turn. Marcus felt time grinding away beneath them, but could not tear himself away from the scene unfolding on that wide bronze shelf. When he spoke, Marcus had to strain to hear the words.

"You are not wrong, Sihn Ve'Yan. We are no longer on the Hoabin path." The little shoulders seemed to slump. "I had hoped to witness the remerged of Humanity. I had hoped that this cycle of violence and oppression was giving way to a rebirth—"

"*Humans*?" It was Angara that spat the word, and caught Marcus completely by surprise. "You thought *Humans* would break a cycle of violence and oppression?" She looked like she wanted to laugh.

Nhan looked sadly up at the dark-skinned woman and nodded. "We study patterns and repetition, Angara Ksaka. We have recorded enough of the galaxy's history to set even a Mhatrong to weeping for its ignorance. And we see more than many today will themselves to see. Yes. I had hoped to see Humans break our current cycle."

Angara shook her head in bewilderment and turned to look Marcus up and down. He didn't like the dismissive curl to her lip any more than he liked the contemptuous tone of her earlier words.

But his friend, the only other Human in the city, was putting himself in great danger to clear their path to freedom. And that would be all for nothing if they didn't get back up to the inhabited sections of the city as soon as possible.

"Look, I don't care what any of you were hoping for, or thinking about, or anything else." He pointed into the shadowy doorway and the corridor beyond. "We don't have much time left now before Justin's going to be on his own up there; throwing God knows what at Taurani's goons. We have to go."

Nhan turned back to Ve'Yan, away from Angara and Marcus. His face was hidden, but his voice was clear. "There comes a time in our study when trust is paramount, Ve'Yan. I promise you, the patterns I see forming here are not complete, and we are not nearly so far off our path as it feels. I would have you with me as we complete the journey, but I cannot force you to abandon your conscience now."

The girl stood still, staring at her teacher long enough that Marcus almost intervened. When she gave a single, violent nod, he didn't know if he was happier to have her back onboard because of her fighting skill, or because it simply meant they could head back to the Concourse now.

They emerged into the tram tunnels to find them filled with smoke. Alarms were sounding their raucous calls, echoing down the service corridors, and violent screams and shouts, muffled by intervening walls, rumbled in their ears.

Marcus smiled. "Sounds like a distraction to me."

# Chapter 20

The tram deposited them just beneath the lowest level of the Concourse, at the nearest access point to the primary docking bay. The smoke had thickened, but there had been no sign of fire or other imminent dangers as they flew through the tunnels. The sounds of panic above them had intensified as they moved toward their goal. Justin had clearly been thinking big when he planned his distraction.

The corridor outside the access station had been empty when they arrived, cleared by Justin's efforts. They began to make their way to the docking bay, hugging the walls and keeping away from main thoroughfares, when the slapping of feet brought them all up short. Everyone tensed, weapons rising, when Justin's slim form came bounding around a corner, pulling up short when he saw them.

"Well, I hope no one objects to my burning down one of my own factories?" His clothing was disheveled and smudged with soot and grease. "It wasn't making much of a profit anyway."

Marcus caught a strange look on Angara's face as Justin came up with them and his eyes narrowed. He looked at his friend and then back to the bodyguard, but either Justin hadn't noticed, or he was feigning ignorance.

For his own part, he was glad they had made it back from the reservoir in time.

"What took you all so long?" Justin nodded back the way he had come. "Although everyone's evacuated this part of the Concourse, there are still patrols. More, actually, in the last few minutes. I was hoping you would be a little early, if I'm going to be honest."

Marcus shot a quick, bitter look at Ve'Yan, but the girl was too wrapped up in her own hostile distaste with Justin for her to notice.

Angara resumed her brisk pace, and the others rushed to catch up.

"It will take me a moment to get the *Na'uka* ready to depart. We should be able to bar the primary access doors from the inside. That will keep patrols out long enough for us to break free." She brought them up to the heavy frame of the main entranceway to the docking bay. "It should not take longer than—"

The enormous door slammed shut in front of them with vicious finality. Its echoing boom was deafening, sending them all reeling back, grabbing for their ears.

"I'm sorry." The voice was tinny, issuing from some small emitter they couldn't see. But it was unmistakably Taurani's. "I'm still familiarizing myself with my new toy. However did you accomplish it, Human?"

Marcus bristled, fighting off the rising despair, realizing that they had been caught.

"It was fortuitous timing, actually." The tone was amused, and made him want to vomit. "I've only just regained control of those lower levels. Had you moved just a touch faster, I fear you would have made good your escape." Even knowing the lipless bastard couldn't smile, Marcus couldn't help but hear a vicious grin in the voice.

The tread of many booted feet shook the floor, and they turned to watch a large contingent of Ntja round a corner and advance on them. Their big rifles were strapped to their broad backs, heavy falchions ready in their hands.

Angara jerked, her shoulder cannon rising and taking quick aim. The lights were dim, however, and the weapon spat out a small gout of sparks and smoke, and then fell silent. She cursed.

A sudden detonation set Marcus's ears ringing violently, as the others clutched at their heads and shrank away from the sound.

An Ntja who had just been struck in the forehead, however, was infinitely more surprised. Briefly, at any rate. The dog soldiers froze in their tracks, staring as their companion toppled slowly backward. The aliens behind the victim stepped quickly out of the way, jostling their compatriots as they tried to avoid the falling body. Even on their fat, canine faces, the shock was plain.

Justin, however, was grinning maniacally as he wielded the little black pistol he had brought all the way from Earth in both hands.

"Get the God damned door open!" He fired two more shots, and the Ntja continued to mill about, trying to decide what to do. Clearly, the Human's weapon was not affected by the suppression field. Perhaps the technology shut down the galactic weapons through some dampening of the energy they used? Maybe good old fashioned gun powder was a little too primitive for the field to address.

Regardless of what made the field ineffectual against Justin's pistol, two more Ntja were down, one dead and the other writhing on the floor with a bloody gut wound, before the rest decided they were better off charging the Human than standing around, waiting to be shot.

Angara pushed Marcus against the door. "Get it open!" she whirled away and was just in time to stop a descending blade with her own crossed knives. The sword blow would have bisected Justin's head, and he grinned a quick thanks to her before dancing around behind, taking random shots as they presented themselves.

Marcus turned to the door, looking for the control panel, when he suddenly realized he had no idea how to open it. During his entire tenure as administrator, the doors of Penumbra opened to him at his approach, like tame puppies. He had never had to press a button, utter a command, or even think hard. It just happened.

He turned back to his friends, ready to beg for help. But they were fully occupied with the assaulting soldiers.

Khet Nhan was holding an entire squad at bay with his staff, now in the form of a long pole sporting a fan-like blade that whistled as he flung it back and forth. Angara and Justin made a formidable pair as she fended off direct attacks while he punched shot after close-range shot into their assailants, building up a prestigious pile of bodies before them. While Marcus watched, he saw his friend switch in a fresh clip. His eyes narrowed in fear for his friend. Hadn't Justin said there were only three of them in his bug out bag?

A scream wrenched Marcus's attention around to his last stalwart, reluctant defender. Sihn Ve'Yan was a spinning vision of death as she danced through the milling throng of shock troopers, her body the only weapon she needed. She knew just where to strike to penetrate their armor. Already, several were down around her. They were moaning, groaning, and rocking feebly as they cradled their injuries, but they were clearly out of the fight.

But none of them were going to be able to help him with the door.

Marcus turned back to the impossible task and searched for buttons he might push, sliders he might slide, or anything else that might be a control he could manipulate and override Taurani's influence.

There was nothing.

He wanted to shout, or scream, or pound his hands against the door, but he knew that wouldn't help anyone, especially his friends fighting desperately behind him. He took a step back, aware of the battle raging only feet away, and looked up at the giant door. The pitted steel stared mutely back at him.

"No!" He screamed despite his resolution. "No, no, no!" He pounded at the door with his hands. He felt like a child, but the knowledge that they were all going to die with their backs to a metal wall had driven him beyond thought.

The door began to grind open.

Marcus's eyes widened. His mouth gaped wide.

The door ground to a halt.

His eyes narrowed, and he pushed his hands against the cold metal with a vicious, "No!"

Somewhere in his mind, he felt something give. Patterns fell into place somewhere beneath his conscious understanding, and he leaned into the door, knowing it would open.

It didn't.

He screamed, pushing all of his frustration and rage into the cold metal. He was not going to die like this. He was not going to fail his friends this late in the day. Taurani was not going to have a Human head to parade around the station as an exclamation point to his farce of conquest.

Behind him, the flat bangs of Justin's gun echoed off the low ceiling. The grunts and cries of close combat were muffled by the wall of flesh, fabric, and armor that pressed in upon them from all sides. The small circle of security was dwindling as Angara, Justin, and the Thien'ha were pushed back one reluctant step at a time.

Marcus's throat was raw, and he dug into himself as deeply as he had ever dug before, his scream rose to painful heights and he pushed forward as if his fingers were going to sink into the metal.

With a stuttering, shaking motion, the blast doors began to retract again into the armored walls.

As soon as the opening was large enough to squeeze through, he bellowed over his shoulder. "Get in! Get in now!"

He had no idea how much longer he could control the door. He felt as if he was wrestling with some contradictory power trying to drive the door closed against him. If he got it open, would he be able to close it?

Justin and Angara pressed close behind him. He had not been keeping track of Justin's shots, but he had to be down to his last clip, and Angara was panting, her dark skin and jacket glistening, her knives and arms drenched in thick, black blood.

The door was about half open before it once again shrieked to a halt. Marcus stood there, one hand on either retracting slab, arms extended to their limit, and shouted for Angara and Justin to go in under his arms.

"You're the only one who can ready the ship!" He shouted into Angara's face, watching her instinct for battle warring with her common sense. Justin nodded without nearly as much thought and pushed her through the door.

"Come on, you two!" As soon as Nhan and Ve'Yan were through, he could try to close the door from the other side. Somehow, he felt that closing it would be easier than forcing it open, as long as he didn't wait too long.

"You go through, Marcus Wells!" Nhan's shrill voice cut above the clangor of battle. "We will hold the door while you begin to close it!"

Marcus wanted to argue, but then he nodded, leaping through the doorway, spinning and placing his hands back on the metal, preparing to lean back into the battle of wills with whatever force had been fighting him, whether program, Ambassador, or inertia.

He stopped as he saw the scene before him. The two mystics were holding back a tidal wave of brown-armored soldiers that pushed toward the door. Their long, heavy blades were inhibiting their ability to fight effectively, which was probably the main reason his four friends had held them off as long as they had. But those fierce, angry faces were pushing ever-closer now, and with the press of bodies, Ve'Yan was finding her own techniques hampered as well.

Nhan's staff, however, was probably the perfect weapon for the situation. In fact, it seemed to be able to become the perfect weapon for any situation.

The furry little being swung the staff around and it blurred into a stubby, wide-barreled shotgun, barked a vicious cloud of green light and death that pushed a wedge of Ntja soldiers back, and then blurred again into a long length of barbed chain fastened to a fluttering cluster of ribbon blades that he swung in a wide arc, sending the rest of the front rank falling backward, swords raised in defense.

The Ntja fell back, giving the two mystics a moment's respite. "Come on! Get in!" Marcus's voice was raw now, but he shouted anyway, ignoring the pain.

Nhan skittered back, his staff resolving itself into a long pike that he brandished in the faces of the closing enemy. Beside him, Ve'Yan moved with graceful steps, her hands before her as a shield.

Then she looked back at Marcus, her eyes narrow, and spun to charge back into the Ntja with an animal shriek.

"Ve'Yan, no!" Nhan took two steps forward, pushing the shining point of his spear into one metal-studded dog face that was getting too close. "Come back!"

"You go!" She grunted as she leapt into the front rank, her hands and feet a constant blur around her as one after another, the nearest soldiers collapsed, clutching at throats, eyes, and groins. "I'll be right behind. Get the door closing!"

Marcus stood for a moment, frozen in indecision. Khet Nhan stepped back to stand beside him, shaking his head with anger. "She blames herself that we were late." He muttered. "The damned fool girl is going to get herself killed."

Marcus blamed her too, and had blamed her from the moment he heard Justin's report. And he seriously doubted that she blamed herself. On the other hand, he wasn't so mad that he wanted her to die …

He bent in against the door and hunched his shoulders, bringing his mind back in line with the door. As it started to shake once again, the panels sliding together, he watched as Ve'Yan continued to make the best use of the space her master's last attack had created. She spun and jumped and dove, attacking first one flank of the enemy and then another so quickly that the swords swinging clumsily at her as she danced away found only empty air.

But there were too many of them, and as they stepped forward, moving over the still bodies of their fallen companions, she was pushed closer and closer to the door.

"Ve'Yan, now! It's closing!" The door was now just barely wide enough to admit her thin body, and it seemed to be closing faster than it had opened, although that might have been merely his perception.

Nhan continued to thrust his spear through the door, keeping any Ntja who attempted to get behind Ve'Yan at bay. One thrust caught a soldier beneath the arm and it grabbed the shaft, pushing through toward the acolyte's back and pulling on the spear. If it had been a normal weapon, both mystics might have been doomed as the beast drove its sword into the Diakk girl's back while pulling the master back into the melee. Instead, however, the spear tip blurred and widened, slicing the fingers from the soldier's hand and digging deeper into its side. The Ntja cried out in surprised pain and staggered back, only to catch Ve'Yan's heel on the jaw with such force that the wet snapping of bones could be heard above the sounds of battle. The alien fell limply to the floor, the spear blurred again, slicing out of its flesh, and reformed to menace the next attacker.

Except that with the distraction of the creature's death, another soldier was able to approach on the far side, out of reach of Master Nhan's spear, and unseen by Ve'Yan who was busy forcing back the enemy on the other flank.

Marcus watched, helpless, as the crude sword rose up behind the acolyte, hanging motionless in the air for a moment that seemed like it would stretch on forever. And then it fell.

The bark of Justin's pistol scared the hell out of Marcus, and he shied away, the door grinding to a halt. The bullet struck the Ntja between its beady eyes and threw its head back, big wet mouth flopping open. But momentum and gravity were harder to stop, and the big chunk of metal continued to fall. It was pulled off of true by the stiffening soldier's dead hands, but nevertheless, it caught Ve'Yan a glancing blow across the back and flung her at the door with a stunned, confused expression on her pale face.

"No!" Nhan's piping voice was furious, and the spear formed once more into a howling chain weapon that gave the enemy a moment's pause. It was enough for him to rush forward and grab his acolyte before she fell. He began to drag her to the door, making little progress until Justin, ducking beneath Marcus's arms, grabbed her around the waist and pulled her through the door. He let her go with one arm and she screamed as she twisted, Nhan catching her as she fell. Justin lashed out behind them without even looking, and several more gunshots sent the pursuing Ntja shrinking back.

They pulled her through the door, a trail of dark blood smearing the floor, and Marcus bent to his work again, pressing his forehead against the cold metal and clenching his eyes painfully shut.

With a dull crunch the metal slabs crashed against each other, muffling the enraged shouts from the other side, and Marcus fell forward onto his knees, no less exhausted than if he had just run a marathon.

He was only dimly aware of the warm wetness beneath him as he collapsed into the trail of Ve'Yan's blood.

*****

As Angara slid into her command chair, she could feel the tension draining from her back. They were still being pursued by an evil mob of thugs, fugitives now without a shred of the power or security they had known. But behind the controls of the *Yud'ahm Na'uka*, it could not be all tragedy and tears.

She could almost feel at one with her people in moments like this.

With several mental signals, the ship began to prepare itself for launch. She released the quantum-gravitic interfaces on the control elements of her wings to faster assume combat profile as soon as they could get clear of the bay. The enormous engines sheltered within the cowlings on either primary wing began to spin up with a hellish roar that warmed her heart. The dim lights of the control deck were soothing after the harrowing gauntlet to get here, and with that thought she peered up over the lip of the vision field to see how things fared at the main blast door.

Justin had returned to the door, as she knew he would, and was standing behind Marcus, peering beneath one arm at whatever was happening outside the docking bay. There was no sign of the Thien'ha, so they must still be holding back Taurani's horde on the other side.

She wished them well. She would never abandon companions in the face of danger, but if they were taken down before her eyes, she would leave Penumbra alone if she had to.

She felt ashamed even as the thought surfaced, and she shook her head with an angry jerk. She *should* leave if they were taken down. She knew she would not. And knew she was a fool for it, too. The *Na'uka* was not some unarmed luxury skiff. She would unleash its full fury on the Ntja below if she was forced to watch her friends die.

There was a sudden rush of motion at the door and she threw herself up and against the viewing field as if she could reach through and affect the outcome. The bang of Justin's primitive firearm was deadened by the distance and the vast space of the docking bay, but clear nonetheless. He fired beneath Marcus's arm and then dove through the door.

The set of Marcus's shoulders, even at this distance, screamed of tension and pain, and his arms seemed to shake as he held them against the metal. Several more detonations rolled back from the battle, and the little Thien'ha master was through, pulling the Diakk girl behind him. Justin came through last, holding her waist and punching his gun back behind him, and her anxiety intensified as she realized it was no longer firing.

As soon as they were clear, Marcus's back tensed up even further and the door resumed its shaking movement, grinding closed until the plates crashed together with an impact she felt rather than heard.

Ve'Yan, the Diakk acolyte, was clearly wounded. Against her dark robes it was impossible to see how badly, but she was limp and still in the arms of her master. They were running to the ship, followed by an exhausted Marcus who kept stumbling as he cast quick glances behind him.

The *Yud'ahm Na'uka* was nearly ready to depart when they dragged

Ve'Yan's limp body into the common room behind the command deck. They eased her down onto her face, taking as much care in their haste as they could. There was an ugly rent clearly visible across the girl's back, the fabric of her robe heavy with blood.

"Get us out of here!" Marcus barked as he came up the ramp. He seemed paler than normal, with deep bruises beneath his eyes.

Angara jumped back into the command chair, setting it bouncing beneath her as it struggled to adjust to her mood and position. Justin and Nhan continued to work on Ve'Yan, trying to stabilize her, while Marcus moved up to stand beside the pilot, looking out at the far blast door while his hands writhed together nervously.

He jerked his chin at the door. "We need to be gone before they get that open."

As they watched, a small sliver of light gleamed out from the center of the door.

Angara bent to the controls and the chair swept her around into a prone position, changing the configuration of the viewing fields, drawing them down and around the nose of the command deck, the better for her to navigate under battle conditions.

"You need to go sit down." She muttered, already lost in the interface with her ship. Icons, information, and graphics flashed before her eyes, and she barely registered his response.

The *Yud'ahm Na'uka* eased itself off the deck and began to hover on the repulsor fields being generated by the two glowing spheres in her wings. She brought it swinging around for the massive entranceway and watched several Ntja pushing their way through the slowly-expanding gap in the door.

Faces flashed behind her eyes. She saw Agha-pa and many others, all dead at Taurani's hands. Well, the damned Kerie was not in front of her, but his thugs were. And for the duration, she was no longer responsible for the well-being of the city or the maintenance of the common docking areas. Her fingers tightened within the control fields. She always preferred to fly by touch when she might need to get fancy or violent.

The ship stopped its spin and floated closer to the opening door. There was a growing party of Ntja on her side of the barrier, and she gritted her teeth, remembering the suppression field. There was little she could do to them while the field was in place.

One of the soldiers brought his weapon to his shoulder and fired a shot that glanced harmlessly off the ship's hardened hull. Somewhere, probably in the control center, someone had realized that the suppression field was more hindrance than help, chasing down such a small party bearing so few galactic weapons.

Her grimace turned to a wide smile as another blast splashed harmlessly off her ship; such unfortunate timing on the Ambassador's part.

The generators on the wings flashed, and massive tendrils of bright energy reached out to caress the mob of Ntja at the door. They died where they stood, frozen in shivering scenes of pain and torture as bolt after bolt flashed through their bodies. The energy grounded into the walls around them, the deck on which they stood, and various small vehicles and pieces of equipment scattered across that end of the vast bay. The first explosion, a small single-person load lifter, ignited others, and soon that entire section was engulfed in vivid orange flames, the walls and floor scorched black and buckled. The soldiers had been reduced to less than ash, leaving no sign of their existence behind.

She refrained from giving voice to the savage glee she felt, and contented herself with an artistic pirouette that brought the nose of the ship thrusting toward the wide entrance. She released the grav-locks and sent the control surfaces flaring out around her ship. Each was capable of creating its own small gravitic fields, allowing her almost preternatural control of the ship's movements through atmosphere or vacuum alike.

The *Yud'ahm Na'uka* soared out of the mouth of the primary docking bay and swept up and around the Red Tower. Taurani had not yet been able to scramble any competent resistance that she could see, and for the first time since that wretched scream in the administrator's office announced Iphini Bha's betrayal, she felt like they might be safe after all. If his control of the city's defenses was no better than his control of the door to the docking bay, they really might have a chance.

A heavy diplomatic shuttle heaved up over the shoulder of the Red Tower. It bore the sigils of the Galactic Council, with flashings for the Kerie delegation: Taurani's personal vehicle. It was against convention for such ships to be armed, but—

Bolts of energy sliced through the void and flashed past her, striking the flank of a tower behind.

Trust Taurani to arm his own diplomatic shuttle.

The thing was a heavy meat animal beside her sleek hunter, though. It was a move of desperation to send such a thing after a Tigan combat craft. She flipped the *Na'uka* on its right wing tip, control surfaces sliding around to provide just the right counter-thrust to pivot in place as she sailed forward, and raked the bottom of the startled shuttle with ravening lightning.

The enemy ship staggered as the energy engulfed it. Jets of atmosphere flashed out, sending the shuttle spinning wildly out of control. She flashed past, bringing the nose of the *Na'uka* swinging back forward again, and flicked a glance sideways to a smaller vision field that now showed her back trail.

The shuttle was drifting toward one of the smaller towers, dark and out of control. She would rather not see it impact the tower and endanger innocent lives. She repeated the excuse to herself as she brought her long-range weapon systems online with a thought. Two tiny projectiles launched out from either side of her ship's nose, arced around, and flew at the drifting wreck behind them. The two tiny pieces of heavy matter collided with the target and instantly converted themselves into a dynamic energy state that devoured the ship in a blinding flash that forced the rearward-facing vision fields to darken.

As she crested the Red Tower she watched, wary, as the defensive cannons rose clumsily from their housings. No matter which way she had steered, they were going to face these defenses sooner or later, and she was more familiar with those of the Red Tower than any of the others.

They had never moved the way they were moving now. They rotated toward the *Na'uka* in fits and starts, juddering as if fighting with themselves. And as they shook in their housings, they remained dark and harmless. She knew this was not Marcus's work, though. It appeared as if Penumbra itself were rebelling against Taurani's control.

That was a thought to warm her heart, but for now, she needed to get them away from the city so they could plan their next move. She was afraid Marcus was planning on giving up, asking to be returned to Earth, and she knew she would have no choice but to grant the request if he made it. She grunted softly in the back of her throat. After trying so long to replace him, it was an uncomfortable, foreign thought, to think she now needed him to stay. They could not leave things here the way they were. She hoped he would see that.

She hoped, too, that Justin would not be quick to surrender. And who knew? Marcus had surprised her often enough in the past.

The *Yud'ahm Na'uka* rocketed off over Penumbra and out toward the system's edge. As soon as they were far enough away she had the ship summon a wormhole, and aimed her nose directly into its coruscating azure heart.

As they were falling into the event horizon of the small black hole, her ship sensed several enormous singularities erupting all around them. Ugly, thick ships fell from them and began to glide toward Penumbra; the Council's Ntja Peacemaker Fleet had arrived, and it was even larger than she had feared.

As the *Na'uka's* wormhole collapsed behind them, she caught one last glimpse of small attack craft swarming toward the city, and then nothing.

# Chapter 21

"What do you mean, 'they're gone'?!?" Taurani's throat was scratchy from the smoke still drifting through the control center. The air scrubbers had been going nonstop since his entrance, but they seemed to be incapable of dealing with the last vestiges of tainted atmosphere.

"They fell away just as Admiral Ochiag's fleet emerged into the system." The Ntja commander's eyes drifted to every corner of the pathetic little office. Anywhere but to the enraged Kerie's face. The bronze domes of the creature's implants shone dully in the overhead lighting with each small movement, underscoring its nervous shuffling. "Your shuttle was destroyed trying to stop them, sir."

He had known that. Iranse, at least, was still competent in his duties. The Kerie delegation would not be pleased that he had lost the shuttle. Their near-sighted goals having been achieved, they would undoubtedly have preferred for him to pull in his horns. But if his race wanted to elevate themselves within the Council, they were going to have to reconcile themselves to losing more than a little skiff or two.

"I thought you had dispatched an entire platoon to keep them from that forsaken outcast's scow." He muttered. He never liked for his underlings to see him upset, but the Humans' escape represented the almost complete failure of his more extensive plans for Penumbra. Now, he would need to share the laurels with Ochiag. And his version of events, casting the bodyguard and the two Humans as the villains of the piece, would seem much less convincing to a discerning eye, without a nice, obvious crime scene, complete with bodies, to present.

He chuffed a breath through his brill and settled back in the throne. He had not even considered the Aijians. They would be quick to believe anything he chose to tell them about the culpability of the Human administrator, but Oo'Juto had been a most prominent member of that prickly species. His loss would mean additional scrutiny, for certain. Without Human bodies to focus their hatred, he would have to move quickly to see that his was the first version of the tale they heard.

"Are the defenses operational again?" Taurani knew he would, eventually, see events here coaxed back to some semblance of his original intentions. But if Ksaka and her tame Humans chose to return at some point, he wanted to be able to take care of them himself rather than being forced to depend on Ochiag for support.

He lifted the Skorahn from his chest and dangled it before his eyes. He had been contemplating the cursed thing since he had put it around his neck. He waved the Ntja away. "Get the mess out there under control." He barked more for something to say than anything else. The administrator's people had put up more of a fight than he had expected, and a great deal of the equipment needed to control the city had been damaged in the process. Ntja made for excellent shock troops and security, but most of them were less than dependable when it came to technical support.

Left alone once again, he lowered his head to stare into the sapphire depths of the jewel. He had known there would be some transitional work to bring the thing completely under his control, but he had poured over countless reports since the Human Marcus Wells's arrival, and knew the filthy animal had been able to manipulate almost every aspects of the city's systems.

His silvered eyes flicked over the desk. There was too much to do. He would need to meet Ochiag at the Tower's executive docking bay if he was going to have any luck getting the admiral to return to his ship and leave the disposition of the city to him. He shook the Skorahn, fighting the urge to dash it against the administrator's desk. The stories about the Human's mastery of the ancient technology rankled more than he would admit. He was no more effective with the damned necklace than that bloated Uduta Virri had been.

He slapped the desk and summoned Iphini Bha from the outer office. He had kept the Iwa'Bantu girl busy since his ascension; the better to keep her mind from focusing on what it was she had done to the city and its inhabitants.

The pale figure stepped through the hissing door and he forced himself not to stare. There would be plenty of time to explore the more intriguing opportunities this situation offered, but at the moment he needed the deputy to provide some modicum of continuity for those few administration workers who remained after Marcus Wells's flight.

"I need you to look at his." He threw the Skorahn at her as he stalked past, sweeping around in a dramatic turn at the door. "You will break through its mysteries before my return or I will know the reason why. Keep it about your person at all times, of course." He forced his face into something that he thought of as a smile. "We would not want the Core to reject us."

The big blue eyes blinked twice, and then dropped to the gleaming gem she held clenched in her weak, long-fingered hands. He could see the thoughts churning there under the surface, and his grimace hardened even as his eyes began to gleam with a more-genuine amusement.

"You can think of turning your coat a second time all you wish, Iphini Bha. But you should know, if you ever betray me, the consequences will be … harsh, and long-reaching." He leaned in close to her, and she cast her eyes down and away. "I am well aware of the reputation I developed among your people during my time on Iwa'Ban as the Council's envoy. I assure you, testing that reputation would be the worst possible thing you could do for yourself and your family at this juncture."

She was shaking visibly as he turned, chuffing a slight breath of amusement, and let the door hiss closed behind him.

Now, if he could only manipulate Ochiag as easily, he would feel much better about this latest turn of events.

*****

Time stretched itself into an attenuated, painful landscape around her before Iphini Bha moved again. Khuboda Taurani did, indeed, have a terrible reputation among the Iwa'Bantu. She was not a brave woman. She knew that. The anger and hatred that had boiled beneath the surface since first laying eyes on Marcus Wells would have driven a more courageous being to action long ago.

Instead, she had smiled, and lowered her head, and done her job. She had even lost track, at times, of her hatred. It was not easy to hold onto such hot emotions in the face of constant, daily contact. But she had never forgotten her ravaged homeworld, nor her memory of the Humans who had nearly destroyed the planet. No matter how innocent Marcus Wells had seemed, he had still been an offshoot of that ravaging stock. Iranse had reminded her of that in their many conversations.

She could not have let a Human destroy everything she had worked so hard to preserve, could she? Virri had been a vast, suppurating wound on the city's soul, but she had kept everything together despite his lack of interest or concern. She had even been able to do a little good, helping the people of Penumbra when she could.

Marcus Wells, no matter his stated goals or seeming purity, threatened all of that by his very existence. Even if he had meant everything he had said, and worked diligently to build the city into something greater than it was, things would have fallen apart eventually under the guidance of a Human. Everyone knew that all they were truly capable of was destruction. It would have meant the ruination of everything she had come to care for in her self-imposed exile.

But no one was supposed to get hurt. Iranse had *promised* no one would be hurt. The Ambassador meant only to remove the Humans, the big Eru had said. She could still remember his soulful red eyes looking down at her. The city would go back to normal. Everyone would be at peace. He had even hinted that she might hope to take on the role of administrator. That was a dream she had never even dared to voice aloud.

Her delicate teeth ground together. Then Angara Ksaka had moved to drag the damned Aijians into the mess. She had known that was not going to please Taurani, but she had never imagined she would have to witness one of them blasted before her very eyes! Right up to the moment the Ambassador had walked in with that giant gun, she had convinced herself everything was going to work out alright.

But with Oo'Juto dead on the floor, smoke everywhere, and the barbaric, metal-studded Ntja howling all around, she had nearly lost consciousness in her terror. When she had regained her wits, the Humans were gone, taking those wretched Thien'ha and Angara Ksaka with them.

That had been more than half a shift ago, now; so much damage and destruction in so little time. Taurani had moved swiftly in consolidating his control of the city. She had watched as the brown-armored Ntja commanders had coordinated strikes against independent-minded conglomerates and neighborhoods before the Humans had even been found. Most of the cartels with a reputation for advanced work had been raided, their operations left in smoking wreckage. One entire tower known for particularly cutting edge research, on the far side of the city, had been blasted off the Relic Core, its twisted remains leaving a trail of glittering wreckage behind as it traced a slow, lazy descent toward the planet below.

And now a massive fleet, larger than anything that had ever been brought against the city, floated overhead. Even if the defenses were brought back online, Marcus Wells would never have stood a chance against them.

Things were not supposed to have happened this way. She wanted to cry, but she felt as if her body had been wrung dry. She collapsed into one of the conference chairs, staring dully at the Skorahn. None of it mattered now. Taurani would bend and twist the city to his will, but he would have to leave eventually.

No prestigious Kerie diplomat would stay this far from civilization any longer than necessary. Whatever he wanted from Penumbra, he would take it, and she would be here to pick up the pieces. She could do that. She had done it often enough when Virri had been in charge.

The jewel gleamed in her hands. There were blemishes across its flat face she did not remember seeing before. It looked like a design, some rune or symbol that she did not recognize.

She lifted it up to the light and squinted into the glittering azure flares. It looked alive. It felt alive. But she had no idea how to unlock its secrets, no matter what kind of threats Taurani leveled against her. Virri had done almost nothing with the medallion the entire time he had possessed it. Marcus Wells had never seemed to work at making it respond at all. It had been more that the city reacted to *him* when he wore it, no matter what he was thinking.

It had started easily enough that none of them had noticed. Lights going on and off for his convenience, doors opening and closing. From there other controls and commands were obeyed that Uduta Virri never would have thought to give. And twice it had seemed as if Penumbra came alive to defend him without his even being aware of it. The destruction of the cloud of nanites in the first attack against him was just one example of things around him working in his favor that no bearer of the Skorahn had seen before.

No one seemed to have noticed until now, when Taurani took such control as a given, and was fearfully angry when it did not manifest.

Would she give him such control, even if she could? She shook her head. A single fat tear finally coalesced in her eye, tracing a warm path down her cheek. Could she *deny* him that control, if she discovered how to unlock it?

She had been running from something most of her life. Her family's perceptions; her homeworld's sad, exhausted soul; her own failures. But how could you run from yourself?

*****

Marcus stared at his folded hands. The surface of the table that had extruded itself from the floor of the ship's common area was hard and smooth. It had a dull shine, like plastic or bone. And yet it had just been deck plating before the need for a table had arisen. He knocked on it with his knuckles, his head tilting curiously at the hollow sound it made, and then shook his head. What the hell did it matter what the damned table was made out of?

They had been floating in deep, empty space for over an hour. Angara had told them her ship did not have sufficient range to follow the wormhole too far without knowing better where they wanted to end up. So she had emerged the ship into a dead system only a few light years from Penumbra; close enough that their options were still open, she said, and far enough away that they could assume that the massive Peacemaker fleet would not be able to find them.

There had been no signals from the city when they had emerged from the wormhole. Angara had been working with the ship the entire time they had floated aimlessly in the empty system, but she had been unable to raise any of her contacts, or the syndicates that had been friendly with Marcus's office. Justin had tried as well, using codes he claimed should have worked no matter what Taurani had done to the systems, but nothing was getting through.

Nhan and Ve'Yan were sitting in a far corner on the floor, staring at each other. The same systems that had put the nanites into Marcus and Justin had made for the acolyte's quick recovery, even from the horrific wound that had laid the girl's back open to the bone. She was still angry with her master over some doctrinal question, however. His own hand in her rescue did not seem to have softened her opinion of him, as far as he could see.

Justin sat across from him, hands also folded, obviously, *painfully* avoiding his eyes. Every now and then, Marcus could feel the weight of his friend's dark gaze upon him, and forced himself not to meet it. He was calm within his own skull. He felt, for the first time in months, as if everything around him was quiet and peaceful. It might well be the peace of the grave, but there was something to be said for knowing you were at the end, as well.

From the moment Angara Ksaka had swept him away from that dusty roadside, he had been running, panting, scrambling, and suffering. He felt like he had been treading shark-infested waters for weeks, and only now was he able to finally rest.

It was over. If the death of the big dolphin; the battle on the cold, echoing shelf of bronze overlooking the vast underground lake; the bloody fight at the gates of the docking bay; and the dogfight as they escaped had not convinced him that his time in Penumbra was at an end, then the sight of the vast fleet falling down toward the fragile-seeming towers of the city had been.

There was no way their single ship was going to be able to penetrate that kind of firepower. They were away, they were safe, apparently, and there was no reason to return after being so forcibly removed from office.

Angara came in with a heavy sigh and dropped down at the table. A chair grew up quickly beneath her and caught her at the perfect height. She kept promising that the *Yud'ahm Na'uka* was not alive, but it was a hard sell when it seemed to read her mind so often.

"There are no signals coming from the city. Either they are jamming the entire spectrum, which would take a great deal of power, or they have destroyed Penumbra." Her voice was flat, but after a quick look to reassure himself, Marcus didn't think she was offering that up as an actual possibility.

"Well, they've got that whole fleet to draw power from now, right?" Justin pointed out. "I mean, there were some big ships coming in. Could they have that kind of capability?"

Angara looked at him, something like a smile playing around her lips, her inhumanly sharp teeth hidden away. "They could have. It could also mean that Khuboda Taurani has gained full control of the Skorahn." She turned back to Marcus. "Could you have done something like this?"

He wanted to laugh. "Have you not been listening to me? I have absolutely no *idea* how I do what you say I do with that necklace!" His hand drifted up to his chest before he forced it back down to the table. "I would approach a door and it would open. I would walk into a dark room and the lights would come on."

"And you would get attacked by a cloud of assassin nanites and a powerful energy burst would turn them all to dust." Her mouth twisted bitterly. "You would look at defenses through a viewing field and they would suddenly activate." That caught him off guard for a moment. He probably had Justin to thank for that one.

A quick glance told him he was right; his friend must have told Angara what had happened during the tour of the defenses.

"Right, and I didn't do anything to make *any* of those things happen!" He barely kept his anger in check. "I thought that's just what the Skorahn did, right? Give someone control of the city?"

Angara's laugh was heavy with scorn. "No, you fool. The Skorahn does not give anything! It takes from its possessor. And we do not even understand what, precisely, it takes!"

He stopped, resting back in his chair. It was frustrating, as the thing kept moving back with him as if avoiding the pressure. He stopped himself with a sigh and leaned forward once more. "Uduta Virri couldn't do any of this?"

She barked another laugh. "Udata Virri could not command his own baser instincts. The doors in Penumbra barely acknowledged his existence."

Well, that was surprising. "Maybe because he was such a sloth? I mean, from what you've told me, maybe the Skorahn was only responding to the kind of person he was? I can't imagine Taurani not wrestling the thing to his will."

She shook her head. "There is no 'wrestling it to your will'. I don't believe the Skorahn has bonded to anyone as deeply as it had to you. I told you, Marcus: the bond that had developed between you and the Skorahn, and thus between you and the city, was beyond anything I had ever seen."

He remembered those last chaotic minutes of the fight at the blast doors. Had he truly manipulated the doors with only his will? When he thought back now it almost seemed as if there was something there responding to him, that he was not so much controlling the door, as reaching into the darkness, and feeling something pushing back at him. And that, whatever that was, had interceded on his behalf.

He had never been overly religious, but as he thought back, those moments resembled nothing in his memory so much as prayer.

"So you're saying that Taurani will have no advantage over us if we return?" He felt that he could sense where she was going with this. He couldn't believe she would even think of returning, but there was little other reason he could think of for them to pull out of the wormhole so close to Penumbra.

"Of course he will have advantages. He will have the entire Peacemaker fleet, for one thing." She leaned back and he envied her that ease of motion.

"Well, I'm glad you're willing to admit that, at least." He could feel his anticipation of the coming argument feeding his anger, and so got even more livid despite the fact that she had not yet said anything questionable.

"Marcus Wells, what are your intentions now?" He saw them exchange a look, and knew that Angara and Justin had discussed this between themselves beforehand. He heard the two mystics rise and join them, seats rising up out of the floor. For a moment his errant brain, refusing to focus, wondered why seats hadn't risen up for them when they had sat on the floor in the corner …

He made himself look into Angara's strange violet eyes. It was easy to forget she was an alien when he was in the middle of things. Easy to forget all of them were. Well, most of them. It was hard to ever forget someone like a Leemuk was alien. Or that big damned fish.

Those thoughts brought him back down again, and he felt his shoulders slump. This was real. He wasn't living some child's fantasy. People had died, again, because of him. He looked back up, and straightened his back.

"I want to go back to Earth." It was what she had threatened all along. Even if there had been moments in the past few months where he had forgotten his home planet all together, when he had entertained thoughts of staying in Penumbra and seeing his reforms to their conclusions, he had always planned on going home eventually, hadn't he? He nodded. "I want to go home."

There was silence for a moment. The Thien'ha exchanged a look, and then looked to Justin who shrugged. But Angara's purple eyes never wavered. "You would retreat, seek the safety of your homeworld, knowing the wider galaxy that exists here and the good you could have done had you stayed?"

It was his turn to laugh, and he would put the bitterness of the sound up against the bitterness of her laugh any day. "What *good* can we do now? We've run. Taurani has won. With that fleet, you said it yourself: he could destroy the city if that's what he wants. And what good could we have done if we'd stayed? No one wanted to listen to me. I was straining, working like a madman, and no one gave a damn for what I saw as the city's potential."

"That's not true!" Justin reached across the table and tapped Marcus's hand. "You have no idea what could have happened! I've lived with them, Marc. I worked with them, I drank with them. I … spent a lot of time with them." His eyes shifted to Angara's in temporary embarrassment, and then he continued. "Things were shifting. The people of Penumbra were just starting to wake up to what you had seen the minute we stepped into that docking bay."

Marcus snorted. "Not enough for them to rise up with us when it mattered. When Taurani's thugs started to work over the city, they all retreated behind their own walls, abandoning the city, me, and each other. No way do we face Taurani and that fleet now. Certainly not without them behind us." He shrugged, muttering. "Why would we even try?"

The Thien'ha had barely spoken since the ship had dropped into the singularity. When Khet Nhan piped up, therefore, it startled Marcus enough to listen.

"There are great things in the offing, Marcus Wells. Sihn Ve'Yan and myself would not have sought you out if we did not think we would be witnessing something of vast importance." He looked at his acolyte and then back to Marcus. "The reemergence of Humanity in the galaxy would be momentous indeed. It would rock the very foundations of civilization as it has rested for thousands of your years."

Ve'Yan leaned forward, almost as if she was being forced, and her voice was low and intense. "It would represent an end to the longest cycle every recorded by our order."

"You are the first Humans to escape Earth in hundreds and hundreds of your years! Your entire species is imprisoned, Marcus Wells. And you would voluntarily take up those chains again?" Angara seemed genuinely angry, but he couldn't understand what she would have to be angry about, that his returning to Penumbra would fix.

"I didn't know it was a prison then." He mumbled, not proud of the position he was taking, but not seeing a way to take another and live. "It's an entire world. I think I'll forget it's a prison soon enough when I get home."

He had been thinking of Clarissa, to be honest. Thinking of going home, of finding her, and seeing if he couldn't maybe fix something a little more personal.

He wouldn't tell her about Penumbra or the insanity that had engulfed him. Not right away, at least. He was already reconciled to the fact that no one would ever believe him. If he returned … *when* he returned, he would be living a lie.

But it was a *lie* he could live with, that was the point. Out here, everywhere he looked, all he saw were truths that were going to get him killed.

"I'm not going back." Justin's voice was low but intense, and when Marcus stared at him, his friend only nodded. "I'm staying out here. Even if I can never go back to Penumbra, it's a wide galaxy."

"Your friend will live like a pirate without a home, Marcus Wells." Angara said. "Penumbra is the only refuge for those with nowhere else to go. It was a beacon for those fleeing oppression and tyranny. It will be gone, forever, if we abandon it now." The anger was building, and he found her more intimidating than ever.

"Well, good luck with that." He pushed himself away from the table and stood. There were sleeping cabins below, along either side of the ship's hull, and he made for the one he had used on their journey out from Earth. "I'm going to try to get some sleep. Let me know when we get back to Earth."

He ignored their looks, their attempts to drag him back into the conversation, and the angry slap of Angara's hand on the table.

Dropping down into the cabin, he lowered himself to the bunk and sighed as the cushion engulfed him.

He had never hated himself more than at that moment.

*****

Angara's eyes were focused painfully on the far bulkhead as Marcus stalked away. She closed them and pushed several deep breaths through her nostrils before opening them again, cocking her head at Justin with a snarl.

"Will you follow him, or shall I?" She snapped the words, narrow eyes glaring.

Justin raised his hands in surrender. "I've never been able to talk to him when he's like this. He's made up his mind." He looked sad, leaning forward over his folded hands. "I haven't seen him this low in many, many years."

Angara had had many fears about bringing the Humans to Penumbra. She had had many chances to rethink her hasty decisions on that darkened roadside. Recently, however, both of them had seemed to be adapting well, and she had even allowed herself to begin to hope that Marcus's vision was something more than a homesick Human's fever dream.

She rose abruptly, shaking out her long hair. "I'm not going to live the rest of my life as a vagabond because your friend is a coward. Our best chance is slipping through our fingers, and we are going to need him if we are to turn things around."

"Good luck." His words were heartfelt, his dark eyes sincere. It was a shock to see the depth of those eyes again after staring through the frosted lenses for so long.

She turned away before she could distract herself again, and made for the dropdown access to the small cabin Marcus had claimed.

There was a small foot pedal that would sound a gentle alarm in the cabin to notify the occupant that someone wished to enter. She ignored it and kicked at the access latch. The door hissed open, and she dropped down, ignoring the ship's ladder.

She landed in the murky darkness of Marcus's cabin, her knees flexing slightly with the impact. Scanning the shadows she saw the Human laid out on his back in the small bunk, sitting up with an expression that combined surprise, fear, and outrage without diluting any of them.

"What the hell—"

Two sharp steps brought her to the edge of the bed, where she stopped, her balled fists at her sides, and glared down at him, her eyes flashing in the darkness.

"I will not allow your cowardice to destroy everything we could have built, Marcus Wells. Our best hope is to return and fight the Council forces from within Penumbra. We cannot do that without you."

He threw his legs over the edge of the bed, his hands buried in the soft blanket. His face was twisted with bitterness and anger as he looked up at her. "How the hell do you expect to do that, eh?" He flung one hand aft to indicate the distant city. "You want to turn this boat around and go back to fight off an entire fleet, and a city full of rabid bulldog aliens? The *five* of us?"

She wanted to slap him. She could not remember the last time she had been so angry. She knew that it was not entirely his fault, and yet there was no denying that without him and his strange bond with the city, her situation was hopeless.

"We can still sneak back in! We can infiltrate the Red Tower, reunite you with the Skorahn, and then, with the power of the city once again with us, we will have a chance! There are others who will rise—"

He shook his head, and she stopped. "Others who will rise up to join us now that we are outnumbered and outgunned, but who did *not* rise up to stand with us when it was just us versus a group of Taurani's thugs?" He looked sad, genuinely disappointed and upset, and she remembered that many of the dreams that were dying behind them had started with this lost, confused Human.

"Look, for a time I thought we were going to be able to do something special." His eyes were shining in the darkness. "I thought everything that had happened to me, every choice I had made, had finally come together for a reason." His shoulders slumped. "I was wrong."

It looked as if he had collapsed in upon himself. Before she had consciously acknowledged the impulse, her hand was stinging, his head was rocking backward, and the darkness in his eyes had been replaced with rage as he surged off the bed, one hand rising to his burning cheek.

"You *bitch!*" He did not reach for her, or prepare for a swing, which she found odd. There were so many preconceptions about Humans she had carried through her whole life. Every time he had failed to live up to them, it had been a shock. But now, with her heart racing and her flesh tingling with anticipation of a battle, his refusal to meet her was the most shocking yet.

She wanted to hit him again.

"What the *hell!*" He looked more hurt now than angry, and that just made her own emotions churn the harder.

She pushed him back onto the bed with enough force that he almost struck the rear wall with his head. "I will tell you what the *hell*, Marcus Wells. What the *hell* is that you are a Human that has escaped Earth! That is what the *hell*. You were the leader of a city that needs you now more than ever! That is what the hell! Without you, a dream that most had never even dared to imagine dies now, here, before it even had a chance to draw breath!"

She was stalking the room, pacing back and forth like a caged beast. "The people of Penumbra had come to know you, to *respect* you! They had come to respect a *Human*!"

She knew her words were meaningless to him. Even after bearing the brunt of the galaxy's discrimination and hatred for all this time, he could not begin to understand what it meant that his words had begun to change the city. And nothing she could say was going to reach him, now.

As the realization struck her, she felt her own anger falter and die. Her shoulders slumped, and she eased herself back against the bulkhead. She was nearly panting with the exertion of a moment before, and could only stare at him.

"Look, Angara." He watched her warily from the bed, but he had rearranged his body so that he could, if necessary, spring up again to defend himself if she rushed him. That was something, anyway. "I know this means a lot to you. I think I might even know why. But you've got the wrong guy. I'm not qualified to run anything, never mind a city. And *really* never mind a floating city full of aliens, for Christ's sake!" He shook his head, resting his elbows on his knees and lowering his head into his hands. "It can't be me, because it was never going to be me. And every being in Penumbra knew it."

For a moment there was nothing but silence in the little cubicle. When he looked up, the guttering light in his eyes was proof that he had no real hope to offer her.

"Why not Justin? He's great with people, every kind of person! He'd be a big help in any sort of desperate scheme you've thought up."

Could he be so obtuse? "I have not yet conceived of any desperate scheme. But anything I could think of would require your presence. You are special, Marcus. I know you don't see it, I know you don't agree. But I've seen your connection with the city. There is something between you, something strange, and unique, and important. And without that bond, any design to retake the city would truly be a desperate, hopeless plan."

He shook his head, looking back down at the deck. "I think you're wrong. It was just dumb luck, and I won't push it again."

Marcus Wells stood up, straightening his back slowly, rolling his shoulders, and looking at her from a stern, steady face. "I want to go home."

She felt the last flickers of hope die within her. They left behind a cold emptiness she had not felt since first being banished from her people's fleet when she was barely more than a child. She was alone again, homeless, without refuge or shelter.

"I cannot make you fight." She pushed off the wall with her shoulders, exhausted. "No one can make you fight."

She turned her back on him and grabbed the top rung of the short ladder. She stopped half way up, and spoke over her shoulder. "We lack the fuel to reach Earth. We will need to take on more, and then we will see you safely home."

He started to say something; to thank her, possibly, or to ask another question. She ignored him and heaved herself the rest of the way up the ladder. She had no interest in further words with a coward.

# Chapter 22

A soft tone echoed off the walls of his cubicle; the ship was falling out of its wormhole and back into real space. They must have arrived at the black market station Angara had mentioned before he had exiled himself to his cabin.

He couldn't deal with the others since the argument over returning to Penumbra. Angara had been nothing but coldly polite since the quarrel. Justin had tried to jolly him out of his dark mood, but he was one man against the weight of truth, two angry females, and an increasingly erratic little ball of fur that seemed to have lost what little contact with reality it had had.

He had made a couple forays out of his tiny cabin, but the pressure was too much. He had been taking his meals below, only venturing out to relieve himself or when the claustrophobia got too much to bear. Whenever he *did* go topside now, everyone avoided his eyes, kept to themselves, and gave off a distinct impression of relief when he headed back down to his cabin.

In theory, each day brought them closer to Earth, but there was no sense of anticipation or excitement. He had been expecting to feel some relief at the very least, that their harrowing experience was nearing its end. Instead, whenever he closed his eyes all he could see were Angara's judging eyes, or the dead, empty gaze of Copic Fa'Orin, staring at him with accusation. Guilt was his ever-present companion. He felt guilty for what he had done, and he felt guilty for what he had refused to do.

It was driving him mad.

He tried to focus on Clarissa's face, but he couldn't seem to conjure it up in his mind no matter how hard he tried. He saw his father and his brother and sister, though. He saw them plenty. And the look in their eyes were stark reminders of the few glancing blows he had caught from Angara's own, violet glares over the past few days.

He was starting to realize that returning home, although appearing to be the coward's road from the Tigan woman's point of view, was going to be no unalloyed joy.

The tone sounded again, and that strange dropping sensation told him they had fallen back into real space.

"What the hell is that?" Justin's tone, excitement and fear mixed, was not lost despite being muffled by the deck plates between them. It sent a chill down his spine, and despite his resolution to avoid them all until they reached Earth, Marcus found himself climbing up into the cool light of the common area.

"It's a ship." Angara's voice was calm, distracted; clearly she was busy piloting the ship.

"That's no ordinary ship." Sihn Ve'Yan spoke in a low voice, as if afraid of being overheard.

"We've got plenty to worry about. It's nothing. It's just a ship." Angara's distracted voice was only slightly hotter than normal. When she was concentrating on her ship, she rarely had attention to spare.

"It's a warship." A manic, chipper voice responded. "Haven't seen one of those in a long time."

"Not in a few days, anyway." Justin muttered darkly.

Marcus moved warily forward, toward the command deck. Angara was controlling the ship from a sitting position, so clearly she did not believe they were in immediate danger of attack. Justin, Sihn Ve'Yan, and Khet Nhan were all gathered around the viewing fields that swept around the forward arch of the chamber, staring out at the mysterious ship.

He was a little sheepish moving forward, but decided that there was no real reason he should be ashamed to take an interest in whatever was happening. He straightened his shoulders and eased past Angara, tossing what he hoped was a casual nod of his head before moving on. He was careful not to look too closely at her, however. He didn't want to be shamed back into his hole before at least checking out what was going on outside the windows.

The others turned at his approach and shifted to make a little room for him in the cramped confines of the ship's nose. Justin was the only one who seemed genuinely happy to see him, however. Ve'Yan looked like she had bitten into something foul, and the little master's soft face was shifting from angry to sad and back again as he watched. He kept his face bland and moved in to take the place they had made for him.

They were approaching what appeared to be a blasted asteroid, half of which had been carved into a fantastical stone building floating in space. Tubes, pipes, poles, and metal lattice stuck out in all directions, and a series of well-lit openings were clearly entranceways for smaller craft like the Yud'ahm Na'uka. Objects that must have been smaller ships were set down upon the wide flat space before the openings, with pipes and tubes connected to them from various bunkers and terminals studding the stonework surface.

But keeping station over the entire compound, nearly as long as the asteroid itself, was a sleek, swept-back shape that had to be a spacecraft of some kind. Aside from the ancient relics of Penumbra, it was the first large ship he had ever seen, and yet something about it seemed eerily familiar.

"What is it?" He tried to ask, but his throat was rusty from lack of use. He coughed and tried again. "What is it?"

"It's nothing." Angara muttered, but when he turned around it was *her* that would not meet *his* eyes. "It won't be a problem."

Marcus turned back to look at the others. There was no help from the two Thien'ha, but Justin seemed troubled, and would not meet his eyes.

"Justin, what the hell is going on?"

His friend shrugged. "Angara's right. It's probably nothing. I'm sure there won't be any problems."

But it was clear by the way that his eyes lingered on that long, shark-like shape, that he wasn't nearly as sure as he was trying to appear.

*****

With some quick words and a hefty credit transfer, she was able to secure them one of the few private berths along the row of docks. They were directed to the far right entrance, and Angara brought the *Yud'ahm Na'uka* in flawlessly, settling it into a wide cradle that immediately began to adjust to the small ship's dimensions. She communicated with the control center through her nanite implants, showing no overt signs as she rose from the flight chair and indulged in a long, slow stretch.

She pretended not to notice Justin's stare, but could not help a little smile from sketching its own way across her lips.

"We will need to negotiate for fuel." She turned to the ship's ventral ramp. "I won't be long. You should all stay onboard while I take care of this."

Marcus raised his hands and moved out of her way, not meeting her eyes. The mystics stepped back, making way for her to move through the common room. Ve'Yan dipped her head as Angara passed, while the little master, his paws rubbing together, smiled at her with wide, wild eyes. She shook her head. Plenty of time to puzzle out what was wrong with the little creature after they were away from the station.

The ship hovering overhead loomed heavily in her thoughts.

"I'm coming." Justin hurried past the lowering command chair and the others, skipping up to her as she activated the ramp. "No reason you should be alone."

She turned, looked him up and down, noting his dark color, his shaven head, and nodded. "You'll need your lenses, though."

Justin hesitated for a moment and then disappeared into his cubicle. He emerged with a pair of dark welding goggles and slipped them over his head with an apologetic shrug. "I don't know that I really want to use those anymore."

She stared at him, then shook her head, turning back down the ramp. As they crossed the docking bay, she could feel the others watching them from the command deck. As nonchalantly as she could, she turned her body to keep her back to the ship as she leaned nearer to Justin.

"You recognized the ship."

He nodded with a sharp jerk of his chin. "I did a little digging after our run in at the fighting pits. I recognized it."

They walked to one of the supply terminals set against the private dock's rear bulkhead. She kept her pace casual. There was no telling what Marcus might do if he understood their current situation.

"It has always been assumed he still had the fleet. But there has never been a sighting of a capital ship since he fled his system. He's never been seen with one, and anyone who tried to follow him back to the mysterious fleet disappeared without a trace." At the terminal she began to outline her resupply request. The process would be mostly automated, and only in the last stages would she have to face a living being for the final negotiations. "He might not be up there. And even if he is, there's no reason for him to seek us out. He can't know who we are, or that either of you are on my ship. We should be fine if we can just get the fuel, the other supplies we will require for the run, and leave."

Justin nodded, a smile firmly planted on his dark face, and pivoted on one heel, surveying the chamber from behind the thick, opaque lenses. It was fairly large, but the *Na'uka* loomed behind them, filling the room with its menacing bulk. "You don't think he'll recognize the ship? Not many independent Tigan swift ships flying about, are there?"

She whirled on him, her eyes flaring. "How—"

He shrugged, his smile a shade more genuine, if a bit sheepish. "I dig. I told you."

She had considered the likelihood of her ship escaping notice, and did not entirely like their chances, but by the time she had seen the big warship it had been too late.

"There is still a chance they will leave us alone. There is no reason for him to assume you are with me. When he left Penumbra, everything was still running as smoothly as it ever did. He might not be suspicious, even if he recognizes my ship."

Justin looked skeptical, but nodded and pivoted again, resting his shoulders against the wall.

"He's a good man." His chin was tucked against his chest, his arms folded, and his eyes fixed on the deck plating. "He's a good man, and I'm not sure it's fair to expect him to rush back into that meat grinder. He's not a fighter. Hasn't been for a long time. And until we met you, *neither* of us had ever seen any real violence up close."

He seemed sad as he said it, and she looked at him, waiting for the next response from the terminal's automated systems. It would have been easier if the pirate station had updated interface programs that would have allowed her to perform these mundane functions from the ship. But those who owned and ran such ventures undoubtedly saw little value in spending hard credits on systems that would make it easier for customers to hide their identity from the station. This way, they were under constant surveillance, their scans were in the station's memory banks, and there would be no doubting who to seek retribution from should something be traced back to them at a later date.

Justin sighed and turned on one shoulder to look at her. "Let's be honest: it's not like we have a plan."

All of the anger she had suppressed since slapping Marcus Wells in his cabin came roaring back. How could these Humans be so obtuse? "With his control of the city's systems, there would be almost no way they could counter us! We would be able to gather resistance, and—"

He reached out, a sad smile on his face, and took her shoulder in a reassuring grip. "There wasn't any resistance, Angara. I understand your desire to go back and save the city. I really do. But just the five of us? And I don't think you're being honest about how that fleet changes the equation, either."

He shook his head and settled back against the wall. "Hell, at least two of those ships were even bigger than the one hanging over our heads!" He jerked a thumb at the ceiling.

Her anger sputtered. She wanted to rant and scream, but something about his touch had defused much of her fury, and his words had done a great deal to douse the rest.

"He was doing it, you know." She bent closer to the terminal, the easier to avoid meeting his hidden eyes. "Marcus was transforming the city into something most of us had never even dreamed of. It might not have been happening quickly, but it was happening. And we saw it."

She closed her eyes, the admission hurting. "And I was taking it away from him."

Justin moved around her, taking her by the shoulders and turning her to look at him. "Angara, this was happening with or without us. Taurani's schemes were in play no matter what we were doing. He wasn't planning to oust Marcus because the city was coming around, he was planning on taking over long before we ever even knew you all existed." He shrugged, looking over at the sleek ship sitting in the cradle. "Hell, if it weren't for us, and you, he might have moved even sooner."

She did not want to believe, but she sensed more truth in his words than she wished she did.

The terminal beeped to life and a shrouded figure appeared on the screen. The negotiation was quick and cursory. She was not requesting anything particularly exotic, and thus prices were more or less fixed. Until word began to spread of the Council's move against Penumbra, anyway. This entire sector of space would be far less hospitable if they maintained their hold.

Automated systems trundled hoses and pipes out to the *Yud'ahm Na'uka*, and lights flashed as the fuel transfer began. Small doors opened in the surrounding bulkheads and materials began to emerge on the backs of low, squat automatons, stacked neatly by the ramp.

She brooded on their situation as she watched the stack of supplies build. Occasionally, she cast a glance back at the shining, opaque surface of the command bridge, wondering if Marcus Wells was watching them. Her anger was still there, simmering beneath the surface, but there was a guilt there now as well, and she could no longer avoid it, thanks to Justin.

Her sullen reverie was broken when a harsh buzz announced an entry request at the main bay doors, just a few paces to her left.

Angara and Justin exchanged looks, his blank stare unnerving. She was surprised how quickly she had become used to his dark, Human eyes.

"It's them." His voice was flat. His head pivoted from the blast door, to the ship behind them, and back again.

"It isn't." She tried to remain calm, to settle his nerves while hiding her own. Nevertheless, she looked over her shoulder, noted the height of the piled supplies, and then turned to cancel the remaining order. They would still lose the credit, but there would be time to worry about that later.

She moved to the door, her pace reluctant.

"What are you doing? You can't let *him* in here!" Justin grabbed her by one shoulder and she let him pull her about. "We need to get out of here, now, before he knows for sure *we're* here!" He gestured with a thumb to his own chest and then to the ship.

"We won't have enough fuel to make Earth, Justin." She was quite proud of her tone. She was having a hard time thinking clearly. "If we leave here, we're just going to have to stop at another pirate station. The terminal here will have a full readout of our current load." She tilted her head at the door. "They will know how far we can go, and so they will be able to follow us. We will have no choice but to meet them again before we can return you to your home." She shrugged, her smile feeling almost genuine. "Better to do so now, when he is hardly certain of our situation, no?"

She didn't wait for his reply, but turned again to head for the door. "I have no intention of letting anyone in. We'll speak through the door comms, and I'll send them away."

She was grateful he did not follow her. The closer she got to the door, the less success she was having schooling her features to stillness.

*****

"What are they doing?" Marcus stood by the viewing fields, looking out at the bay to where his friend and the purple-skinned warrior woman stood by a console, apparently lost in a casual conversation while automated systems refueled and resupplied the ship.

"It would appear they are preparing for your return home, Marcus Wells." The high pitched voice caught him by surprise. He hadn't noticed the little mystic approaching him, and had spoken aloud without thinking. "Why, what is it you think you see?"

He gave the creature a quick glance and then looked back out. Ever since they had fled from Penumbra, Khet Nhan had been acting unstable. His knowing little smile had been replaced with a wide, rictus-like grin, his twinkling eyes now shone as if he were in the grip of some terrible fever. His movements, once graceful and flowing, were jerky and uncoordinated. And he rubbed his agile little hands together constantly, as if eager for some anticipated event.

"Nothing, I guess." Marcus murmured after a moment's uncomfortable silence. The last thing he wanted to do was have a conversation with the little alien now.

Outside, Angara and Justin had moved, and were now standing a few paces from a large blast door that must lead further into the station. A flashing light was pulsing by the door, and he thought he could hear a buzzing sound in the distance.

Khet Nhan stopped his fidgeting. The stillness was more alarming than the ceaseless motion had been.

Marcus jerked around to look at the mystic. "What?"

Nhan shook his head roughly back and forth, the pale grin fur of his fringe beard waving wildly. "It's nothing. Probably nothing. I'm sure it's nothing."

Sihn Ve'Yan came over from her position of meditation in the common area. "What is it?" She seemed to have sensed her master's concern, and spared a look for neither of them as she moved over to the field and gazed out. "Someone wants in."

Angara was moving toward the door, leaving Justin standing still behind her, one hand half raised as if he had thought to stop her, and then decided better of it.

Something about the way Ve'Yan and Nhan were acting had set him more on edge than he had been, and Marcus stepped away from the viewing field. "Who could it be? What would someone want, coming to a bay like this?"

They looked at each other, and then back out without turning around. "Could be almost anything." Ve'Yan spoke as if each word caused her discomfort. "Could be merchants, could be people requesting passage. Could be station administration, looking for a bribe."

Marcus knew that Angara had paid for their docking bay with her dwindling personal credit, but he hadn't thought of it as a bribe.

A sound like a distant gong rang out through the docking bay outside, and he hurried to join the other two at the field. As always, he felt as if he was looking through a window with no glass, a clear view of everything outside laid out before him.

Justin moved toward Angara, while the woman was gesticulating wildly to a small screen set in the grimy wall beside it. Another impact echoed across the bay. Someone was banging on the other side of the door. Someone was *beating* on the other side of the door, and they were either very big, or very angry, or both.

"Of course, it might be something else entirely." Ve'Yan finished lamely. Her smile was wan, her eyes flat.

"One way or another, this is about to get very interesting." Master Khet Nhan rubbed his hands together, his sharp little teeth gleaming.

Marcus was trying to decide how troubled he should be by the disturbing little display when a deep-throated shout, buzzing with feedback, burst through the stillness outside.

Angara was arguing with Justin now, her movements sending her fine white hair flying. But his friend was unmoved, nodding slowly in that infuriating way he had when he knew he was right. Marcus felt a moment's compassion for the woman. There was nothing so frustrating as trying to shake Justin's faith in himself when he was that certain.

His friend reached one hand out to press against a sensor in the wall, and the door shot up and out of sight.

Marcus wanted to vomit.

Standing on the other side of the door, his huge frame draped in red robes over bulky armor, stood the demon-faced monster they called K'hzan Modath, the red king. His black horns were shining, his rigid, twisted face furious, and he stared down at Justin with opaque, black eyes.

Behind the giant alien stood an honor guard of creatures nearly as tall as their king, holding heavy rifles in the place of the big polearms they had carried in Penumbra. He assumed this station, small by comparison, didn't have a similar suppression system. Somehow, the guns seemed even more threatening than the gleaming steel of their cruel blades.

Justin stood before K'hzan Modath, straightening to his full height, just over six feet.

It fell sadly short of the red king, who was more than a foot taller.

The demon beast snarled something to Justin, and Justin shook his head, gesturing vaguely behind him toward the ship. Angara was now standing with him, shoulder to shoulder, and nodded her own head, clearly in support of the Human.

But whatever they were saying, K'hzan was unconvinced. He sneered at Justin, his face particularly suited for the expression. The beast leaned in, mouth working, and then lashed out with one huge hand, slapping Justin aside with a casual backhand blow.

Angara fell into a fighter's crouch, the weapons on her shoulders emerging with lightning speed. But not soon enough. The king's honor guard had her dead to rights before she could even turn, and as she looked down their barrels, Justin shifted on the floor, shaking his dazed head, and she relaxed. The weapon snouts withdrew, and she straightened.

K'hzan looked at them both, as if waiting for them to proceed. When neither moved, he stalked past them toward the ship.

"He's coming here." Marcus muttered under his breath. He remembered the tales he had been told about K'hzan's hatred for Humans. He staggered away from the viewing field, despite knowing that anyone outside was seeing only the featureless metal of the hull.

"He's coming for me." His breath was coming in short, sharp gasps.

"Well, he's not coming for *us*, that's for sure." Nhan rubbed his hands again, looking at him with a vicious grin.

Marcus glared at the creature, but before he could muster a reply, a gravelly voice outside the ship echoed hollowly off the surrounding bulkheads.

"Come out, *Human*!" It was guttural, vicious. "I know you are within. I could smell your foul stench through the void from my own ship."

Marcus crept back to the field, peeking out over the lower lip. Below him, K'hzan was frowning up. Even knowing the demon couldn't see him, he felt a cold hand twisting his guts. The empty black eyes seemed to be staring right through the armored hide of the ship, pinning him to the spot.

"I know what you have done, coward! Come and face me, or I will root you out of your cage and drag you into the light!"

Marcus cringed at the words. He could sense the Thien'ha staring at him, and knew there would be no help to be had from either of them. He looked back out. K'hzan stood below, clawed hands flexing at his sides, and sneered up at him.

"I can smell your fear, craven. I would look you in the eye as I declare you a wretched worm, and have of you an explanation of your intentions now that your destruction of my home is complete."

Marcus started at that. Could Penumbra have been destroyed? He couldn't imagine even Taurani would have destroyed the entire city in so short a time. The thought banished all the personal fear from his body, replacing it with a sudden, unreasoning dread that the city was gone.

He turned and moved so quickly between the two mystics that even they could not have stopped him had they wanted to. He stalked through the common room and down the ramp, working his jaw as his inner ear equalized with the pressure in the bay, and then moved around the ramp, toward the tall, dominating figure of the red king.

"What?" He spat the word as if it was a curse; adrenaline overcompensating for his terror. "Let's hear it."

He had never spoken two words to this creature before, but there had been those in the administrator's office who had taken a positive glee in telling and retelling the stories. This fierce and barbaric warrior king had been exiled by his own people for denying to bow down to the Galactic Council when they came to disarm his race, the Variyar. He had been living in exile in Penumbra, disappearing for long stretches of time on mysterious errands, for what he had to guess was over a century.

Through all that, his reputation as a brutal fighter in the pits and a terrible foe in both business and war had been forged.

And here Marcus stood, screaming up at the monster from the questionable shelter of the *Yud'ahm Na'uka*'s shadow.

K'hzan looked down at him for a moment in surprise. He shook his head, the rack of horns gleaming, and widened his stance.

"Your cowardice disgusts me, Human." The hot, foreign breath washed over him, and his shaking adrenal courage wavered. "All my life I have heard the tales. I was raised on the myths and legends of Human power and fury. I was taught that the sad, pathetic remnants that wandered the galaxy were nothing but an attenuated shadow of the might of the primeval Humans." He snorted. "I harbored in my heart of hearts the belief that such greatness could still be found among the Humans of Earth. That one day, perhaps, they would surge forth and the great, ancient war would erupt once again, washing the tyranny of the weak away once and for all."

He reared up on his massive, reverse-jointed legs and spat a gobbet of black phlegm that slapped against the deck at Marcus's feet. "My disappointment in your failure knows no bounds, Marcus Wells."

That brought Marcus up short. How could this enormous demon-beast out of his worst nightmares possibly be disappointed in *him*? He looked up into that horrific face, confusion roiling through his mind. When K'hzan leaned down toward him, he didn't think to back away.

"The Humans of Earth have loomed large in the tales of the Variyar for uncountable ages. There was a time when the galaxy trembled at the tread of your people's feet, Human. The foundations of the universe shook at your will! And *now* look at you." One clawed hand reached out and cuffed him backward, pushing almost negligently at his shoulder. "A pathetic coward that runs from the weak and the feeble as if chased by the very hounds of hell."

Well, that hardly sounded fair. People had died because of him! Did this giant red shit-head not understand that? For a moment he wanted to push the big alien back, but thought better of it. Still, however, he burned with the need to respond. His mouth, as always, ran far ahead of his thoughts.

"What do you want me to do, you asshole? Would it make things better for anyone if I went back and let those psychotic basset hounds kill me? Would it make the city safer? Would it bring back Copic Fa'Orin and his son?" It was his turn to sneer, his adrenaline in full control again. "You'll forgive me if any sense of racial guilt on *your* part isn't enough for me to feel better about dying."

The black eyes reflected warped images of himself. He hoped the fear he could see in his own eyes wasn't as easily read by someone less familiar with Human emotions.

"Fear of dying is the refuge of the weak. There are far worse things than dying, worm." It was uncanny, the way the towering monster seemed able to read his mind.

"It's probably easier to say that from some positions than from others." Marcus stood his ground, trying to ignore his own reflections.

The rack of horns swept back and forth as K'hzan Modath shook his head. "I could easily have stood and died when they came to disarm my people. There were many who expected me to do so. Many believed the old ways *demanded* it. Instead, I ran." Something in the eyes shifted, and Marcus had the impression the big monster's thoughts were far away. "When you run from some things, there is no stopping. You will run for the rest of your life."

Marcus snorted. "Running might just be a little more comfortable as a king than as a beggar, though, I'd imagine."

Those black, inscrutable eyes narrowed and fell with their full force upon him. "You might think that. You would be wrong."

"Leave him alone!" Justin's voice was a little strident, and he was holding his arm stiffly across his chest. The goggles were askew, and a single dark, Human eye stared out, hot with anger. He tried to insinuate himself between Marcus and the big alien, but Marcus put his hand on his friend's shoulder and gently kept him out.

"I can take care of myself, Justin." He focused on bringing his breathing under control, but his growing anger at K'hzan's assault worked steadily against him.

Angara came up on the big alien's other side, the enormous honor guards behind her. "There's nothing here for you, K'hzan. You should leave."

Neither of them drew the red king's attention away from Marcus, however. He was breathing heavily, chest heaving with his own pent-up emotions. As the moment stretched into uncomfortable territory, Marcus found he could not look away, his anger fueling his innate stubborn nature.

He could hardly believe it when, with a last eloquent snort of derision, K'hzan straightened, peering down at him from his daunting height.

"Very well. I had hoped to find a legend hidden away within the breast of this creature. Instead I find a worm." He shook his head in disgust and turned away. "The galaxy is a poorer place for it."

"Wait!" The piping voice cried out from behind them all. Everyone but Marcus turned to stare at the diminutive mystic in his fluttering white robes running toward them with an erratic gait, his thin, furry arms flailing wildly. "You can't leave! This is it! This *must* be it!"

Marcus was still in shock at his adversary's surrender. As things unfolded around him, he could only stare at K'hzan with an open mouth.

"Master, stop!" Ve'Yan shouted, following the little alien at a full run. "Please, you *must* end this!"

But she was too late, and Khet Nhan skidded into the space between K'hzan and Marcus, his little chest heaving, his hands fluttering about without purpose or direction, and his head craning first to the Human, then to the Variyar king. The wide red eyes were pleading, and as he turned his full attention on K'hzan, the hands curled around each other and began to rub viciously.

"You cannot leave him like this. He cannot be allowed to render all that has happened here worthless!" The voice was high and beseeching.

"Master, come away." Ve'Yan took the small master under her right arm and tried to guide him gently back toward the ship.

"No!" Nhan sounded like a child as he pulled himself out of the Diakk woman's grip. "This cannot be how this ends! We cannot have dived headlong off the path only to see him fade into oblivion!" He jerked a small thumb viciously in Marcus's direction.

Marcus's mouth twisted: someone else shoving their baggage onto his shoulders.

The anger burning within him churned hotter, sending sparks of fire swirling through his chest and up into his head.

"This cannot be the end!" The high-pitched shriek echoed off the belly of the ship looming above them. Angara and Justin looked embarrassed as they hovered behind Sihn Ve'Yan. The acolyte, however, was obviously far more concerned for her master than for anything else.

The Diakk woman kneeled to soothe the little master, and his vibrating beard began to wilt, his shoulders slumping. He looked up at her with sad, wide eyes. "This cannot be the end."

Ve'Yan nodded but said nothing as she led him back toward the ramp.

Marcus watched them go, and then turned back to the enormous form of K'hzan Modath. The red king was staring at him again, and the look on his face was cold and distant. "I trusted in the wrong tales, Human. You bring misery and destruction with you wherever you travel. We are well rid of you. The Earth is welcome to your poison. Good riddance."

The towering alien spun away, sending his heavy red cloak swirling, and stalked toward the distant doorway. The two honor guards backed up behind him, keeping their eyes, and their weapons, trained on the trio beneath the ship.

Marcus heard everything with a faint, echoing quality. There was a rushing in his ears that threatened to drown out all other sounds. He had been spat upon and dismissed from the moment Angara had forced them onto her ship. He had clawed his way toward respectability, not understanding the pressure mounting against him, but determined to do his best as his understanding of Penumbra's potential had grown within him.

And he had lost it all. Every goal he had formed was dust. The people he had tried to help were dead or scattered. And the contempt piled upon him continued to mount.

He was worthless. He was less than worthless, he was a detriment to the only good thing he had ever tried to do in his life.

He was exactly what his father thought him to be.

"Stop!" He barked the single word and it echoed harshly around the cavernous chamber.

K'hzan paused, his horned head tilting like a hunting dog catching a new scent. But he did not turn around.

"I won't go back there to die." He approached the red king, ignoring the wide bores of the honor guards' weapons thrusting at him. "If I go back there alone, I *will* die. And it will serve no purpose at all."

K'hzan turned, regarding him with a flat, emotionless glare.

"If I'm not alone, though, there might be more to discuss." The anger was still there, but now it was oriented with equal parts against himself. "If you're willing to offer more than your contempt and disdain, we might not be done here yet."

Within those dark, soulless orbs, something flickered.

# Chapter 23

The common area of the *Yud'ahm Na'uka*, never terribly spacious, was positively cramped with the bulk of K'hzan Modath crouched in the corner. Even the ship's mutable decking could not provide the red king with a seat suitable for his large frame. If the Variyar's horns scraped across her ceiling again, she was going to scream.

They sat around the low table, no one wanting to be the first to speak. Master Khet Nhan sat upon his hands, refusing to fidget, his eyes firmly fixed on the table top. He was clearly embarrassed by his outburst in the bay, although no one seemed inclined to acknowledge it.

Marcus Wells sat at the head of the table with Justin next to him. Justin was uncomfortable, shooting an occasional glance at K'hzan. But it was Marcus Wells that dominated her thoughts. His pale-skinned face was distracted and brooding behind his dark stubble. His hair, as always, was artlessly tousled, lending to his air of grim, wild energy.

The Human she had put on the administrator's throne, the Human that had nearly driven her to violent rage with his lackadaisical response to their abject failure, had found his courage at the sharp end of K'hzan's low regard. Where the begging and pleading of his friends had had no discernible effect, the harsh words of this demonic stranger had stoked something within him that she had not seen before.

She could admit now, with K'hzan sitting across from her, his massive warship floating somewhere above, that her initial reaction to Taurani's plot and Iphini Bha's treachery had been emotional. They would have died if they had returned to fight alone. Marcus Wells's points against that had been well-made. She was honest enough with herself that in the silence of her own mind, she could confess to those things.

She did not dare, however, assume that K'hzan Modath might take their side against the Council, even with the Variyar exile grudgingly agreeing to sit with them. But if by some miracle they could persuade him, maybe the situation had changed enough to make a return to Penumbra something less than a suicidal proposition.

"The way I see it, with your help, returning to Penumbra is just feasible enough for us to discuss." Marcus inclined his head toward K'hzan. There was clearly no love lost between the two, especially after their shouting match in the bay. But the Variyar exile, whatever his reasons, was listening, and that was a victory in and of itself.

"I am still not convinced that this is anything but a forlorn hope, but there are possible avenues, if we can agree on how to approach them."

"The city is completely enveloped by the Council fleet." The Variyar's voice grated harshly against her ears in the confined space. "There will be no access to Penumbra without first engaging those ships."

Marcus's eyes were fever bright as he leaned forward over the table. "Well, I was sort of hoping that would be where you came in."

K'hzan quirked a single eyebrow up, the deep ridges of his forehead writhing around his horns. "Please, by all means, elaborate."

"That's not the only ship you have." Justin broke in, jerking a thumb at the ceiling. "Your fleet is out here somewhere. That's got to be worth something."

K'hzan inhaled slowly, nostrils flaring, before his eyes slid to Justin's face. "I suffer you to sit upon these proceedings at the behest of your administrator, coward." He sniffed, eyes roving up and down the dark-skinned Human's form. "You lacked the courage to embrace your heritage in the face of the scorn of lesser races. You are beneath contempt or regard."

Marcus slapped the table with one hand. "Oh, God damn it! I am *so* fed up with this *bullshit*! What the hell has got you all so hung up on the Human race?" He screamed the words, finally giving in to the frustration that had been building within him for months. "Every single soul in that damned city hated me from the moment I walked onto the decking because I'm a Human. Even those who I came to call my *friends* had nothing kind to say about my species! What, in a galaxy so full of the strange, bizarre, and downright disgusting, is so very wrong with Humans?"

He was nearly panting as he finished. He glared at everyone around the table, obviously unsurprised that none of the aliens would meet his gaze. None of them, that is, except for the giant demon king.

K'hzan's smile was something out of a nightmare. The way it caused his coarse features to shift and ripple would stay with her for the rest of her life. The deep-set black eyes widened in mock surprise, and a black tongue lashed out to moisten the grinning lips.

"Is it possible that none of your compatriots here revealed to you the weight of history that bears down upon your delicate shoulders?" He looked at Angara and then the two Thien'ha, all of whom cast sheepish, sideways glances toward Marcus and Justin and then away.

The Variyar's laugh echoed through the small chamber. "My friends, you have given me my first joyful moments in more than an age." Angara could not tell if the creature's eyes were tearing up or if they had always shined that way. His clawed hand tapped gently on the table with an unnerving scraping, as he shook his head in disbelief.

"You have lived among those who hate you all this time, and none of your precious advisors thought to enlighten you regarding the source of this odium?" The smile faded slightly, and the look he gave Angara was more judgmental than before. "That was no kindness, girl."

Angara felt the need to defend herself rise in her chest, but tamped it down. She forced herself to settle back into her chair, waving the comment away.

K'hzan Modath turned on Marcus and fixed him with a flat stare. "You have a galaxy of history to learn, Marcus Wells. It will take you a lifetime to absorb it completely." The smile returned, but there was no kindness in it. "However, I will take great pleasure in summating for you the salient points."

She watched Justin lean forward in fascination. Marcus, too, was fixated upon the big Variyar, barely able to control his eagerness.

"Your tale begins in a time now lost in the mists of myth and legend. For make no mistake, Humans, this is your tale." One clawed finger stabbed out first at Marcus, then at Justin.

"Many sentients rose from their homeworlds to contest for mastery of the galaxy, meeting in battle, forming alliances and federations, and negotiating a new reality as sentients have always done." He leaned on one elbow and brought his head closer to his rapt audience.

"One race rose more swiftly than any other. There is almost no way to know now what combination of traits and strengths attributed to their rise, but very soon, in galactic terms, *Humanity* was the near-undisputed ruler of the known universe."

Marcus and Justin straightened at this. A faint smile spread across Marcus's pale face. Obviously, he liked where he thought the story was going. She almost cringed, knowing its true destination. And with a Variyar telling the tale, especially *this* Variyar, she knew it would not be easy to hear.

"This is nothing to rejoice in, Humans." The demon's face became stone. "Your ancestors were not kind. Their rule was not one to bring joy to those they ruled. The galaxy was their plaything, and they were as unruly children, incautious with their possessions. Their cruelty knew no bounds, and despite the fact that only whispered legend remains of those dark times, it says much that the hatred instilled then continues to run true to this very day."

Marcus must have realized his mouth was open and forced it shut with a click. Justin seemed even more affected.

"Among their many lasting cruelties were those the unkind refer to now as the Children." The horns glinted dully as he inclined his head to Angara, then Ve'Yan. She did not know about the Thien'ha, but she could have lived without the recognition. "Also known as the Children of Man. Entire races created as the ideal servants, soldiers, and even idle works of art."

Justin started at that, shooting a quick look at Angara with an expression she was too preoccupied to translate.

Marcus's eyes were narrowed, a deep crease forming between them. "But Earth—"

K'hzan silenced him with a single upraised finger. "My tale, Human. To be completed in my time." The smile would have taken some of the sting from the words, she thought, had it featured fewer sharp teeth.

"One race dared to contest with these tyrannical overlords. My own people, the Variyar of old, were proud warriors in their own right, and refused to be subjugated. They rose up against the Humans and contended with them for the fate of the galaxy. The war that then raged across the face of the heavens was mighty indeed, and entire systems were laid waste by the power unleashed by both sides. An age of war descended upon the galactic civilization, and entire generations were born, raised, and died knowing only violence, hatred, and death. The scars of this great war have never fully faded, and are the true source of your difficulties today."

K'hzan waved a hand toward Khet Nhan. "For the Variyar were not alone. An alliance of races that had not dared face the Humans unaided coalesced over time. These sentients stood beside my own ancestors, compensating for their lack of strength and numbers by slowly calling to themselves the many disparate peoples who had been wronged by Humanity. Their assistance was unasked for and unwanted, but the war had ground down into a bloody stalemate, and my people, for all their strength, could not end it alone. The alliance of the weak asserted itself in the final stages of the conflict. Now numbering far greater than the Variyar, they

were in a position of great strength and influence in the end. With some small jus-
tification, they were able to declare themselves essential to the final victory over
the Humans and lay the groundwork for a supposed democratic alliance of equals
to rule in place of the defeated tyrants."

Marcus's eyes widened as he put the pieces together. K'hzan met his
gaze and nodded slowly. "The Galactic Council is the spiritual descendant of that
ancient alliance. They have since spent millennia consolidating their power in the
name of equality and justice for all beings." The red king's sneer spoke volumes
on his regard for that pursuit. "Behind the pretext of democracy and manumission,
some few of the more energetic of these weakling races guided the formation of
the Council, replacing the dispossessed Humans with a new tyranny: the tyranny
of the weak."

This turn in the story had changed the big creature's demeanor, and he
now looked as if he wanted to spit onto her table in his anger. His eyes drifted into
the middle distance as he contemplated something that obviously twisted bitterly
within him.

"But what about Earth?" Justin asked after a moment. Marcus nodded,
mutely.

K'hzan seemed to shake himself, and then looked between the two Humans as he brought his mind back to the present. "Ah, yes. Earth. Have you not
guessed? Under the control of that ancient, fledgling council, those remnants of
the Human race who surrendered in the final days of the war were deposited on
what you think of as your home planet. They were given no advanced support or
assistance. My speculation is that those kind hearted sophists of old expected
your ancestors to wither and die of their own accord. In the likelihood that these
survivors thrived, the entire planet was seeded with genetic markers that would,
over time, bring the DNA of the defeated Humans in line with the lifeforms indigenous to the planet. A false fossil record was laid down, with no small amount of
amusement, to make it appear that Humans had been on Earth far longer than
their actual tenancy."

"And the damned dolphins were sent to keep an eye on us." Marcus was
obviously numb with the successive revelations, but that last piece slid home with
an almost audible sound.

K'hzan shrugged. "The Aijians volunteered to take that duty upon themselves in perpetuity when it became clear that the Humans had survived, and
would most likely continue to do so. The Aijians negotiated for a larger share of
power within the forming Council for their services."

Marcus and Justin shared a look, and Angara could almost feel sorry for
them both. At least she knew the true history of her wretched people.

Justin raised a hand, the other holding his head upright. "What about all
the other worlds the Humans had occupied?"

The red king frowned. "There must have been great anger in the final
days of the conflagration. Humans had nearly burned the galaxy down around us
all. The Council, in their *wisdom*, decreed that no single work of Man would survive the ending of the war. Planets were scoured, millennia worth of development
and production were plunged into uncaring suns. In the final, desperate days, Humanity had almost unlocked the secret to unleashing a new, devastating form of
weaponized energy that might well have turned the tide of the war. Fearing what

might have happened should another race continue their research, no vestige of their technology was allowed to survive." The crimson face fell once again into its habitual sneer. "I'm certain the Council would have never held back any of that technology for its own study, of course."

"There is no proof that the Humans even had such knowledge." Angara said abruptly. "You speak of myth as if fact, and legend as if it were written in stone, not smoke."

K'hzan smiled at her with an unnerving expression. Angara met him head on, not willing to allow him to editorialize further. Much to everyone's relief and surprise, the big alien shrugged again, settling back into his seat.

"My people know what they know, and believe what they believe. I am certain the Tigan have their own variations of these tales, princess?"

Justin's eyes widened at that, and she felt a nervous flutter in her stomach, but K'hzan was not finished with his diatribe.

"Still, it is true that much is speculation and guesswork at this late time." He looked back at the Humans, his eyes cold. "But rest assured, the weight of opprobrium you have felt from the first moment your feet left the mud of Earth behind finds its root in the tale I have told you here." He looked at Angara and the mystics, then back to Marcus. "What parts are true or fable matters little. Your people are hated and feared in equal measure for what they are perceived to have done."

"But all things change!" Khet Nhan muttered, his eyes still wild. "And the return of Humanity onto the galactic stage could well signal the end of a cycle of stagnation and torpor, and a dynamic reawakening in the galaxy!"

"Or it could herald the destruction of everything." Sihn Ve'Yan spat under her breath.

Marcus shook his head. "This doesn't make any sense." He seemed less convinced than his words might indicate; she had come to know his tones and facial expressions well since forcing him from his home, she realized. "I've spent months looking for anything like this story, and the data stacks throughout Penumbra don't say anything about any great war, or Humanity as the evil overlords of the galaxy, or the Variyar as the plucky down-and-out saviors." He looked as if he had bitten into something rotten. "If this is so well-known, why wasn't there so much of a hint anywhere I looked?"

That seemed to truly puzzle K'hzan, and she herself found it odd. She had never looked for any such information, of course. Every naive youth knew these stories. Every species had their versions, and in ever one, Humanity loomed large as the dark forces of evil and slavery. The rare splinter fleets of feral Humans, the descendants of those ancient fleets that had escaped the end of the great war, had always been taken as proof enough. But, because everyone believed it, she had had no reason to ever look into the Penumbran records for the information.

The horns gleamed dully as the red king shook his head. "I do not know the worth of your research, Marcus Wells. Nor do I know the depth of the information available in Penumbra in this regard. But I can assure you, as I said, these tales are the fuel that feeds the fires of hatred you have been fighting since you arrived."

"Enough." Marcus's seemed tired, his shoulders slumped. He turned back to K'hzan. "There's no denying that the story's interesting, and will bear future thought. But as far as our problems here and now, it doesn't matter at all. What

Justin said is true. We've heard you have a fleet, somewhere out here in the fringe. Is that true? One ship will hardly be sufficient, no matter who commands it, or what brilliant scheme we concoct."

K'hzan nodded, eyes narrow. "I have access to more ships. In aid of what?"

"This cannot be a battle between Variyar and Council!" Khet Nhan had jumped off his chair, his hands gripping the edge of the table. "History has already witnessed that folly." The little pink eyes glared at K'hzan. "You have already witnessed that folly." One small finger rose to point, dark nail gleaming, at Marcus. "This moment must rest on the shoulders of the Human."

Marcus stared at the little master in silence. His eyes blinked once, and then again, and then he smiled. He dipped his head as if to acknowledge the point, and then looked at each of them in turn.

"Our only real chance is if I can bring the city's systems to our side. And the only real chance we have of that is if I can get the Skorahn back." He shrugged, looking a little lost. "Whatever was happening with my bond to the Relic Core on our way out of Penumbra, we cannot gamble our lives, and the future of the city, on such a weak hope. Only with the medallion do we know, for a fact, that we will have the city's power working for us, not against us."

"And you can't get to the city with the fleet in the way." She wanted to nail down K'hzan's support as soon as possible. There was almost no way they were going to be able to make any of this work without somehow dealing with the Council fleet, and there was no way a single Tigan swift ship was going to be able to do that. She turned to the red king. "How many ships can you bring to our cause? Will they be enough?"

He smiled at her as if he could see into her mind. "I have reviewed the sensor data from your flight. The Council has sent an entire Peacemaker fleet to Penumbra; a formidable adversary." His smile tightened, and his sharp teeth glistened wetly behind thin lips. "I will not bring to bear power sufficient to meet them in open battle, but I believe I will be able to make such a show as to draw them off long enough for you to insert yourselves into the city." He leaned back, massive shoulders heaving beneath the cloak. "As for securing your Skorahn, of course, that will be up to you."

"Between the Ntja he smuggled into the city, and the marines from the Peacemaker fleet he has surely added to his force, there will be an army waiting for us as soon as we land." Sihn Ve'Yan's bitter face had hardened as the plan took shape. It was unheard of for Thien'ha to take a hand in events the way Khet Nhan was suggesting. It must have been eating at the girl since they had first taken steps to watch over Marcus Wells. Now that her master's support was so patently stated, it was most likely driving her mad. "And what good will taking the city do us if at the end of the battle, the Council fleet still commands the system?"

"We can help with those Ntja, anyway!" The little master slapped the table. "They'll know they're on the wrong side of history!"

The Diakk girl shook her head, her dark eyes gleaming, but said nothing more.

"Once the city's defenses are engaged, there is little the fleet will be able to do, even if my people retreat from the system. As for the Ntja, you will need more than an eager scholar and a couple of uppity Humans to defeat them."

K'hzan waved one hand. "I can provide a small strike force that will see you to where you need to be."

Marcus nodded his wary thanks for this unlooked-for largesse. Angara, however, had her doubts. Command of that strike force would be important. And although K'hzan seemed inclined to take their side in this venture, there would be nothing to stop him from seizing the city after they drove out the Council forces, if that was what he truly wished.

But without him, there was no hope at all. If Angara was going to salvage the mess she made of this situation, she needed to be willing to work with whatever tools fate saw fit to provide her. She could imagine what each of them saw on the other side of the blood and flame. Justin's world had been opened wide through his exposure to Galactic civilization. Marcus would be free to pursue his dreams for the city. For whatever reason, the Thien'ha would be happy to see a Human presence in the galaxy once more. But what was K'hzan hoping to benefit from such a horribly risky venture?

Her eyes tightened as she watched him smiling amiably at the rest of the table. His hatred for the Council was well known. He might very well be willing to throw his power behind this fight just for the chance to taste some of their blood in open combat. But he had bided his time for nearly an Earth century. What was changed now, that made him willing to expose his carefully-hoarded assets against Taurani and the Council's Peacemaker fleet?

Her eyes slid to where Marcus was sitting, high in his chair, looked relieved and rather proud of himself.

A coldness gripped her gut as she looked at him. Humans; that's what had changed.

She wished she knew why that made such a difference to the red king, who was said to hate Humans more than anyone. Why had the presence of a Human, here and now, goaded him into this long-awaited action?

A cold certainty gripped her. Somehow, the answer to that question was going to matter a great deal more, in the long run, than most of the other questions they had wrestled with that day.

*****

Iphini Bha stared at the medallion in her hands, sitting dull and empty against her white skin. She had spent days with the jewel, searching its sapphire depths in every kind of lighting she could find. The symbol still floated there, just out of her ability to comprehend, but other than that, the rock was lifeless and dead. Since Marcus Wells had run away, the Skorahn had been no more responsive for Khuboda Taurani than it had for Uduta Virri or any of the other administrators who had sat the command throne in living memory.

Security systems had come back under the control of the administrator's office, rather than the seemingly semi-autonomous responses they had begun to exhibit when Marcus had been present. Taurani's Ntja were in full control of the suppression fields, doors, defensive cannons, and other systems. At least, she thought they were Taurani's. The black-clad soldiers that had arrived with the Council fleet were all Ntja as well. They wore uniforms of a more severe cut, and the bulbous metal domes sunk into their heads to shield their crude implants were polished to a high sheen. But they were still the same brutish monsters that had been tearing the city apart since the incident began.

She sighed, sinking back against the hard back of the chair in the administrator's office. Taurani had all-but abandoned the control center since his coup. He was out in the city, directing the efforts of the soldiers in seizing the assets of those he deemed dangerous, and incarcerating the most troublesome in a series of storage halls buried beside the reservoir far below.

She had been following his progress, and had noticed an alarming trend in those enterprises he felt were dangerous: each of them had been researching or manufacturing the most advanced, potentially aggressive technologies, far more innovative than anything in Council space. It had aroused her suspicion enough that she had looked further back, to the earliest days of his takeover. Those first two syndicates his thugs had raided had not been random either, and she wondered what he might want with time dilation technology or the advanced energy field projectors of the Numanu architects.

But she had far more personal worries, and had no time for more esoteric concerns. His threats had been getting progressively more graphic, as it became more and more obvious she would be unable to unlock the mysteries of the Skorahn. He had worn it for the first day or so, but he soon lost interest in the 'bauble', as he called it, when he realized that it was not conveying upon him any more power than it had given to the detested Virri. He had thrown it at her, demanded she unravel its powers, and turned his attention to other matters.

She could feel the psychoactive art looming all around her. She knew, without looking, what she would see. The canvases were nearly empty, dark and bleak landscapes with sad figures wandering along them, lost and alone.

The city had been a hell since Taurani had taken over. All of the worst fears of Angara and Marcus Wells had been realized. The black-armored shock troopers were everywhere, controlling movement through the city, issuing credentials to those willing to play their games, keeping others under tight confinement in their specific towers.

There had been no more serious fighting. That was something she could be thankful for, at least. When the fleet had first arrived, Taurani and the Ntja admiral had used it as a tool of terror, going so far as to flatten one of the smaller towers on the underside of the city. Hundreds of sentients had been killed in what Taurani was claiming was a preemptive attack on a dissident cell.

Iphini knew that the tower in question had housed only older residents of the city, many of them requiring the charitable assistance of their neighbors to even survive.

But since that attack, resistance had been all but extinguished. Taurani and the Peacemaker soldiers had been at liberty do whatever they liked. The oppressive pall that had fallen across Penumbra was a stark, painful contrast to the city's former, chaotic energy. It was an occupied camp now, no better than any other recalcitrant system subjugated by the Galactic Council.

And they never would have been able to succeed if it had not been for her.

She felt her eyes fill once again. It seemed to her that she spent most of every day weeping, now that her actions had born their inevitable fruit.

Penumbra under the vague and inattentive eye of Uduta Virri had been a violent, unruly place, but its soul had been intact. She had come to the city herself as a last resort, running from a past she could never have escaped elsewhere. Iwa'Ban had been nearly destroyed by feral Human raiders but it had been the depredations of the Council minions who had descended upon her homeworld to *help them recover* that had been the real horror. She had seen, first hand, Peacemaker officers savaging her people without repercussion. When a council- or that had been granted administrative rights over her family's province took an unwholesome fancy to her, her own parents had urged her to flee.

But everywhere she went within Council space, she was reminded of those last dark days and her flight from her ravaged home. She had tried to convince herself that what she had seen had been anomalies, that the servants of the Galactic Council were, on the whole, the heroes she had always believed them to be. But with each revealed abuse, she had been forced to lower her head further, to shut her eyes to the reality developing all around her. She had been at her wit's end by the time she had been advised to seek out Penumbra. It had been her refuge and her sanctuary, but she had never lost the feeling of the unwilling exile, and had grounded that resentment and sadness into the city that had nurtured her since her arrival.

In her heart she had never reconciled her endemic hatred of the Humans who had ravaged Iwa'Ban and the Council enforcers who had made it their own personal preserve. When Angara had brought her two Humans back to the city, she had been horrified, as had every other right-thinking being in Penumbra. When the thoughtful Eru had approached her with his soulful red eyes and his attentive demeanor, she had eventually revealed all of her doubts and fears to him. He had been the kindly hero she wanted to see, despite his instructions to keep their friendship secret. He had been patient, she could see that now. He had slowly steered their conversations away from the Council and deeper into her fear of the Humans. She had been blinded to everything that Marcus Wells was attempting to achieve, as well as the horrors inflicted upon Iwa'Ban by Taurani's ilk, and instead saw only the shattered ruins of her homeworld, overlaid with the destruction of this new home that had accepted her.

She had been a fool. Each time she tried to sleep now, she was haunted by thoughts of Marcus Wells, and the dark and empty corridors of Penumbra in its present state. The realization that she had helped to destroy this place that had been her home was crushing her.

She closed her eyes to access the time through her implants. Khuboda Taurani was scheduled to address the entire city soon from the Council Chamber where Marcus Wells had spoken so often of his hopes and dreams. The old Mhatrong arena would be filled with the most prominent survivors of Penumbra, forced at gunpoint to provide a suitable backdrop for what was sure to be a historic moment.

He had not bothered to tell her any of his plans, of course. There was little reason to do so. She knew, in fact, that she was only still alive on the off chance that she could puzzle out some last little glimmer of power from the medallion. She also served as its bearer while Taurani strengthened his hold on the city, so that the services and systems would not fail.

She had not been told what the speech would reveal, but any rational being could guess what Taurani was going to say. A great deal of effort had gone into filling the chamber with all the right beings.

The Council Ambassador was going to announce the final disposition of the city. He was going to reveal to them their ultimate fate; a fate she had helped to orchestrate. A fate she had no hope now of averting.

There were whispered rumors that the Humans would return. The irony was palpable: that the once-hated and reviled creatures were now seen as the only possible saviors of the city. But she did not believe them. How would Marcus Wells return? That he had escaped in the first place was a miracle. Even though she had been blinded by her own prejudice, she knew too well; he was too smart to return to such a hopeless situation. Even if he did return, what could he possibly do against such overwhelming force?

Her head fell forward. Marcus Wells was a Human, and in her heart, more suited to be a destroyer than a savior.

And that was the true tragedy of her position: even her best hope was empty.

*****

Khuboda Taurani stood at the podium in the vast Mhatrong hall and gazed out over the fruits of his labor. The most prominent citizens of Penumbra were crammed cheek to jowl in the big room; well, at least the most prominent citizens that could be trusted to remain cowed and submissive. He had dreamed of this moment since long before being stationed in the wild, unruly city. The Council's instructions had been fulfilled in the first moments of his attack. The technology he had been sent for was secure, its creators dead or captive, and all transferred to Ochiag's ships overhead. Now he was working for himself and his people.

The hall was silent as all the sentients stared. Some eyes were curious and alive. Those would be the inhabitants not invested overmuch in the city, without a great deal to lose. Many more, however, were sullen and hostile. Those would be the beings who had left everything in Council space behind, to come here and begin anew. Those pathetic vermin would lose everything today.

Because today the last sanctuary against the power and wisdom of the Galactic Council would fall. He had consolidated his control over Penumbra, and with Ochiag's help, those most likely to make things difficult were no longer able to do so. Now, with the power of the Peacemaker fleet behind his words, he would confirm his place in the historical files of the Council and take the first step toward establishing the Kerie as the preeminent race in the galaxy. First among equals, leaders of the great and enlightened push into the future, his people would be the lords of known space one day soon. And it will have all started here.

It was almost enough to bring a smile to the rigid flesh of his face.

He drank in the despair in those eyes for a moment longer, savoring the heady taste of victory and subjugation. These fools had believed themselves beyond the power of the Council, and above the wisdom of the greatest minds of the galaxy working in concert for the greater good. They had put themselves, their ambitions, and their goals ahead of all the other sentients in existence. Today they, too, would reap the rewards of their choices.

"Citizens of Penumbra," Taurani's voice was strong and full. It was being broadcast to every corner of the city, so that even the most cowardly worm skulking in the lowest service tunnels would not miss the message. "I come here to speak to you today light of heart, looking out at a future for this city, and for the galaxy as a whole, that is far brighter and richer than any of us might have imagined even a short while ago."

There was nothing but silence in the room. Out of sight of the visual recorders, hugging the far walls and staying to the deep shadows, Ochiag's Ntja troopers watched the crowd with leveled weapons. The audience had been warned to remain silent. There would be plenty of time to add the joyous sounds of celebration and adulation after the fact, should such things be called for in the future.

"Under the guidance and protection of the Galactic Council, Penumbra is going to know an unprecedented period of growth, prosperity, and safety! No dream will be too big to dream here out on the rim, and the Council will help you all to make those dreams a magnificent reality."

They were silent still, of course. But he could see the confusion in many of the eyes now. He could see tenuous hope glowing to life where before there had only been despair. He could feel his lip twitch with the effort not to indulge in a sneer.

"Now, under a partnership agreement between the free city of Penumbra and the Galactic Council, those ancient treaties that so rigidly controlled our relationships to date will be replaced! We shall forge the bonds between us anew, here and now! And to assist you all in keeping the peace, and making sure you are not victimized by any of the myriad dangers of the galaxy, I hereby announce that the free city of Penumbra will henceforth be known as a Protectorate of the Council!"

Despite instructions, a low, soft, murmur arose from the crowd. He allowed it, reveling in their sudden realization. He had noticed that their interest had been truly kindled when he had used the term 'free city'. He knew the light of amusement was bright in his silvery eyes, and he knew that no one in the chamber would be able to decipher it.

Let them keep their foolish name, he thought. 'Free city' ... he wanted to laugh. And of course, as a Protectorate, the Council would have complete control over all policies and statutes within Penumbra. The very lawlessness that had attracted these vagabonds to the back of beyond would be gone, and with it, the incentive to come so far from the center of civilization. He had just killed their city, and the fools were too ignorant, or too numb, to realize it. The energy and innovation Penumbra had sapped from Council space would return to where it could be more carefully husbanded and controlled.

As he indulged in his moment of glory, the lighting within the hall dropped slightly, taking on a reddish tinge. It was the most dramatic signal he had been willing to allow his watchdogs to use during his grand announcement. It means something had gone truly, horribly wrong.

"My friends, duty calls me away." He shrugged, putting the mask of reluctant public servant on with practiced ease. "I had really hoped to share more of my vision of Penumbra's future with you today. Perhaps I may impose upon you all in the days ahead. For now, thank you for your attention, and may we all look to a brighter future, walking the path of civilization together."

With a nod he had Iranse cut recording feeds, and then directed Ochiag's ground commanders to see the chamber emptied, the citizens returned to their proper places. He turned, clicking shut his eyes to access the communication network through his implants, and demanded information from whoever was on the other side of the connection.

"Please explain the terrible crisis that necessitated the interruption of my announcement." He snarled as he pushed his way through the hidden door into the preparation room. Never had a position been better defended than Penumbra was now. And besides, other than the single Tigan swift ship the Humans had used to escape, their enemies had no access to more potent forces. The question was not so much *who* would possibly be attacking the city, but *why* would anyone *attack* it, under the current circumstances.

"It's the Peacemaker fleet!" When Iphini Bha's shrill voice erupted in his ear, he almost snorted with derision. The Iwa'Bantu were always timid creatures. If she had sounded the alarm, it could be almost anything. Perhaps she had outlived her usefulness. There had been no movement with the medallion, and he found it more and more difficult to control his hunger around the little creature. Perhaps this lapse in judgement would be the catalyst he needed to take a more direct hand in her instruction. He would have to find someone else to wear the worthless gem until the city was dismantled, of course, but that would hardly be troublesome.

"Someone is attacking the fleet!" Bha continued, and this time, Taurani was brought up short.

"Attacking?" He was incredulous, and spat the word out as if it tasted bad. "Who?"

"I don't know! They just emerged from a single wormhole! A whole fleet from a single singularity! It's a slaughter!"

Taurani felt the bristles of his brill grind together as his jaws clenched. Orchestrating a simultaneous singularity transit was incredibly difficult and dangerous. Outside of the surprise impact delivering an entire fleet in tight formation might have in war, there was no good reason for anyone to even attempt such a feat.

In fact, as far as he knew, in all of known galactic history, only one race had perfected the tactic.

His eyes widened, and he shoved two brown-uniformed Ntja ahead of him to clear a path through the milling crowd. The denizens of Penumbra were muttering quietly about his announcement, but fell silent as they felt the pressure of his bodyguards pushing down the corridor. He followed at a trot, not caring in the least what the peasants of this pathetic backwater might be saying now.

# Chapter 24

Iphini Bha could only stare at the viewing field floating over the communications station in awe. The city could be seen in all of its chaotic glory in the lower quadrant of the image, with the Peacemaker fleet floating in a globe around it. The three massive warships that formed the core of the fleet were each stationed within the defensive sphere, one third of a turn from each other, halfway between the plane of the city and the upper pole of the formation.

A massive singularity had ripped into being right in the teeth of one of the biggest ships. A fleet of sleek, aggressive-looking attackers had stormed out, and the battle had erupted before either the Ntja commanders or Iphini had known what was happening.

At the core of the attacking fleet was a ship almost as big as the biggest Council vessels. There was something eerily familiar about the lines of the vessel, but her agitated mind could not tell her why, and abandoned the thought in favor of the more immediate concern of a full-blown war erupting over her head.

The defenses of the city began to spit coherent light into the teeth of the attackers, but the ships had fell out of their huge wormhole so fast, the city's systems were having a hard time tracking its targets. The guns seemed to be moving sluggishly, but she was no expert, and assumed it was merely the speed of the attackers causing the difficulties.

The entire attacking fleet concentrated their fire on the nearest of the large Ntja warships. Bolts of green and blue and red flashed out from every ship, streaking vapor trails traced the arcing flights of missile weapons as they sliced through the empty void at incredible speeds, slamming through defensive fire and gravitic shields alike.

She understood almost nothing of what she was seeing. She had never witnessed a battle in her life. Aside from the occasional feral Human fleets hunted down by Council Peacemakers, it had been an age since a battle such as this had occurred. Still, it was clear that the attackers were concentrating all of their weapons on that one beleaguered ship, and that their chosen prey's defenses were weakening under the onslaught.

Blue flares outlined the hard planes of the ship's gravitic shields, pounded down, closer and closer to their parent with each impact. Bolts of searing energy snapped into the shields and were deflected off and away by the amplified, near-solid gravity. The Peacemaker fleet was so densely packed into their globular formation that many of these redirected blasts struck other ships, glancing again off their own shields. One smaller ship, weaker or more unlucky than those around it, caught one of these powerful streams of light and its shield failed in a coronal flash. The ship imploded around the sinking bolt, and then wreckage blasted outward in a flash of orange fire that rapidly dwindled to a wisp of glittering fog.

Around her, the black-uniformed Ntja that had been left to watch over the control center were barking orders at each other, snarling into communication stations in an effort to redirect the fleet units deployed opposite the vector of the attack. Her eyes were fixed upon the viewing field, however, watching the concentrated effort of the attack as it pummeled the larger ship mercilessly. Her grip was pale and tight around her ancient stylus, its constant motion stilled.

It was painfully obvious when the first gravitic shield went down. The flaring blue light went lightning-bright, outlining the shield, and then it shattered like an enormous plate of glass. An entire swarm of missiles, sensing the opening, altered course and flashed through the hole, each slamming into the unprotected hull beneath in terrible, rapid succession. Gouts of burning wreckage spewed out into space and the ship began to fall out of formation trailing a stream of sparkling white condensate.

With the failure of the first shield, the entire system had clearly become compromised, and a cascade of shimmering blue plates flashed and shattered, scattering sparks back against the squat hull. Bolts of energy flew through the widening gap, accompanying another shoal of missiles, and suddenly where a massive, proud warship had struggled for existence, nothing but a brief, fiery star and an expanding field of debris remained.

A collective moan rose up around her as the ship died. She searched her heart for her own reaction. Was she sad to see the Council ship brought low? Glad? All she could feel was the cold despair of the helpless observer, as terrible violence crashed around her.

The wreckage spun off in all directions, wreaking havoc with the Peacemaker fleet formation. Much of it was caught in the weak gravity field of Penumbra itself, and tumbling chunks of warship fell among the towers, sowing their own crop of destruction and misery. One section, it looked like it had been the bow from what she could remember of the ship's configuration, fell, spinning, into the city and, accompanying the small, sterile visual on the display, the decking beneath her lurched. She reached out for support and ended up holding onto the rough-furred arm of an Ntja soldier. He looked at her, his thick lips pulled back in a sneer, and shook her off.

She turned back to the display just in time to watch the attacking fleet alter its flight pattern, engines tilting downward and pushing the ships in a smooth, choreographed maneuver that sent them skimming along the top of the Peacemaker formation. The two remaining Council battleships began to come about, but the bulk of the fleet hung between them and the fleeing attackers. More and more of the smaller Council ships fell out of formation to give chase, and soon the attackers were streaking down toward the distant planet, a tail of Peacemaker ships in their wake.

A constant cascade of colored bolts and streaking missiles continued to pour out of the attackers' weapons, goading the Ntja into a thoughtless, headlong pursuit. The battle was not entirely one-sided, however, as the Ntja ships finally began to return fire, and space between the two formations was bright with streaks of death and destruction, with countless small suns erupting and dying within the clouds of the two fleets as smaller ships succumbed to the onslaught.

As she watched, the defensive fleet was stripped away as if by a strong wind. The skies above Penumbra were clear, her eyes widened as she saw something none of the commanders around her had yet noticed.

Another singularity had opened up, almost exactly where the first had been. A much smaller fleet of ships fell through as she watched. These were squat, ugly ships, not nearly as large as the warships in the first wave. And leading the charge was a ship she recognized. Its sleek lines, the swept-back configuration of its wings, and its outthrust command module were familiar to any citizen of Penumbra.

Her lips quirked into a tentative smile.

Angara Ksaka had returned.

*****

Angara was prone in the command chair, hands tight within the interface fields and mind lost to the symbiotic relay of information and power she shared with the *Yud'ahm Na'uka*. The sensitive instruments of her ship told her that K'hzan's plan had worked. The Council fleet, embarrassed and enraged by the sudden attack and the loss of one of its most prominent components, had followed the Variyar attack force as it inserted itself into a high orbit around the planet below.

The defenders would be gone for a while. Even if they realized what was happening, they were now committed to their current course. They would have to follow their orbital path around the planet and come at the city from the reciprocal angle. By then, if everything worked according to the next phase of their plan, it would be too late.

Behind her, strapped into reaction chairs, Justin watched over her shoulders with wide eyes, along with four of K'hzan's honor guard, uncomfortably cramped within the confines of a ship made for much smaller creatures.

Marcus and the two Thien'ha were with one of the Variyar transports sticking closely to her flank. K'hzan had made it a condition of his involvement that Marcus make the approach in one of the more heavily armed and armored troop transports. She had fought him, but when he had also pointed out that Justin and Marcus needed to be split, in case another Earth Human was capable of engaging the Skorahn if Marcus was lost, she gave in. She would not consider that too closely, but she had noticed the look Justin had given her when K'hzan had mentioned the Children back at the pirate station, and for some reason, that moment had stuck with her through all the planning, exhaustive waiting, and gut-wrenching action since then. In the end, she was carrying Justin, and the thick-bodied transport hugging her glittering back trail held Marcus Wells and the mystics.

Far overhead, the Variyar fleet was leading the defenders off on a merry chase. The massive warship that had been destroyed was an unlooked for bonus, although the collateral damage its destruction caused was going to make things more difficult for whoever won the battle, when it came time to recover and rebuild Penumbra.

Angara made for the wide entranceway to the main docking bay beneath the Red Tower. The plan called for them to drive straight in, make a landing in force, and push their way up through the Tower to the control center with the power of the Variyar warriors as the tip of their spear. They expected Taurani to be directing the defenses from there, with the medallion around his neck. If Marcus could get his hands on the Skorahn, the whole battle would, theoretically, be over.

As she swept around the shoulder of one squat tower, however, she saw things were not going to be quite that simple. Boxy defensive turrets that had remained dormant for longer than the oldest denizen of the city could remember were swiveling back and forth, searching for targets. A black mob of soldiers, many shouldering heavy weapon systems, were massed just behind the bay's containment field. The field kept the vacuum out and the atmosphere in, but would do nothing to stop those weapons from ravaging what she had come to think of as her own little fleet.

Behind the mob of Ntja soldiers were even bigger shapes, looming in the background, indistinct behind the fog of the field. Seeing them made her blood run cold: Ntja heavy infantry. Just one would be more than a match for several Variyar, even at their peak. And she thought she saw an entire unit readying to repel them as they attempted to land.

Splashes of color began to streak up past them as the more overeager troopers below unleashed their attacks. One lucky blast caught the Na'uka on the nose, and the cabin lights dimmed with the power transfer to her gravitic shielding. The turrets were slower to engage, zeroing in on chosen targets based upon ancient formulae of threat assessment and battlefield conditions.

"Primary landing zone is closed." She thought of her squadron channel and murmured her assessment. Her implants would enhance the signal and see that the correct commanders received her message. "Shifting course for alternate entrance point."

The control surfaces of her swift ship slid around the fuselage and pushed the ship away from the docking bay. Skimming the surface of a tower, she swept around the glittering hull. Behind her, the heavy Variyar transports followed, although several of them, emotionally charged with their first taste of real battle, launched spiteful attacks on the troops lined up against them as they flew past.

Darts of energy and streaking flashes of heat snapped through the containment field with scintillating ripples of silver, falling among the Ntja soldiers, blasting holes in their ranks and sowing chaos throughout the bay. Even the towering heavy infantry ran for cover from the ship-borne ordnance falling among them.

The turrets opened fire as soon as the transports attacked, and three of the large ships were shattered in a matter of moments, wreckage flung back away from the city, spiraling off into space. A quick flicker of a closed eye ensured her that Marcus's ship was not among the lost.

"They waited until the ships actually fired!" Marcus's voice was loud over the link. "They were engaging much faster when we tested them."

She had had the same thought. The city was supposed to engage hostiles immediately when in active defensive mode. Something was causing the system to slow down.

Maybe they had more than a forlorn hope after all.

"We are heading for the executive landing bay." She checked her status, her ship remained unharmed. The one lucky blast had not overloaded her systems or caused other ancillary damage. "They will be ready for us. It will be more heavily defended and we will not be able to land as many shuttles, but if the city's systems are hesitating, we might be able to get in."

Acknowledgments came in from the surviving assault ships. To avoid the highest concentrations of defensive turrets, most of which were oriented against attacks from above rather than enemies that had already penetrated the city itself, she decided to get closer to the Red Tower before they were required to confront the full force of Penumbra's defenses.

Before she had even finished the thought, solid beams of light flashed down from above, spearing through her formation. With a muttered curse she jerked the *Na'uka* into a tight spiral. Nevertheless, one of the bolts fell on her ship. It exploded against her shields in multicolored sparks. Several of the transports had been hit as well.

Most of the gravitic fields held, but one ship, at the tail of their formation, was struck a glancing blow to its flank and began to stagger out of the line. Its commander reported that they were losing flight integrity, but were going to attempt to land on the surface of the Concourse and make some trouble for the Council forces from there.

She acknowledged the report, wished the warriors luck, and turned her mind back to the matter at hand. The defensive turrets around the Red Tower obviously had greater flexibility than they had anticipated. Nearly every one of her ships had taken fire now. In fact, her eyes narrowed as she flicked through information scrolling by her peripheral vision; only one ship had made it through the gauntlet unscathed.

"It's going to get worse as we approach the bay." Marcus shouted again. The adrenaline had gotten the better of him, clearly. "And there's too many of us to all fit."

"Not if we keep losing ships at this rate!" Justin's voice was harsh with emotion, but she took a strange sense of comfort from the fact that the sound of his voice was in her ears rather than through her implants. "We're not all lucky enough to have a Tigan princess for a pilot, you know!"

She gritted her teeth. Not only were the Variyar on the channel not likely to appreciate the joke, but she hated it when anyone called her that. Trust Justin to pick up on K'hzan's little barb. Still, she had more to occupy her mind than petty bickering, and bent to it.

She had never been fully comfortable with their back-up plan. Although there were auxiliary bays scattered up and down the Tower, each could only handle a single oversized transport. The administrator's executive bay would be able to hold three at least, four if the follow-on pilots were any good. But even four ships would not carry enough warriors to blast their way into the control center alone.

This, admittedly less-well-thought-out contingency plan, called for them to swarm the Tower and gather at one of the lift tube foyers before pushing on. It would be even more dangerous given the versatility of the defenses and the warning Taurani's forces now had.

"We don't have a choice." She spoke in her calm battle voice, trusting to her implants to convey the proper tone. "It's the best way to reach him, Marcus."

There was a pause, and for a moment she was afraid an errant shot might have brought Marcus's transport down behind her. A quick check showed that it was still soaring, its flanks unmarred by damage or shield overload. She shook her head, hoping no one up above them was noticing.

"Understood." Marcus's tone was softer. She wondered if someone might have told him to temper his volume. "Let's send in a transport first, then us, then you, then another transport, if it fits?"

The *Yud'ahm Na'uka*'s sensors had already determined that there would be room enough, depending on the skill of the pilots. But one thing bothered her about that plan. "I will follow the lead transport in. That will give the warriors more time to secure the bay, and assure us of a tighter landing pattern."

Another pause brought her teeth grinding together. Was she going to have to force his hand every step of the way? When he finally responded, it was with a grudging tone. "Fine. Just get down quickly so we can all get back together. I'm not enjoying this separation."

She smiled, and knew that Justin was smiling behind her. "I agree, Marcus Wells. We will see you in the bay."

A curt order brought the Variyar formation more tightly into her wake, and they swept up and around, effectively reversing their approach vector. More shots rained down on them from above, as well as occasional blasts from smaller access ports scattered around the surrounding towers. None of the automatic fire hit Marcus's transport.

She gritted her teeth as she prepared to come flaring up before the executive docking bay, ready to plunge her treasured ship into the heart of the Red Tower.

As she flew, she took a moment to wonder if Marcus had realized his charmed status.

*****

"Iphini Bha, where are they!" The roar was attenuated through the communications system, and it was clear that Ambassador Taurani was out of breath, rushing to the control center from the Mhatrong meeting chamber.

"I swear, girl, if you do not respond—"She could sense his burning anger through the signal even without visual confirmation.

"Assault ships have been turned back from an attack on the main docking bay. They have suffered severe casualties moving through the city, following an erratic pattern." She kept her voice steady despite the growing fear and tension building in her chest. The stylus was once again spinning smoothly around her fingers as if it moved of its own accord.

She had every piece of information concerning the attackers scattered in front of her, but her stomach burned at any thought of giving further assistance to the beast. The medallion hung around her neck, dragging her head down with its useless weight.

If she could only manage to die in this counterattack, she would be done with the whole mess, and no more decisions would be required of her.

"Where are they *now*!" the Kerie barked, and even the Ntja commanders recoiled from the console. They exchanged looks over Iphini's head, and then glanced down at her, waiting for her to respond.

She blinked, shaking her head. "It looks like they are coming back around to try to assault the Tower. Here. This tower. The Red Tower." Her voice stuttered to a halt.

"Are the city's defenses fighting them? Have you dispatched combat teams to the executive landing bay? *Damnit*, Bha, I can't conduct the defense of the city while I sprint down corridors!"

She nodded, although he could not see her. "The automatic defenses have engaged the attackers." She tilted her head to access the relevant information. "They have lost five transports, with two others forced into emergency landings." The stylus continued to spin.

One of the Ntja cleared its throat with a low, rumbling growl and tapped a small portable pad with one gnarled claw. The display was flashing with an urgent message she had been doing her best to ignore.

"The systems are reporting more sluggish response times than we had anticipated." She straightened her back and spoke with as clear a voice as she could muster.

The claw tapped on the display by her elbow again, this time with enough force to nick the screen.

Iphini Bha closed her eyes with a sad, pain-filled sigh. She spoke without opening them. "Analysis of the systems indicates they are avoiding engagement of a single, particular transport."

She could hear Taurani's heavy breathing through the link. When that breathing suddenly stopped, her eyes popped open. Somewhere beneath her, the Council Ambassador had stopped his headlong dash for the control center.

"The system itself is avoiding one of the shuttles?" The words were flat and emotionless.

She could feel the hulking soldiers looming over her to either side. She had no choice. "Yes, sir."

"The Human." Taurani filled the words with venom. The breathing resumed, even harsher if possible than before. "Dispatch support weapon teams to the area! Identify this lucky transport and destroy it at all costs!"

She stared down at the console. She knew this would happen if she gave him that information. She had avoided doing that for as long as possible, trying to give the attackers as much lead time as she could. Even now, she could not bring herself to relay the order to the commanders standing over her.

"Sir, most of your forces are deployed around the bay. Redeploying them now will weaken the defenses—"

"None of that will matter if that damned Human filth is allowed to tread on the decks of this city again! Send the teams!"

Her shoulders lifted slightly, her head tilting. "What weapons were you thinking, sir? I assume—"

"Commander Bochia, are you there?" A chill went up her spine as he addressed one of the Ntja commanders, ignoring her at last.

The Ntja stiffened. "Yes, Ambassador."

The commander had the black uniform of a fleet officer. His manner was not as obsequious as the brown-suited diplomatic guards. Likewise, unfortunately, there was nothing in his tone that gave her hope he would not follow orders, either.

"You have heard the order I just gave Deputy Bha?" Taurani bit the words out, their edges sharp.

"Yes, Ambassador."

"See that it is carried out immediately."

"Yes, Ambassador." The hulking creature turned away to follow the instructions, but was drawn back as Taurani's voice barked out again.

"See to it personally, Commander. Everything we do here is in jeopardy if that craft is allowed to land."

"Yes, Ambassador." Bochia stumped off without a backward glance, gesturing into the shadows with one arm as he made for the door. Several soldiers who had been standing there moved off with him.

Iphini Bha stared down at the console again, hoping the time she had purchased for Marcus Wells would be enough. The knowledge that she was helping a Human twisted in her gut, but it helped when she thought of him by name. There were brief moments when she wished she could do more.

"Bha, we *will* discuss this, when circumstances allow."

The voice was soft. She had thought Taurani had cut the connection after sending off his killers. The threat stopped her heart.

"Bha?"

She swallowed, and then forced the words through tight lips. "Yes, sir." The stylus was still, hanging limply from her hand.

"I know what just happened, girl. I am sending Iranse to relieve you. You will give him the Skorahn, and await my arrival. When I reach you, we will have words, you and I."

With a sharp hiss, he ended the connection.

She touched the medallion at her throat again. Surrounded by enemies, distrusted by the very creatures for which she had betrayed her home and friends, there was nowhere for her to turn, nothing more she could do. At least he was sending Iranse. There was a slight comfort in that, at least, even now that she knew she had been manipulated all through their clandestine friendship.

But the old, whispered stories of Khuboda Taurani's excesses on Iwa'Ban began to claw their way out from the shadows of her mind. Her grip on the stylus tightened.

Behind closed lids her eyes fluttered. It was almost as if she could sense his approach, through miles of steel and vacuum; inexorable as death.

*****

Marcus squeezed his eyes shut as the heavy transport completed its latest turn, angling upward toward the executive docking bay near the top of the Red Tower. Memories of his time as administrator clung to the edges of his consciousness as he tried to focus on not losing control of his stomach. He had taken interstellar travel quite for granted since his abduction, with his only experience being aboard Angara Ksaka's personal ship. The combat transport lacked so many of the amenities of the *Yud'ahm Na'uka*, but of them all, he missed whatever the little ship used to compensate for inertia the most.

He felt like a child sitting at the adult table, strapped into a hard metal chair designed for the hulking body of a Variyar warrior. In the troop bay behind him, thirty such warriors stood easily, only resorting to the overhead grid of grips and bars for the most violent or sudden maneuvers. A row of seats had been bolted down to the rear of the command deck to give Marcus and his two escorting mystics a good view of flight operations and out the vision screens in the nose of the ship.

Through those screens he had seen two other Variyar transports shattered by defensive fire, and several bolts strike the dancing shape of Angara's ship, leading them in their weaving path through the city. The beautiful screens that seemed to flash into existence to save the ships from fire, usually, had so far kept the swift ship from harm, but his heart was in his throat each time he saw another attack slash in.

"Approaching the Red Tower." The Variyar pilot, a fierce female warrior named As'vhikudu, growled. Although, to be fair, anything they said sounded like growling. He had not realized how much effort K'hzan must have put into articulating his speech around those enormous fangs. Either that, or for some reason his nanite implants were having a harder time translating these lower-caste warriors.

The familiar, angular tower emerged from around a tall, bulbous structure that must have once been a tanker of some kind. The Tower was bright with defensive fire, tracing an interlocking pattern of hard light all around its crest. He remembered his tour of the Tower's defenses, Justin and the mystics in tow. He had worked the guns, put them through their paces. There was something wrong with the way they were performing against him today. They were scoring hits, of course, they had lost too many ships to deny that. But he thought they should have been dealing out more damage. He was fine with the fact that they were not, he just wished he knew why.

It had occurred to him, not long after they first diverted from the main bay, that his own ship was leading a charmed life. All around him, the small fleet was being pummeled. But not even an incidental, glancing blow had landed against his transport. He was afraid to attribute any significance to that, knowing that the minute he took something like that for granted, he was going to get dashed from the city's sky. He knew, even from his narrow experience, that As'vhikudu was a good pilot; maybe even almost as good as Angara. But she was not good enough to account for their continued immunity.

"Lead element is heading in." As'vhikudu ground out.

Marcus hunched forward in the massive chair, pushing at the uncomfortably wide restraining belt. He watched as Angara's *Yud'ahm Na'uka* dropped back, allowing one of the thick-bodied transports to lurch ahead and then drive in for the long, narrow slit of the executive docking bay.

He didn't know if it was just bad luck or if attempting to land in the Tower had triggered more aggressive subroutines in the defensive systems, but a sleet of devastating bolts flashed down from every direction, shattering the ship's shields, pummeling it into scrap and dashing it against the side of the Tower where it burst into a brief, brilliant flare and then darkened; charred wreckage spinning down into the darkness.

"Shit!" Marcus screeched, recoiling from the sudden deaths of over thirty warriors. But before he could say more, another transport heeled over and plunged through the drifting mist of its sister's death, smashing through the containment field of the dock and filling the darkness within with strobing blasts of energy.

A seething mass of dog soldiers filled the docking bay, and a solid wall of light rose up from them to stagger the attacking ship. But it landed, roughly, with a dazzling pulse of blue-white lightning that flattened the nearest warriors and blinded the rest. The Variyar warriors, even more intimidating than usual in their hulking vacuum armor, rushed from the forward deployment ramp and swept into the Council forces.

Even while he watched the first big Ntja soldiers go down beneath a hail of Variyar rifle blasts, the *Na'uka* flashed through his field of vision, the panels and plates of its floating components sliding all over the fuselage in a dizzying ballet. Another searing wave of blasts struck Angara's ship, but its shields were far more effective, apparently, and it sailed through the opening with its shields fully visible, trailing blue sparks.

Another burst of illumination heralded the lightning orb weapons on the ship's wings, as fans of electricity stabbed out at another contingent of Ntja.

"Go! Go in now!" He was straining at the belt, pushing forward while he shouted at As'vhikudu. "What are you waiting for?"

"The firing pattern from those towers is regular." The pilot pointed one gauntleted hand to indicate the surrounding structures. "We should be clear in—"

"We're clear now! They're not shooting at me! Go in *now*!" He wanted to growl, but he realized it would only sound pathetic to these creatures. He hadn't wanted to say it out loud, but he could see tiny figures struggling along the floor of the docking bay, and as he watched, one fell through the twinkling containment field and plummeted down to the surface of the Concourse far below. He wasn't going to fly around out here while his friends fought and died trying to get him inside.

Suddenly, the flaring light show within the slit died as if someone had hit a switch. There was a moment's pause in the chaotic movement, and then the forces rushed toward each other.

"Suppression field." The pilot's assistant muttered to the Variyar commander. "Close work, now."

Marcus was not sure, but he could almost convince himself that he saw the quick, tiny flashes of an Earth handgun popping off in the melee. He wondered how Justin had found more ammunition.

"We need to get in *now*!" He howled, seeing Sihn Ve'Yan's lip curl from the corner of his eye and not caring. On the other side it looked like Nhan was almost as eager to come to grips with the enemy as he was. He swallowed, realizing that both of the Thien'ha were far more *capable*, at least.

As'vhikudu grunted something that might have been assent and throttled forward, sliding them toward the battle.

A streak of light flashed in from his right and grazed the forward viewing screens. The pilot jerked back from the contact and the ship lurched. Marcus was suddenly reminded of how much he disliked traveling in the big flying box.

Then he realized: they had just been shot at. What about his immunity? What about his connection with the city? Suddenly, he felt more vulnerable than he had ever felt before.

Several more blasts slashed in, engaging the shields and draining power from the internal illumination.

"Multiple origination points." The pilot muttered as she pushed the ship toward the docking bay. "Off-pattern."

Marcus craned his head around to try to see what was going on through the distant viewing screens. Although he could see straight ahead of the transport well enough, his peripheral vision was awful. How could the city be shooting at him? How could *his* city be shooting at *him*?

He caught a flash of light high and to the right: a small opening, barely large enough to admit a single small ship. One of the auxiliary bays their slipshod plan called for the follow-on transports to use. But why was it open?

Then another blast slashed out and took his transport on the nose.

Movement in the small bay revealed the presence of enemy infantry. It wasn't the city shooting at him; it was more of the damned Council troopers.

Other shots were coming in from other private docking ports. And all of them were targeting his ship. His eyes widened, and then narrowed. Someone in there had figured out that the city wouldn't fire on him. Whether that had been enough to figure out where he was, or if they just decided on general principal not to let that stand, didn't matter. They'd decided to see to it that the city didn't have the last word on that score.

One of the aft flank shields was the first to go down. Sparks flew through the passenger compartment as the overloaded gravitic circuitry exploded. A horrible rending sound tore through the ship next as first one, and then a second blast caught the transport through the hole in its defenses. His stomach fell away as the ship flipped over with a shuddering, reluctant heave.

"Controls not responding." As'vhikudu's hands floated through the control interfaces with an admirable calm. Her assistant was also collected as he accessed a river of data coming at him through various screens and fields. "We've lost our window."

Marcus watched as the entrance to the executive bay slid away. Even as that happened, however, another transport rose up to take their place, ramming itself into the opening and disgorging its payload of warriors.

By now, the other ships in the flotilla had realized what was happening. They were peeling off to claim their own auxiliary landing sites, pouring fire into the bays to silence the portable weapons deployed there.

But all that was going to happen without him, he realized, as his own ship continued to fall out of the battle.

After all this, he wasn't going to get to the control center. He was going to crash into the Concourse, probably *through* the Concourse, and smash into paste on the surface of the Relic Core far below.

He shook himself out of his useless histrionics as he realized that As'vhikudu had managed to level out their descent. They were still going downward, but they were no longer in freefall, and they seemed to have wrested some control from the situation.

"Can we get back up there?" He jammed his palm against the belt release and staggered forward, holding onto anything he could reach to keep his footing. "Can we get back up to the battle?"

"No." The pilot was preoccupied, but the assistant glared at him over a wide, armored shoulder.

"What are we doing, then?" He refused to be cowed by these red-skinned demons and their glossy black eyes.

The pilot was still lost in her effort to maintain control, but through gritted teeth she managed to grind out, "We are going to have to land somewhere. We cannot maintain altitude."

Marcus had another flashing image of crashing into the Relic Core, and then jerked up as other memories flooded into his mind.

He leaned down close to shout into the pilot's ear, trying to ignore the giant horns. "Where is Sanctum from here?"

As'vhikudu scowled out of the corner of her eye, which struck Marcus as a pretty impressive feat, and muttered, "What?"

"Sanctum! The big bronze ship in the middle of the city! Where is it from here?"

The pilot thought for a moment, still straining to keep the bucking ship moving forward.

"That way." The pilot's assistant gestured with a claw to the left. Marcus would have sworn it was in the other direction, but then at this point he had no idea where they were.

"Go that way! Get us as close as you can!" The image of a strange, glossy black wall loomed large in his mind. A lot had happened since the last time he had stood before it. He couldn't explain it, but the sudden urge to head for that ancient ship was stronger than anything he had felt in a long time. It was the best he could think of.

The damaged transport left the flashing, smoke-wreathed Red Tower behind, losing altitude with each moment, its rough flight tracing an erratic line among the structures of Penumbra, toward the center of the city.

Coming between two tall towers, Marcus could see the sudden drop off at the edge of the Concourse, the Ring Wall, and beyond that, the flat expanse of the bronze field that surrounded Sanctum. In the far distance he could just make out the massive dome of glinting crystal that marked the observation deck of the big ship.

The transport gave another lurch and As'vhikudu cursed. Marcus was knocked off his feet and slammed down painfully onto the ridged decking.

A rasping alarm began to sound. He heard more Variyar cursing from the back, but his nanites could make no sense of the chaos. Behind him, he heard the warriors scramble for crash positions and wrap themselves in restraining harnesses.

He thought he was dead when he was hoisted up into the air. Something was wrapped around his chest, thick, iron-hard bundles of steel rod tilted him to the side and then flung him at his abandoned chair. He flew backward and saw the pilot's assistant standing there, arms outstretched from having thrown him. Over the warrior's shoulder he saw the flank of a squat tower growing larger in the view fields at an alarming rate. With an impact that drove the wind from his lungs he hit the hard chair, and hands on both sides began to scrabble around him, searching for his restraining belts.

The assistant leapt straight at him, and Marcus cringed back. The Variyar found the belts with practiced speed, wrenched them around Marcus and drove them locked with a definitive snap.

He turned back for his own chair then, but it was too late.

The transport must have struck the building a glancing blow, but it was enough to slew its forward momentum violently to the side. Marcus could feel his neck strain as he was whipped sideways. The pilot's assistant, without benefit of seat or harness, was thrown violently against the bulkhead where he crashed with bone-breaking force.

The ship sailed on sideways, but then some part of its exterior anatomy snagged against the roof of the Concourse and they began tumbling, shedding speed and bits of spacecraft as they roared across the surface. He clenched his eyes shut against the noise and the twisting motion, but nothing he did would dampen the scream of tortured material as the ship was torn apart around him.

# Chapter 25

Smoke was pouring into the air faster than the atmosphere regulators could clear it away. Shapes loomed out of the thick, soupy air as the fleeing Ntja scrambled up a stairway to the level above the flight deck. She leapt toward them, her knives glinting dully in the subdued lighting, and another towering warrior fell back with a yelp, its thick, black blood spraying up into the ceiling.

Angara came down in a predatory crouch and paused for a moment, lowering herself against a skeletal stairway leading from the flight deck of the executive docking bay up to the entrances on the raised mezzanine level. The chaos swirling around them was nearly complete, with shouts and cries echoing off the low ceiling as the Variyar warriors pushed the Ntja defenders back toward the exits.

The deck behind her was littered with dead; rivulets of blood tracing a many-colored pattern over the floor plating. In the drifting smoke it was impossible to tell if they were doing well. Except that they must have been, given that the resistance was falling back, and the surviving horned warriors with their heavy armor and tall, bladed weapons were pressing up the stairs and grav-lifts onto the raised area around the sunken ship deck. But the bodies were piled high around her, those sporting the bronze enhancement blisters of the Ntja and the black, back-swept horns of the Variyar in near-equal numbers.

The flight deck had been filled with Council soldiers, their squat transports forming defensive positions along the outer lip of the chamber. The pilot of the first Variyar attack ship had placed his heavy, armored charge directly between two of the ships on the deck and smashed through, ripping a hole in the defensive perimeter. Warriors had poured out, taking the Ntja line from behind, and opened more holes in their defenses. She had been able to slip the *Yud'ahm Na'uka* up and over the tangled mess, sweeping it around, defensive weapons blazing, to touch down gracefully in the open space beside the bent and smoking hull of the first Variyar ship.

The battle had devolved quickly after that, as K'hzan's demonic forces flooded the bay. The suppression shields had dropped soon after they arrived, silencing her shoulder guns before she even got a chance to use them, and the work had gotten close and bloody. The crash and clang of heavy swords on graceful polearms had echoed through the chamber, a glittering counterpoint to the shouts, screams, and moans of the fighters. But even this chaos was to be expected. The only dissonant note in the battle had been Justin, whose barely-contained nervous laughter had surged to prominent, puzzling life several times since they had jumped onto the deck.

In the noise and violence of the moment, she had been unable to ask him what he found so amusing, but she assumed it had something to do with the war cries of the Ntja, as the laughter would invariably slip his control each time a particularly loud sample erupted from their foes. She had never seen the large, snub-nosed fighters in action before, but she saw nothing particularly funny about their howling, barking challenges.

Justin, apparently, found it hilarious.

Once again the dark-skinned Human had been enjoying the efficacy of his small handgun, saving his shots for pivotal moments in the fighting while hovering around just behind her for most of the battle. She knew he had saved her life at least twice. The Ntja had threated to overrun her forward position, only to be blasted off their feet by the small Earth weapon wielded by the cackling Human.

"How close are we to the control center?" It was taking some getting used to, seeing Justin without the implants that had leached the color from his eyes. She was finding that she preferred their dark, natural color.

She shook her head. What business did she have with any kind of preference? And for a *Human*?

But there was too much to do, and not so much time she could waste any examining her own confusing feelings.

"Very close, only a few moments' walk." She put one hand up to temper his growing smile. "But there will be many Ntja between here and there." She nodded up to the mezzanine, nearly empty now as the Council forces fell back to defend the control center. "We've still got quite a bit of fighting left to go before we can get you through those doors."

She did not want to think about what might happen if they made it to the control center and found the blast door closed. They needed the Skorahn more than ever, without Marcus. Justin had shown no affinity for the medallion at all, and only the defenses of Penumbra, under their control, were going to save them when the Council fleet came back around.

"Commander." The guttural voice caused Justin to jump, but it was just another piece of information to her mind, as she tried to maintain some semblance of control around herself. She turned and nodded to the Variyar warrior standing behind her.

She was not sure when they had started calling her 'commander', but she could appreciate their confusion. She was not entirely sure what she should be called, either. She certainly was not acting as a very good bodyguard for Marcus, anyway.

A moment of despair threatened to crack her battle focus, and she shook it off. Right now it did not matter what her place here was, only that she was defending the city that had provided her a home when nowhere else would.

Commander had a pretty nice ring to it, though.

"The administrator's shuttle has reported in." It was hard to read a Variyar's expression; the hard, flat planes of their face barely moving from the snarling sneer nature had given them. But whether it was something in his eyes, or his tone, or maybe she was just getting better at understanding her stoic allies, she thought this one seemed uneasy.

His words came back to her and a cold knot in her stomach she had been doing the best to ignore loosened just a little bit. "Are they safe? How are they? *Where* are they?"

The Variyar's black eyes widened in an expression she really wished she could understand, and he looked away. "The administrator's transport failed before they could reach their destination. It was forced into an improvised landing some distance away."

"Improvised landing?" Justin pushed his way between her and the towering warrior. "What the hell does that mean? They *crashed*?"

The flat black stare failed to subdue the Human, and the Variyar blinked once before replying. "Yes." He said, his gravelly voice low. "They crashed."

The look Justin gave her as he turned away was haunted. But there was no comfort she could give at the moment, and she only touched him lightly on the shoulder while turning back to the warrior.

"Was there any report after the landing?"

"Nothing, Commander."

That meant, for all they knew, Justin was their only hope now. They needed to fight their way through to the control center as quickly as possible and get that medallion around his neck. With luck, he might be able to get the defensive array to turn on the Council's forces yet.

She felt her stomach drop. It wasn't much of a hope, she knew.

*****

There was no air left in the transport. There had been a moment of horrific, cyclonic winds as they crashed, everything had gone dark, and then the smoke had been whisked away, along with the last remnants of atmosphere. Something snapped over Marcus's face, wreaking havoc again on his night vision, and then everything came into stark relief as a bright, sharp light flooded into the tumbled passenger compartment through several rents in the hull of their downed ship.

There were no internal lights, none of the viewing fields were active, and without windows, there would have been no light at all. He heard the coughing and the shuffling of bodies nearby, but the sounds came to him muffled as if heard from a great distance. He turned and saw many of the Variyar warriors rising, shaking off the effects of the crash and reaching for their stored weapons. Many more remained scattered across the cabin, unmoving.

Turning back to the nose of the craft he was shocked to see the pilot's chair empty, an enormous slumped shadow collapsed in the angle of the floor and the bulkhead. Marcus stared at the shape in confused silence and then made to rise, but his body would not obey him. As he looked down at his restraints in mild confusion, a shape maneuvered past him and bent down to the check on As'vhikudu. Sihn Ve'Yan's dark robes created an odd effect as she moved through the slashes of hard light, sliding in and out of shadow.

"You need to get up now, my friend." Marcus looked dumbly to the side, mildly alarmed at how slowly his head seemed to be responding, to find the bright little form of Khet Nhan bending over him. The little alien's face looked worried, his big eyes reflecting vermillion light back from the bright bars hanging in the air around them.

He felt the restraints across his lap and chest give way. He slumped forward, almost falling onto his face, but the little mystic caught him with strong, wiry arms and coaxed him up into a standing position. "We need to leave here, I think. You mentioned the Sanctuary, to As'vhikudu?"

Marcus looked down at the furry features, then over to where the robed and hooded figure of the little creature's neophyte was rising like the Grim Reaper over the body of the pilot.

He *had* mentioned Sanctum, hadn't he? But why? He couldn't remember. In fact, he couldn't remember much. He wrinkled his face up in thought, trying to batter at his memory, to dredge any little detail up that might explain his current situation. It felt like something sticky was stretched across his face.

Suddenly, Marcus felt like there was a plastic bag stretched over his head. He stopped breathing, convincing himself that he couldn't, and his body dropped into a terrified crouch. He panicked, hands rising to claw the thing off before it could suffocate him.

"No!" Nhan said, slapping his hands away and then grabbing his wrists. "It's just the emergency rebreather membrane!"

Marcus stared at the creature in uncomprehending dismay. He grunted with the effort, trying to raise his hands to his face. Why was Khet Nhan trying to kill him?

The slap rocked him back on his heels and he staggered, looking up in shocked pain to see Ve'Yan standing before him. Her mouth twitched as if she was having a very hard time fending off a smile.

"It's a field generated by your collar." She said the words slowly, and that helped. It didn't help that she said them as if she was talking to an idiot child. "It's the reason you're not dead right now." She gestured to the hull breaches, and the true horror of his situation came crashing down on him.

He should be dead. They should *all* be dead. They were exposed to vacuum, to the unforgiving void that surrounded the city beyond the safety of its towers and the Concourse.

"No one told you about the emergency systems built into almost all clothing worn in Penumbra?" The genuine curiosity in Nhan's voice did nothing for the Human's self-esteem.

And as he stood there, being held up by the diminutive but terrifying little mystic, the sting of the girl's slap still tingling across his cheek, he remembered. Remembered the briefings, one of the first conversations he had, in fact, with …

His heart skipped a beat. Iphini Bha had told him about these emergency precautions. He had been impressed with a technology that would have seemed like magic on Earth, but was so simple to the Galactics that they sewed them into the collars and cuffs of their everyday clothing.

He looked down and now he could see the faintest shimmer of a field surrounding his hands as well.

He was safe from the vacuum.

"Administrator, we cannot stay here." One of the Variyar had approached while he was suffering his minor breakdown. The surviving warriors, about ten in all, were gathering at the rear of the transport, around the main access hatch. He tried to see some rank insignia or some other way to tell the demon-faced fighter from his friends, but there wasn't anything Marcus could see.

"Where did we land? Are we close to Sanctum?" It was coming back to him now, although he still couldn't tell why, exactly, he had suddenly decided the ancient ship in the middle of the city was where he should be headed. Something was pulling him toward that silent, slick black wall.

"We have landed midway between the Red Tower and the Ring Wall. We have a long walk ahead of us if you wish to reach Sanctum."

"And the Ntja will not be cooperative." Another Variyar called out from the group, his angry-looking face looming from the shadows.

"They will come, and soon." Nhan nodded with a quick, jerking motion, rubbing his hands together. "Ambassador Taurani will want confirmation of your death. Time has never been our ally in this endeavor, but our situation is far bleaker now than it was before we were forced to alter our course."

"If we are going to run," Ve'Yan looked sour as she spoke. "We have to run now. But why Sanctum? An ancient ship, with no defenses, and countless vulnerabilities? What possible significance can it have for us now?"

Marcus stared at her, his mouth open. In this harsh light she looked far less Human than she normally did. Her skin, milk-pale, was too smooth, and the black designs that traced down the sides of her nose and across her cheeks looked far more like scales or plates than tattoos, this close. He shook his head. "I don't know."

Her eyes flared at his honesty, and then narrowed, but as she leaned forward to respond, one of the Variyar shouted.

"Here they are!" The words echoed dully through their tactical communications net, and the Variyar warriors hefted their weapons, using the tears in the ship's body to peer out into the harsh light. Several detonations rocked the wrecked hulk that surrounded them, and the tall demons pushed the muzzles of their weapons through the cracks to return fire, their black eyes flaring with eager light.

"We need to leave now." Nhan pulled him toward a large gap where the entrance hatch had been twisted partly away. "Plenty of time to discuss contingency plans once we survive the current crisis."

More impacts rocked the dead transport, and the bolts sizzling from the Variyar rifles was a near constant hiss in the background.

Marcus was staring at the Variyar weapons in confused fear. "Why are the guns working? Why isn't the city suppressing them?"

The little creature continued to pull him toward the hatch. "I imagine, outside of the city's halls and walls, there is nothing Penumbra can do. A suppression field takes a great deal of energy, and usually requires a massive array to project. The city must use the materials of the towers and corridors to project its internal fields." He waved a paw vaguely around them. "Out here there's not enough of the substance of the city around us to suppress the weapons."

He didn't know why, but hearing about limitations of the city always bothered Marcus. He paused, but Nhan pulled him more forcefully, and Ve'Yan gave him an ungracious push from behind.

"Where are we going?!" Marcus shouted, adrenaline pumping furiously through his veins despite the sounds of battle being nearly muted in the vacuum. "We can't run all the way to Sanctum!"

The hatch crashed open, again with far less sound that he felt it should have, and they rushed out, moving behind the ship where its bulk would provide cover from the incoming fire. Marcus glanced back at the track the transport had made as it crashed, and he paused in awe at the devastation. The scar on the roof of the Concourse beneath them stretched back for more than a hundred yards, and passed through the corner of a tower, strewing wreckage in a wide fan stretching out from the point of impact.

It was a miracle the pilot had managed to save as many of them as she had.

Marcus looked around, but nothing he could see was familiar. When he had worn the medallion, knowledge of the city had seemed second nature to him. Once he had gained some familiarity with the Skorahn, he had only needed to wonder about something and he knew immediately where it was and how to get there. Here, wandering the outside of the city, he felt hopelessly disconnected from any kind of help or safety. And this far from the control center, moving farther away with each step, he wasn't likely to regain access to the medallion anytime soon, either.

An expanse stretched all around him, towers rising from it, reminding him of the streets of a city back home, but only in the vaguest sense. There was no regular grid pattern, no long thoroughfares or boulevards. The towers rose up all around, and the flat spaces in between, if he thought of them as streets, were zig-zagging, random affairs.

Above them stretched the towers, and then the empty blackness of space. Marcus's mind spun as the sensation crashed down upon him. For months he had been surrounded by the materials of the city. A faint crawling sensation along his spine made him wonder if he hadn't developed the beginnings of agoraphobia in his time in Penumbra.

The light around them had a harsh quality, with no air or dust to defuse it. Shadows were harsh and razor-sharp, giving the whole scene a more alien aspect than anything he had seen since Angara had forced him from Earth.

Several towering warriors kept to the edges of the crumpled ship, snapping shots off into the bright, hard-lined distance. The rest of the Variyar formed up around Marcus and the mystics, looking to him with their flat black eyes for guidance. Nhan looked hopeful and curious, Ve'Yan's lip was curled in disdain.

More impacts struck the far side of the transport; it was only a matter of time before they found themselves flanked, taking fire from either side. He closed his eyes, trying to cudgel useful information out of his brain. He didn't have the medallion anymore, but he couldn't shake the feeling that the city wanted to help him, if he could only find the right way to ask.

His head jerked back up. "We need to get down into the Concourse." He pointed to the building they had struck as they augured in, its interior blasted open to the void. "Through there, and then down." He turned to Nhan. "The rail line looked pretty extensive. We should be able to catch a car nearby. How close does it come to Sanctum?"

Nhan shook his head, his hands raised as if fending off an attack. "We have not been here long, Administrator. We know less about the city than you do."

One of the Variyar stepped forward. "The rail lines do not stretch out into the bronze plains. They end at the reservoir ring, at the Ring Wall."

Marcus nodded. "Well, if we get that far, we'll worry about the next step." He pointed at the blasted hole in the tower again. "Get us there, first."

*****

Angara wedged herself into the corner at the latest jog in the long hallway leading to the control center. The red-tinged shadows provided only the illusion of safety, however. They had been able to force the Ntja back, but they had paid for each step. She checked her knives, her lip curling in anger as she saw that one of the monomolecular blades was chipped, probably from the metal bubble she had forced it through to brain her latest victim.

Justin was panting heavily beside her. He had run out of his last reserve of ammunition for his primitive firearm some time before, and had picked up one of the heavy falchions carried by the Council troopers. She smiled at that. He had chosen one of the massive weapons in an attempt to impress her; she was almost certain. And ever since, he had been dragging the clumsy chunk of metal, completely incapable of wielding it effectively, but too embarrassed to leave it behind in favor of a more realistic blade.

"We're almost there." He was trying very hard not to appear winded, but his eyes were weary, and his dark skin had taken on a grayish pallor.

Around the corner they could hear the Ntja working themselves up into another countercharge. Justin seemed to find no further amusement in their harsh, barking shouts.

This time, when they came, there would be no Variyar with them to help blunt the attack. K'hzan's warriors were forming up several jogs behind them, not yet ready to make the next attempt against the enemy. She had moved up to check on the Ntja, and Justin had followed her.

"I think we should go back." She turned to him, jerking her head back the way they had come. "We will be of no use here alone if they attack now."

Justin tried to give her a reassuring grin and hefted the slab-like sword in what he probably thought was a jaunty manner. "You don't think we can take one for the team, give the big boys a rest?"

She was not sure if he was making a joke or if he had lost his senses, but the question was rendered moot as the howling down the hall rose to a crescendo that shook the walls. They were upon her before she could brace herself.

The first Ntja to come skittering around the corner was holding his falchion in two hands like a spear, thrusting it at them before he had even cleared the edge. His slobbering lips were pulled back from sharp, glistening teeth, and the small dark eyes gleamed with malice. He only sported a couple of the metallic enhancement domes, smaller than others they had seen. He was a low-status line soldier, incapable of higher-level tactical reasoning.

She allowed the long blade to slide past her, hyper-aware that Justin was on the other side, and then simply dipped one knife into his eye socket with a graceful gesture that saw the thug stumbling forward, dead on his feet. She spun beneath the next slash, hearing it whistling in before she could turn, and rammed the other knife up into the folds of flesh that covered that soldier's neck. Dark blood sprayed out in a fan and he slumped to the side.

She stayed low, her knees bent in a crouch, and the blades flashed out, slicing upward and gutting the next two to pound around the corner. She stood, but three of the soldiers rushed her at the same time and she was overwhelmed. There was no way they could bring their long swords to bear against her in the tight confines of the hall, but their sheer weight bore her down to the hard deck plating. Shadows flashed above her as others jumped over their tangled pile, and her eyes flared as she realized they were going for Justin.

"Get the Human!" The voice was guttural, muffled by the bodies piled above her, but the words were unmistakable. "Kill him!"

They knew who the real threat was.

Angara screamed in frustrated rage, pushing her knives over and over again into the unyielding flesh that surrounded her. They writhed and pummeled at her, but could do nothing to stop the little blades. Unfortunately, even as she killed them, they slumped down over her, pressing her even more forcefully into the floor.

Somewhere above her she could hear shouts and growls and the dull clang of heavy Ntja falchions against each other. With each sound, her desperation grew, and she pushed herself through the tangle of leather-clad arms and legs, rising at last from the pile of bodies as if she were emerging from some foul ocean.

Justin grinned at her. His shoulders were heaving with his labored breathing, his face and arms were running with black Ntja blood, and he was using his stolen sword as a prop to hold himself up, surrounded by the hacked and mangled bodies of the remaining Council troops.

"You didn't think I could do it." It wasn't a question, but he smiled wider, and she was nearly overcome with the desire to wrap him in her arms.

She forced herself to shrug. "I figured you'd hold your own."

That got a reaction, and he stood a little straighter, gesturing to the bodies at his feet. "That's it? I don't get any credit for all this?"

His eyes had a wild cast to them, and she reminded herself that he was not a warrior. The Human before her had never killed another living being before this day. Given that, it was nearly miraculous that he was holding up as well as he was.

"You were incredible." She kept the smile off her face, looking into his dark eyes with all the sincerity she could muster. But there was no repressing her instincts completely. "Of course, these were all small ones."

He was sputtering, his returning smile faltering, when her ear began to itch with a warning of an incoming message. She held up her hand to silence Justin, nodding to the Variyar now moving up past them in the corridor, and listened to the report.

"Sanctum?" She tried to make sense of that. "Why would they go to Sanctum?" It was an old, decrepit ship; the oldest in the city. There was nothing to lend it any sort of strategic value at all.

Unless …

An image of the Alcove and its ancient black wall flashed into her mind; a towering doorway that had never opened to anyone in the history of the city.

No one knew what was behind the wall. Maybe Marcus knew something she did not? At least she knew he had survived the crash.

She turned back to the task at hand. The control center was close, and the resistance was folding. She looked over at Justin, collapsed against the wall behind her. He straightened again as she turned, pretending he had been standing tall all along, and looked around him with a nonchalance that would fool no one.

"Marcus is okay." She owed him that news before they continued. "I think he's got an idea."

Justin's face lit with relief, but then hardened. "Is he coming back this way? I'd rather not have to try to use the damned necklace if there's any other option."

She shook her head. "He's got another idea, but there's no telling if it will work, even if he can get through. We need to keep working to get you to the Skorahn, in case he fails, or..."

He looked at her for a moment, but then nodded before she was forced to finish the thought.

"Okay, well, let's get to it, then." He jerked his chin down the hall. "Care to take the lead? I don't feel like I have anything else to prove at the moment."

She looked at him, and half a dozen possible retorts fought for space on her tongue. But then she looked down at the dead enemies he had stacked on the floor, and she nodded with a slight smile.

"I can do that."

Around them, the Variyar prepared for the final assault on the control center.

*****

The hatch over his head seemed innocuous considering what could lay on the other side. Marcus looked back at the line of beings following him. The two mystics stood nearest, Khet Nhan eager to continue, Sihn Ve'Yan resigned to whatever lunacy he forced upon them next. The young Thien'ha had turned sullen as they moved. Her dour anger seemed to grow, however, whenever they clashed with Council soldiers.

They had made it to the breached tower by eliminating the small squad of Ntja that had first come to investigate their crash scene. He had never actually seen the enemy, beyond the flashes of energy slashing out from an entranceway to a nearby tower. The Variyar had saturated the shadows beneath the overhang with their own rifle fire, and soon the blasts had slackened off.

Once inside the damaged tower, Marcus had followed his instincts, feeling almost as if he were moving through familiar territory again, although he had never visited this part of the city. They had gone down through the service tunnels, into the vast, echoing space of the empty Concourse. Apparently, Taurani had locked the city down, and once the fighting started, even those few who had been allowed to roam freely had retreated behind whatever safety they could find.

The rail line was as he remembered ... or thought it should be. His memories and his expectations were blurring in a confusing way that he did not even try to articulate to the others. They took two of the service cars, which responded quickly to verbal commands, and met only token resistance from two more parties of Ntja.

Sooner than he wanted, the service rail had brought them to the very edge of the Concourse, and they were now standing at the Ring Wall. On the far side was the bronze expanse of the empty plains surrounding Sanctum. In his overflight with Iphini Bha, he had been distracted during their approach and departure, but he was almost certain that they had quite a long walk ahead of them, with no cover at all to hide them from the wary eyes of the Council forces.

He shrugged. There wasn't much else they could do at this point. They had seen the Ntja shadowing them, and he knew by now the corridors between him and the Red Tower were probably filled with the enemy.

"If we turn back now, we die." Ve'Yan's spat the words in a bitter tone. "We don't have a choice."

Marcus turned back to the wall before them, stretching over thirty feet up to the roof of the Concourse far overhead. The hatch was similar to the blast doors that protected the control center or the primary docking bay, but there was no heavy security system that he could see. He put his hands up against the cool metal, fingers splayed, and bowed his head.

He intended to search for the deep, prayerful center of thought that had allowed him to operate the doors to the docking bay when they were making their escape. But as soon as he closed his eyes he felt a click behind his forehead and the surface beneath his hands gave one quick jerk and then fell away from his hands, rising up and away, into the wall.

The unmistakable shimmer of an energy field buzzed into being over the doorway, and the harshly-lit expanse of burnished bronze stretched out before them.

"We will need to watch for air cover." The tallest of the Variyar muttered. He kept looking back at the vague figures lurking in the shadows behind them. "They will be in contact with their other forces. They will know where we are, and where we are going."

Marcus nodded, his eyes fixed on the tiny lump of bronze glittering in the distance. The outer Wall of the Concourse swept away to either side, the tall shapes of the city's towers rising up behind it in both directions. To the right the Wall diminished into the distance until it ended abruptly, over a mile away, at the precipitous Gulf. To the left, though, the wall stretched away, and then curved forward, encircling the vast empty space, until it reached the Gulf on the far side of Sanctum, tiny in the distance.

There was nowhere to hide out on that plain.

"There's nowhere to hide in here, Marcus." Khet Nhan's voice was soft; it was as if the little creature had read his thoughts. He put a soft paw on Marcus's shoulder. "If we stay here, this is where our cycle will end."

Ve'Yan snorted, shaking her head with a violence that surprised him. "As if you have any further care at all for the cycles." She shoved Marcus's shoulder and pointed with one long finger out into the glaring light. "If we are going to go, let us go. Let us not dress it up in mystical terms, or pretend we are struggling valiantly in the service of something greater than ourselves." She glared at Marcus, her face more pale than usual. "If we turn back now, we die."

He didn't fully understand her anger, but he nodded. What she said was true.

Glancing back over his little band, he was heartened to see the brawny Variyar ready to follow him out into the stark light. Their horns gleamed, their eyes aglow with the prospect of more violence.

With a nod, he pushed one shoulder through the energy field, felt the plane of the surface pass over his body, and the small field snap into place over his head. Flexing his fingers, he was glad to feel the now-familiar tightness there as well.

Outside on the bronze plain they moved at a brisk trot, the Variyar spreading out before and around him, seeking for targets. No avalanche of blaster shots fell upon them from the top of the Ring Wall behind them, but glancing back he could make out the shapes of Ntja standing there, watching, their weapons held ready across their chests.

"Why aren't they shooting?" The flesh between his shoulder blades crawled.

"I believe that is a question best left to the dark silence." The leader of the Variyar muttered. "So long as they are not shooting, the answer can do nothing but discomfit us."

"Perhaps they know our quest is useless." Ve'Yan spat.

"Perhaps they do not know enough to fear our quest," offered Nhan.

Marcus found himself wishing he had a stronger impression one way or the other.

If there was some threat to the Council in his visiting Sanctum, with the amulet locked away in the control center with Taurani, he didn't know what it was.

*****

The sounds of battle rang down the hall, as if the fighting might round one of the corners before them at any moment. Khuboda Taurani, Ambassador Plenipotentiary of the Galactic Council to the Free City of Penumbra, ran his tongue over the stiff brush of his brill in satisfaction. They had not yet reached the control center.

And now they never would.

He gestured with one arm, enjoying the dramatic sweep of the sleeve as he moved, and a score of Ntja soldiers in the black uniforms of Ochiag's fleet moved past, holstering their guns and drawing their heavy, clumsy blades. Judging from the clangor down the corridor, the suppression field was in full effect here.

"Ambassador," an Ntja soldier with extensive enhancement domes pushed through the reserve squads guarding him. The creature sketched a vague salute and stood stiffly, waiting to be recognized.

Taurani's reputation for strict discipline and decorum had clearly spread to the fleet.

"Yes?" He turned to the newcomer, keeping his glittering eyes down the hall. As soon as he heard from his vanguard, he would be moving out toward the control center, where the Skorahn awaited him with the prospect of a well-deserved distraction in the person of the cowering Iwa'Bantu deputy.

"We have reports from some of the striker teams moving through the city. The Human administrator has broken through the cordon and is making for the center of the city."

"*Former administrator.*" He spat the words at the cretin, and was gratified to see the beast cringe at his tone.

Sanctum. Why would Marcus Wells be heading to Sanctum? The barbarian had surprised him at every turn, so he tried not to set too much credence in his initial impulse to dismiss the move as a hopeless ploy. Certainly without the Skorahn there was nothing the Human could do at the old wreck.

And yet, for some reason, the idea twisted at something in the back of his mind.

"Well, at least we'll know where to find him when we clear things up here." He shrugged, forcing himself to relax. There was nothing the Human could do without the medallion, no matter where he was. "Tell the striker teams to follow, but not to engage unless he leaves them no choice. When the time comes, I very much intend to be in on the hunt."

"Yes, Ambassador." The big soldier nodded and backed away before turning and trotting down the hall.

"Ambassador, the way is clear." One of the Ntja formed up around him tapped a gleaming bronze hemisphere erupting from the flesh near his ear. "The Variyar are being held several jogs down the corridor. We are cleared through to the control center."

The rigid lines of Taurani's face twitched, as if they intended to form a Human smile, and he would almost have been willing to let them, if they could. Everything came down to this moment. K'hzan Modath had revealed himself to be the recidivist traitor everyone in the Council had always known him to be; his clandestine fleet had been revealed at last, and when Penumbra was awakened against him, he would be crushed between the city's defenses and Ochiag's Peacemaker fleet.

His long strides took him past the point guards and to the control center. The scars from the escape of the Humans and their allies were still dark around the blast doors and along the walls of the corridor. He almost told one of the following soldiers to make a note to have the mess cleared up, but then his spirits lifted even higher as he realized that he would soon be gone, with no further need to suffer the ugliness. As soon as he took care of Marcus Wells and his people, Taurani intended to leave this benighted backwater behind and return to the Council for his reward.

As he moved to enter the control center he met an Ntja soldier coming out. It was dressed in the brown uniform of the diplomatic guard, a puzzled look on its animal face.

"What?" He barked, trying to ignore the cold grip on the back of his neck.

The soldier cocked its head at his tone or his word, looking blankly at him through its rheumy little eyes, but said nothing.

With a snarl, Taurani pushed past the big oaf and into the beating heart of Penumbra. The bodies had been removed, the mess cleaned up as best the soldiers were able. All was silent at the moment, as the battle was being controlled from advanced command nodes throughout the city, and, until it had followed the Variyar fleet, from Ochiag's command ship overhead.

The light was dim, the viewing fields of the various stations humming and glowing with a neutral gray. A bar of only slightly brighter light was falling out of the administrator's office, where the security door was open, and the privacy door ajar.

With a sinking feeling Taurani moved toward the door. Iphini Bha should have been at the door, cringing and groveling for his amusement, holding the Skorahn up in shaking hands.

The cold had risen up and over the crown of his head. He rushed the last few steps and threw the door open, a savage curse for Bha in his throat.

A curse that died, its ghost escaping as a whisper, as he surveyed the room.

The towering, purple-furred form of his body servant Iranse lay stretched out on the floor. His face bore a vague expression of surprise, somehow also conveying mild annoyance. But he stared up at the low ceiling with a single dull, unmoving eye. His other eye was a red ruin, the butt of an ancient stylus standing proud of the wet, wrinkled flesh as pale blood traced a gentle stream from the corner of the eye, matting the fur there, and flowed to the small puddle gathering beneath his head.

The paintings on the wall were jagged, filled with angry reds and yellows, but they were sinking as he watched, a dark blue, almost black shadow seeping up through them, drowning out the brighter colors. He paid the art no mind and scanned the room for the sake of form. He already knew what he would find.

Of Iphini Bha and the Skorahn there was no sign.

# Chapter 26

The material was dead and cold against his forehead. Unyielding beneath his desperately probing fingers, there was nothing but the heavy, leaden blackness. No sensation of energy stirred within. No sense of purpose or awareness touched his mind through the contact. The massive black wall was cold, solid, and dead.

They had crossed the bronze plains without incident. The towering Ring Wall of the Concourse surrounded them like the bowl of a massive arena. Council forces had shadowed them, watching from the top of the Wall and following in their wake, but keeping their distance, not engaging them as they ran desperately for the derelict space ship in the center of the flat void.

But now that they were here, Marcus feared that the impulse that had driven them had proven as empty and pointless as Sihn Ve'Yan had declared.

The stations of the ancient bridge remained dead. The spectacular view of the Gulf was still there, the glittering ribbon of curling water being drawn up from the planet continued to coil its eternal way upward into the Furnace far beneath them. But Sanctum itself, aside from the life support structures, lights, and heat, was still and lifeless.

The Variyar had established a perimeter around the base of the bridge chamber, where the tall windows swept down to meet the textured floor plating on a level with the ground outside. They were keeping watch on the Council forces approaching all around them now, as if their vigilance would mean anything when the Ntja got the order to close the noose.

And all to bring him to the Alcove and this silent wall of ancient darkness. He pressed his forehead once again into the wall, denying the impulse to dash his head against its surface. He pummeled his brain, trying to force it back onto the pathways that had worked the doors of the docking bay, and the wall behind them, but there was no echo of the contact he had felt before. This blackness was as cold and dead as the Variyar who had fallen all around him to bring him to this moment.

It was the medallion. It had to be. Whatever residual contact had made it possible to open the blast doors during their flight was gone now. Taurani must have attuned himself to the gem, and their entire battle plan was pointless. There was no awareness here that they might negotiate with, threaten, or cajole. Without the Skorahn, he was no more special than any of the other sentients wandering the city.

"We're going to die here." Ve'Yan's voice was calm. She leaned against one of the ancient console stands, staring out over the empty expanse of bronze. For some reason, he thought she wasn't even seeing the gathering forces beyond the crystalline panes. "This cycle ends." She looked down at where Khet Nhan sat on a tiered step, his head in his agile little hands. "Nothing you've done has mattered at all. You wandered off the path, betrayed your life's work, and the path has swept right back beneath your feet."

Nhan made a delicate snorting noise and turned his head away from his apprentice.

"You have turned your back on everything you believed in, everything you taught me to believe, and it will all be for nothing." The bitterness in her voice was painful to hear. She cast one last venomous look down at the diminished master and then turned away to pace along the viewing windows, continuing to watch out over the empty expanse.

Nhan slumped in his place, staring at the ancient floor, his head moving slightly back and forth in denial. Marcus looked back at the immovable wall, gave it one last spiteful push, and then moved over to collapse down beside the Thien'ha master.

"She seems more upset than usual." He tried to keep his tone light, but Ve'Yan had never been gentle with him, and it wasn't easy.

"She is not wrong." The little head remained down, the fine fingers woven into the fur at its back. "She is not wrong."

Marcus knew very little of the Thien'ha philosophy, or what had motivated Master Khet Nhan to assist him. But the little creature had been a friend in the short time they had known one another, and he hated to see him in such pain. "Is there anything I can do?"

Nhan barked a cruel laugh, and his red eyes rose and pierced Marcus with a heat he didn't remember seeing there before. "You could rise above your nature, bend the realities of space and time, and shatter the interminable cycle that has frozen entropy out of the galaxy for thousands of years!"

With that, the little creature leapt to its feet and stormed off to find a quiet corner, leaving Marcus behind, mouth open, brows down in bewilderment.

"Administrator!" The rumbling voice of the lead Variyar almost made him jump. "They're coming!"

He sighed, his own head falling between his knees, the hopelessness that had gripped him at the wall's stubborn silence slamming back into his mind full force.

*****

"They're falling back!" Justin's voice was harsh with exhaustion as he shouted over his shoulder at the waiting Variyar. Angara shook her head but did not stop him from yelling back the report. She was not entirely convinced that the Ntja were actually retreating, and she was not about to have any of her people rush into a trap. But as long as no one sprinted past her, they should be fine.

The last pitched battle had left four more Council soldiers bleeding out onto the decking while one of the tall Variyar had taken a falchion across one arm and looked as if he might lose the limb if they did not get him treatment in time. Luckily, they held the Tower all the way back to the executive docking bay, and a triage center had been established near the shuttles to care for the wounded.

"They're falling back, right?" This time he almost whispered it, as if her failure to join in his celebration had him doubting his assessment.

"They're not pushing anymore." She leaned around the corner and scanned the next stretch of corridor; clear to the next jog. She could not even detect movement in the red shadows beyond. As far as she could tell, the Ntja had fallen back. The next question, of course, was why?

"We will need to rush the control center in force." She rocked back behind the shallow curve in the wall, turning to look at the warriors looming up behind

Justin. "They will be ready for us, but we serve no good purpose sitting here in safety."

The big warrior at the front of the party nodded, gripping his polearm in two clawed hands, an unmistakably hungry flash lighting up his black eyes. There were at least twenty of the horned nightmares gathering behind them now, ready to rush into the control center and wreak a bloody havoc on the Council defenders.

"We need to keep the communications gear intact so we can reach your fleet. And whatever you do, don't damage the Skorahn!" She sank back into a ready crouch, preparing to sprint toward the control center, but then rose again. "If you see Iphini Bha, spare her. I'll have answers from her own lips before I give her the release of death."

They growled and nodded, and she looked at Justin. "Would you rather go in with the second wave?" She did not want him hurt in the initial fury of battle when they pushed Taurani's creatures into the larger killing ground of the center. But she knew his answer before she asked the question.

"No, I'll go in with you." He hefted the Ntja belt knife he had been wielding instead of his discarded falchion. The belt knife was the length of his forearm, almost as long as one of her own blades, and looked far more comfortable in his Human-sized hand.

She nodded again, put her back to the wall, and took one last glance down the corridor. She spun and was running before she could have really known it was empty. K'hzan was due to return, pursued by the Council fleet, very soon. If they did not have control of the city's defenses by then, there would be no choice but for the Variyar fleet to abandon their cause. When the Council warships resumed their position around Penumbra, it would be over for all of them.

She gripped her knives tightly, her arms pumping with all the strength her exhausted body could provide, and she tore into the small alcove area before the blast doors to the control center. There were no Ntja in evidence, and she leapt for the doorway, sailing through, scanning for threats as she flew.

She tucked at the last minute and took the impact of her landing on her shoulder, arms folded across her chest, knives tucked under her chin, and rolled. She bounced up into a corner, shrinking into a fighter's crouch, ready to start laying about her into the surprised and confused soldiers.

The room was empty.

As she stood, knees still bent with unrelieved tension, not really believing the enemy was gone, a score of Variyar came pounding in, Justin howling along beside them. They came sliding to a halt, their horns gleaming as they cast their black gazes in all directions. They were arrayed in a perfect attack pattern that quartered the command center, defending each other's flanks while presenting monomolecular blades in all directions.

The room remained stubbornly empty.

"What the hell?" Justin stood up, relief and disappointment battling for pride of place on his face. "Where is everybody?"

Angara shook her head. She moved quickly through the chamber, gesturing for the Variyar to post guards at the doors, keeping a watch further down the hall, while the rest of them were to maintain their position.

The observation and control stations were all active, but on standby, their viewing fields a hazy gray. She looked quickly to the bulkhead where Agha-pa's body had come to rest the day Taurani had made his move. Aside from a faded stain on the floor, there was no sign that day had even happened.

She continued to move through the dark room, her eyes sliding from point to point, catching everything. The doors to the administrator's office were both wide open, and she sidled up to the doorframe, back to the wall, knives held tight, and then spun in, her face fierce, her breath held, and her blades ready.

But there was no need.

The room was empty except for a body stretched across the floor beside the long table. She recognized the purple fur and coarse black hair of an Eru, and knew at once who she had found. It was Iranse, Taurani's body servant. He was laid out on his back, something sticking up out of the ruin of one eye. She leaned closer and almost smiled; Bha's old stylus. She shook her head. There was more going on here than she had time to process. One thing was sure, though. The Skorahn was not here.

As she turned to leave, she noticed that the paintings were a strange, swirling blue that she did not believe reflected her own emotions at all. It seemed to carry hints of worry and fear, but a slow, deep, churning sensation of potential energy as well, like the swelling of a great ocean tide.

She shrugged. She had always hated those damned pictures.

"Commander." By now she did not give the title a second thought, only nodded to the Variyar seated at one of the communication stations. "A diplomatic shuttle has just taken off from the auxiliary bay beneath us." He turned black eyes to her. "From the readouts, it was running heavy."

"Taurani." It had to be. She had no idea why Iphini Bha had killed Iranse, or why her own body was not slumped next to his. The Ambassador must have a reason for dragging her with him. They must have decided the Skorahn needed to be moved. She cursed herself, sheathing her daggers and kicking at the floor as she rested her hands on her hips. She should have known that Taurani would see the danger and flee.

"That is all, then." She shook her head, disgusted. "There is no telling where he has gone. All he has to do is hide until the damned Council fleet returns, and we are beaten."

"Sanctum." The Variyar at the console muttered, his claws swiping back and forth through the interface field, searching for more data.

"What?"

"The shuttle has assumed a direct course for Sanctum, at the center of the city." He continued to work.

"Marcus." Lacking a sheath, Justin was holding the big dagger in one hand, waving it about to make his point. "Marcus is at Sanctum. It can't be a coincidence, can it?"

She shook her head. "But why? It makes no sense! Taurani has the medallion. There is no reason for him go hunting after Marcus before the battle overhead is won, and that is all but a formality if we cannot win the city's defenses over to our side."

Justin shrugged. He tried to fold his arms casually as he leaned back against a console, but it proved more difficult with the long knife than he might have thought. With a frustrated snort, he put the blade down. "You can't tell me you know everything there is to know about all of this." He waved one hand over his head. "If Taurani is headed out that way, there's a reason, and it means we missed something, and things aren't as hopeless as we might think." He smiled, his teeth bright against his dark skin. "If Taurani is running scared, there's something to be scared *of*, and we might just be able to make that work for us."

She shook her head, but his words seemed to click into something in her own mind, something that gave off just the faintest wash of warm hope.

"Commander, K'hzan Modath is clearing the planet's shadow." The big Variyar turned to her, continuing his adjustments and calling up the viewing field. He cast one claw up and the field swelled to fill the space, floor to ceiling, before his station. "The Council fleet is moving faster than we anticipated."

In the field she watched the dun-colored shoulder of the planet for a moment, and then saw the flickering eruption of the Variyar fleet as it flashed over the horizon, hulls glittering in the hard light. What appeared to be a dust-cloud rose up behind them, with two massive bull-shapes leading the charge: the Council fleet, narrowing the gap between them even as she watched.

"He's going to run." She muttered under her breath, but everyone in the control center heard her. "He's going to have to run."

"Penumbra, are you receiving?" The voice echoed through the chamber, and the display shivered, darkening, and then the unmistakable nightmare visage of K'hzan Modath loomed out of the flat plane. "Penumbra, respond."

Angara shifted around so that she would be in the pickup field of the active station's communications array, and dipped her head to the massive image. "We are in possession of the control center, but we do not have the Skorahn." She forced herself to meet his gaze, but felt relieved when he took his massive eyes off her to scan around the half of the room he could see.

"Where is Administrator Wells? Is he not with you?" There was an edge to K'hzan Modath's voice, and she forced herself to keep in mind he was engaged in a lethal battle of his own.

"The administrator was unable to join us. He is currently at Sanctum." She turned to look at Justin, and then shrugged. "We think Taurani is headed there as well."

There was a flash from the viewing field, and the scene shifted slightly. In the background, behind K'hzan's calm, cold tones, they could hear agitated voices, warning klaxons, and distant detonations.

"We are taking fire from the Council fleet. Are you reporting that the city's defenses are not in your hands?" He glared for a moment at Justin, and then his eyes slid back to Angara's.

"They are not." The words tasted like hot dust. "But they might not be under Taurani's control either!" She saw what was happening, and had to stop it, no matter what the cost. "The city may not fire on you if you seek shelter behind it! If we—"

"I must preserve my main strength, Angara Ksaka." Another detonation echoed through the link. "That must be my first priority. I cannot depend upon your assumptions to keep my ships safe."

She tried to get angry at that, but she understood his position perfectly. She tried another tack. "You have warriors down here! You have people that will die if you abandon them now!"

"And we are perfectly capable of looking after ourselves." One of the taller Variyar was standing beside her, somehow conveying disappointment and sadness at her choice of ploy.

"My warriors will follow the paths fate has set before them." The massive head in the field nodded. "For now, we flee."

She knew those words must not have tasted sweet to K'hzan, but he was doing what he must. Whatever Taurani was afraid of, could they utilize it with the Council fleet over their heads?

"Be well, Angara Ksaka. We will return if we are able." Without waiting for a reply, the field switched back to the wider view of the fleets as they hurtled around the planet, their orbits rising, and the Variyar ships began to disperse, taking up a scattered disposition that would ensure that most of them made it away safely.

The largest ship, K'hzan Modath's flagship most likely, would skim close to the city before launching off into the empty reaches of the system to drop its wormhole and escape.

She watched as their last hope scattered out and away.

The trouble started with one of the farthest ships, smaller than most of the others. It dropped a wormhole that formed and grew before it became the distinctive, ravening hole in time and space that Angara had seen a thousand times before. But even as the ship began to disappear into safety, the hole collapsed, crushing the forward sections of the ship with its infinite gravity.

The rest of the ship coasted onward for several lengths, shedding glittering pieces of itself as it went, and then detonated as the damage became too great for the structure to hold any longer.

The Variyar around her began to scream and shout all at once, and her own eyes widened as she saw three more Variyar ships devoured by their own singularities.

Somehow, the Council fleet was collapsing the holes, trapping them in the system where they could be destroyed in detail. K'hzan and the fleet he had hidden for a lifetime would be eliminated in one stroke.

"There is some form of suppression field emanating from the largest Council ship." The Variyar at the station said as his hands writhed within the interface field. "It is somehow quashing our singularities as quickly as our ships can summon them."

"We are making for the outer system." K'hzan's reappeared in the visual display. His voice was still calm, but behind him it seemed like his bridge was erupting in utter chaos. "We will come back around for another attack pass after we have regrouped and assumed a more offensive formation."

She was still no good at understanding Variyar facial expressions, but she did not think she was far off the mark in assuming that K'hzan was furious, not afraid.

"We are going to go to Sanctum!" She gestured for the Variyar warriors around her to move out. "Keep the Council fleet off our backs until we can sort this out, and we may yet salvage something from all this."

"Apparently I have no choice, Angara Ksaka." His stiff face was always rigid, but with his tone it seemed even more so. "It may just be that this admiral has undone himself by forcing my hand."

She nodded, but she was already out the door. "We need to get to the auxiliary docking bay." She said over her shoulder. "There should be at least one more ship there. We can take it to Sanctum."

Justin ran past her, empty hands pumping. "I can get it started!"

She spared a moment's thought to thank whatever powers were shaping that day. By taking his Ntja with him, Taurani might just have left them an opening.

Around the next bend there was a gasp, and a sick, half-hearted cry.

The Variyar with her raced around the corner with shouted war cries, and she sped up. Her stomach dropped, and she shivered with a sudden, violent cold. She had been a fool; she knew it before she even came around into the next straight passage. The corridor was full of Ntja soldiers, their swords swinging wildly as they met the Variyar in combat once again.

At their feet, jostled by their maneuvering but bereft of any directed motion of its own, was the body of Justin Shaw.

*****

The diplomatic shuttle was a crude, military model; nothing like the luxurious craft he had become accustomed to in his work for the Council. But Ochiag's fleet was a hunting formation, designed and equipped to enforce Council policy and eradicate Human splinter fleets. There was little call for the niceties of a fully-appointed shuttle for civilian diplomats.

Taurani stared into the depths of a viewing field oriented forward, showing the view flashing over the towers of the city, the glittering dome of Sanctum growing larger in the distance. He occupied a small bubble of space in the crowded ship, almost entirely filled with elite Ntja soldiers and their equipment. He could have crammed a few more in if he was willing to forego his own comfort, but even under battle conditions, there were some standards he refused to lower. He justified the move by thinking that the added strength of the rearguard would make it harder on the Variyar barbarians nipping at his heels.

He figured that the mess in the command center would give them pause as well, as they tried to puzzle out what had happened to the big Eru stretched out on the floor of the administrator's office. He cursed Iranse in the silence of his mind, but the creature had clearly reaped the rewards of his folly, and was now beyond the Ambassador's wrath.

What was Iphini Bha thinking? He had always been such a gifted judge of character. And the timid little thing had never even registered as a threat as he developed his plans. He had taken the innate passivity of her race for granted. What had possessed him to let her have the Skorahn?

He wanted to strike the bulkhead beside him in his anger, but refused to reveal the depth of his frustration to the soldiers around him. He sat back, his shoulders straight, and concentrated on his breathing.

Why was Marcus Wells at Sanctum? The fury of the storm of questions rose again in his mind, upsetting his feeble attempts at meditation. There was nothing there for the Human. Even with the cursed medallion, if that was in fact where Bha was headed, there was nothing they could do.

He had done extensive research before accepting the assignment to this filthy hole in space. The mysteries of Sanctum were minor compared to many of the other unknowns associated with Penumbra. He knew about the ancient wall in its Alcove, of course. He had even visited the site once, during his early time in the city. He was aware of the extensive efforts to open the doorway throughout the recorded history of the place. Various administrators had even attempted to use the Skorahn, and all of them had met with nothing but the cold, immovable silence of the sealed blackness.

He snorted. No one even knew what was *behind* the wall! The chain of wildly improbable events that would bring Iphini Bha and Marcus Wells together again and see the door open was still no real threat to his designs. Nothing hidden beneath the dust of the ages could match the forces he was bringing to bear. He would wrest control of the city away from the ragtag crew of misfits once and for all, and nothing a Human could do would stop him.

"Ambassador, Admiral Ochiag requests a word, sir." The Ntja sitting at the control console turned around to address him. The pilot's enhancements were extensive, but then those Ntja who had survived the running battles through the Tower with him were mostly high-ranking, this late in the battle.

He nodded without a word, and turned back to the viewing field, its spherical shimmer glittering for a moment, and then Ochiag's craggy features peered down at him.

"Ambassador, the technology you provided was most effective." Wet teeth gleamed within the folds of the admiral's smile. "The Variyar are trapped." The heavy brows dropped. "I cannot help but notice, however, that the defenses have not yet begun to engage them?"

He frowned. This is what came of relying upon such a crass species. "No, Admiral. The city's defenses seem to have defaulted to a ready state."

"I trust they will pose no risks to my fleet as we pass to engage the enemy?" There was a gleam in the Ntja's eyes that Taurani did not care for.

"Hardly, Admiral." He reached into the interface field beneath the image and called up a status report. "Your heavy infantry are redeploying from the prime docking bay toward the insurgents. The rest of our forces have contained them within their fallback position. There is nowhere for them to run, and they lack the power to withstand our forces. The defenses of the city will be back under our control very soon now."

A burning sensation rose up in his throat as he forced the words out, keeping his tone reasonable. Nothing galled him more than having to treat with a being of such markedly inferior social position. And he could tell that Ochiag was enjoying the reversal of roles.

"See that they are, Ambassador." Ochiag had the grace to keep the grin from his jowly face, but that light was still dancing in the small, dark eyes.

Without a formal farewell, the field jumped, and he was once again looking out past the nose of his shuttle.

He sank back into the crash couch and looked up at the nearest Ntja. "Make sure the heavy infantry are converging on Sanctum. I want everything in place by the time we arrive."

The creature nodded, turning to push its way forward to the control console against the forward bulkhead.

Part of him wanted to level the ancient ship from a distance and just have done with the entire, sordid affair. Of course, he could not endanger the Skorahn that way. And besides, he wanted to look into Marcus Wells' eyes as the Human died, preferably a slow death, choking on his own blood. And if he could walk beside the corpses of the rest of his little band, seeing their lifeless eyes for himself, even better.

He coveted a private hope as well, that he might catch up to Iphini Bha and thank her personally for this latest little twist to his path.

*****

Another blast slapped against the networked crystalline panes spread out before them. Whatever the ancient viewports were made of, it had been standing up to the Ntja weapons quite well. Although, Marcus had to admit, sheltering behind a transparent wall during a firefight was not helping his nerves any.

From his position near the Alcove and its sunken, unresponsive door, he watched as the Variyar took shelter behind the foremost consoles of the ancient bridge, firing through holes they had bored through the crystal with their hand weapons. The brilliant flashes of blue and red strobed almost constantly now as the Council troopers closed the distance. Many were following walls of portable barricade, while others were in low-slung vehicles carrying heavier weaponry.

Above Sanctum soared several Ntja transports working as ground attack craft. He thought he had seen a Variyar ship off in the distance at one point, but it had been run off by the Council forces.

There were eight Variyar left, snapping off suppressive fire meant to slow the Ntja as much as possible. He wasn't sure why they were bothering, to be honest. It looked like there was an army out there swarming toward them, with a fleet of ships overhead. If Angara and Justin had had any luck at the Red Tower, he felt sure the pressure would have eased by now.

Instead, this was pretty much the end.

He looked over to where Sihn Ve'Yan stood, near the end of the wall of glass. She stared out at the approaching forces, her face blank. The flashes of plasma blasts winked in her eyes as they locked on a distant horizon only she could see.

Khet Nhan had collapsed again by the black wall, cradling his head in his hands. The little mystic had not spoken since his last outburst against Marcus, and he would just as soon not suffer another. There was something profound going on between the Thien'ha, he knew, but given their current situation, he couldn't bring himself to care what it might be.

Ever since he had been dragged to Penumbra, he had been treated like shit. Now that he knew why, it wasn't making it any easier to bear. So Humans had once ruled the galaxy and done a shitty job of it. So what? What did that have to do with *him*? How bad must they have been, though, to have left such a thick psychic stink behind them after thousands upon thousands of years?

He thought back to some of the darker moments in his history classes. Human history had more than its fair share of monsters, of course. Was there any doubt that, if the wrong people got in charge, given the technology these Humans must have had at their disposal, some truly terrible things might have happened?

Maybe it was best that he end here, with his back to the damned wall, before he could do any serious harm.

It was hard to maintain that internal dialogue with the Council's dogs showering the massive wall of glass with blaster fire.

Screw that. If they wanted him dead, they were going to have to fight their way in and route him out. And he was going to do his damnedest to find out what was behind the high black wall before he died, as well.

He heaved himself to his feet and gestured with his head toward the door when a nearby Variyar looked up from his firing position at the sound. He jogged down the ramp into the Alcove, looking back up at the wall as if he hadn't spent hours staring at it already. It was cold and black and smooth, obviously of a different material than the rest of the ship that made up Sanctum.

An explosion across the broad expanse of windows caused him to duck in place, whipping his head around, assuming the Ntja had just breached the chamber. But whatever had hit the windows was fading away outside, its heat and light bleeding off into the void. The Variyar continued to fire, and return shots continued to spall off the glass.

Turning back to the door, he sighed, sliding to his knees, forehead on the cool metal. He was going to die up against this damned wall; he just knew it.

# Chapter 27

The shuttle was a dilapidated old scow; it handled like an asteroid and offered all the comfort of an eggshell. She skimmed the surface of the Concourse on the west wing of the city, far from the Red Tower and danger represented by the Variyar fleet's arrival. She had been flying since she ran from the Tower. She made sure to keep beneath the city's defenses in case Taurani somehow managed to regain control of them.

Although, without the Skorahn, she had no idea how he might do that.

Still, better safe than sorry.

She had no idea where to run. She had no real friends in the city; not anymore. Her coworkers in the administrator's office were either dead, fled, or looked at her as the worst kind of traitor.

Around her neck, the Skorahn pulled with a weight out of all proportion to its appearance. She could not be sure, but it felt like it had been getting heavier since the Variyar had dropped onto the control center viewing fields. As soon as she had realized what she was seeing, she knew that Marcus Wells had returned. And she knew what he must have returned *for*. She had no idea what the Human thought he could accomplish with the gem, but there was no other reason for him to come back.

She picked up the Skorahn and stared into its blue depths. The shuttle was flying through a preprogramed flight pattern that circled around a series of towers, low enough that she would not have to worry about anyone on the east wing seeing her unless they were looking very carefully. She laughed at that, but stifled the ghastly sound as the sharp edges of panic grated in her own ears. Taurani would be looking for her, of course. And for more reasons than one.

She looked down at her pale hands, still stained with Eru blood. Iranse had pretended to be her friend, he had stolen his way into her confidences, manipulated her past and her fears, and moved her onto a course that had destroyed her life and everything that had come to mean anything to her.

She could see it now, of course, after it was too late. All of the dark and mysterious motivations Iranse had hinted at were nothing more than illusions, made large by her own fears and preconceptions. Marcus had only been doing his best in what almost any being would find an intolerable situation. And he had been even more alone than she. With Justin forging his false life among the denizens of the city, Marcus had been left alone to come to grips with an almost impossible task.

He had tried, too. What he had done for the Diakk man and his boy had been inspired. It would have saved the boy's life—

Except that Taurani had then killed them both. The Kerie had then pulled her own strings, and tricked her into putting a blade into Marcus's back.

The medallion got heavier around her neck.

If she knew where he was, she would give it back to him. The thought struck her without warning. She had not had any luck with the Skorahn herself, but Marcus had always had an uncanny affinity for Penumbra. The city had responded to him more strongly than it ever had for Uduta Virri, at least. Maybe, if she could have given him the necklace, he could have salvaged something from all of this.

Maybe he could keep Taurani from her as well. She knew better than to think the Ambassador was going to forget her betrayal, or forgive her. It was fear of him, more than anything else, that kept her flying now. The impenetrable, glittering eyes seemed to stare out at her from every shadow. She knew she would see that face for the rest of her life, no matter how this day played out.

She looked down at her hands, at the sticky fluid that drenched her long, agile fingers. Maybe she did not deserve any better than that.

Iphini Bha had never even dreamed of taking another life before that day. But when she realized what was happening, and what Iranse was threatening, something had risen up inside her that she had never experienced before. And when she saw the contempt twist the giant Eru's muzzle, when he had regarded her fear with nothing but cold amusement, whatever it was rising within her had surged forward, and she had lost all control.

The stylus she had carried with her ever since leaving Iwa'Ban had been in her hands, idly flipping from finger to finger. It had been so easy to slightly alter the pattern so that the point emerged from within her suddenly hard fist. It had been even easier to plunge it into his eye.

She had had not thoughts of murder even a moment before. The wild, animalistic desire that had surged up inside her had only wanted to wipe that look off his face. She had succeeded.

Iranse had just enough time for his eyes to widen in shocked surprise before the stylus plunged into his brain. He had stood there, still as a statue, for longer than she would have thought possible, while she crouched, spent, near the door, waiting for him to pull the needle out and come after her. Instead, he had teetered and then slowly toppled over backward, his head cracking against the hard floor, his remaining eye wide and distant.

And then she had run. She thought the Variyar might be making a move for the control center, and he did not want to be there when they arrived. So she had fled. She had run down to the tower's auxiliary docking bay and taken the service shuttle kept there for emergencies.

And she had been flying ever since. Marcus Wells was somewhere in Penumbra, if he was still alive. She figured Angara had probably returned as well. Justin Shaw was probably back also, and maybe even those thrice-damned Thein'ha that had adopted Marcus as their own.

She stared into the middle distance with an empty heart. She had followed the wrong path, and her adopted home was going to pay the price. She had allowed herself to be fooled and manipulated by an evil being, and there was no returning to the safety of her old life. As the realizations crashed down upon her, one after another, she saw the majestic form of Warder Alab Oo'Juto collapse again to the floor, the water of his personal preservation field cascading down around him.

That death, too, was on her head. Just as much as Iranse and every being who had died since Taurani and his thugs had taken over the city, and every being who had died this day, both in the city and above it, as brave people tried to undo her mistake.

Almost without realizing what she was doing, the view through the forward fields tilted and the shuttle came around.

If Marcus was after the Skorahn, he would assume Taurani had it, and was commanding things from the control center in the Red Tower. That is where the battle would be joined in earnest. Given how much strength the Council fleet had been dumping into the city, and how big the Variyar fleet that dropped into the system had been, things around the Tower must be terrible now. But she might be able to get close, land in a nearby tower and cross through the Concourse or one of the smaller bridges, and move up from there.

If she could get Marcus the Skorahn, he might be able to set things right.

She came up over the Ring Wall, planning on skimming across the bronze surface of the central plain to cut the distance to the Tower, when she saw forces arrayed all around Sanctum.

The medallion pulsed against her chest. He was there. Somewhere within that swirling, colorful, violent storm, Marcus was there. She brought the shuttle around and pointed it toward the ancient ship.

As the plain flashed beneath her, she confirmed that the forces surrounding Sanctum were Ntja, mostly in the black armor and uniforms of the Peacemaker fleet. A second force, the towering shapes of heavily armored troopers, were emerging from the Concourse's Ring Wall, sprinting ponderously toward the battle.

She leaned into the controls as if that might give her some advantage, her sudden resolve bringing a grim curl to her lips. The fight was centered around the massive bulbous observation arena at the fore of the old ship. There were two auxiliary docking bays on the flanks; neither of them seemed to have attracted much attention. She saw a few breaching parties tearing into the ancient hull with actinic cutting lasers, their blinding light sending shadows swooping crazily around them.

The first shot that hit her shuttle took her completely by surprise. She had not even considered that the Council army would try to stop her.     They had seemed so fixed on Sanctum, and she so above the distant, silent action, that the threat had not occurred to her at all.

Then the second shot struck, and the shuttle bucked as it lost power. She realized that she would not have to worry about seeing Taurani's face in the shadows for long.

She felt tears on her cheeks, but sat up straighter despite her fear. Her hands clenched into fists within the interface, wrestling with the old ship as it started to list dangerously to the right. She tried to force it back up and away, desperate to escape the claws of vicious light that raked her flanks.

Ahead of her, Sanctum loomed up out of the viewing field. The army seething around it looked like a surging tide of vermin, and she suddenly realized that there was more truth to the random thought than she would have assumed. The galaxy belonged to those vermin, and the masters that held their leashes. The last refuge against that unholy alliance was Penumbra, and she may well have surrendered it to them herself.

The shuttle changed course, bringing its nose in line with the rear of Sanctum's bridge section. She did not need to survive the impending crash, only the Skorahn did. If Marcus Wells was here, there had to be a reason. The administrator needed the Skorahn, no matter what else transpired.

She wanted to see images of Iwa'Ban rise up in her mind as she leaned into the coming impact. She wanted one last glimpse of her homeworld, scars and all, before she died. But all she saw was the pale purple face of Iranse, glaring at her through a single eye, and then the black, fathomless eyes of Alab Oo'Juto. He looked sadly at her as her own eyes widened. Then there was a jarring shock, a distant, rending crash, and a heavy blackness rose up to engulf her.

*****

There were several breaches in the vast expanse of crystalline window now, the shimmer of emergency integrity fields distorting what lay beyond. The surviving Variyar crouched low at their own self-made firing ports, keeping the overwhelming forces of the Council at bay for as long as they could. Already several were stretched out on the floor where they had fallen, the grievous wounds of galactic energy weapons horrifically, obviously fatal.

Marcus found that even in moments of mortal stress, his brain lacked the discipline to focus completely. He wondered why the city allowed the Variyar weapons to fire without locking them down with a suppression field? There must be a very strange, convoluted logic behind when Penumbra decided its inhabitants required its help in saving them from themselves.

"Small craft incoming!" A rough voice, he couldn't have said whose, shouted. It snapped him back to the despondent moment, and he looked up from where he had sunk down against the wall in the Alcove, waiting for the inevitable.

"Ours or theirs?" His mind still refused to grasp many elements of their situation. One of them, he was learning, was that the concepts of 'us' and 'them' was much harder to differentiate when you were one of only two Humans within thousands upon thousands of light years, and everyone between you and Earth seemed to hate you.

"Civilian model." One of the Variyar had donned his helmet, which must have offered many more enhancements to his senses than even the nanite technology that infested his own brain. "Older model, well-maintained."

Well, at least it probably wasn't armed. He had been wondering when the Ntja would get around to bringing airpower to bear.

"Changing course." The reports came in a passionless monotone. "It appeared to be skimming the fields, heading back to the Red Tower. It is now coming around, heading in this direction."

Well, that was it, then. Even if it didn't have weapons, they could crash the thing into Sanctum and breach the wall anywhere along the perimeter. There were only seven Variyar holding the line against them now; no way they could hold a full breach.

"It is taking fire from the Ntja!" Others were peering up from behind cover as the incoming fire slacked off, sheets of plasma rising up to meet the boxy, ungainly-looking craft that hove gracelessly into view.

He could see it now; the old standby shuttle from the administrator's private bay. It was trailing sparks and venting air in glittering plumes that flash-froze in fan-shaped swathes of ice along the old hull. Even as he watched, the shuttle took several more hits, staggering in its flight as its trajectory was tortured by the battering. The craft followed an erratic course toward Sanctum as the pilot struggled to keep it in line with the ancient starship. It soon became clear that he intended to bring it right up against the forward observation bubble.

Did he intend to land out there, in front of the entire enemy army? Marcus looked down at the bronze surface outside Sanctum. The Ntja were pressing in close on all sides, offering very little room for such an effort.

But the shuttle was not slowing its approach, nor was it slewing around for a landing. Its nose continued to point directly at Sanctum, heading for the rear of the bridge area where the dome's wall of windows met with the metal bulkheads and blast doors that led to the rest of the ancient ship.

His eyes went wide as he realized the shuttle was still not slowing down. It continued to take a beating from the Ntja arrayed outside, withering away under the fire as he watched.

"Take cover!" The piping voice of Khet Nhan was huge in the silence that had descended as they all stood at their stations to watch the drama outside unfold.

The silence was shattered when the enormous bulk of the service shuttle, now lacking even a pretext at directed flight, crashed through the crystalline matrix that had kept the vacuum at bay for longer than any Galactic race could remember.

Marcus dove down beneath the lip of the sunken Alcove. From the corner of his eyes he saw the others crouching behind control consoles or minute contours in the floor for what little cover they could find.

Sihn Ve'Yan was blasted off her feet by the concussion of the shuttle's impact, smashing into a Variyar warrior who had raised his hands to catch her. They both crashed to the deck, rolling with the vicious momentum.

For a moment, Marcus's ears whined with a painful change in air pressure. A geyser of atmosphere flashed out from the ragged wound in the crystal windows and metal pains before a large emergency containment field flashed into existence, halting the flood of air, and distant, unseen fans churned into life to replace what been lost.

It was a testament to the Variyar that they were back against their barriers, weapons once again blasting away, before the smoke had even begun to rise from the wreckage. The Ntja were still holding back, not approaching despite all their advantages. Marcus was no student of military tactics, but he didn't think it boded well that the enemy, given their clearly superior position, were waiting for something more before they moved.

Looking up over the lip of the Alcove's pit, Marcus watched Khet Nhan rise shakily to his feet, dusting off his white robes, and pull the metal rod from his sash. The thing shivered and grew into a long staff of the same thickness. The little mystic never took his red eyes off the crumpled, smoking wreck.

Sihn Ve'Yan limped up behind her master, favoring one leg, her arm curled up at her side. Her enmity and disappointment was obviously not enough to drive her from her place at Nhan's side. She, too, was staring at the ship, moving forward in a crouch that promised more mayhem than a dozen guns or swords.

Marcus did not stir. His ears were ringing with the concussive blast of the ship's crash, his eyes were squinting against an accumulation of acrid smoke Sanctum's systems seemed incapable of clearing away. The flashes of light from his defenders' weapons lit up the drifting banks of stinging fog, giving the whole scene a surreal, hellish cast.

As Nhan and Ve'Yan disappeared into a massive, jagged rent in the shuttle's side, Marcus stayed where he was. He couldn't imagine who would have wanted to reach Sanctum so badly they would brave the gauntlet of Ntja soldiers outside only to crash here. He was afraid who he might find behind the controls. He was more afraid of what state they might be in.

Khet Nhan staggered back out of the shuttle with none of his usual grace, his little eyes wide. He cast around the chamber, eyes blinking, and then settled on Marcus. He was leaning on his metal staff as he gestured for Marcus to join him with one paw.

When Marcus didn't move, Nhan snapped, and gave one more violent gesture. "Now, Administrator!"

Marcus was fairly sure he shouldn't be spoken to like that, but eased out of his cover and walked hesitantly toward the little Goagoi mystic.

Nhan huffed, shook his head, and rushed at him, taking one sleeve in a strong grip. "Quickly, Administrator, before it's too late."

Marcus found himself dragged down the tiered steps of the ancient bridge to where the service shuttle lay in a cradle of buckled decking and a nest of window frame and wires.

"Hurry. *Hurry!*" Somehow, Nhan was behind him, pushing him through the jagged hole and into the dark core compartment of the shuttle.

"Forward. *Now!*" The pushing continued, and he almost spun around to growl at the little creature, until he saw the thin fluid splashed all over the forward bulkheads, and the pale shape huddled within the restraints of the command couch. Sihn Ve'Yan crouched down beside the couch, and her eyes flicked from the still form to Marcus, as if waiting for some violent reaction.

The lighting was poor, reminding him uncomfortably of the interior of his own Variyar transport after their crash. But there was something about the diminutive form he saw there that narrowed his eyes. The head, tilted away from him, was hairless and pale. As his vision adjusted to the dim lighting, he saw the tracery of black lines, like cracks in fine porcelain, and his heart froze into a painful lump in his chest. He stopped moving, staring at the back of her head, and nothing Nhan did would drag him closer.

At last, the little mystic turned with an exasperated sigh. "You must finish this journey. You must go now!"

Marcus shook his head, unable to speak. At the little Thien'ha's voice, though, the form in the couch stirred slightly, and her head tilted listlessly to the side. Wide, pale blue eyes searched the shadows as her hands, curled in her lap like little claws, twitched aimlessly.

The pale, thin lips moved but no sound emerged. There was no doubting the excruciating pain in those eyes.

"It's okay." Ve'Yan, her voice almost unrecognizable in its tenderness, reached out and rested one hand on the figure's shoulder. "He is coming."

Marcus felt his head shaking. The cold lump in his chest was rising, filling his throat, and he didn't know if he was going to vomit or scream.

Turning her head had clearly been the most she could do, and she settled back into the couch with a soft, hissing sigh. Still, the hands twitched.

Ve'Yan stood and looked at him coldly. "There is little enough you can do now, Human. The cycle is nearly complete."

He wanted to shout at her, to curse her God damned cycles. Didn't she remember what this traitor had done to them all? What she had done to the dolphin that was supposed to be their savior? Until he had met Angara Ksaka, Marcus had lived an extremely normal life, his understanding of the term 'betrayal' blessedly mundane. He was finding that your first, much like your first love, was a deep, impactful experience you were not likely to forget. He shook his head again.

Ve'Yan sneered at him, and then looked down at the being that had been her master with a look no less filled with contempt. "And so it falls to you, *master.*" Marcus cringed from the venom she managed to pack into that word. She gestured at the still body with a graceful hand. "Complete your apostasy, and walk the rest of your life alone."

Marcus could not believe that now, of all times, he was once again caught between the two fanatics and whatever internal discord they were struggling with. The tension was a nearly-visible force stretching between the two as a heavy silence almost seemed to drown out the sounds of battle beyond the fractured hull.

"Please." The voice was nearly lost in that imperative stillness. It was weak and breathy, and in its near-silence, it managed to convey an entire world of pain.

Ve'Yan's eyes softened, and the look she then shot at both Nhan and Marcus was almost pleading.

Marcus felt a small hand slip into his own and almost jerked away, but he stayed still, looking down at the little master.

"There is no more harm to be done here, Marcus Wells." The soft white robes shuffled as the creature shrugged. "And perhaps a little good?"

He shook his head again, but there was no conviction in it. She seemed to be growing smaller as he watched, her body diminishing before his eyes. He looked down again at Khet Nhan. The little creature did not speak, but his soulful red eyes were eloquent.

Marcus closed his own eyes and took a deep breath, almost coughing on air thick with smoke and worse. He opened them and tried to force himself to move forward. His legs refused the order.

She had betrayed him! She had betrayed them all! He didn't know why she had flown through the enemy fleet, the very enemy she had handed them to with her treachery, and a very large part of him didn't care. But Nhan was right. There was very little she could do now.

He forced himself to move forward, easing past a silent Sihn Ve'Yan, to stand at last in front the wounded, dying, Iphini Bha.

She was torn and bleeding, her porcelain skin almost white. Her body was bent into a painful, unnatural pose, curled around those twitching hands, and her eyes were larger and more luminous than ever.

She tried to talk, but then shuddered in a pain-wracked cough. There was thin blood on her lips, and running down from one small nostril. She tried to talk again, her chest fluttering, and again collapsed into a twisted, hunched misery. He saw that there were tears coursing down her cheeks, mingling with the blood, and the lump in his throat receded just a little.

"Hello, Iphini." He didn't know what else to say, but that seemed pathetic as soon as he heard himself. She almost smiled, though, and so it seemed like it might have been enough.

She tried to speak again, and this time got a few words out, but for some reason they were registering as nothing but gibberish to him, his nanite enhancements failing him with that strange tickle he got in his inner ear sometimes when they were unable to translate something.

He shook his head. "I don't know what you're trying to say."

Suddenly, the desire to hear her words was almost overwhelming. He felt like she was trying to communicate to him from across some vast gulf of understanding and enlightenment. He *needed* to know what she was trying to say. She subsided back into the couch again, and desperation began to thaw the anger in his chest.

"I can't understand what she's trying to say!" He looked over at Khet Nhan in fear.

The little creature moved up beside him and crouched down next to the wrenched and twisted couch. He muttered something to the Iwa'Bantu girl, caressing her smooth head with one gentle paw. She leaned into his touch, the big eyes closing. Her lips moved, but even as close as he was, Marcus couldn't hear a sound.

Nhan nodded, and then looked up at Marcus. "She sees that her cycle is ending. She passes knowing that she strayed from her path." He looked away, not able to meet Marcus's eyes. "She dies fully aware of her betrayal."

One twisted hand floated up to snag the collar of the little mystic's robe and drag him back down, and again her chest fluttered, her lips trembled, moving very little, and then she settled back again, one hand curled up higher on her chest.

Nhan's eyes looked up again at Marcus. "She came here to set things right."

The hand fumbled at the neck of her tunic, and a gleaming flash of sapphire glittered in the dust-laden shaft of light.

Marcus felt his heart leap into his throat again, but this time it seemed to pulse there, threatening to choke him, and there was no anger or fear in it.

Her eyes, barely slits now, found him out, and she lifted the familiar medallion just about an inch off her chest before it fell back, her strength exhausted.

The medallion. The Skorahn. The only thing that offered them even a hint of hope.

There was a cold, distant part of his mind that refused even now to believe what he was seeing. That medallion was around Khuboda Taurani's neck, he knew. He knew it with all of the certainty of dread. There was no way that egomaniacal bastard would have ever let the mysterious Skorahn out of his grasp.

He knew that as he knew his own name.

Iphini Bha was staring up at him, a wordless message that he could not read in her eyes. He stared down at her, but his mind was twisting around his disbelief and fear of further betrayal.

But what if Taurani didn't know the true power of the medallion? Marcus tried to put himself back to when almost every entity in the known galaxy assumed the position of administrator was a pointless, powerless sinecure. The officeholder was nothing more than a living battery for the city's systems.

What if Taurani still believed that? What if the Ambassador still believed that the Skorahn was nothing more than the degraded symbol of an impotent office?

Marcus had made a classic mistake, and he could hear that younger version of himself scolding him in harsh, unforgiving tones.

Taurani had not learned the lessons he and his friends had learned. Not until it was too late, apparently.

Marcus lowered himself to one knee. Part of him wanted to take the medallion now and run for the wall in the Alcove. But he forced himself to rest his hand upon hers instead. "I understand, Iphini." He didn't, not really, but he no longer doubted the sincerity of her regret. There would be plenty of time to ponder Bha's motives and actions later if they all survived.

For now, for just a moment, he knew that this little woman deserved for him to stand beside her, one last time.

He was shocked, in truth, to realize that he *did* forgive her. It is hard, he learned, to look into the dying eyes of a truly penitent being and not be moved to compassion, no matter what the crime.

"It's alright, Iphini. It's going to be alright." He placed one hand on the side of her head.

She shook her head, new tears welling up in her eyes and spilling down. Her claw-like hand grasped the medallion and pulled at it, yanking down and away.

Marcus's heart lurched as he saw the desperation and fear in her eyes, and he put one hand over hers.

"No! It's okay, Iphini. I'm here. I have it. I'll get it." He didn't know what to tell her to ease her mind in these last, desperate moments. He would have told her anything at that point, if he thought it might soothe her pain.

But she continued to thrash weakly against him, pulling at the medallion's chain beneath his hand. Finally, deciding he was going to cause her more pain by fighting her, he nodded and helped her to move it over her head. She thrust it at him, into his hands, and then with an incredible effort of will, threw her other hand on top of his.

She rose with a jerking motion, her eyes boring into his. Beneath the glossy sheen of tears they were bright, laser-focused. Their soft blue was blended now with blood flooding slowly into the sclera.

She trembled beneath him, her hands gripping his with a strength he never would have thought possible. Sitting up, shaking, she stared into his eyes and spoke two words, her voice vibrating with emotion and pain and effort.

"So … sorry …"

She settled back into the couch then, her eyes never leaving his, but her hairless brows twitched, begging again for forgiveness. Then her body relaxed, the eyes seemed to shift focus slightly, looking off over his left shoulder, and she was gone.

Marcus sat there for what seemed like a long time, staring into the dead woman's face. The medallion was warm and heavy in his hands, but he could not pull himself away.

What had led her down such a dark and lonesome path? Why had she betrayed them, only to sacrifice herself like this now?

He was lost in that hopeless, never-ending loop of speculation when a cry went up among the Variyar outside the crumpled shuttle. He couldn't make out the words, but the warriors seemed agitated.

He turned to where Ve'Yan and Nhan were standing by the large tear in the hull. "What are they saying?"

Ve'Yan shook her head, her face a mask, but Nhan ducked out, shouted something, and then was moving back in before the reply was finished. His eyes were round with fear.

"There's another one coming. We need to get you to that wall."

# Chapter 28

The view through the piloting field was shifting alarmingly, but she ignored it, knowing that her instincts were equal to the task. It was a minor annoyance, however, and one she would have expected to be addressed by the usually detail-conscious Council techs.

It was only when she shifted her eyes from the viewing field to the bloody falchion on the seat beside her that she realized it was her eyes at fault, not the equipment. She shook it off, wiped the moisture from her face, and focused on the moment at hand.

The Ntja shuttle handled nothing like her beloved *Na'uka*, but it was armed, and had the benefit of being available while her own ship was busy on a much more important mission. This chunky little bitch had been docked off to the side, refueling in case the Ntja needed to make an emergency trip out to the fleet. It was fully loaded with ordnance, in accordance with Peacemaker combat doctrine. She had made sure before she ignited the engines.

She had no intention of flying over the whoreson bastards without dropping a little pain on them as she went by.

She shook her head again. There was no point in worrying at the moment. She was slipping through the towers, keeping low to avoid the city's defenses and the notice of the Council forces. Somewhere above her, she knew, K'hzan was fighting for his life, and for his precious fleet. And the Ntja fleet was going to be coming back around to lock Penumbra down tight as soon as they were done with him.

There was almost nothing left for her to do. Taurani was racing toward Sanctum, where she knew Marcus and the others had headed after their crash. She did not think there was going to be anything she could do against the Kerie murderer and his thugs, but she could kill as many as possible before the end, and die beside those who had proven to be true companions, against all odds.

Her mouth twisted at the thought. This is exactly why her father had exiled her. This last stand nonsense made no sense. There was nothing to be gained by a pointless, principled death. No good Tigan threw her life away for anything so ephemeral.

The Ntja transport wove through the towers. There was no sign of pursuit to distract her from her thoughts.

Why would Taurani go to Sanctum? Even knowing that Marcus was there, the move made no sense, and was completely out of character. The Ambassador's type never put themselves in danger when there was any other option. They stayed far from the fighting until the last remnants of resistance were wiped clean. Her father would have approved, she realized with another bitter twist of her lips.

She closed her eyes to consult with her implants. The interface with the Ntja technology was not ideal, but she could see ahead of her, the map of the eastern wing of the city dropping away beneath her mind's eye as the flashing icon that marked her own position raced for the end of the Concourse, the Ring Wall forming an arena around the bronze plains and the Sanctuary in their center.

The plains were covered with Council forces, all moving for the ancient ship that had started it all. She opened her eyes again, rubbing the haze from them, and watched the edge approach. She was pushing the old crate for all it was worth, and the featureless gray expanse of the Concourse flashed by beneath her. It made for a marked contrast between the relatively modern construction and the dark bronze of the visible Relic Core. The line was an arc, actually, leaping ahead and away in either direction.

As she soared out onto the plains, she noticed a second wave of attackers swarming toward her friends. They were much taller than the soldiers around them, thicker and squatter-looking; the heavy infantry that had held the primary public docking bay against them during their initial assault.

The Council did not use such heavy shock troopers often or lightly. Their deployment here meant that Taurani intended for his control of the city to be absolute, but brief.

She refused to consider the further ramifications of their presence.

With a thought, she dropped two incendiary bombs off the stubby wings and watched with grim amusement as they tumbled down, small assist drives directing them in the absence of appreciable gravity.

As the two weapons fell, they began to emit a glittering mist, spreading outward in spiraling tubes that traced their trajectories. The heavy infantrymen below scrambled off to either side; trying to avoid what they realized was coming.

Just before each bomb struck the metal of the plain, they erupted in a fountain of chemical fire that ignited the glittering clouds around them despite the complete lack of atmosphere. Flowers of blinding light unfolded behind her, devouring several of the slower Ntja and dashing the rest into low-trajectory flights that ended as they crashed down in slow motion in a wide circle around the points of impact.

A low sound, suspiciously like a snarl, rumbled in her chest and she kicked the shuttle around in a spin so that it was pointing back the way it had come, angling the craft down at the scrambling soldiers. She keyed the cannons in the nose and sent a cascade of glowing plasma bolts into their ranks before bringing the ship spinning back around to orient on Sanctum.

Ahead of her, the core of the Ntja army was now aware of her presence and man-portable heavy weaponry erupted within their ranks. Winding contrails traced through the void as missiles rose up to meet her, and she threw the shuttle into a series of erratic maneuvers that would throw off all but the most tenacious weapons. For those, she saved her nose cannons, again swiveling the ship around on its axis to bring the weapons to bear, shattering the pursuing missiles and then sliding back to face forward once again. She unleashed the nose cannons on the compact formations before her now, keeping them too busy for a second volley.

Her first pass was satisfactory. Two more incendiary weapons blew massive ragged holes in the formations, and the cannons punched through light armor and heavy armor alike. She had no complaints concerning the performance of the Council's hardware beneath her hands.

As she flashed past Sanctum, she was alarmed to see a sizable hole punched through the enormous, bulbous wall of viewing crystal. A containment field formed a thin skin over the hole, but something had obviously crashed through. Something large. She could see movement within, however, and an occasional shot snap out through jury-rigged firing ports, so she knew someone was still alive inside.

Her second pass proved one too many, as a lucky missile strike tore her left wing free to spiral away, forcibly making the case for the futility of her current impulse. There were hundreds upon hundreds of them down there. Probably close to the entire contingent of troopers from the orbiting fleet. One old shuttle was not going to put a dent in a force that size, while sheer numbers would eventually bring her down.

She came back around, pivoting upon her forward vector again to hose her nose cannon back and forth, keeping them down, and then rocketed through the massive hole in the dome. A chaotic scene flashed before her eyes, registering on her senses at an instinctual level.

The old standby shuttle that had been missing from the administrator's executive docking bay was resting in a crater of ancient metal, its hull blasted, twisted, and holed in a thousand places. She kicked her own maneuvering thrusters in, taking up the momentum of her entrance and then spinning down for a fast but controlled landing nearer to the bottom of the tiered deck, where the observation dome came down to meet the floor plating along the old ship's nose.

As she drifted toward her chosen landing site, she saw four Variyar warriors move quickly out of the way, standing back to avoid the wash of her drives. Higher up, back where a ramp led down to the legendary Alcove at the rear of the chamber, she saw the two mystics, a tall figure in black and a shorter one in white, standing together, watching her descend. There was a long bundle wrapped in fabric at their feet. It might be her imagination, or the energy surging through her body, she knew, but something about the way the two figures stood seemed odd, and she reassessed her first impression: they stood near each other, not together. And by them, standing by the Alcove, stood Marcus Wells.

Seeing him brought it all back to her, and her vision blurred once again. She bowed her head down over the interface field as the shuttle settled gently onto its landing jacks. Without looking, her hand reached out and grasped the cold metal of the ugly sword beside her.

*****

Marcus watched the Ntja ship settle down on the big hydraulic-looking legs. Whoever had landed that had done a much better job than Iphini Bha had managed. He had a suspicion who it might be even before the door in the shuttle's flank snapped open and Angara Ksaka dropped out. She was carrying something across one shoulder, but he wasn't paying attention. He wanted to speak with Justin. He wanted the comfort of the only other Human nearby at his side.

But no one else emerged from the shuttle. And as Angara made her way up the tiered flooring, Marcus looked at her again, his eyes narrowing. Had she been *crying*?

Angara Ksaka was as exotic as ever. Her deep purple skin and the contrast of her long, wild mane of white hair were distracting when trying to read her emotions or reactions. Her violet eyes were red, however, and there was moisture on her dark cheeks.

Marcus felt light headed. Nhan reached out to steady him before he even realized he needed it.

"Where's Justin?" He demanded, his tone harsher than he had intended, but he didn't care.

Angara was silent as she closed the distance between them. When she stood before him, she dropped the heavy sword she had been holding, and as he looked down at the weapon he saw that the blade was slick with bright red blood. Something about the situation told him everything he needed to know; it was Human blood. He looked up again, and this time there was no doubting what he saw there. Tears coursed shamelessly down the Tigan woman's face.

Marcus shook his head. The draw to the shimmering blackness was strong. They had only paused at the top of the ramp when they saw the shuttle coming straight for the dome, thinking they might all die before he even got a chance to try. Now, knowing that it was Angara and not more of Taurani's creatures, he wanted to go finish the quest, whatever it might be. He needed to finish it.

But he couldn't turn away.

"Where's Justin." He repeated the words. He wouldn't ask anything more pointed, terrified where it might lead.

Justin had been his best friend for almost his entire life. And now, since they had been kidnapped and dragged out to this insane asylum among the stars, he had also been the only Human in his life for months and months. That had come to mean even more since K'hzan had made his cruel revelations of ancient history.

She remained silent, however, her head moving minutely from side to side.

"Where ... Is ... Justin." He wanted to take her by the shoulders and shake her, even knowing how lethal she was.

But at the same time his mind was whispering to him, reminding him of half a hundred signs he had noticed over the last couple of months. There was something between Angara and Justin, even if they might not know it yet. And so he patted Nhan on the shoulder, stood straighter under his own power, and reached out for the tall woman's arm. He had to know, before they could move on.

"What happened?"

She looked into his eyes for a moment, then away. When she spoke, her voice was harsh, full of self-recrimination and pain.

"We had cleared the Red Tower. Taurani was gone. No one was there. We were moving on the executive bay, to follow, when Justin ran ahead." She looked down at the sword and nudged it with her foot. "This was in his belly when I caught up. They had struck him down and moved on to the Variyar without a second thought. I don't even think they realized what they had done."

Since Taurani had taken over Penumbra, it had been his fondest wish to see the only two Humans within it dead. Every one of his servants had lived only to serve that purpose. The irony of his best friend being randomly cut down in the heat of battle was not lost on him.

He nodded. "He's dead."

Her face twisted. "I don't know." She shook her head, and again refused to meet his gaze. "I rushed him back to my ship, dropped him into the medical cist, and had the ship fly him back up to rendezvous with K'hzan's flagship."

Marcus's brain struggled to make sense of the words. "He's not dead?"

It was her turn to glare at him. "I don't know!" She kicked the sword, and he recognized it now as one of the heavy blades the Ntja carried for work beneath a suppression field. "This was *sticking* out of his *belly*!"

Marcus shook his head. None of it mattered now. There was hope, and that was all he was likely to get at the moment, so he needed to turn back to the more important matters at hand.

"I have the Skorahn." He held it up, the sapphire gleaming as it dangled from his fist. He had not put it over his head yet, but even in his hand it conveyed a feeling of warmth. He felt better just holding it. He gestured to the huddled form at the feet of the mystics. "Iphini had it." He felt his own eyes well up at the thought, and shook the tears away, confused and angry at the same time. "I need to go to the door."

She stared in a disbelief that managed, in part at least, to penetrate her grief, and nodded. "Do what you need to do."

He shook his head, almost smiling at that, and cursing himself all the more for it. "I have no idea what I think is going to happen, or if the wall will open, or if there will be anything more than a broom closet on the other side. What I *do* know is that there's nothing else left to do here." He looked down the ramp at the silent door. "Everyone agrees, the city's defenses have never seen off a force the size Taurani's come up with, even with one of their big ships down. I'm terrified that, even with the Skorahn, there's not much we can do."

He was going to feel like a complete asshole if wall didn't open.

Briefly.

With a deep breath, trying to focus on the moment, Marcus walked down the steep ramp, raising the medallion and dropping it over his head.

He immediately fell to his knees in agony. A glaring white light exploded behind his eyes, a screeching whine pierced his ears, and everything around him faded into insignificance beneath the sensory avalanche.

He didn't know how long he huddled there on the ramp, but when he came back to his senses, Angara and Khet Nhan were crouching beside him, holding him upright and speaking to him in hushed whispers.

He didn't pay them any attention. The torrent of light and noise had settled down to a steady stream of information pumping through his mind from some unknown source. Something immense moved in his mind behind his eyes. It stirred sluggishly, as if waking up from a long slumber, but it was enormous nonetheless. And with it, the information rose unbidden and nearly overwhelming, into his mind.

There were nine thousand, five hundred and eighty-three Ntja surging across the bronze plains. One hundred and twenty of them were carrying the weight of heavy infantry armor. There were six shuttles or assault craft in the airspace above them, including a diplomatic shuttle that most probably held Khuboda Taurani, standing off at a distance, observing the ebb and flow of the fighting around the Sanctuary. There were eight hundred and seventy-three other Ntja located in various spots throughout the city.

He focused on those scattered remnants and knew, immediately, where each one was. He knew, as well, that if he closed his eyes he would be able to conjure an image of them in real time.

The Skorahn burned against his chest, the heat palpable through the tunic. He recognized its touch in his mind, but he had never felt it so strongly before. He recognized, also, the echoes of the power he had touched dealing with the blast door into the primary docking bay during their escape. Somehow, through either his own heightened need, their separation, or whatever Taurani had been doing while he had been away, the medallion was establishing its connection to him more strongly than it ever had before. He felt almost as if the thing were staking a claim on his soul.

Beneath the constant murmur of information, anything he could think to wonder about throughout the city, there was a soft whispering that he could not decipher. These whispers seemed to carry even more weight than the initial surge of information that had flattened him, and it sent a chill down his spine.

He looked down at the glowing blue jewel in wonder, and recoiled slightly as he saw that the image cut deep within the gem, the shape that had been swimming toward the surface since he first looked at it, was clear now. It was shaped like an X, with intricate details within each of the bars. There was something at the junction of the two lines, like a swelling or a circle.

Looking at it gave him a headache. He felt like the thing was trying to drive the design into his brain, but it wouldn't fit.

He heard words as if from a great distance. Shaking off the mesmerizing hold of the Skorahn, he looked up to see Angara shouting into his face. As he focused on her, her voice came pounding at him with full volume.

"We need to get moving! They're coming!" She gestured back to her downed shuttle with one glittering knife. When had she drawn her weapons?

But just the mention of the approaching enemy was enough to call them to mind, and he was presented with a mental map of the Sanctuary and the surrounding plains. The Ntja were, indeed, moving forward. They were going to be inundated by alien dog soldiers within a matter of moments if he didn't do something.

He looked from the crazed and fractured windows and the glowing mosaic of containment fields back to the enormous wall that had stood, silent and inviolate at the bottom of the ramp for more thousands of years than anyone could know. When he looked at the wall he felt a faint pull, the medallion drawing gently at his hand.

A calm part of his brain wondered why the detailed map he could conjure up in his head stopped at the slick black wall. He didn't know if that was bad, but he couldn't come up with any reason to think that it was good.

He took several hesitant steps down the ramp into the Alcove, the others huddled together just behind him, and finally stood before the wall. He felt as if he had spent hours staring at the featureless darkness before him, pleading, to no avail, for it to open.

It opened.

At the first thought of the wall opening, the heavy black surface shuddered apart, a fall away like a layer of thick water that washed up either side, forming a doorframe that beckoned silently before them.

Beyond was only darkness. He moved up to the verge of the doorway and tried to pierce the shadows with the force of his will. The map in his mind had not expanded as the door opened, but as he squinted into the gloom, a series of bars overhead began to glow with a soft, green-tinged light.

It was a hall, the walls, floor, and high ceiling made of the same bronze-like material of the plains around them. The lights appeared in a haphazard pattern that made him think not all of the bars were functional. The sheer height of the opening made him wonder who it might have been built for.

"We don't have a choice. We have to follow it." Angara edged past him to stand just inside the doorway. She looked back at him, her dark skin blending into the hollow behind her, her white hair and light eyes giving her the aspect of a ghost, emerging from a tomb on some mysterious, vengeful mission. The sorrow was still there, locked silently behind her eyes, giving her an even more frightening visage.

A blast shook Sanctum, and as he shrank away from the sound and the pressure wave, he was treated with the distinct image of the Council forces blasting a hole in the crystalline wall, taking advantage of the breach Iphini's shuttle had made when it crashed through.

Scores of the soldiers were forming up to flood through as soon as the smoke cleared.

He gasped as he emerged from the vision, nodding his head frantically. "We do."

Ve'Yan spun him around, her face cold and hard. "What's down there? What are we running into?"

"What does it matter?" Angara's exasperation was almost a physical force in the confined space. Behind them, the surviving Variyar got off several shots, accompanied by the gruff screams of their targets, before the air around them took on the heavy, oily feel of a suppression field. He could probably raise it, he realized, but didn't think that would be wise, given how badly they were outnumbered.

"I'd rather not die cornered in some dusty old tunnel like a trapped rodent!" The Diakk woman's face was twisted with rage. "I'd rather not die here at all! But that path has been closed to me!"

The enraged mask turned on master Nhan, who cringed away, unable to meet her eyes.

"We need to get in now." The Ntja were surging toward them with their howling, barking war cries. The Variyar discarded their own rifles, rising to meet them. Angara grabbed Marcus by the arm and pulled him into the tunnel. "We shall keep going until we cannot. There is always time for a hopeless last stand when you have tried everything else first."

Marcus and Angara were several steps into the tunnel now, Khet Nhan near them, looking despondent. Outside, the Variyar were fighting with fatal abandon, the clash of their long blades ringing off the crystal roof high overhead.

"Go!" One of the warriors called over his shoulder, a terrible grin twisting his hard lips. "We will hold them here!"

Sihn Ve'Yan stood between the two groups, looking first at the press of battle at the top of the ramp, then back at the three of them standing in the shadows.

She shook her head, and a hard, cold fire igniting in her eyes. "I will stay with the Variyar."

That brought Nhan out of his silence and he looked up at her with wide, disbelieving eyes. "No! Sihn, you cannot! Do not throw your life away because of my mistakes!" He moved to her, his little hands clenched together in a silent plea.

"Your path must not end here, like this!"

Marcus winced away from the scornful edge to her voice as she snarled her reply. "You held all of my trust, master. I followed you willingly across the galaxy, taking your words to heart and seeing the galaxy through your eyes." She flicked her glance back to Marcus and then away. "You have betrayed everything you have ever taught me. You have broken the cycles through your intervention. You have shattered everything." She shook her head, looking down, a soft disappointment visible for just a moment through the armor of her anger and distress. "I do not wish to live in a cycle rendered worthless through the failure and apostasy of the very being who gifted me with my faith and knowledge."

"No ... no ..." Nhan's head was shaking back and forth as if he was having a fit. "No. Sihn, you can't."

She stood up straighter, her balled fists clenched at her sides. "I can. It is the only choice you have left me."

She turned without another word, and they watched her leap up to the lip of the recessed area, coming around to take the attacking Ntja in the flank. She bounded into the air with a terrifying shriek and her foot lashed out to take one soldier in his massive head. The force shattered an enhancement dome and sent pressurized gas boiling out of the rent in the metal. She was a whirl of fists and feet. She fell deeper into surging battle, and disappeared.

Nhan collapsed, one hand grasping out after his novice as if he could pull her back through sheer force of will.

But she was gone.

"Go!" The Variyar's voice was a growl, exhaustion obvious in it despite the fierce joy of combat.

Angara nodded, pulling Nhan's loose frame in after them, and Marcus turned back to the door. He imagined the doorway surging closed behind them, sealing them into the dimly lit corridor, coming between the onrushing enemy and whatever mystery lay behind them.

Aside from a slight tremor that shook loose a streamer of dust from above, the glistening substance did not move.

"No." Marcus jerked toward them, placing a hand on the cool material of the door. "No!" He tried to imagine it slamming closed with all the power of his mind, but there was no response. The doorway was not going to close again. He knew, without knowing how, that some mechanism deep within the Relic Core had broken, succumbing to the weight of millennia.

"Go!" The battle had pressed the last three Variyar down the ramp, there was no room now for doubt or hesitation.

"Go!" Angara shoved him roughly down the hall and he began to stumble into the darkness. She pulled Nhan after her, and the three of them were soon dashing down the high metal corridors, lights snapping on before them and fading into darkness behind. They moved through a bubble of greenish light, the sounds of deadly battle behind, nothing but cold, mysterious emptiness ahead.

# Chapter 29

The stink of the Ntja soldiers was starting to wear on his nerves. He had been forced to growl more than once, now, to keep them out of his space. He had never been able to abide having his elbow jogged while he was working, and now, as everything fell into place for him, he found it rankled his dignity even more.

With the final dissolution of Marcus Wells and his compatriots, Penumbra would be his, for as long as he wanted it. The last refuge of those too obtuse, archaic, or ignorant to understand the full benefit of living beneath Council rule would be removed. In the scale of the galaxy as a whole it was a small thing, really. Fewer than fifty thousand souls resided within the dusty towers of this outpost of egotism. But as a symbol, its impact was incalculable.

As would be the glory of removing it, once and for all, from the galactic game board.

The Kerie, in the ascendant within the halls of the Galactic Council now for generations, would be the first among equals. They would take their rightful place at the head of the galaxy's sentients, and he, as the being placing the last great keystone upon the successes of his race, would reap the greatest of the rewards. With the treasures even now stored in the holds of Ochiag's command ship, the shape of the galaxy itself was about to shift.

And as there were those races and systems the Kerie knew needed to be more firmly put in their place once the power was there, Khuboda Taurani knew of many of his fellow Kerie who likewise could stand for a reminder of the true order of things.

And all of that would fall into place with the death of a single Human barbarian, here and now.

His viewing field was keyed to Sanctum and the forces raging around it. The ancient ship was laid out beneath him like the subject of a dissection, its bulbous forward observation bridge the distended head of the diseased body. Even from this height, he could see several breaches in the complex of clear panes that made up the enormous forward bulkhead of the chamber.

Ochiag's forces were pressing in close. There had been no visible blaster fire since right after the second shuttle had crashed through the entrance wound of the first. He could admit, now, that the appearance of that second shuttle had been harrowing. Clearly an Ntja attack craft, his soldiers had not fired upon it as it approached. But when it dropped the fire bombs upon his heavy infantry, gunning them down with its chin gun and then swerving back around to attack the main body of his force, it had wreaked havoc with their formations.

He had feared treachery for a moment. He had worked with Laksamara Ochiag before, and had never known the Ntja admiral to betray an ally. But the stakes had never been higher, if the admiral was aware of them, and he dared take nothing for granted. Ochiag most likely did not understand the rewards on offer here today, but still: rivals could be hiding anywhere, and Ochiag might well be a cat's paw for another player that had not yet made their presence known.

But no other space craft had arrived. The lone Ntja shuttle had taken a second run at his main force and then plunged into Sanctum ... admittedly with far more grace than the civilian craft that had crashed through earlier.

He watched as the Ntja swarmed around the forward section of Sanctum like metal filings around an activated electromagnet. They were disappearing through breaches in the crystal wall, but he could not follow their movements within Sanctum, unable to pierce the combination of solar glare off the surviving panes and the shimmering blue of straining containment fields.

"Ambassador, they seem to have breached Sanctum. Shall we approach?" The pilot's voice was muffled by a large enhancement dome emerging from the side of his cheek.

Taurani leaned in to his viewing field. The fighting appeared to be over. Also, he needed to keep in mind that Ntja did not follow blatant cowards. It would do his reputation no harm to be seen heading into the battle before the all clear was officially given.

"Take us down. Land just outside the dome, however. I feel no need to prove points of heroism or superior ship handling today, if you please." The skin around his bright eyes tightened in amusement. Word of his calm demeanor and soft words would enhance his reputation as well. When the time came in Council, it would help to have as many loyal soldiers at his back as possible.

The diplomatic shuttle drifted down over the blackened wreckage and field triage centers that had been hastily thrown up to deal with the casualties of the shuttle's recent attack. His ship made a gentle landing before the devastated exterior shell of Sanctum's observatory, and his detail leapt out to take up defensive positions, their heavy rifles seeking targets as if an entire friendly army had not scoured the site clean only moments before.

He stepped from the shuttle lightly, almost oblivious to the personal field that snapped up over his head. He did not venture into hard vacuum often, but he had done it enough that he felt no fear of the sensation.

Ntja sentries stood at each of the breach points, and they all saluted him as he approached, dipping his head to receive their homage. He had only visited Sanctum once, but he was shocked at the state in which he found it as he stooped to enter through the blasted hole. There were Ntja bodies piled up all along the lower tiers, and almost every ancient command console had been shredded, either by the crashing civilian shuttle or during the fire fight that had engulfed the chamber. One entire side of the huge hall had collapsed, a tangle of metal and glittering crystalline shards burying more bodies of both sides.

The enemy dead had been left where they fell, and he gazed with grim satisfaction upon the twisted and still forms of the giant Variyar warriors. Their armor was distinctly individual, not the comforting, disciplined uniformity of a true military force. Their rifles and tall long blades were scattered across the floor.

One body lay at the head of the dead-end ramp at the back of the bridge chamber, wrapped in sheeting and far too small to be a Variyar. One of his soldiers had torn the wrappings aside, and the serene, still face of Iphini Bha had been revealed. Her big eyes were shut, her skin unmarred by any visible wounds, but pale pink stains seeped through the wrappings.

His stiff mouth twisted. He had envisioned some amazing things he wanted to have done to the Iwa'Bantu woman for all of the annoyance and frustration she had caused. It was some relief that she was dead, however. And there were always more Iwa'Bantu to be found to slake his needs.

He resolved to find one as soon as he returned to the core systems, to celebrate his victories and leaving the benighted rim behind.

"Ambassador, should we follow?" A high-ranking Ntja with many facial enhancement blisters of varying sizes lurched up to him. "We've secured the rest of Sanctum, sir."

Taurani glanced around. He had expected to see Marcus and his minions laid out before him, their bodies torn and cold. There were less than ten Variyar, and the little Iwa'Bantu body, but other than those, the visible dead were all Ntja. They might be beneath the collapsed portion of the dome, he thought.

"What? Follow who? Follow them where?" His innate sense of self-preservation was starting to tingle. If the Human and his allies were not here, safely dead, then where were they? And if Sanctum had been secured, where had they fled?

"The doorway, Ambassador. There is a hall leading downward? It would appear from the placement of the bodies that the final Variyar were guarding that doorway when they fell."

Taurani's body temperature dropped. He whirled, his robes flaring about him, and rushed up the tiers to the highest level. A veritable wall of Ntja bodies surrounded the recessed area known as the Alcove, heaped around the fallen Variyar defenders. They were scattered across the ramp leading down to the bronze wall with its door, as well.

The door that had never been opened.

The door that all records and myths said *could* never be opened.

The door that was open now, nothing but darkness beckoning beyond.

His mouth fell open and he nearly choked on the fear rising in his throat.

He tried to reason with himself. There was no telling what was down there. The city was thousands upon thousands of years old. Anything down there was probably eons past its time of usefulness.

But still … why take any chances?

A cold hand gripped his heart and without a word he strode up to the tiny, shrouded form of Iphini Bha's corpse. He knelt down beside it and wrenched the sheeting away.

Her throat was bare.

"Go! Get in there now! Send the heavy infantry and kill them! Now, before they find anything!" He could hear the edge of fear in his voice. There was nothing in that voice to earn the admiration and loyalty of these soldiers now. But damn them, anyway. They were little more than slaves, in the grand scheme of things. "And bring me back that damned medallion!"

His glittering eyes narrowed as he realized it would all come down to this. It was a race, his Ntja against the Human. And although he had no idea what they were racing *toward*, he had no doubts about one thing: everything for which he had struggled was now at risk.

*****

They followed the narrow passage further and further into the substance of the Relic Core. The lighting continued to follow their descent, reminding her of the service corridors receiving Marcus upon his arrival in Penumbra.

The light here was a soft yellow with just a touch of green, and reminded her of light filtered through the leaves of some great forest high overhead. Even the air seemed clearer here, and there was no sign of the dust and deterioration that had marked the first few paces of the entrance tunnel.

There was no sound of pursuit; the clash of battle had faded away soon after they had turned to run. She could hear her own breathing echoing in her ears, and the others were not much better off.

Master Nhan looked stricken, still leaning against her as if incapable of holding himself upright. His mouth writhed like he was delivering some impassioned harangue, but no sound escaped his lips. She grimaced, hitching up her grip on his arm, and tried to move faster. Having a friend sacrifice herself for you was one thing, and would be hard enough. But the anger and indictment in Sihn Ve'Yan's eyes as she had turned away to throw herself into the battle would haunt Angara for a long time, she knew. And Ve'Yan had not even been directing her hatred at her!

A slight change in the atmosphere around them brought her out of the dark reveries, and she paused to look around them. The walls had darkened, and here they widened out, doubling the width of the corridor. Some irregularities marked the walls ahead, flat objects to either side, and as they approached, she felt her brow furrow in confusion.

They were images. She thought they might be paintings at first, but as she came up even with Marcus, who had stopped to stare, she saw that they appeared to be built into the walls themselves. Mosaics, maybe? Or some kind of sculpture …

But as she slowed to a halt before them, looking more closely, the subjects of the two images were far more interesting than their composition.

In each image, several Humanoid figures stood upon a horizon, looking upward. The details were sparse, and they could have been nearly any of the countless races known as the Children of Man. In each image, the skies over the figures were marred with stylized visions of warfare. There was almost no way that warships in orbit would be visible at this scale, but the basic shapes, and the slashes of beam weapons, were unmistakable.

Marcus turned away from the images to look a mute question at her. She shrugged. "I've never seen anything like it."

And yet there was something about the figures, standing there looking up at the sky, that made her uneasy. Something about the way they stood, or the set of their shoulders, seemed to hint at emotions or intentions that struck her as ominous for reasons she could not articulate.

With a gruff sound, Marcus pushed on down into the gloom. After a moment Angara moved off after him, nudging Nhan before her.

She had seen lights popping off and on for Marcus before, but for some reason this time she felt a growing unease. As each bar overhead faded into luminescence, and as each one faded away into the darkness behind them, she knew they were being watched; that somewhere nearby something was marking their movement. She could not shake off the feeling that whatever entity was following their progress, it was not her friend.

They came to several junctions as they moved. Each time the lights above all the available corridors would brighten. She had no idea how Marcus was choosing their path, but he hardly hesitated at each intersection, and as soon as he began to move down a new hall, the lights in the side passages dimmed just like those behind them.

Something was guiding the Human, or facilitating his advance. Her head constantly pivoted from side to side as she tried to open all of her senses to their surroundings. The deeper they moved, the heavier the air seemed. The feeling that they were under constant observation would not be shaken, and she checked that her knives were loosened in their sheaths.

Somehow, she knew that she would not be allowed to use her energy weapons within the Relic Core.

Even Khet Nhan was responding to the pressure. He had come out of his depression enough to take an interest in their surroundings, and judging by the way his wide red eyes scanned the shadows around them, he felt no more at his ease here than she did.

They came to several more images on the walls, and in each one Humanoid figures were transposed with fiery depictions of violence and war. And again, as she looked at each image, those figures troubled her. She looked down to Nhan when they passed their fourth set, and saw that the little Thien'ha was fascinated, staring up at the pictures with his mouth open and his eyes wide. She wanted to ask him what he was seeing, but something about the silence around them stopped her from speaking.

Her head jerked up at that thought, and she craned her neck back the way they had come. The silence had suddenly become more brittle, as if it threatened to shatter at any moment. Did she hear pursuit, soft and distant? She thought she could almost hear the clang of metal, the guttural mumblings and yelpings of Ntja soldiers hounding them down into the depths. As she focused, the sounds became louder, more distinct. It was easy to forget, here in the cool darkness, that they were fleeing from crushing defeat and certain death.

"Come on." Marcus muttered, and moved off. Angara was still looking behind her, but when the light over her head snapped off, threatening to leave her in darkness, she hurried to catch up.

The sounds behind them, whatever they had been, had disappeared with his words.

Angara found herself moving closer to Marcus as they descended, and noticed that Nhan was doing the same. Whatever she sensed pressing in around them, he obviously felt something similar.

Marcus, however, continued to move with a purpose he did not share with them. His footsteps were clear, echoing dully off distant, unseen walls. If anything, he was moving faster now than when they first braved the hall behind the mysterious door. He was walking as if driven forward by some force she could not feel.

Unless it was the force she felt all around her, watching them from the shadows.

She was ready to scream by the time the corridor opened out into a wide chamber around them. It seemed to emerge from the darkness as lights pulsed into life along the ceiling and embedded within support columns standing out from the walls. A vibration shook the air; a sound just beneath her ability to hear, or a pulsating power just out of sight. It did nothing for her peace of mind, and she wondered if the others sensed it too.

The chamber was empty, the walls featureless dark metal except for the raised pillars and the glowing beams within. Between each pair of columns was a large mosaic, similar to the others except in scale and scope. Each of these portrayed enormous crowds of figures, and in each, a lowering sky threatened them with bolts of brilliant lightning. She felt like there was some symbolism at work that was beyond her understanding, but she could not pull her gaze away from the figures themselves, who still filled her with a formless dread.

It was not a huge room, probably similar in size to the control center in the distant Red Tower. The high-ceilinged hallway ended here, and a big, heavy-looking door sealed the only visible exit on the far wall. Marcus moved forward more slowly now, as if in a trance, and barely spared a glance to any of the images as he stalked past. He walked to the door set into the center of the opposite wall, and when it failed to open for him, he stopped, staring up at it like a small, disappointed child.

"Won't it open?" Khet Nhan moved to Marcus's side, staring at the door as well; the weight of mystery and menace drawing him out of his melancholy.

Marcus looked down at the little mystic, his head jerking from side to side. "No."

Angara glanced back the way they had come. Was she imagining those sounds again? Then she joined them in the center of the strange room. "There's got to be some way to open it. It would not have brought you this far with no way to move forward."

He looked at her, a dimple deepening the shadows of one stubbled cheek. "It?"

She shrugged, gesturing toward the glowing medallion on his chest. "I'm assuming the Skorahn is to thank for our continuing escape?"

He looked down as if he had forgotten the gem. The design floating just beneath the surface was darker than it had been, the 'X' more pronounced. She had no idea what it might be, but there was no doubt that the image was resolving.

The feeling that gave her was a stark reminder of the sensation she had, looking at the mosaics.

Marcus lifted the glowing medallion with one hand, looking deeper into the stone. Then he looked back at her, down to Khet Nhan, and then back to the door. He moved toward it with hesitant steps as if expecting it to open at any moment. It did not, and when he finally reached the door, he looked back at them, then turned, dropped the medallion back onto his chest, and placed both of his hands upon the door. He lowered his head a few degrees, and his shoulders rolled as he began to push slightly upon the metal.

Without a sound, it slid up into the low ceiling.

A brighter light, still with the same greenish cast, fell into the small antechamber where they stood. The sensation of power grew, the low rumble becoming more distinct. Marcus lowered his hands, straightened, and then stepped into the new room without looking back.

Angara felt herself being drawn forward, and decided not to fight it. Nhan moved forward beside her. Whatever happened to them in this mysterious chamber deep beneath the surface of Penumbra, at least she would not be alone.

*****

After the dim lighting in the corridor, Marcus wanted to squint as he peered into this new chamber. Whatever had been pulling him along through the halls had died away when he had entered the antechamber outside, but now that he had reached out once again to whatever it was, the feeling had surged with the opening of this door; this door that he felt certain in his bones was the last.

The room on the other side of the door was much larger. The ceiling soared up into shadows, and he could not have said with any certainty what the source of the light might be. Enormous shapes hung down from above, with pipes, tubes and wires dangling farther still. Three gigantic pillars rose up from the floor and joined the shapes in the dark. Wide, softly glowing bars of green light providing the only illumination to those upper areas.

There was a heavy feeling to the cool air, as if everything was vibrating. A deep thrum of power dominated it all, almost too potent to experience on a conscious level. The air was cool and fresh, nothing like the musty closeness he had anticipated. He felt like the chamber existed on more than one level; there was the empty, quiet room he occupied, but there was also a bustling, surging power present just below the surface.

The walls were a metal honeycomb of large, spherical hollows that reminded him of viewing fields, now shadowy and dark. Between each set of hollows was a deep alcove buried in shadow, and within those shadows loomed enormous Humanoid figures that seemed to watch them from the darkness. There was no other ornamentation, no mosaics or other statues; only those huge sculptures, standing guard across the long, lost millennia.

He shook himself and went back to the hollows. As he looked at them he saw a sort of sense to the layout of the room, separated into distinct areas by the placement of the fields and the shapes hanging from above. There seemed to be an open space before each cluster of hollows, and the image of a group of beings standing in that space, watching images flicker within the hollows, flashed in his mind.

In the center of the room a series of metal steps led up to a platform about five feet off the ground. More pipes and hoses were gathered around the sides of the platform, feeding into it and down into the floor. A few of them dropped down from the ceiling, connecting the platform to the mysteries above. And upon the platform itself was the only piece of recognizable furniture in the entire chamber. An elaborate metal seat was placed there, umbilicals dangling from it and connecting to the platform itself.

It was a massive chair, more than eight feet tall and four feet wide. The back swept up into a leaf shape that housed a huge jade plaque marked with a symbol that at first did not register in his mind. He stared at it, his eyes narrowing, and a shiver shot through his body as his blood ran cold with sudden recognition.

Two stylized swords crossed before what might have been a rounded helmet, tilted downward as it regarded the viewer with enigmatic, empty eyes.

He grabbed the medallion and held it up. The symbol was there, as clear as if it had been there all along. The swords, the helmet, all sharply defined and unmistakable.

"They're the same." Angara murmured, looking over his shoulder and then back up at the colossal seat.

"The same." Nhan appeared to agree, but it was hard to tell exactly what he was talking about as he stood at the base of the platform, his shoulders slumped and his eyes wide, staring up at the green plaque high above him.

Marcus shook it off and looked around again. There were flickering lights here or there around the chamber, and the thrum deep in the air definitely gave the sense of potential power permeating the room. But other than those lights and the presence of the cool, clean air, nothing seemed to have acknowledged their presence in any way.

Angara moved away to pace along the edges of the room, looking up into the hollows, while Nhan remained, standing stock still at the bottom of the dais.

No matter what he did or thought, there was no response from the vast room. His eyes kept drifting back to the giant chair, but then he would turn away, shaking his head. Something about the thing was weighing heavily on his mind, and he was developing a desperate desire not to sit on it.

Angara, having circled the big chamber and returned to the wide door, stopped, her head cocked toward the outer room, and then turned to him.

"I think they're coming, Marcus." Her face was calm considering the implications of her words. If they were caught down here, helpless and alone, there was no way they would survive to see the surface again. Taurani would never give them another chance to escape.

He went to the door and peered out into the shaded exterior room. He wasn't sure if the thrumming in the air was stronger than it had been, but it was definitely keeping him from differentiating any sounds that might be coming at them from down the long metallic corridors. In fact, as Angara turned to speak to him, he found that he had to concentrate to hear even her, standing by his side.

"I'm sorry, what?" He tried to force his attention through the thick air, but it was getting harder and harder.

She gave him an exasperated look and shook her head, but repeated what she had said. "We need to do something, Marcus." She gestured to the room around them. "This is a control center of some kind, like the one in the Red Tower. Can you not get any of this equipment to respond? It does not appear to lack for power."

He shook his head, his own eyes raking across the hollows in the walls again. "I'm not getting any sense of connection with anything here. But there's something…"

Nhan shook himself out of his trance and lifted his voice to be heard over the deep humming. "You know what you have to do, Marcus Wells. You know where you must go." He gestured up to the chair. "Hesitate now and we are all lost."

The haunted look in his eyes that had faded during their descent was back. "Our path narrows, our choices are gone." He pointed up the stepped dais. "All of our actions and choices have led to this. You must take your rightful place."

He shook his head, the dread rising. "No." His head vibrated back and forth. "Not me. Why not one of you?"

Angara's eyes were narrow as she looked back at the little mystic, and then she stalked past him, up onto the dais, and stood before the chair itself. Whatever she saw there stopped her, and she stood, elbows slightly bent as if ready to fight, staring at the seat itself.

Her lithe body seemed almost clumsy as she turned to look down at Marcus. "It needs to be you." She spoke as if in a trance, or emerging from a sudden and profound realization.

"Why, because of the Skorahn?" He slipped it over his head, willing to do anything to avoid taking the chair. "Here, take it!" He held it up, dangling from its chain and taking on a richer sapphire flare from the sourceless green illumination all around. "I don't want it! Take it, sit your ass on the damned throne, and let's get out of here!"

She stared at him, a strange sorrow shadowing her eyes. He looked at Nhan, and saw the sadness in his eyes as well.

"It cannot be us, Marcus." She shook her head, gesturing around them, then back to the antechamber. "This does not belong to us. It does not belong to any of us. It belongs to you."

The words made no sense. Even as the Administrator of Penumbra, he didn't own any part of the city. Hell, he didn't own *anything*! He shook his head, a cloud rising up in his mind that shadowed the implications of her words.

"Please." He begged her, his voice soft. The medallion fell as he lowered his arm. "I don't want to."

"You must, Marcus." Nhan was beside him, guiding him gently to the dais. "There is no one else. This journey is yours and yours alone."

He couldn't remember going up the steps, but suddenly he was standing taller than he remembered, looking down at the shadowy shapes around him. The chair was even larger standing before it, and as he looked down, he saw that the size had been misleading. Clearly crafted into the material of the chair, hidden within the recess for a titanic host, was a shape intended to sit a single being. A single, averaged-sized Human being. It shouldn't have meant anything. There were countless races he had seen in his time in Penumbra that would have fit equally well in the seat; including all the various Children of Man.

The Children of Man. They would fit in that seat. But it was not meant for them. The cloud in his mind parted completely, and his own eyes widened. The chair was not meant for the Children of Man, or for any of the other myriad species who had risen to dominance across the galaxy. It was meant for Man. And Man alone.

Amidst the buffeting storm of grief, fear, and anger, a smile curved the corners of his lips.

Angara noticed and her brows dropped. "Why do you smile now?"

He shook his head, not even wanting to voice the thought that had intruded upon this solemn, terrifying moment. But he couldn't help it.

"All the shit I've been getting from all of you since before you even dragged me here … Every snide comment, dark look, and condescending smile … and you assholes have been squatting in my back yard for how many thousands of years?"

She recoiled a little at the venom in his voice, but then her eyes narrowed, she settled back into a more relaxed posture, and nodded. She might have even smiled a little smile, but he wasn't paying enough attention to see.

He was staring at the chair again. "So, what we're basically saying is that Humans built the Relic Core thousands upon thousands of years ago, and then abandoned it. Penumbra was raised up around it sometime between then and now, and here we are, being chased by an army of dog aliens howling for our blood, and it all comes down to me sitting in this chair and hoping that something happens to save us all?"

She nodded slightly. "It would appear so."

The fear was a physical presence freezing his limbs into immobility. The chair loomed over him, the strange symbol seeming to mock him with its silence. But, even if no one had followed them down into the Core yet, they would be soon. And there was nothing that any of them could do to survive their arrival when they came.

They had killed Iphini Bha, they had probably killed Sihn Ve'Yan. And Angara obviously thought they had killed Justin. Justin, his best friend, who had stood beside him through most of his adult life, and been there for him in every moment of need. Justin, who he had failed, running instead to Sanctum following some strange siren's call he couldn't have explained if he had tried.

The siren's call that had led him to this moment.

He was shaking as he forced his body to take a step toward the chair. The tremors grew worse with the next step. The next was nearly impossible as his muscles locked in terror against his obvious intentions.

But they had killed Justin. They had destroyed every good thing he had tried to accomplish.

And he would be damned if he was going to let them kill *him* before he found out what he had been running toward all this time.

He forced his body to turn, aware of Angara and Nhan staring at him in fascination as his body trembled with effort. He felt as if he had aged a hundred years, as if the shaking was the failure of an infirm body to respond to his simplest commands. But he wrestled control from his own terrified hindbrain and lowered himself into the vast, encompassing seat.

And fell right through it into darkness.

# Chapter 30

He landed on his back, hard. The air rushed from his lungs in a painful gasp and his back and ribs throbbed with sudden, dull pain. But even in the depths of that sting, he knew something more was wrong. He hadn't landed on the hard metal surface of the dais. His mind was confused, sending him mixed signals. It was a wooden floor. It was dirt and grass. It was a hard, flat, smooth surface, cool to the touch.

He touched the ground on either side with his hands. He still wasn't sure what it was.

"Damn, that looked like it hurt!" The voice sounded familiar, and he opened his eyes to peer up at the shape looming over him. Beyond the figure's head he thought he could see the shifting light of sun through leaves, or maybe bright, artificial light. It seemed as unsure as the surface beneath him.

"What?" He tried to talk, but his tortured lungs subjected him to a coughing fit instead, trying to suck air back in despite the insult he had done to them by falling on his back. When he was breathing more easily he repeated, "What?"

"That fall." The voice was soft and kind, and for some reason, that worried him. And that worry further underscored that absence of the paralyzing fear that had gripped him only moments before.

The fear … What had he been afraid of?

"Are you okay?" A gentle hand took his shoulder in a comforting grip. "Can you stand?"

His vision was still blurry, and he couldn't make out the face. Unkempt dark hair, five o'clock shadow along strong, well-defined jawline. He shook his head, trying to sit up. A friendly shoulder settled into his back, steadying him.

"Take it easy, now. That couldn't have felt good." The voice continued to speak in soothing tones. And that difference, rather than any similarity to past experiences, put it all into place.

"What the hell do you care?" He snapped, pushing the helping hand away.

The response, when it came, was not angry. Instead, it sounded almost amused. "Took you long enough."

Marcus pushed himself to his feet, feeling an overwhelming urge to cry foul. Why should he feel such pain in his own fevered fantasy world?

"I'm not in the mood for a lecture or a threat." He looked around them, but the details of their surroundings were fuzzy. He felt as if he was seeing a kaleidoscope impression of shifting foggy, obscured battlements, plywood backings with two by four supports, and distant fields in the corner of his vision, but whenever he turned to look directly at something, there was nothing there at all. They were encircled by gray, featureless fog and only the hints and illusions of surroundings.

His younger self gave him that smile that made him want to punch himself, and shrugged. "Nothing much to lecture you about now, big boy." The smile became more of a smirk, and Marcus felt the first stirrings of the fear he had only recently left behind. At his double's next words, the fear surged up, threatening once again to choke him. "You've gone and made the big move. Now all we can do is wait it out and see what happens."

Marcus felt his hands tighten up into fists. "What the hell is that supposed to mean?"

His younger self shrugged again and paced around him, looking out into the fog as if he was seeing more than the swirling mists. "Something's happening to you, again. Something a lot more profound than last time." He turned to Marcus and reached out to tap him gently on the forehead. "They're *really* messing with *our* brain this time, old son."

Marcus sneered. "Now it's our brain, is it?"

Again, that maddening shrug. "I told you, if you die, I die. Whatever you might want to think, the brain belongs to both of us." He flinched as if something horrific had lunged at him out of the surrounding clouds. "And it's taking a beating."

Marcus paused, his brow furrowed, and tried to feel his mind, to sense whatever the doppelganger was claiming was being done to him, to the real him, *wherever* he was. He couldn't feel anything.

"Who is it this time?" The memories before his fall were dim, he remembered standing with Angara and the little mystic. Had she done something to him again? Last time it had been her fault, he remembered. But at least now he understood her motives from the time before. Now, what would she be doing?

He remembered the big chair, and the fear rose up in his throat again. He remembered sitting down …

"It was that damned chair, wasn't it." It was a statement, not a question, and Marcus didn't even need the other version of himself to respond. He knew it.

"I'd call it more of a throne than a chair, really, but yeah, that'd be my guess." Those familiar dark eyes were peering into his again, looking around as if trying to see something. "You really can't feel a thing? It's crazy, what's being done to us."

He shook his head with exasperation. "No, I can't!" he took a couple steps away to put some distance between them, but it did no good. The fog followed him, and so did the other figure, without apparent effort. He gave up. "Who the hell is doing this to me?"

"To us." The other's voice was smug.

Marcus decided not to rise to the bait. "Who?"

The other shrugged again. "There's something here with us, much more powerful than last time." He walked around, again looking out into the fog. "We've never encountered anything like this. In fact," he tossed over his shoulder, "I don't think anyone has encountered anything like this in a very, very long time."

Marcus thought about that for a moment. "Angara seems to think the Relic Core was built by Humans."

The younger man smiled again. "Well, that's what you've thought for a while now, but you lacked the faith to admit it to yourself." The smile widened. "Or, should I say, *I've* thought it for a while, but *you* wouldn't listen."

Marcus ignored him. "So, what does that mean?"

The smile on the other man's face faded and he grew thoughtful. That was enough to bring the fear right back to full strength. "Well, I've been thinking a lot about everything the big red bastard said at that refueling station. About Humans being the ascendant species in the galaxy, and screwing it all up by being total assholes." His face dismissed the concept with an eloquent expression. "Not that I have any trouble imagining that to be possible, but it doesn't matter much now." He gestured at the fog and turned back to Marcus. "Looks to me like we're inheriting more than just that bad bogeyman rap, now."

Marcus thought about that. "So, you *do* think this is some kind of greater bequest? It's not just going to eat me?"

"I think something very powerful and very old is trying to communicate with us. And I think, for some reason, it's got to change your brain to do so." The smile was back. "I didn't say it wasn't going to eat you, too, however."

Marcus felt the overwhelming urge to slap his younger self again, but before he could make any response, the young familiar face contorted in sudden pain, jerking around again as if he thought someone was sneaking up behind him.

"What's wrong?" He didn't want to care, but honestly, if something was stalking that version of himself in here, it was probably hunting him as well, he just hadn't sensed it yet.

But the other made no reply, a look of confusion and fear swept across his features, his eyes twitched around him one more time, and then he fell backward into the fog.

"Hey!" Marcus scrambled over to follow him down, dropping to one knee to help, but when the swirling mist eddied out of the way, the ground, whatever it was, was bare.

Marcus was alone.

"Hey!" The fog sent back a thin echo of his own voice, but no reply from his other self. "Where'd you go?"

He turned one way, then the other, but nothing but featureless fog lay in every direction.

"*This will do.*"

He spun, looking frantically behind him. He hadn't recognized the voice. It hadn't even really sounded Human. It was heavy and almost painful to hear. There had been a grainy burr to it that sounded almost like an insect's wings. The buzzing seemed to resonate oddly with his implanted enhancements, and he found himself opening and closing his jaw to try and alleviate the annoying pressure.

His double walked out of the fog in front of him, but his movements were all wrong. It was the same face, the same hair, the same body; but the motivating force within it was completely different. The body moved with a flowing, unnatural grace. It regarded him with an empty, enigmatic expression, its eyes dark, hollow depths.

Marcus stared at this new figment his subconscious had apparently thrown up, and his face tightened. He really wasn't in the mood.

"And who are you, now?" He would have hoped his imagination would do better than to just reuse his own face for multiple repressed manifestations.

The figure cocked its eerie head to one side. "*You may as well call me ... Penumbra.*"

He felt like someone had punched him in the stomach, and the fog dropped away without warning. The floor was a smooth, featureless black. And all around them was an infinite vastness, dark and empty.

He realized he was no longer trapped in his own mind. He swallowed. Apparently, wherever they were, when he got nervous, his throat still got dry.

"What do you want?" He was fairly proud he managed to get the words out in an even tone.

The eyes stared at him, lacking any Human expression. "**We do not have much time. I am afraid the enhancements I required took longer than anticipated, and events within the command chamber have proceeded apace.**"

That didn't sound good. "What enhancements? What events? What the hell are you talking about?"

"**Please.**" The word was polite, but the voice didn't carry an ounce of concern. "**I know I must explain myself before we begin.**"

Marcus shook his head. "That's what I'm saying! What the hell are you doing? Who are you? What's going on?"

The other cocked his head as if listening to something Marcus couldn't hear. He wanted to scream again.

"**There is no time.**" The thing wearing his image stepped toward him without warning and reached out to grasp his wrist. There was a sharp shock, a jerking sensation, and then the harrowing sense of falling all over again. He squeezed his eyes shut, bracing himself for the impact –

*****

Marcus was floating in space. He gasped in fear; his emergency rebreathing membrane had not engaged. It was a moment before he realized that despite floating freely in open space, he appeared to be breathing normally, with no troubles at all. Then he looked around and realized that although he was seeing the empty void, he was not, after all, floating in it. He was observing things from some disembodied vantage, as if he were in a dream.

This just got stranger and stranger.

"**There are seventy two hostile contacts within sensor range.**" The strange voice was speaking in his ear, although the being that had called itself Penumbra was no more visible than he was. "**Actions?**"

Marcus looked down and saw the horseshoe shape of Penumbra floating beneath him. The city's towers glittered with lights, looking warm and safe. But between his vantage and that safety swarmed a mass of starships engaged in desperate battle.

K'hzan's forces had clearly not been able to escape, and had been pinned against the city while trying to extricate their comrades who had accompanied him in the assault. The city's defenses were active, and fighting on the right side again, as far as he was concerned. The batteries sent bolts of coherent light up at the larger Council fleet. It was clear, though, that the fire from the city was less effectual than they had hoped. The combined power of the various towers was not enough to penetrate the fields of the larger ships, and the smaller Ntja vessels merely sheltered behind their more massive brethren.

Somehow, he knew that the last time anyone had attacked the city, shield technology had not been so advanced.

He could feel his mouth tightening into a cruel grin, wherever it was. Suddenly, he knew what Penumbra was asking of him. And there was no way it would be asking if it couldn't deliver.

He opened his mouth to give it the order to destroy the Council fleet, but then stopped.

There was no way there were seventy two Ntja ships down there. He focused on them, intending to count them, and suddenly they were separated out of the snarling tangle by glowing lines and icons. There were forty eight Council ships in all. The two large warships at the core of the fleet were pounding the life out of the Variyar, their twenty four smaller ships being forced into a tighter and tighter formation.

Their defensive fields were crazing with each hit, close to giving out. K'hzan was using the larger ships to shelter the smaller ones, their fields overlapping in what he somehow knew was a dangerous, desperate maneuver, but the only gambit the demon-faced alien had open to him.

And then it hit him. God knew how long Penumbra had been dormant, or inoperative, or in whatever inactive state it had been in. To the entity curled within the Relic Core of the city, anything that was not Human was a hostile contact. It was offering him the chance to destroy them all.

"Stop!" He shouted, although he knew there was no need. Wherever he was, he was within Penumbra's power, and there was little doubt that the entity would be able to hear him. "The Variyar are our allies! Don't destroy them!"

There was a hesitation in the strange voice that lasted less than half a heart-beat, but it was nice to know the creature wasn't entirely unflappable. He would have liked nothing more than for the voice to question his statement, but in that he was disappointed.

"*Designate hostile contacts.*"

Marcus shook his head, but then looked down again at the battle unfolding below. The squat, ugly forms of the Ntja ships were easy to spot, and without even thinking about it, all forty eight ships were glowing with individual angry red haloes.

"*Targets designated. Activate defenses?*" He was forced once again to work his jaw against the annoying buzz, but he nodded with savage satisfaction. He had fought his way through an enemy army, been chased down through the tunnels behind the door that had not opened in millennia, and lost too many good friends to bring him to this point. He hoped the results were spectacular.

He had no need to fear.

The image of Penumbra floating below him started to change. The glowing blue cavern at the apex of the Gulf, known as the Furnace for millennia, began to pulse. With each beat, it became brighter, more intense, and Marcus imagined beams of power leaping out and scorching the Ntja. Somewhere, his teeth gritted with expectation.

He was not alone, however, and the Ntja commanders were not blind. The fleet began to drift away from the city as they saw the flaring light. The bolts flashing between the two fleets dropped off as the distance opened up, and Marcus was glad that K'hzan did not pursue. He had been careful to instruct the entity to target only the Council fleet, but the way the Furnace was glowing didn't seem to indicate a fine-tuned, precision weapon. The farther away the Variyar were, the better.

He looked again to the brilliant sapphire glow now streaming from the Furnace, but although it continued to build, there was no obvious offensive capability about the column of light.

And then it flashed out in a coherent bar that stopped in the center of the Gulf. It formed a sphere there that began to burn like a tiny sun, and the Ntja surged even farther away. The smaller ships closed up around the two largest as they moved.

The Variyar, no longer content to merely stand their ground, began to retreat as well, swinging behind the plane of the city, getting the bulk of the Relic Core between their vulnerable ships and the churning sphere of cobalt power.

Marcus focused his attention back on that globe, and saw a deep, cold blackness growing at the center. It started as a small dark knot, but grew quickly, swelling and darkening until its true, black nature was unmistakable. It was clear as he watched that the blue sphere was harnessing the blackness, holding it in check somehow.

As he watched, he felt an awareness far larger than his own all around him. It felt as if the entity calling itself Penumbra was straining forward, eager for the kill. And Marcus shared that taste for vengeance. The more immediate wrongs he had suffered at the hands of Taurani and his dog-faced minions were subsumed into far more ancient grudges. His paltry dead were joined by an endless legion of the fallen, each one screaming out for vengeance and justice.

The sensation overwhelmed him and he felt himself swoon beneath the pounding hatred and passion for revenge. It began to beat within his mind, the rhythm falling quickly into sync with the tempo of the pulsating energy emanating from the Furnace. He felt his eyes open wide in anticipation.

A small window in the churning blue orb released a lash of utter blackness. A branch of vicious dark lightning reached out, visible only as a void before the stars, and caressed several of the nearest Ntja starships. They came apart in an instant. Their protective fields disappeared without a murmur, their hulls disintegrated like sand castles before an incoming tide, and soon they were nothing more than glittering flotsam, expanding off into the void.

A visible panic gripped the survivors, and the tight Ntja formation broke apart as each ship's captain tried to save himself from the terrible wrath of the thing that had lived beneath the city.

Marcus laughed with the heady power of it. Somehow, he knew that no being had ever unleashed the energies he now lashed at his enemies.

But it wasn't enough. More windows opened and more black lightning flashed out. More Ntja ships died. In their panic they grew careless, and collisions began to take almost as heavy a toll as the weapon beneath the city. One of the large battleships was struck several times by its smaller kin, and began to drift downward, back toward the city, as its light flickered with damage to its reactors. It drifted too close, and the lightning kissed it, and it died the same, stately death as its consorts.

Only three of the Ntja ships survived to fall into their wormholes. The sole remaining battleship, bleeding fuel and atmosphere in a glittering wake, was the last to drop away. Only the Variyar were left.

Marcus felt a nearly overwhelming urge to then focus the city's terrible lash upon those usurpers as well. Every slight, every belittling glance, offensive comment, and poisonous sneer came back to him in a rush. The pathetic, envious, wormlike aliens of the city, bloated with self-importance and filled with their own misplaced righteousness, deserved nothing less. His eyes narrowed and he focused on the largest Variyar warship; the one that would be carrying K'hzan Modath, self-styled king of that upstart race.

As he bent his destructive will toward the ship, he tightened one fist, preparing to lash out with the full power of the beast within the city, and then he blinked. His fist. He felt his fist, and his arm, and the rest of his body. He came back to himself in a rush, although his awareness was still locked outside, floating in the cold of space.

He recoiled from what he had nearly done, or allowed the city to do. He ordered the thing in his mind to stand down, gratified that it did so without a fight, and then forced his own mind to settle, clearing the echoes of frustration and anger that had fed the reaction.

He shook his head, casting about one last time to ensure they had scoured the system clean of Council vessels, and then closed his eyes.

The alien presence had withdrawn, but he could still feel it. It was no longer all around him. Now, it was crouched somewhere within his mind, looking through his eyes, and dissatisfied with what it was seeing.

A desperate shout echoed off walls that were somehow far away and close at hand at the same time. He recoiled from the sound, and he felt the awareness within him surge up again.

The brilliant sapphire cage began to dwindle, the darkness within receding, even as his vision of the space around the city faded.

That fleet was not the only danger, he remembered. There was an entire army bearing down upon him, wherever his body was, even now.

The call had been Angara's. He was sure of it.

And the anger within him surged to the fore again, merging with the awareness that had taken up residence behind his eyes, and burning with a dreadful light, fear for his friends adding fuel to the fire.

He felt as if he were falling down a great shaft, leaving the darkness of space behind him, the soft green glow of the command chamber below.

A small part of him knew fear as he fell. Fear not of falling, but of what new power he would find at the bottom.

But a larger portion of his mind hungered for that new power, and the anticipation of further revenge stoked the heat in his chest to an almost painful degree.

*****

Angara had watched as Marcus drop onto the giant seat. When the back of his legs touched the metal, his body had gone rigid, his back arching painfully, and his mouth had opened in what appeared to be a silent scream.

Then he had stopped moving completely.

She was not sure how long he had been like that, because soon after he had stopped moving, the viewing fields had begun to snap to life all around them. She had watched Marcus for several moments, but there was nothing she could do for him. He did not react to her shouts, and when she tried to nudge his body she found him frozen in place as if everything about him, his flesh, his hair, even the fabric of his clothing, had been transmuted into metal.

Nhan would not move, staring at Marcus with something moving deep behind his eyes that might have been hope, or might have been despair.

In the end, she had told the little mystic to watch the Human trapped within the stasis of the chair, and she had gone to see what the viewing fields were showing.

From the top of the dais she had been able to make out the view on the main screen. It showed Penumbra as if seen from above, with the battle raging in its skies as the remaining Variyar, unable to hide from their pursuers, had turned to fight. She watched as shuttles rose toward the fleet amidst the towers of the city, and realized they were trying to recover as many of their people as they could. It was a brave attempt, and entirely Variyar in its sensibilities. They would rather die in battle, standing on the decks of their warships, than hunted down through the corridors of Penumbra.

She took the dais stairs two at a time and walked along the wall of shifting images. Every one carried a different view of the battle overhead, or the army of Ntja soldiers milling about the shattered wreck of Sanctum.

Her eyes flicked back to the main screen, as a flare of blue light dominated the image. The Furnace, that mysterious glowing cavern that had been the object of inquiry and myth for as long as Penumbra had existed, was pulsating with sapphire brightness. Countless beings had investigated the Furnace down through the ages, but the intensity of the fires that burned within had defeated every technology brought against it. The theories concerning the purpose of that fire were as numerous as the grains of sand blowing across the dead planet below. None of them, however, had imagined this.

She had never seen anything like the stream of light that flooded from the Furnace to fill the Gulf. The sphere that formed next looked like a brilliant blue sun, with a darkness beating at its heart. Her eyes widened with the first blast of power. Ntja ships shivered into oblivion at the touch of that black fire, and she realized there was only one thing she could be seeing.

The primordial power that bound the universe itself together had somehow been harnessed by the beings that first made the Relic Core. That energy was now being unleashed with gleeful abandon upon the Galactic Council's Peacemaker fleet, and the warships were simply disintegrating beneath its caress.

No race in the history of the galaxy had been able to harness this dark energy. But somehow, the Humans had done it. Puzzle pieces began to fit into place in her mind. She saw Humans, pushed back to the very brink of defeat, desperately clawing at the boundaries of known science for some technology that would save them. It seemed they had found it, but too late.

She wondered what had happened to those last Humans, huddled here at the end of nowhere while the rest of their race was being pushed back and relocated on that evil little ball of mud and misery they had come to call Earth. Somehow, they had disentangled the secrets of dark energy from the interstices of the universe, but it had been too late. They had never had the opportunity to use this weapon, she knew, or the history of the galaxy would have been very different.

Within the fields before her, the last Ntja ships had made good their desperate escape. There was clearly no defense against the jagged death stabbing out from that brilliant blue ball. The wreckage of nearly their entire fleet floated in the skies above Penumbra, and the Variyar were already moving back into position, redeploying their ships and their recovered warriors to address the force now churning, confused, around Sanctum far above.

She found herself caught within the silence that followed the destruction of the Ntja fleet. Despite the odds, it looked like they were going to be victorious after all. Marcus, somehow, had protected them. His faith in whatever had been drawing him along had been vindicated.

They were saved.

The thought caught in her mind. It was a comforting one. It was a warm realization. And it was utterly wrong.

Distant sounds intruded upon her sudden realization. Heavy, echoing footfalls, muttered orders, and the scrape of metal on metal surged toward her, growing louder and louder with each passing moment.

She turned quickly to Nhan. It would not matter if the Variyar above destroyed the remnants of the Ntja army if enough of them made it down here to kill them before help could arrive.

The little mystic was still standing before the massive chair, staring at Marcus.

Except that Marcus was not there anymore.

A huge, stylized, metal statue sat in Marcus's place. Where Marcus's body had taken up the small, Human-sized recess within the seat, this shape now filled the throne completely. It was not smooth metal, she saw, but rather formed from countless angular grains of steel, each shining in the cool green light.

The face was majestic. It was not Marcus's face, but rather the ideal Human face, strong and regal. Within it were isolated elements that might have been gifted to the Children of Man; the resolve of the Mnymians, the wit of the Namanu, the haughty power of the Subbotines. All of them were somewhere within that stately face, and yet clearly this was the master of them all. It was also completely still.

"What happened?" She cried as she ran back up the steps, forgetting, for the moment, the approaching enemy.

"I don't know." The little creature's voice was soft and hollow, filled with pain and loss. "It looked like dust, sifting upward over his body." He pointed to the statue with a trembling finger. "It only took a moment, and he was gone."

The statue was cold to the touch; grainy and rough. She stared down, completely at a loss, when the first Ntja rushed in, a heavy falchion gripped in both hands, staring around, the whites of its narrow eyes gleaming. When it saw them both standing on the dais, it barked a command to soldiers following behind, and ran at her, heavy weapon raised to strike.

# Chapter 31

Marcus continued to fall into darkness. The sensation of freefall ended abruptly, replaced with a strange, remote sense of cold. He could hear some sort of commotion in the distance, but he felt no urgency toward it. The cold was all-consuming, leaving no room for distractions.

The anger was still there within him; a flicker of warmth in the all-pervasive ice. He wanted nothing more than to destroy, to crush, to kill those who had hurt him, hurt his friends, and denied him his rightful place. He felt, surging beneath his own anger and hatred, a much larger animosity, like a great sea monster gliding through the darkness of the deep ocean of his mind. It was alien to him, different from him. But it was kindred, somehow, and he welcomed its support and vindication of his own black thoughts.

The fact that he could not move only fueled the rage. Something was holding him back from his vengeance, and he threw all of his being against those chains, straining for the freedom to destroy.

He felt something coil behind his eyes, some strange intrusion that was somehow a part of himself and yet different. Whatever it was, he felt a click somewhere in his mind, and his eyes flared open.

His vision had a blueish cast, making everything appear more distant and cold. He was in a vast hall, with mysterious shapes dropping down from a ceiling lost in shadow. Large pillars rose up around him, lost in the gloom overhead. He saw banks of shifting images all along the walls, showing scenes of chaos, devastation, and combat. None of the particulars of any image registered in his mind, but he was nearly overwhelmed with a sense of joy as he saw red-skinned terrors battling dog-faced monstrosities across the city.

Echoes of those battles were playing out right before him, he realized slowly, but instead of the horned Variyar, there was a ferocious girl and a diminutive furry creature battling the hulking, black-clad dogs. She had the purple skin and white hair of one of the slave races, the Tigan, if he was not mistaken. The creature by her side, wielding a nanostaff with something more than adequate skill, looked more like a Goagoi than anything else, in the fluttering robes of some priest or mystic.

He watched as the Tigan girl spun through the howling attackers. A glittering knife sparkled in either hand, and as she danced through them, glistening arcs of vitae sprayed out behind her, and dogs died.

The Goagoi was a blur as he kept the nano-weapon spinning in constant arcs, defending himself from clumsy attacks and then riposting, the weapon changing shape countless times. It was a long staff to accept a blow from one sword, then slid off that blade and lengthened into a delicate war spear to flash out and stab a distant soldier in the face. As it withdrew it became a squat weight of spiked metal that raked another of the enemy across its wrinkled snout, tearing what looked like metal domes affixed to the thing's face free from the flesh.

There were over a dozen dead soldiers heaped on the floor, their blood flowing freely and rendering the footing tricky for the surviving combatants. The purple-skinned Tigan was grinning maniacally as she fought, each blow striking home with a triumphant grunt before she was on to her next victim. The Goagoi, though, did not look to be taking any joy from the battle.

He continued to watch from his high seat as the enemy poured through the wide door, pressing the Tigan and her little ally most sorely. He saw a lucky strike slide through the woman's defenses, her flesh parting in a spray of blood high on her left shoulder. She staggered back, her face a mask of anger. She unwisely launched one knife through the air, taking the lucky assailant in the eye and pitching him back into death. But that left her with only one weapon, and she obviously regretted her decision before her enemy had fallen.

It was a foolish thing to do, to relinquish half of her limited arsenal. But it had been brave as well, and he understood the motivation behind it. His approval, however, would not save her from the odds now terribly stacked against her.

The Goagoi howled as he saw his friend's blood, and the little creature redoubled his own efforts, pushing the encircling enemy back with the fury of his attacks. Clearly the beast was a worthy friend and ally despite its debased genetic stock. The nanostaff was now nothing but a vibrating cloud of matter in his hands, shifting shape and size too quickly to see. Towering enemy figures were spinning away shedding sheets of blood in every direction, but he could tell even this would not be enough. There were simply too many of the ugly adversaries pushing in from all sides.

The girl staggered, ducking beneath a wild slash and slipping to one knee with a grunt of pain. Her knife drove out and caught the arm wielding the sword in the elbow, but as the momentum of the heavy weapon dragged the limb around, her dagger was plucked from her exhausted grasp, wedged in the bones and gristle of her victim.

A howl went up among the attackers and they surged forward. The Goagoi stumbled forward, pushing the Tigan girl behind him, ready to defend her with his last breath, and something swelled in his heart.

"**Angara**!" The name issued from stiff lips before he even remembered it, and the voice terrified him. But when he said it, when he heard it, the strange, foreign filter over his eyes dropped away, and he surged forward, raising one hand to reach for her.

Except that it was not his hand. The arm that responded to his desperate impulse was heavy, a grainy, gritty metal that threw off tiny emerald flashes from a million miniscule facets scattered across the surface. It was a statuesque arm, well-muscled and well-proportioned to the strong hand whose fingers now flexed out toward Angara Ksaka, bowed down before the Ntja.

And beyond that hand he saw then that the attackers had stopped, every flat-nosed face turning in confusion and growing fear toward him.

Behind them, peering through their bulky bodies, Khet Nhan rose, his red eyes wide and his little mouth open in amazement.

Marcus looked down at his body. It was the form of a metal Adonis, all rippling muscle and clean lines, crafted from the same metallic grain of the arm. It reminded him of Nhan's staff, somehow, and a world of possibilities coursed through his mind at the thought. He was towering over the rest of the room, he realized. Looking behind him, he saw that he was taller than the enormous chair that had somehow done this to him. Then he froze.

There was a body seated in the chair. A familiar body, still and cold as death. His body.

He looked back down at the statue, a moment of fear rising up and threatening to break his intense focus. But there was no time now to wonder. He turned his back on his own body, metal eyes narrowing, and scanned the room for foes.

All around the chamber the alcoves flared into life, green brilliance bursting from them, illuminating the figures within. Each was the mirror image of himself, and he realized how godlike he must now appear. He wanted to laugh, but it was choked with bitterness.

Fear pushed the anger and hunger down as he felt his eyes widen at the sight of this new body. Had the city turned him into some metal monster? Had his consciousness somehow been transferred from his own body into this form of molten metal? Had he lost his Humanity completely? The irony of that was painful. To have learned so much of what it meant to be Human, and then lose it all?

And then the anger surged back to the fore.

He roared a vicious, hunter's cry. The unreasoning hatred returned, the alien presence surged up in his mind again, and he lurched forward a ponderous, clumsy step. All around him, the statues emerged from their niches a single step as well. He looked at them, his eyes narrowed, and saw that they were all looking at him with glowing blue eyes.

He smiled.

With another atavistic roar he took a second step, and then a third. Each was easier than the last. Finally, he stood at the very edge of the dais. It was not nearly so high as it had first appeared. He leapt down, landing with a grace he felt he never could have matched in his natural body, and rose to stare down at the Ntja, gathered in stillness around his friends.

With wild, ferocious abandon he fell upon the soldiers. He was fully aware of the other statues following his lead, and soon there were screaming dog soldiers running in every direction, trying desperately to escape the doom that had risen up to consume them. He found that he could change the shape of his limbs at will; his hands could form any weapon he could imagine. He lashed out with spears, and whips, and swords with more skill than he ever should have possessed. At one point, curious to see what might happen, he formed an enormous cannon barrel with his left hand, leveled it at one tall soldier, and a mighty sapphire pulse leapt out and devoured the target's head.

Marcus laughed, and the gruesome sound bounced off the surrounding walls with an evil sound.

Several Ntja, their cruel faces twisted with dread, swung their own rifles around and jabbed them at the statues.

Nothing happened, as the suppression field, managed by the entity living within the Relic Core, fine-tuned the energy to dampen only the weapons of the enemy.

Some of the soldiers, braver or more foolish than the rest, tried to rush the metal men, swords flashing. Falchions clanged off steel flesh, sending sparks and glittering shards of weaponry flying into the air. He relished the looks in the creatures' eyes as realization dawned there. There was no hope to be found in resistance. Others tried to surrender, and found to their brief dismay that there was no hope on that path either.

He saw one statue rear up behind Angara and Nhan, its hands elongating and shimmering into two huge sword blades, and he raised a hand. "***No!***"

The statues, as one, paused in their mayhem.

"***Tigan and Goagoi are inviolate.***" The voice was affirming what he said, not asking a question. He recognized its buzzing tones from the early conversation he had had in his head, but this time it was echoing all around him.

The last few Ntja were scrambling for the door, metal statues following them, casually cutting them down with elongated weapons, spears, and an occasional blast of cobalt energy. Two or three made it away, disappearing through the antechamber and into the corridor beyond, but he found now that if he merely thought of them, he could see them fleeing, their weapons forgotten, their terror palpable in their filthy animal cries.

As he followed them, however, he saw them brought to an undignified halt, crushing themselves to the walls of the corridors to allow enormous, stooped shadows to pass. These newcomers were stalking down the high-ceilinged corridor toward the command chamber with a slow, ponderous gait.

The Ntja heavy infantry. He had seen them from afar, but had not seen them fight. They were much larger than a standard Ntja soldier, bulked out with armor and life support equipment, and an ungainly power pack on their backs that made them look liked huge hunch-backed gorillas.

He looked back to where Nhan was dressing Angara's wounded shoulder, and tried to speak. He didn't feel his lips moving, but the room echoed with a booming rendition of his voice, much like the voice that had spoken moments ago.

"***Heavy infantry heading this way.***" He felt certain that his cohort of giants would be able to handle the new threat, but he knew it was going to be much more of a challenge.

He was looking forward to it.

*****

Angara gritted her teeth against the pain. Her brain was wrestling with too many things at once, and she felt dizzy. There at the end she really thought she was going to die. She was looking up at that big ugly brute, the sword coming down, and knew it was over.

She had almost not recognized Marcus's voice when it first echoed through the room, halting the beast above her and granting her a reprieve.

Everything in the strange chamber had paused, and they had all looked up at the statue that seemed to be addressing them from the dais. She had not known whether she should be terrified, horrified, or grateful. Something about the way the statue stood up there by the throne was unmistakably Marcus. But a quick glance at the throne had shown her Marcus's motionless body, back on the giant seat. And as the metal figure had leapt down onto the floor and swept into the Ntja, it had moved like nothing she had seen before.

At first she had not even noticed the other automatons come to life. And then she had been in the middle of a swirling death machine, somehow spared each time a blade or limb or gaze came her way. They moved with an unnatural grace, their faceted metal skin shining, and there was nothing the Ntja could do to stop them.

The last of the enemy was down before she realized it, and the adrenaline abandoned her to the pain. She leaned heavily against a pillar as Nhan bandaged her shoulder with a strip torn from his own robe. He had been silent, throwing terrified glances at any of the statues that came too close, while he worked on her wound. The one time a metal giant had approached them, nearly cutting them down from behind, Marcus's voice had stopped it in its tracks. Their guardians had not bothered to notice them since.

The warning of heavy infantry heading their way had seemed almost laughable. Marcus's giant statues had had no difficulties with these regular soldiers. How much more dangerous could the heavy infantry be? She had heard stories, of course, of the elite shock troopers of the Council. Everyone had heard *stories*. But they were rarely actually seen, and almost never in action.

But as the first of them shouldered its way through the door, she realized she should have given more credence to the tales. The whimper that escaped her lips might have been from Nhan giving the bandage a last pull to tighten it, but then it might not have.

The thing was huge, enormous shoulder pads giving it even more width than it would have had. The thick armor plating gave it twice the bulk of a non-armored Ntja, and the hump of a generator on its back made it look like some giant, feral animal. The helmets were contoured to resemble a ferocious Ntja's face, glaring implacably around the room with glowing red eyes.

The first one carried a huge pole in two hands, dull metal throwing back soft green highlights. There was no sign of any power generators or other force enhancers, but it was huge. With a grunting war cry, the beast took a powerful swing at the nearest statue, putting all of its considerable strength behind the blow. She realized in an instant that this monster did not need to wield a powered weapon. The armor it wore would provide all the power it needed.

The bludgeon went whistling in at the statue, and the metal man straightened as it came, cold face uncaring. It raised a single hand to stop the blow, and for a moment she thought it would actually work. But the weight of the Ntja's weapon shattered the upraised limb, turning the hand and arm to glittering dust as it carried through and caught the statue in the chest. The metal figure flew backward, shedding clouds of dust, and crashed to the ground with a hollow, empty sound.

It did not move again.

Another statue standing nearby jerked as if its awareness had suddenly shifted, and it turned to regard the armored Ntja striding into the room. Without preparation or warning, this statue leapt, and raised its arm to take the brunt of a hasty blow of the bludgeon on its forearm. The metal arm shattered much as the first's had, but the metal pole lacked the force to sweep on through and strike the body, and so the automaton was able to sidestep the dropping weapon, sidle up beside the soldier, and raise its other arm.

From her vantage point on the floor it was hard for her to see what happened next, but it appeared that the arm changed into a massive piston shape, a heavily reinforced cage enclosing a huge, heavy striking arm. As the lip of the cage made contact with the helmet, the striking arm blurred into motion, battering against the reinforced armor again and again, faster than she could see. The staccato blows rang through the chamber as the helmet deformed beneath the punishing blows, finally crumpling down into the neck of the armored suit, which then collapsed into a loose pile of armor and splashed blood.

There was no time for celebration, however, as three more heavy shapes pushed into the room and the statues rushed to join them. This time the battle was not nearly so one sided. The one-armed statue that had killed the first trooper fell to the combined attention of two heavy infantry, while a ferocious duel on the far side of the room saw another statue locked with another suit of armor, both pummeling the other mercilessly. It quickly became clear to her that whichever survived would be of little use to its allies in the rest of the fight.

In the center of the melee the statue that had been Marcus roared another challenge. Wherever he had come across the knowledge, he was wielding the nanotechnology in his limbs as if he had been born to it. At the moment, one arm had taken the shape of a huge hammer, pounding at the cringing Ntja before him. The other was a long thin lance, and as his opponent winced away from a particularly telling blow, he plunged the lance between its helmet and shoulder, yanking it out in a spray of blood.

More shapes crowded into the antechamber outside, pushing their brothers deeper into the room, and Angara realized that their situation had once again deteriorated. The Ntja would not stop, despite the loss of their fleet. Even with the Variyar on their way, even with the aid of these enormous metal men, there was no way they could survive. The Ntja would never surrender.

Her head came up and she shot a look at Nhan. He was watching the battle with horrified fascination, but glanced down at her as her head turned toward him. She tilted her head at the crashing violence, and then jerked her chin to the ceiling. "Taurani!" She shouted over the sounds of brutal death all around.

His eyes were wide already, but managed to convey a surge of surprised energy all the same. He nodded, and then looked to where the statue that was Marcus had stepped up to take on the next Ntja through the door.

She understood. To get to Taurani, they would need to get through the crush of enemy waiting to face them. How would any of them, even the enormous statues, move past that crowd? And what would happen to her and Nhan if they did?

But it did not matter. Death here together, or death alone with the hope of victory against her enemies. It was no question at all. If anyone could get away from this death trap and hunt down the Ambassador, it was Marcus.

"Marcus!" She shouted, her voice cracking with the strain. "Marcus, Taurani!"

The Marcus statue looked back at her, and as it turned, another Ntja reared up behind it, another massive bludgeon raised high.

"No!" She screamed, pointing behind her. The statue turned back, but it was too late. The enormous metal weight came crashing down on the statue's head, smashing it to the ground. The metal figure staggered, going first to one knee and then the other as its head, shattered by the blow, ruptured into a cloud of glittering dust that cascaded down onto the floor. The bludgeon sheered through neck and chest to finally stop buried deep in the statue's core.

The Ntja steadied itself, yanking the bludgeon out and raising it for a final blow.

The giant club caught the statue on its shoulder and dashed it to the floor in a flood of metal grit.

Angara heard herself scream. The statue was stretched out on the floor, lifeless. But beyond it she watched as another metal figure jerked upright as if shocked, and then turned to look at her. Something in the way this statue moved reminded her of the Human, and she breathed again. This statue nodded to her once, and then turned to the massive, armored Ntja that had destroyed the first Marcus statue.

As the heavy soldier turned toward the new threat, the statue grabbed its helmet with one huge hand. With a blur the hand became a solid block of metal and there was a muffled crunch. The headless suit of armor tumbled lifelessly onto its side.

The new Marcus statue turned to nod to her once again, and then made a sudden rush for the door. This time he was not trying to meet any of the suited Ntja in battle, but rather snaking through them, shouldering them aside as his body became a long, sinuous shape that wove through them like a serpent through tall grass.

The remaining statues formed up into a line before Angara and Nhan. There were only six of them left, and every one of them was showing damage from the battle. But even as she watched, their bodies seemed to be reforming, repairing themselves as they took up their positions.

Marcus had done what he could for them, and she was grateful. Now all he had to do was fight through the tunnels and find Taurani before these last statues were overwhelmed.

She reached out and recovered the knife she had lost earlier. If this was the end, she would not die whimpering on the floor without a weapon in her hand.

*****

Marcus flew through the tunnel, heedless of the obstacles in his way. He had pushed past the last armored Ntja, driving the thing's head into a mosaic as he passed. Now he was catching up with fleeing foot soldiers who cried out as he gained on them. He wanted desperately to take his time killing them, but settled for those blows the urgency of his mission would allow. With his speed, strength, and the ability to turn his hand into a sword blade with a thought, that was usually enough.

Soon, however, he had outpaced even the fleeing soldiers, and found himself pumping through the corridor, his glaring eyes fixed before him, moving as fast as the metal body would allow.

He came tearing through the doorway in the rear of Sanctum like the ash cloud of a detonating volcano. He landed heavily upon the tiered surface of the floor and came to rest with one fist and one knee denting the floor plating. He rose, glancing around him, and found most of the Ntja soldiers at the wall, defending against a foe pressing them from outside. Most of the observation dome had come down at some point, leaving only a slow breastwork that provided little protection to the dog soldiers trying to fend off the furious Variyar assault.

None of the Ntja had noticed him in the heat of battle, and so he took his time surveying the situation. He knew Angara was right. He needed to find Taurani to finish this. Even as the thought settled into his mind, he saw two heavy-armored Ntja standing guard behind Iphini Bha's brutalized shuttle. There, in the lee of the wreck, cowered Khuboda Taurani, his robes smudged, thin blood tracing a dark path down one gray cheek.

The creature's noseless face was hard to read, its canted, metallic eyes glittering strangely in the dust-filled air. But Marcus wanted to think there was fear there, given the current situation.

Marcus stalked toward the two bodyguards and formed his arms into two monomolecular lances, weapons he had found most effective down below. The two Ntja turned to him as they sensed his approach, and as they recoiled from him, only raising their enormous clubs as he continued to close, he punched a lance through each of their necks. He felt his weapon extensions pierce the weak armor, and pushed blades of fine wire out of the lances and up into the helmets, where they flashed and scraped against the insides of the suits.

In less than a second, his weapons were the only things holding the dead weight upright, and he withdrew the lances back into metal hands, allowing the bodies to drop to either side. He straightened, looking down at Taurani, and smiled.

Those eyes were never built to widen in fear, but the way the lipless mouth opened and shut, there was no hiding the panic rising there. It tasted delicious.

The full weight of the hatred and distrust that had been heaped upon him rose up again, and he looked down at the creature responsible for nearly all of the pain and suffering that had occurred in Penumbra since Marcus had arrived. He saw the faces of a Diakk man and boy, he saw Iphini Bha, and Angara's pained expression as she tried to ignore her wound in the command chamber far beneath their feet. And he saw Justin, countless scenarios flashing through his mind, each one ending in his best friend's death by an Ntja sword.

Marcus took a step toward the Ambassador, a low growling shaking the scattered wreckage around them.

Taurani raised his arms, his wide, expressionless eyes throwing back a reflection of the statue reaching toward him with one enormous hand.

"No!" The voice was not Taurani's, but it was vaguely familiar. With a snarl, Marcus looked up to see a huge Variyar running at him. K'hzan's gravitic armor was shuddering as he ran, pivoting around his body to guard against the occasional blow aimed his way by the Ntja between them. The red king spun once on his heel, his battle staff flashing, its blade taking one enemy soldier in the gut before he spun it away, throwing up an arc of blood, and plunging it into the neck of the next as he sprinted past.

Soon enough, K'hzan Modath was standing before Marcus, his breath deep and even, and this time the Variyar had to look up at *him*, which was a nice change. Although they were closer in height than he would have liked.

K'hzan looked up at him, his staff held warily across his body. "I am speaking to Marcus Wells, Administrator of Penumbra?"

How he had known Marcus was inside the metal he could not know. But he found himself nodding a heartbeat before the thought occurred to him that maybe he should have just pretended he didn't understand.

"You cannot kill this beast, alone and unarmed." K'hzan gestured to Taurani, who now craned his head from one to the other in confusion. "To do so would be wrong, placing us in the same damned and doomed camp as his masters."

Marcus felt metal eyes narrow as he looked down at K'hzan. From his appearance, there was nothing to tell that this alien king had grappled through a desperate deep space battle, and now had fought his way through half an Ntja army to come to stand before him.

Who was he, this little thing, to tell him what he *could* do? Ancient hatreds rose once more, and he sneered down at K'hzan. He felt his hand begin to vibrate itself into a broad-bladed sword.

K'hzan noticed the movement and took a step back, raising his staff. "Marcus Wells, we have much to discuss. Much and more has happened here today. But please listen to my words. If you end Taurani this way, there will be a grave price to pay. We will be no better than our rivals. Do we not strive to be better than those with which we contend? Otherwise, why do we fight at all?"

The words made sense to a part of Marcus, and he settled back in his stance, his hand reforming. The thought of all the death he had dealt out so far that day suddenly weighed heavily in his mind. He had never killed more than a mosquito in his life, and now he was literally drenched with blood. He looked down at his hands. The metal hands of the statue he had somehow become.

Once again it was all too much. This was all too far from his old life for him to even grasp at a frame of reference. He wanted to weep. He wanted to vomit. He wanted to scream.

The ancient, alien hatred in his mind rose up, and he pushed it back down. This wasn't him. He wasn't a killer, despite the evidence to the contrary. He needed to master this new thing that was coiled behind his eyes, or he would be gone as surely as if he had died in the chamber below.

He was no killer.

Then his eyes settled on a dull metal object lost amidst the tumbled debris on the floor. An Ntja falchion. The sword Angara had tossed at his feet.

The sword was tiny in his huge metal hand, but he managed to spin it in his fingers until he was holding it by the base, its hilt fully engulfed in one massive fist, the blade gleaming dully as it stretched out before him.

There was almost no resistance as he pushed it through Taurani's robed body.

The Ambassador looked down at the blade emerging from his chest in confusion. The glittering eyes flared, the mouth opened wide, and fine, long fingers rose to grip weakly at the blade. Then the eyes dulled, the mouth fell slack, and the fingers relaxed as the body slid to the floor, a dark stain spreading through the pearlescent fabric.

Marcus looked down at the dead Ambassador. He had expected to feel a rush of joy, or shame. He had desperately wanted to feel vindication. Instead, he felt nothing. If there was to be a price to be paid, it wouldn't come due today. He forced himself to raise his eyes to meet the empty blackness of K'hzan's burning glare. He opened his steely mouth, but there was nothing he could say.

A sudden wave of exhaustion swept over him and he felt himself collapsing onto his knees. There was a sensation across his skin as if water or sand were streaming over him. His vision blurred, faded, and dimmed. The harsh light around him was suffused with green, and he found himself slumped into the huge command throne deep beneath the surface of Penumbra. Only a moment ago he had been a colossus, striding uncaring through battle and crushing his enemies before him. Now he was collapsed in the massive chair, surrounded by the stench of death, in the center of the ancient control chamber.

A thousand aches and pains made themselves immediately known, and he sank further into the throne in exhaustion. He shook his head, unwilling to open his eyes.

Somewhere overhead, K'hzan still stood, burning with his righteous anger.

# Chapter 32

The cavern was cool and dark. The vague, soft sounds of distant water were soothing counterpoints to the thoughts surging through his head. The low, bronze ceiling loomed overhead, but he found it more comforting than confining. The reservoir had swiftly become the only place in the city he could go to escape the burdens of his duties and the expectations of others.

Sadly, from the expectations of the city itself, there was no escape.

The heavy thoughts of the thing that lived coiled within the Relic Core were always there, lurking in the back of his mind, inextricably entwined with his own thoughts and emotions. At least, he thought they were his own. Telling them apart was getting more and more difficult with each passing day.

It took all of the discipline he had ever possessed to keep his mind focused on matters at hand when the ancient voice in his head clamored for revenge and the return of Human domination to the galaxy.

Trying to reestablish normalized relations with countless alien species calling Penumbra their home, this devolved into quite a distraction.

He missed Iphini Bha more than he would have thought possible, now that he was the ruler of the city in truth as well as name; and there was no one standing beside him whose advice he knew he could trust. He often found himself thinking about their time together and wondering if he could have done anything to alter their paths.

Those were the hardest thoughts. The foreign voice in his head did not take kindly to soft recollections about alien traitors.

The scuff on the metallic floor behind him came exactly as he knew it would.

He lowered his head and shook it gently. Even the surprise of happy reunions had been taken from him.

"Hey, hero." The voice was rough and weak, but welcome nonetheless.

He turned smoothly, rising to his feet, and smiled at Justin. He kept his face schooled to pleasant stillness against the surge of emotions he felt at his friend's condition.

Justin's wounds had very nearly killed him, he knew. Angara had barely gotten him into the medical cist of her ship in time, and even then it had been close. He had stayed in close contact with her since the battle, and knew how much effort the Variyar expended to save his friend's life.

But once he learned that Justin was out of danger, he had turned his mind to other matters. He had not thought what that kind of injury and convalescence might do to a person.

Justin's dark skin was ashy pale, the flesh of his face was limp; the hard, chiseled lines softened from his long recovery. Somehow, though, he had found the time to shave his head, and it gleamed in the light of the reservoir cavern. It had been almost a month since the last Ntja had surrendered, and Justin had spent all of that time in a medical ward aboard K'hzan's flagship.

"I know, I look like shit." Justin smiled as he said it, but he winced a little as he shrugged, closing the distance between them with a slight limp. He lowered himself beside Marcus with a grunt of effort, shifting slightly around something on his hip, and then took a few slow breaths as if he had just run a great distance.

"You don't look like shit." Marcus tried to sound reassuring, but he had never been able to fool Justin. "Well, you don't look like total shit. You look ..., vaguely shit-like? I see you're wearing a new accessory with your outfit."

His friend looked down at the pistol settled on his hip and shrugged. "You're not the only hero, turns out. I've got to look the part of the intrepid gunslinger, now that I've got the rep to go with it."

Marcus shook his head. "I thought you ran out of bullets shooting your way out the first time."

Justin's smile widened. "I told you I had three *clips*. I didn't mention there were a couple extra boxes in there as well. Of course, I'm going to have to find some more soon, if you're planning on continuing with your vigorous diplomatic efforts."

Marcus could only laugh. It was one of the first times he could remember doing that in a long time, and it reminded him of his friend's injuries. "Speaking of looking like shit, or not, how's the belly?"

Justin grinned, and his shoulders gave a slight tremor as he tried to suppress a laugh. He shook his head and turned to look out over the dark water. "You'd think these aliens and all their futuristic technomagic would be able to deal with a simple stab wound." He propped himself up with one arm.

"A simple stab wound?" Marcus didn't try to suppress his own laughter. "From what Angara said, that damned dog-face spitted you. And don't try to deny it. I saw the skewer." His smile faltered at a moment as the words echoed out over the subterranean lake.

Justin didn't appear to notice, and chuckled. "Yeah, well, you'd still think they could patch me up quicker with some of their hocus pocus."

Marcus forced the smile back in place and shrugged. "Angara said it was something in the metal the Ntja use for their weapons. I guess it interferes with the nanites, or something like that."

Justin shook his head. "Well, whatever it was, K'hzan's people set me to rights soon enough. I won't complain too much." He smiled again.
"Not where any of them can hear me, anyway. There's not a lot of room for thinking when you look down at your stomach and see the dull end of a giant alien sword sticking out, but I wasn't thinking anything good."

"So, you're best friends with K'hzan Modath now? You going to go sailing about the galaxy wearing matching outfits?"

Justin lowered his head with a smile and cast a sideways look at Marcus from beneath his heavy eyebrows. "Jealous?"

Marcus sat up. "What's there to be jealous about? Penumbra's a hell of a lot bigger than anything the red king can claim to rule."

Justin's smile slipped a little, and Marcus realized that maybe he was jealous; just a little bit. He shrugged. "Sorry. Anyway, didn't he want to kill you the last time you were face to face?"

Justin looked at him a moment longer then turned back to look out over the water. "Yeah, well, he might have come around on the whole 'Human issue' just a little bit."

They could both smile at that. "They do like to fight. He probably would have been willing to share a drink with an Ntja, if they'd let him fight."

"They were willing enough, at the end, to oblige him." Marcus joked, but his heart wasn't in it. The comment about ruling Penumbra hadn't been his. He was pretty sure of that, and he resented the thing interfering in his reunion with his friend.

"Yeah, so I hear." His smile got a little thin and he patted his belly gently. "I was a little distracted at the time."

Marcus turned to his friend. "You're lucky she got you back to the ship, you know. In the middle of all that craziness, no way were you going to get out of there otherwise."

Justin turned back to look out over the reservoir. "Yeah, she's got her good points."

Marcus watched his friend's dark eyes, and then nodded to himself. "So; you and Angara?"

Justin's smile widened. "Me and Angara what?"

"You're a ... You're a thing?" Marcus made a vague gesture with his hand. His feelings on the situation were decidedly mixed, and he was honest enough with himself to admit that not all of the negativity could be blamed on the new awareness sharing his mind.

Justin's face softened as he continued to watch the ripple of the lights on the distant water. "A thing? Well, we're something, I guess you could say. Going to give it some time, see what develops."

Marcus settled back, turning out in the same direction and resting back on his locked arms. "Until the next one comes along, right?"

Justin shook his head, his face serious, and shifted around to face him. "No. I don't think so. Not this time."

Marcus smiled. "Good," he said, his face straight ahead. "Because if you piss her off, she's more than capable of slaughtering both of us." Then he smiled, giving Justin a quick push with his shoulder that almost knocked the other man over.

"Well, she might be able to slaughter me, weak as I am. But I hear she might have a harder time getting at the hero of the hour." Justin pushed him back, with considerably more force. "Where's your big metal suit? I heard you had a big badass metal suit." He tilted his head back the way he had come, and continued with narrowed eyes. "And I noticed you brought friends down with you?"

Marcus didn't look back. He didn't have to. All he had to do was close his eyes and he knew exactly where the two automatons were standing, one on either side of the low entrance to the reservoir's observation point.

They were always with him now, standing guard outside his rooms at night, and following him wherever he went during the day. Two had approached him in the command chamber after the battle, and taken up positions on either side. They never talked, of course, and he couldn't be sure if they were the same ones all the time or not. All of the alcoves in that frightening room deep beneath Sanctum were filled again, and not a single statue had the slightest sign of damage.

It had taken him a while to figure it out, but he knew, now, that whatever the voice was that he heard in his head, it was the motivating force behind the statues, and pretty much everything else in Penumbra.

He grunted. "Nanites." He lowered himself onto his back so he was star-ing at the bronze ceiling. Because of the width and breadth of the room, the height often seemed low. But that gleaming metal surface was more than thirty feet over his head. "Just like the stuff Nhan's staff is made out of."

Justin adjusted himself, rolling onto one hip to look down at him. "You were covered in that stuff?"

He took a deep breath. "Still not sure, to be honest. Covered? Coated? Sealed? I didn't know what was going on."

He had not told anyone about all of the drama that had apparently taken place in his head that day. He would have spoken to Justin, except that Justin was preoccupied by his continued refusal to die. Everyone else assumed that he had somehow used the Skorahn to unlock further abilities of the city's defenses. No one knew about the conversations he had been having within the silence of his own skull. He had hoped to talk to Justin about it when his friend was feeling better, but now that the time had come, he was reluctant. How do you talk about a person, or an entity at least, when you literally cannot get away from them?

Justin saw it, though, and was too good a friend to let it go. "Marc, I know there's a lot of heavy shit coming down right now, but you look like you've got more to say, and if I can drag my sorry, wounded ass all the way over here, you can damn well open up." He smiled, taking some of the sting from the words. "It's not like there's another Human within a billion miles that gives a shit."

Marcus shook his head and looked at his friend. "It's not so simple."

He was startled as Justin barked a harsh, loud laugh that echoed eerily around the enormous cavern. "Not simple?" He sat up and gestured all around them with one hand. "We're sitting on the metal shore of an underground lake located within a floating city in space a billion light years from Earth after getting kidnapped by a purple-skinned warrior woman who saved us from a squid driving a Prius." His eyes were intense. "So, since we're starting at a pretty screwed up baseline for 'not simple', why don't you just tell me what the hell is going on? I've heard stories, and believe me, if you don't tell me what it is, I'm going to make some shit up that will put a serious dent in your reputation."

Marcus smiled, slowly sitting up, and shook his head. Justin always got what he wanted out of him. And so, on the shore of that strange lake, he told his friend all about the conversations that had taken place in the place that wasn't anyplace, and about what had happened during and after the battle. He even shared with him the impulses he believed the voice placed in his mind, and his growing alarm at the realization that he was having a harder and harder time differentiating between his own thoughts and those of the voice. He kept the last moments of the battle to himself; K'hzan's words, and his slaughtering of the help-less Taurani. He wasn't sure the Variyar king was right or not, but somehow, he did feel as if he had surrendered something, in that vengeful, violent moment.

When he had finished, Justin stared at him with wide eyes for a mo-ment before speaking. When he did, his ragged voice was even more noticeable. "Damn. That's … not so simple."

Marcus wanted to hit him, and almost did before remembering his inju-ries. "You're an asshole. You know that, right?"

Justin's teeth were bright against his dark skin as he grinned a manic grin. "It's part of my charm." But, having gotten a smile out of Marcus, he turned serious quickly. "So, you have some ancient alien racist in your head, is what you're telling me?"

Marcus shook his head. "No, exactly *not* that. I think I have an ancient Human racist, or speciest, or shapist, or whatever the hell it would be, in my head."

Justin gave the two statues standing motionless by the entrance a sidelong glance before continuing in a lower voice. "What the hell is it?"

Marcus shrugged. "I don't know. It won't tell me. I don't know if it knows what it is."

Justin searched Marcus's face, but there wasn't even the hint of a smile there now. "And you caught it, or whatever, down in that room below the old ship?"

"The *oldest* ship, and yeah. Whatever it is, it got ahold of me down in the command chamber."

Justin nodded absently, turning away. "Why do you think it's Human?"

Marcus got up and stretched his back out, glancing absently at the statues. "The thoughts are Human, for sure. They don't like any of the other people we've met out here all that much. In fact, whatever it is seems to be pretty upset at the current status quo."

"And we built Penumbra?" Justin looked up, not quite ready to rise.

"Humans? Yeah, looks it. Well, not Penumbra. But the Relic Core, whatever it was." He moved down toward the water's edge, where the liquid lapped softly against the metal shore. "I think it must have been some kind of research facility, or last-ditch secret weapon at the end of the war between Humans and the Variyar and … everyone else, I guess."

"And they never used it, despite losing the war, and left a ghost behind to haunt the first Human to stumble into their little museum thousands of years later?"

"Tens of thousands of years later, and I never said it was a ghost." Marcus looked down at his friend. "I think it might have been something like the base computer, artificial intelligence, or whatever. Although a lot of the thoughts have different … I don't know … different flavors, to them? Like they're from different people."

Justin grinned again. "So you have a schizophrenic computer ghost in your head."

Marcus was getting angry, and didn't know if it was him getting angry, or the voice again, and forced himself to take several deep breaths before responding. "I don't know. And it's not just in my head. It's everywhere. It's been here, and aware, since long before the ship we now call Sanctum landed, long before all the other ships were fused with the Relic Core and the city was born. From what I can figure out, the AI, or whatever, can pass through nearly any conductive material. As new ships were added to the city, it simply locked them into the system it had created. That's why they all got power; this force, or being, or whatever made itself useful, so it could spread its network. At this point, it's everywhere."

"And you have everywhere in your head." Justin rose unsteadily to his feet, and Marcus moved to help him.

"No, but if I close my eyes, I know pretty much anything there is to know in the city. It's like it used to be with the Skorahn, but a thousand times more sensitive. And it happens without me thinking about it half the time."

"So, you knew when I landed?" Justin rubbed his hands together as if there might have been sand or dirt on them.

"Yeah. I've known where you were since you docked."

"And you didn't motivate your sorry ass up to meet me? Damaged as I am?"

"I'm going to push you into the water if you don't take this seriously." Marcus's face was expressionless, his voice flat.

Justin only smiled wider. "Meh, a swim might be just the thing. So, what are you planning on doing with the..." He made a circle with the tip of one finger pointing at his ear. "What are you planning on doing with the thing, then?"

Marcus gave him another flat look and then turned away. "I don't know."

"But you're not going back to Earth?" There was more of an edge to Justin's voice now, of fear or something else, Marcus couldn't tell. "You thinking of going home?"

This time it was Marcus's turn to laugh, but it was a hard, dark sound, nothing like the genuine mirth Justin had given voice to moments before. "With *this* in my head?" It was his turn to trace the little circles around his ear. "I don't think that would be such a great plan. It's not really happy with the idea of Earth right now. I could go insane and try to take over the world if I went back right now."

Justin nodded as if reassured. "Without Taurani or any other Council assholes screwing with you, you could probably do some real good around here, by staying."

Marcus looked at him. "Have you not heard anything I've said?" He was almost shouting, and Justin cast another nervous glance at the statues, but they remained still. "This thing in my head hates all of them! Everyone on this station but you and me! It's looking at the galaxy through a lens that's tens of thousands of years old! Everyone is either an enemy or a traitor, and it's railing against them *day* and *night*!"

Justin backed away for a moment. "That sounds ... bad."

Marcus shook his head and stalked off, his hands in tight fists. "I can ignore it when I'm busy, or focused on other things. I've been working, just like you said, trying to build those networks, bringing people together, tying Penumbra back into a community. I've even had some success. The Kot'i are responsive, and of course the Namanu, Diakk, and," he tilted his head back at Justin. "The Mnymians, are willing to work with me. The Leemuk and other staff have returned to the control center as well." He shrugged. "So, I'm making progress. But every night, when I go back to my rooms, the thoughts are there, and it's angry at me for working with our ancient enemies!"

Justin put a hand on Marcus's shoulder. "That's not right." He nodded to the Skorahn, laying against Marcus's chest. "Have you tried to take that off? Maybe have Angara fly you out-system, see if the voices leave you alone?"

Marcus felt his shoulders fall, exhaustion sweeping over him. He looked down at the amulet, the icon clear on its gleaming surface. "I don't want to take any chances. And I haven't had time to leave the city. Like I said, I've been trying to keep busy."

"And you're running from something." Justin said it quickly, almost interrupting him. When he looked up at his friend, those dark eyes were burning into his, but his stance was hesitant, almost as if he were gauging whether he should be ready to flee.

"Running from what?" His eyes narrowed, focusing intently on Justin's face.

"From what happened at the end of your battle."

That struck a chord, and he shot his friend a hooded look. "I don't know what you're talking about."

Justin reached out and laid a hand on his shoulder. "We've both done a lot of crazy shit since we got here. How many Ntja have we killed? Before we got here, neither of had killed anything bigger than that cat you hit with your car back in high school. Now, we both have too much of that thick, black blood on our hands. That's going to mess with your head no matter how you slice it, Marc." He hesitated, looking away, and then met his gaze with more force. "And I heard what happened with Taurani."

"Taurani was a bastard! He deserved what he got! Who told you about that, K'hzan? He's just angry that he didn't get to preside over some dog and pony show trial!"

Justin raised both his hands to ward off the anger, eyes wide and white with surprise. "Whoa! No! I don't talk much to K'hzan, even if I *am* on his ship. No, Angara told me. And I know you. I know how something like that would haunt you."

"Something like *that*? Something like *what*? I put down the dog that caused *all* of this!" Marcus stormed away, flinging one arm wide to indicate the entire city, or maybe the whole mess his world had become. "I put an end to the monster that drenched this city in blood!"

"And killed him as he knelt before you, unarmed and helpless." Justin's words were flat, but there was no anger in them. They brought Marcus up short. "You think I don't see those dog-faced bastards in my dreams? You don't think I have nightmares about all the blood I spilled? I was a damned businessman, for Christ's sake! I've heard how many of those armored assholes you killed, and I've heard how you did it. It must have been even bloodier. That can't be leaving you alone at night." He shrugged. "And striking down an unarmed man, or whatever, isn't something the Marcus I know would be easy with either."

"Maybe I'm not the Marcus you knew." He spat the words before he could think, but when they were out, he realized how true they might be. He was afraid of how true they might be.

"Nope, that won't work. You're you, no matter who else might be rattling around in that head of yours. And I know you can't be right with the way that went down."

And as he heard the words, he knew they were true. Deep in his mind he felt the alien presence stir at the suggestion that Taurani's death had been anything but proper, but he forced it back down. He looked down at his hands, curled into claws, and forced them to relax. Then he turned away and folded back down to sit, legs crossed, looking out over the water once more.

He didn't speak for a while, and Justin settled down beside him, willing to give him the space he needed. They sat side by side on the alien shore, watching the oily surface of the water undulate off into the distance.

"It wasn't right." The words were muffled. He wasn't proud, and the words came hard. But he forced them out. "I know. But so many people died! And I thought you had died, and I saw the sword Angara had thrown at my feet …"

"Well, you should probably know, not everyone thinks you made a mistake. Angara happens to agree with what you did completely. It's made for some ... heated debates."

The silence stretched on again, and Marcus didn't want to fill it, but knew he had to. He needed to.

"So, what should I do?" It was almost a whisper. Half of him was afraid Justin wouldn't hear him, while the other half was afraid of the reply.

"Well, I'm no priest, but I think you just go forward, doing the best you can. All this talk about voices in your head actually makes me feel *better* about what happened." Justin turned toward him, his face sober. "And if you know this thing is whispering to you, you know to watch for its influence. Have you thought about talking to Master Nhan? I don't know much about the Thien'ha, but he is sort of mysterious ... maybe that's close enough to a priest?"

Marcus shook his head. "No, he hasn't been much use since the battle. Helping us defied some ancient belief of his, some pledge of neutrality or something like that. And he still blames himself for Ve'Yan's death."

Justin sat in silence for a moment, then nodded. "Well, you can always talk to me, man." He felt the hand on his shoulder again, and it meant more than he could have said.

Again they lapsed into silence, but this time there was more peace, and a little less pain. Or, at least, a little less isolation.

"So, what's next?" He knew, or guessed, that Justin was relieved he didn't want to go back to Earth. But it was only natural that his friend would want to know where they might go from here.

"Well, there's a lot of damage to be repaired, both physical and emotional." He tilted his head back, his eyes unfocused as he thought. "A lot of trust to rebuild. Taurani spent a lot of time and effort sewing discord the whole time he was here. The scars from the battle and its aftermath won't go away anytime soon."

Justin nodded. "And when you've set everything right? What's the future hold for the Savior of Penumbra?"

He felt his face twist in a sour frown, but shook it off. "Well, I hope to get things back on track. Bring everyone back together, and try to make this place more of what it could be; a place where folks who'd rather not live in the Council's utopia can come and forge their own future."

"They're not going to leave us alone, you know. They're going to come back. No way was Taurani out here on his own. Not with an entire fleet at his beck and call. And they can't let an insult to their rule like this exist, not after the slapping you just gave them."

Marcus sighed. "I know. And K'hzan thinks that their admiral, Ochiag or whatever, was on that big ship that got away. So, they'll know what happened. When they come back, they won't just stumble blindly into whatever meat grinder caught them this time."

"I heard it was pretty spectacular. Some kind of antimatter ray gun or something like that?" Justin couldn't keep the excitement at such a prospect from his voice, and it brought a smile to Marcus's face despite the turmoil churning in his gut. "No one seems to know what it was, really. I figured the lord of the manor might have a clue."

He snorted at that. Between the two of them, science had never really been his strong suit. "I'm not sure either. It was nothing anyone can seem to identify. The best the Kot'i can guess, it was something called dark energy, which even to Galactic science, is only theoretical."

"Tell that to the dogs you blasted out of the sky." It was nice to hear Justin's excitement. There was enough guilt associated with the battle already. Knowing his friend didn't see the whole thing as a moral failing was a small comfort. Of course, the fact that he had been unconscious on one of the Variyar ships threatened by the Council fleet might have something to do with that. Justin had always been something of a pragmatist.

"Well, it did the trick, anyway." Marcus agreed.

"But you don't think it'll be enough if they come back?" Justin had turned to face him as the conversation wandered farther from the emotionally charged topics.

"Well, who knows what the range of the weapon is? _I_ don't." Once he started talking, the words rushed out of him like a flood. "The Council could send a fleet in to stand off at a distance and launch something at us from half way across the system. They might be able to strike us with beam weapons from even farther away. They could shatter the planet with something while hiding behind its shadow, and we could be destroyed in the resulting cataclysm before we even know they're there. As far as anyone can tell, Penumbra has always been a static target, and will always _be_ a static target. If we can't move, eventually, they're going to hit us with something we can't deal with."

"As far as anyone can tell?" Justin perked up at that. His face had fallen as Marcus had ticked off all the possible attacks they might be facing. "There's a chance it might not be static? That it might be able to _move_?"

"Well, if you think about it, it's not a great secret weapon if its trapped in a backwater system with no ability to get to where it can do _some_ damage. So, one theory goes that if it is the secret weapon it appears to be, there has to be some way to move it. You'd think I would know how to do it. I seem to know everything else. But apparently there are some secrets the big scary voice wants to keep to itself for now."

Justin nodded at that and settled back, his face lost in thought. "You're not going to be able to deal with the Council alone, no matter how mobile the city might turn out to be."

Marcus frowned. "No. Even if we try to take a live and let live approach, and I'm not at all convinced that's an option, we'll need friends to help watch our backs, and stand the Council back if they try to make another run at us."

"Any ideas?"

Marcus looked at his friend out of the corner of his eye with a thin smile. "Well, I might need your help with that."

That seemed to amuse Justin. "Oh yeah? With what?"

He settled back on his hands. "The Variyar, for one. K'hzan threw in with us on this one, but almost everyone agrees that the fleet that he brought against the Council here can't be everything he's got. Most of us are hoping that he's in for the long haul now. It's not like he was going home anyway."

Justin nodded thoughtfully. "He _is_ sort of stuck. Not that I think he minds." He smiled at Marcus with a wide, open grin. "I think he sort of likes you, but God knows what the price for his help might be, down the road. I don't get the impression he's big on charity."

Marcus shrugged. "We'll deal with that when it comes up. And that was the easy one. I've got another idea that I was hoping you might be able to help me with."

"Yeah? Anything. You know that."

Marcus paused, looked at his friend almost in apology, and then said, "Angara's people."

That seemed to give Justin pause. He blinked a couple times, a line of confusion appeared between his eyes, and then his head tilted to the side. "Angara's people?"

Marcus nodded, rushing forward before his friend could stop him. "Angara's people; the Tigan. They're supposed to be amazing fighters. They *live* on their ships, for God's sake! And they're independent. They sound perfect, if we're trying to build an alliance against the Council."

Justin's eyes stayed wide, drifting off as he thought about Marcus's words. "Angara and I haven't spoken much about her people. They kicked her out, you know. She won't talk about the details, but they can't be good. And I'm pretty sure they're not in the Council because no one on the Council trusts them. I didn't get the impression anyone can trust them. Hardly sounds like an ideal alliance to me."

Marcus shook his head, warming to the topic. "No, but beggars can't be choosers. And if they're good fighters, and we can get them to fight beside us, can't we work around any other problems that come up along the way?"

Justin looked skeptical "I can think of good fighters from our own history that we wouldn't want beside us, just for starters." He shrugged. "I don't know, Marc. All I know is that Angara doesn't trust them, and they raised her. And I trust Angara. So, if possible, I think we might want to look elsewhere for allies, if we're really desperate."

Marcus bowed his head. "That's just it. We *are* desperate. I don't think there *is* anywhere else to look."

The mere thought of even asking for help from K'hzan Modath, or the Tigan fleet, or any other alien or Human half-blood drove the voice in his head half-mad, and he gritted his teeth against the pain. He knew there was no way to keep Penumbra free from an enraged Galactic Council now, but –

"What about Earth?"

He looked up. "What?"

Justin looked him in the eye. "Earth. What about them? It's still a prison, whether they know it or not. Are we going to just leave Earth as it is, oblivious and isolated? The punch line for a thousand alien jokes?"

That stung, and the thing in his head surged at the thought. He realized now that it had been sidling in that direction all along. Now that he saw it, he realized he should have recognized it much sooner. The entity in his head, whatever it was, was vehemently pro-Human. It wanted to reestablish a galactic order that had existed tens of thousands of years ago, with Humans as the preeminent species. As much as he hated the thought of Earth as a prison, and his people trapped there against their will, by all the reports he had found, the galaxy at the mercy of Humanity had not ended well for anyone, including the Humans.

"Can you imagine what would happen if we just rode Angara's ship down onto the lawn of the White House and announced that aliens were real? Not only that, but that we were outnumbered millions to one, and the rest of the galaxy wanted us all dead?" He shook his head and made a sweeping gesture with one hand. "No. I don't think that's an option right now. With Earth as an isolated prison colony content to spin along on its own, it's no threat. If we bring them into this right now, with no way to defend them? They'll be dropping rocks down on London before we know what's going on."

"Okay." Justin was quicker to let the point go than Marcus had feared he would be. But he was still wary. His friend wasn't finished, he could tell. "But what about your brother and sister? What about your father? What about Clarissa?"

Clarissa. He felt like he'd been punched in the gut. He hadn't thought about her since before Taurani's takeover. But when he *did* think about her, it hurt.

"Clarissa and I were done before we ever left Earth, remember? That's why we were at that damned casino in the first place?"

Justin laughed, and he was surprised to hear no judgment or anger in the sound. "You were, maybe. I was there to win a little cash, have a little fun..." He gestured around them. "Mission accomplished, I guess."

Marcus stared at him, and soon Justin raised his hands in surrender. "Okay. But still, I know you're not over her. You usually take a lot longer than this to get over a girl. Doesn't it bother you, knowing that her, and the rest of your family, are trapped in a *prison*? That they have no idea what's going on?"

Marcus settled back, exploring the emotions that had churned up at Justin's questions. He had been so lonely. He hadn't gotten along with his father in over a decade, and even his brother and sister weren't too close anymore. But they were family. They would understand what he was going through better than anyone except maybe Justin. Hell, they'd even be assets, given what he felt for sure was coming down the pike.

And Clarissa ...

"Just something to think about, I guess." Justin murmured as he settled back on his own hands, looking out over the lake.

And in the distance, as they sat in companionable silence, green flecks glistened on the distant water.

# Epilogue

The dead system spun through its accustomed patterns, unaware of time's passage beyond its decaying borders.

Circling the blasted remains of a once-mighty gas giant, the enormous hunter once again powered up to perform its accustomed watch. The massive hatch opened, the armature extended out past the expanding cloud of cosmic dust. The collected, collimated light of a thousand stars pounded down into the melted sphere below, pounding the field of craters with yet another indignity to heap upon the rest. And the eternal bell was struck once more.

And once again, the wave fronts of countless forms of energy and particles were cast outward into the vastness of space.

The column vanished, plunging the planetoid and the gargantuan ship back into utter darkness. The armature retracted, bringing with it the huge energy projector, and nestled back into its internal cradle. Another skeletal arm moved into position, reaching out, and extended the silvery orb of its receiver array into the void.

The automated monster waited with the infinite patience of a machine as time passed. As the decaying messengers returned home once more, many having crossed the length and breadth of the galaxy, systems within the juggernaut began to analyze and collate the data provided by the rebounding waves. The armature shivered, the silver ball began to withdraw once again.

Soon, the matte black finish of the behemoth's hull was unbroken once more, and it continued its eternal dance with the black ball of slag. It spun through the crypt system, oblivious to the ancient death and tragedy around it.

And then it trembled. Deep beneath its armored flanks, the crystal matrices of its mind, sifting through the minutia of the latest reports, found an anomaly. Somewhere in a distant corner of the galaxy, something had been detected. The sentinel's systems began to power up beyond the limits of its caretaker duties. Huge shields opened upon the aft sections of the hull and engines that could swallow an Ntja battleship flashed to life as they came back online for the first time in millennia.

The data was vague. The return was weak, the tachyon wave that had carried it had only tasted the remnants of an event; the shadow of a moment that had occurred before the particles had passed through that region of space. But that taste had been enough. That moment had been captured, reported, and now logged.

Somewhere, the ancient enemy was stirring. The weapon that had been feared had, indeed, been unleashed. And now, it was a danger to the leviathan's creators.

The great, stupid brute had no concern for the passage of eons. It had no knowledge of the rise and fall of empires, or the turning of galactic seasons. It had been created for a purpose. It had tirelessly worked toward that purpose for more millennia than its creators could have imagined. In fact, in the intervening ages, the tumultuous history of living beings had wiped the leviathan's existence from living memory. It had been forgotten.

But it had not forgotten.

Using the returned particle waves to plot its course, it sent power to those enormous engines and began to lift itself away from the broken planetary core that had been its home since before the first man had stepped foot upon the Earth. The thrust to move such a massive object was unimaginable, and the roar of its mighty engines would have shivered the heart of any living being who might have witnessed its departure.

But there was no living being to watch as the monster slid upward, orienting itself past the white dwarf, spinning away its last millennia of life in the distance. Weapons designed to devastate continents began to run their system checks, bringing colossal projectiles and energy capacitors out of their dormant state and preparing them to be fired in anger for the first time.

The enemy had revealed itself, and if the behemoth, charging out of the dead system at its best speed, lacked the furious, burning anger of a mortal combatant, it nonetheless went forth with all of the same focused intensity and fatal intent.

The enemy had revealed itself, and the enemy must be eliminated.

# A Survey of Member Races
## Within the Galactic Council

**Aijians**  Large aquatic gray mammals originally from the planet Omiaye, the Aijians are known to be loyal subjects of the Council. Thousands of years ago a great sacrifice was made by Aijians, to assist the council in containing a terrible evil. They are held in high esteem in no small part due to this sacrifice.

**Diakk**  One of the Humanoid races, the Diakk are not easy to generally categorize, but are looked upon with some small amount of suspicion by the Council. Marked by jaundiced skin and dark, scale-like markings across exposed areas of skin, few Diakk wander from their home planet of Varra.

**Eru**  The Eru are a race most comfortable in a servile position. Their squat, powerful bodies are usually covered in a fine coat of pale, purple fur, with coarse black growing from their heads. They are true citizens of the galaxy, as few of their number remain on their homeworld of Heimurin.

**Gogoi**  Their diminutive stature and dexterous limbs combine to make this species considered to be one of the more mechanically apt in the galaxy, although many also pursue more scholarly paths. A coat of soft green fur covers most of their bodies, while a fringe   of white tendrils covers their lower jawline.

**Iwa'Bantu**  A gentle species, usually given to careers in poetry, music, and philosophy, the Iwa'Bantu have never been prominent within the Council, caring little for Galactic politics. Relatively recently, a marauder raid on their home planet of Iwa'Ban caused terrible damage, from they have yet to fully recover.

**Kerie**  Prominent within the Galactic Council, the Kerie were instrumen tal in the administration of the ruling body since itsinception. Their nearly featureless gray faces are generally considered to be unreadable by almost any other race, and thus they are considered to be among the best diplomats in the galaxy.

**Kot'i**  The Kot'i are some of the best engineers and craftsmen in the galaxy. Content to allow others to administer the Council, the Kot'I have been behind some of the most important technologi cal advances in recent memory. Their shaggy fur and long, somber-seeming faces belay their generally light, wry personalities.

**Leemuk**  The most salient feature of a Leemuk, upon first encountering one of these massive creatures, is their enor

mous, lipless mouths. With a huge expanse of glisten
ing gum above and below long, yellowed teeth, they are
truly a fearsome-looking race, at odds with seemingly
genetic bureaucratic bent.

**Matabessi**     Their spatulated heads and serrated beaks seem more at home
in a deep oceanthan the deserts of their homeworld, Lamanta.
The heavy, armored lids of their large eyes only add to this im
pression. However, the Matabessi are among the most savvy
traders in the galaxy.

**Mhatrong**      One of the oldest denizens of the galaxy on record, the Mha
trongare a true oddity in that they seem to monolithically follow a
standard racial archetype; that of historian and philosopher. The
bone mask that hides all but the hollows of their milky eyes only
adds to their air of aloof detachment.

**Mnymian**       These Humanoids have a terrifying reputation that they seem
determined to maintain. Jet-black skin, fiery red hair, and white,
featureless eyes make them out, even other Humanoids. Few
Mnymians who venture off their home world of Ekaya do so as
anything other than mercenaries or guards.

**Namanu**        Another Humanoid race, their skin is a marked orange color,
their hair black, and their eyes unnatural large for their heads.
As a race, the Namanu appear to be ideally suited to the hard
sciences, their skin particularly resistant to many types of radia-
tion, as befits the children of a blasted planet such as Lefatsia

**Nan'Se La**     With their rearward-facing knee joints, heavy skulls, and of
course, the second, albeit generally clumsy pair of arms, the
Nan'Se La hardly seem Humanoid. However, the best Council
scientists have proven their provenance beyond question. The
absence of a home world of record only adds to their mystery.

**Ntja**          One of the most loyal of galactic races, the Ntja of Ntj have
served selflessly through some of the Council's greatest crises.
Foregoing the nano technology used by most of the galaxy,
a mature Ntja will have several metal domes affixed to their
heavy-featured heads, housing all manner of intellectual enhancements.

**Rayabell**      These amorphous gastropods are often particularly gifted in bu
reaucratic or administrative positions, found in organizations
across the galaxy. Most evince a mild to severe sociopathy that
often makes them more effective when properly supervised.

**Subbotine**     One of the most highly-regarded of the Humanoid races, the pale skin, regular features, and stark white hair of the Subbotine are often acknowledged as aesthetically pleasing by even the most rigid galactic loyalist. Many grow bored of their homeworld, AlyonaSubbotina, and leave for more sophisticated climes.

**Tigan**  Not, strictly speaking, members of the Galactic Council, the Tigan are anarchist nomads who travel across the galaxy in an enormous flotilla they refer to as PrapaVimala. With their deep purple skin, they can be mistaken for Mnymians if shorn of their brilliant white hair, often with temperaments to match.

**Tsiiki**  The somewhat vapid-looking half-smile that is the Tsiiki default expression, along with the drooping cephalic nodes over their eyes, combine to give the Tsiiki the appearance of amused, idiot children. Their sharp, insightful minds, however, often mean they have the last laugh in any negotiations.

**Variyar**  Their crimson skin, twisted, sneering expressions, and impressive ebony horns give them the Variyar a frightening appearance that their racial history does little to dismiss. A large percentage of the Variyar have eschewed their homeworld of Variya to follow their disgraced ruler into mysterious exile.

Look for more books from Winged Hussar Publishing, LLC – E-books, paperbacks and Limited Edition hardcovers.  The best in history, science fiction and fantasy at:

**https://wingedhussarpublishing.com**

or follow us on Facebook at:

**Winged Hussar Publishing LLC**

Or on twitter at:

**WingHusPubLLC**

For information and upcoming publications

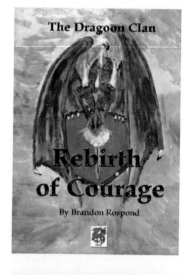

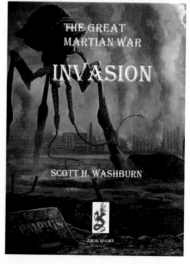

# About the Author

Craig is from Bedford New Hampshire where he does his best to warp space and time to fit far more activity into each day than anyone, including his wife, thinks would be advisable. During the day Craig teaches Theatre and Literature courses to the intrepid students of Milford High School. After hours Craig actively pursues kickboxing and mixed martial arts, and is one of the two hosts of the wildly mediocre and not-too-horrible general gaming podcast The D6 Generation. He is husband to a remarkably supportive wife and father to clearly the smartest, cutest, and most promising three year old on the planet (an entirely objective assessment). Craig plays games whenever he can find the time and the opponents, ranging from his recent favorite, a classic South American dice game called Perudo, to whatever the local tabletop war-game flavor of the month happens to be. And in all the voluminous free-time this schedule allows, Craig writes.

Always an avid reader and a writer for his own pleasure, recently Craig has been able to parlay that dream into a stunningly-exciting reality. For two years now Craig has written articles, rules, short stories, and background fiction for companies such as Spartan Games and Fantasy Flight Games. In August of 2012 Craig partnered up with the freshly-minted Outlaw Miniatures, where he spent the next nine months writing over 100,000 words worth of supportive fiction establishing the entire game universe for their new Wild West Exodus. In that time he was also hired as the lead writer for a line of comic books taking place in the same universe. And now, the most recent chapter in this ever-rising rollercoaster of coolness, Craig prepares to embark on his newest adventure, more excited than words can convey to set his keyboard to bringing the shattered Wild West even further to life in a new series of novels for Wild West Exodus. Legacy of Shadow is his first independent story.

Zmok Books